THE WORLD'S CLASSICS

THE PROFESSOR

CHARLOTTE BRONTË was born at Thornton, Yorkshire in 1816, the third child of Patrick and Maria Brontë. Her father was perpetual curate of Haworth, Yorkshire from 1820 until his death in 1861. Her mother died in 1821, leaving five daughters and a son. All of the girls except Anne were sent to a clergymen's daughters' boarding school (recalled as Lowood in *Jane Eyre*). The eldest sisters, Maria ('Helen Burns') and Elizabeth, became ill there, were taken home, and died soon after at Haworth. Charlotte was employed as a teacher from 1835 to 1838, was subsequently a governess, and in 1842 went with her sister Emily to study languages in Brussels, where during 1843 she again worked as a teacher. She returned to Haworth in the following year, and in 1846 there appeared *Poems by Currer, Ellis, and Acton Bell*, the pseudonyms of Charlotte, Emily, and Anne. Charlotte's first novel, *The Professor*, was rejected by several publishers, and was not published until 1857. *Jane Eyre* was published (under the pseudonym Currer Bell) in 1847 and achieved immediate success. In 1848 Branwell Brontë died, as did Emily before the end of the same year, and Anne in the following summer, so that Charlotte alone survived of the six children. *Shirley* was published in 1849, and *Villette* in 1853, both pseudonymously. Charlotte married in 1854 the Revd A. B. Nicholls, her father's curate, but died in March 1855.

MARGARET SMITH is one of the editors of the Clarendon Editions of the novels of the Brontës: *Jane Eyre* (with Jane Jack, 1969; revised reprint, 1975), *Shirley* (1979), *Villette* (1984), and *The Professor* (1987), all with Herbert Rosengarten.

HERBERT ROSENGARTEN is Head of the English Department at the University of British Columbia, Vancouver.

THE WORLD'S CLASSICS

CHARLOTTE BRONTË

The Professor

Edited by

MARGARET SMITH

and

HERBERT ROSENGARTEN

with an Introduction by

MARGARET SMITH

Oxford New York

OXFORD UNIVERSITY PRESS

Oxford University Press, Walton Street, Oxford OX2 6DP

Oxford New York Toronto
Delhi Bombay Calcutta Madras Karachi
Petaling Jaya Singapore Hong Kong Tokyo
Nairobi Dar es Salaam Cape Town
Melbourne Auckland

and associated companies in
Berlin Ibadan

Oxford is a trade mark of Oxford University Press

First published by Oxford University Press 1987
First issued with a new introduction as a World's Classics paperback 1991
Reprinted 1992

British Library Cataloguing in Publication Data

Brontë, Charlotte 1816–1855
The professor.—(The world's classics).
I. Title II. Smith, Margaret 1931– III. Rosengarten, Herbert
823.8

ISBN 0–19–282741–3

Library of Congress Cataloging in Publication Data

Brontë, Charlotte, 1816–1855.
The Professor / Charlotte Brontë; edited by Margaret Smith and Herbert Rosengarten; with an introd. by Margaret Smith.
p. cm.—(The world's classics)
Includes bibliographical references.
I. Smith, Margaret, 1931– . II. Rosengarten, Herbert.
III. Title. IV. Series.
PR4167.P7 1990 823'.8—dc20 90–23043
ISBN 0–19–282741–3

Printed in Great Britain by
BPCC Hazells Ltd
Aylesbury, Bucks.

CONTENTS

ABBREVIATIONS USED IN THIS EDITION

BCP	The Book of Common Prayer.
BPM	Brontë Parsonage Museum, Haworth, Yorkshire.
BST	*Brontë Society Transactions.*
CP	*The Letters of Mrs Gaskell*, edited by J. A. V. Chapple and Arthur Pollard (1966).
Gérin	*Charlotte Brontë*, by Winifred Gérin (1967).
Life	*The Life of Charlotte Brontë*, by E. C. Gaskell, 3rd edition, 'revised and corrected', 2 volumes (1857).
LL	*The Brontës; Their Lives, Friendships and Correspondence: In Four Volumes*, edited by T. J. Wise and J. A. Symington (1932).
ODEP	*Oxford Dictionary of English Proverbs*, 3rd edition, revised (1970).
OED	*Oxford English Dictionary.*
TLS	*The Times Literary Supplement.*
⟨ ⟩	Deleted in MS

References to Charlotte Brontë's other novels in the Explanatory Notes are to volumes in the Clarendon edition, 1969–84

INTRODUCTION

As Victorian novels go, *The Professor* is surprising. It is short, no main character dies, its hero is a bespectacled schoolteacher with tufts of dun hair, and its heroine, who is admired for 'twanging off' the word 'hell' with an 'uncompromising sort of accent', insists on continuing to teach after her marriage. Mrs Gaskell, at work on *The Life of Charlotte Brontë* in 1856, was charmed by the heroine but worried by the occasional coarseness and profanity she detected in the unedited manuscript of the novel, and she took care to add to her biography a defence of Charlotte Brontë's essential purity of mind. *The Professor* was finally published in June 1857, rather more than two years after Charlotte's death, and two months after the *Life*, when there was an eager audience not only aware of her power as a novelist, but aroused and moved by the strange sad lives of the whole Brontë family.

As the work of a virtually unknown 'Currer Bell' in 1846, the novel had seemed to publishers too deficient in 'thrilling excitement' to suit the circulating libraries on which success largely depended. Charlotte had determined that her hero 'should work his way through life' as she had seen 'real living men work theirs'; but, as she ruefully admitted, 'Publishers, in general—scarcely approved this system, but would have liked something more imaginative and poetical.'[1] Six of them rejected it before it reached Smith, Elder, who at least saw its promise. In 1847 the best-selling *Jane Eyre*, which *was* more imaginative and poetical, spoiled the market for its quieter forerunner. After two or three attempts to rewrite *The Professor*, Charlotte reluctantly acquiesced in its ninth rejection, but refused to let her 'martyrized M.S.' depart into the dusty oblivion of the publishing house for safe keeping. She wrote to George Smith on 5 February 1851:

[1] See Preface, p. 1.

You kindly propose to take 'the Professor' into custody. Ah—No! His modest merit shrinks at the thought of going alone and unbefriended to a spirited Publisher. Perhaps with slips of him you might light an occasional cigar—or you might remember to lose him some day ... No—I have put him by and locked him up—not indeed in my desk, where I could not tolerate the monotony of his demure quaker countenance, but in a cupboard by himself.[2]

So *The Professor* was laid aside, and its central Brussels episodes were recreated, with the compelling power born of tragic experience, in *Villette*.

Yet *The Professor* has its own value. It contains, as the reviewers were quick to point out, the 'germ' of the later novels. It is also the climax of a long period of private writing. Scores of tales, rapidly composed and lovingly set down in minute handwriting, give evidence of the ardent creative talent of the Brontë children. Charlotte and Branwell wrote of their imaginary kingdom of Angria, Emily and Anne of the Gondals. For Charlotte especially the Angrians came to have almost a real existence. Until 1840, when she sent the opening chapters of a novel to Hartley Coleridge for criticism, the Angrians belonged only to her private world, shared by Branwell and possibly by her sisters, but created primarily for her own enjoyment. She turned to these earlier stories for material when she wrote *The Professor*, and, in the early part of the novel, her attempt to break open the intimate world of her imagination seems to have left traces of the effort involved. The later Angrian tales, such as *Mina Laury* (1838) and *Caroline Vernon* (probably 1839) have an assured fluency of style and mastery of dialogue. Charlotte is perfectly at ease with her characters and situations: their relationships need not be explained afresh, for they are motivated by passions and repulsions developed through many years. But *The Professor* has to meet an unfamiliar audience, and the story begins in a stiff, self-conscious style. The awkward device of a letter to a school-friend, who never afterwards reappears, is in part an attempt to set the real audience at a distance.

[2] BPM MS SG 45. (See p. vii for abbreviations used in this edition.)

Apart from these initial difficulties of presentation, Charlotte's insistence on the 'real' instead of the 'wild wonderful and thrilling' would limit both plot and characters. Theoretically the real in fiction was desirable in the early 1840s. Mrs Trollope's *One Fault* (1840) begins with a declaration which closely anticipates Charlotte's preface:

> The persons of the story I am about to tell were neither of high rank, nor of distinguished fashion; and worse still, the narrative cannot by possibility be forced to become one of romantic interest. Ordinary every day human beings, and ordinary every day events are my theme . . . That they shall be such men and women as I have seen and known, is the only fact . . . that can be urged as an apology for introducing them at all.[3]

In practice these everyday events prove to be attempted murder, intended seduction, sudden death in a duel, and the highly coincidental meeting of two long-parted lovers on storm-swept cliffs where they are cut off by the tide. The social range of the characters excludes the aristocracy, but is otherwise limited to the genteel middle class whose work, if any, is irrelevant to the plot.

Charlotte Brontë certainly considered that she would be breaking new ground in making her main characters working schoolteachers, and in portraying at least two of them sympathetically. Looking back on *The Professor* after the publication of *Jane Eyre*, she thought it gave a 'new view of a grade, an occupation, and a class of characters—all very common-place, very insignificant in themselves'. Whereas fictional tutors and governesses had been presented with understanding—in for example Harriet Martineau's *Deerbrook* (1839), which Charlotte Brontë admired—the resolute concentration on schoolteachers was unusual. In 1836 E. G. G. Howard wrote of 'ushers' (i.e. assistant teachers) in *Rattlin the Reefer*: 'It would be an amusing work, to write a biography of some of the most remarkable ushers. They seem to be the bats of the social scheme.

[3] Frances Trollope, *One Fault*, i. 1.

Gentlemen will not own them, and the classes beneath reject them.'[4]

It was not surprising that Charlotte felt that her recent experience of real life might be a source of compelling fiction. In 1842 and 1843, as a pupil of M. Heger in Brussels, and later as a teacher, she had known both exhilaration and near-despair. On her return to England she suffered intensely from her separation from Heger and from his lack of response to her letters in 1845. In 1845 too, like her sisters, she was shocked by her brother Branwell's dismissal from his post as tutor, the result, as they believed, of 'domestic treachery' involving his employer's wife. Interweaving comparable material with existing Angrian fiction could not be easy, but it was not impossible, for there was a continuity in technique as well as in theme between her early writings and *The Professor*.

The progress of the Angrian cycle, and more especially of the stories written from 1839 onwards, was toward greater realism. From fantastic Arabian Nights adventures, through Scott-inspired romantic heroisms and Byronic soul-searchings and amours, she had developed a society in which characters moved with a recognizable and plausible individuality, in which emotions—not only those of passionate love, but those of private and public loyalties, of parental affection, of friendship with its complexities of *odi et amo*—had been minutely analysed. Her portrayal of character and feeling in *The Professor* is therefore the work of a practised hand.

There are two main themes in the novel: the hostile tension between William and Edward Crimsworth, and the master–pupil relationship developing into love between William Crimsworth and Frances Henri. Christine Alexander notes that 'antagonism between two brothers existed in Charlotte's stories from the beginning'.[5] She and Branwell each developed the theme in different ways. Branwell's 'The Wool is Rising, or, The Angrian Adventurer' (begun before 12 June and finished

[4] E. G. G. Howard, *Rattlin the Reefer*, ch. 19.

[5] C. Alexander, *The Early Writings of Charlotte Brontë* (1983) 219.

on 26 June 1834) reflects in its portrait of a slave-driving, tyrannical mill-owner, something of the violence of the Ten Hours Bill controversy over working conditions in the mills and factories in the 1830s. According to Branwell, the arch-villain Alexander Percy orders his children Edward and William to be put to death. Saved from this fate, they and the foundling Steaton (the precursor of the sly and heavy-looking Steighton of *The Professor*) endure degrading poverty until they set themselves up as wool-combers. Edward, coarser and stronger than William, makes himself the master. Nevertheless William is already a rebel, though not a successful one. He is amused by Edward's anger and Steaton's prayers: 'William sat at his desk with his hand to his mouth, striving to smother that laughter, which had his brother heard might have perchance in its effects smothered himself.'[6] He attempts open defiance, too, for after one of Edward's harsh orders, William turns red with anger and exclaims, 'Will I obey you Will I turn your slave. Ill die rather.'[7] Branwell describes Edward as handsome, ambitious, and unscrupulous. In success he becomes a tyrant: '. . . this morning his behaviour to the work people was almost insufferable curses and threats and maledictions he poured out without mercy.'[8] He soon acquires a fortune, marries a haughty princess, and becomes Secretary of Trade to the Angrian cabinet.

Realizing the potentialities of this situation, Charlotte developed the theme in *The Spell: an Extravaganza in Eight Chapters* (21 June–21 July 1834), and in Sir William Percy's diary and letters. In *The Spell*, Edward Percy's energy and eloquence are described. He is athletic and of a 'fiery beauty', and we see him surrounded by a 'brilliant ring of ladies',[9] while William, as in *The Professor*, is excluded. Charlotte explains that William is little known, for he is overshadowed by Edward; and,

[6] P. B. Brontë, 'The Wool is Rising', ch. 3, in *Miscellaneous and Unpublished Writings of Charlotte and Patrick Branwell Brontë*, ed. A. Symington and T. J. Wise (1936) i. 420. We retain the unconventional punctuation and capitalization of the juvenilia.

[7] Ibid. ch. 3.

[8] Ibid. ch. 8.

[9] C. Brontë, *The Spell* (1931) 125.

as Miss Ratchford wrote in *The Brontës' Web of Childhood*, 'she employs all her skill to show how William, Edward's superior in intelligence, taste and refinement, grew to hate his tyrant all the more because of his enforced submission.'[10]

By about 1839 Charlotte felt she had stayed for too long in the 'burning clime' of Angria, and sought to conjure up new creatures of her imagination in 'a cooler region where the dawn breaks grey and sober'. She recast the story of the Percy brothers in an English setting, calling the heroes Ashworth. Abandoned by their father, they were brought up by their grandmother, Lady Helen. After her death they 'soon went down into obscurity—dived as their father had done—but into a worse gulf than he had ever visited'.[11] The standards by which she measures their characters are those of *The Professor*: Edward is active and talented, but 'some might fail to perceive the traces of generous feeling or chivalric honour'.[12] Her sketch of William Ashworth is, in outline, the character of William Crimsworth, though this is modified as she adapts it to her later feelings and experiences in *The Professor*:

> William Ashworth differed considerably from Edward yet he was scarcely better liked—he was quieter in manner but not more cordial in feeling—his temper was not so violent it was cool and well controuled He had not Edward's disposition for bullying & fighting because he was not so muscular . . . his forte lay rather in endurance than action.[13]

William Crimsworth has a similar quietness, and opposes a 'buckler of impenetrable indifference' to his brother Edward's attacks. Again, in William Ashworth 'you soon discovered a want of candour, of openess, of frankness in his character—he told you nothing of his own feelings'.[14] In the same way William Crimsworth, guarded by his 'three faculties—Caution, Tact, Observation', refused to reveal his real feelings and hopes to Edward, or, later, to Mlle Reuter.

[10] F. E. Ratchford, *The Brontës' Web of Childhood* (1941) 191.
[11] C. Brontë, '*Ashworth*: an unfinished novel', ed. Melodie Monahan, *Studies in Philology: Texts and Studies 1983*, University of North Carolina Press, 52.
[12] Ibid. 50. [13] Ibid. 51. [14] Ibid. 51.

Though some of the characters in *The Ashworths* are still exotic and eccentric, it is clear that Charlotte's aim is realism. She is not 'writing a novel', she says, and so she must be a faithful chronicler of these 'real events'.[15] She takes care to give the action a local background—Mr Ashworth senior reappears at the 'Strafford's Arms Inn in Wakefield, Yorkshire', and is 'a popular man in the commercial districts. the smutty—intelligent mechanics of Manchester & of the West-Riding of Yorkshire adored him.'[16]

Thus the story has been progressively brought within the bounds of 'reality': the threat of death to the children, Edward's marriage with a princess, his gaining a position in the Cabinet, have given place to tamer events in a more or less credible English society. *The Professor* retains and further develops this tendency. William's self-denying economies, his work in the counting-house, his cold, star-lit walks through the streets of X——sound authentic. So also does the vivid picture of the northern manufacturing town, set in the midst of country from which 'Steam, Trade, Machinery had long banished . . . all romance and seclusion' and brooded over by 'a dense, permanent vapour' of sooty smoke vomited from long chimneys. Thus far Angria makes a positive contribution.

Unfortunately the Angrian heritage is also responsible for some of the weaknesses of the first six chapters of *The Professor*. For Charlotte the Seacombes and Crimsworths had a substantial existence in Angria: but, not yet accustomed to a strange audience, she has failed to give them enough semblance of life in *The Professor*. William's youth at Eton and Seacombe Hall appears vague and shadowy. Edward has in his quarrels with William a disproportionate violence, a motiveless malignity deriving from the violent, amoral world of Angria, but inadequately explained in the later novel.

Charlotte herself soon came to think the beginning 'very feeble', and in December 1847, after the success of *Jane Eyre*, proposed to recast the whole novel—'add as well as I can, what

[15] Ibid. 37. [16] Ibid. 46, 49.

is deficient, retrench some parts, develop others—and make of it a 3-vol. work'.[17] Her plans involved drastic cuts. In her rough draft of a preface for *The Professor*, probably written at about this time but left incomplete, she writes, as Crimsworth's 'editor', '. . . upon his entrusting it to me for correction and retrenchment . . . I took the liberty of cutting out the whole of the first seven [originally 'six'] chapters with one stroke of the scissars—A brief summary of the import of these chapters will content the reader—'.[18]

The fragment known as 'John Henry' may well be another attempt to carry out her plan for a three-volume work. It testifies to Charlotte's continuing preoccupation with the two brothers theme: Edward becomes John Henry Moore, a forceful and handsome mill-owner with a sensitive younger brother and a lively, self-centred wife. The marital relationship is more fully developed, there is a rather factitious spasmodic energy in the style, and an obvious attempt to brighten and extend the dialogue and to introduce at an early stage a new emotional entanglement for William Moore.[19] Charlotte abandoned this version at the beginning of the third chapter, and, dropping the element of antagonism between the brothers, planned *Shirley* to involve the elder of the two in a wider social conflict which would give full scope for his forceful energy, and to leave the introspective younger brother, his rival only in love, as a secondary character.

In *The Professor* she virtually discards the elder brother after the first six chapters. He has served his purpose as a foil for William; and since he is merely harsh and repellent, without the flamboyance and complexity of his Angrian prototypes, he offers little scope for development. Charlotte has deliberately simplified his personality, for she is interested not in the tyrant, but the underdog, the rebel younger brother. She has shown Edward as a harsh and cruel master—her first title for the novel

[17] Letter to W. S. Williams, 14 Dec. 1847; Princeton University Library MS.

[18] BPM MS Bonnell 109; printed in the Clarendon *Professor* as Appendix III, 295–6.

[19] See Appendix D in the Clarendon *Shirley* (1979) 805–35.

was *The Master*—but she has already begun to reveal William's attainment of a truer 'mastery', that of self-control. William is established as sensitive, reserved, yet ardently desiring freedom, and proudly courageous in defying Edward—a character near to her own heart, through whom her own feelings could be expressed. Like her, he gains the freedom of a new life abroad. With the transition to Brussels, Charlotte's writing also seems to gain greater freedom and fluency, for William now speaks in the voice of his creator:

> Belgium! I repeat the word, now as I sit alone near midnight. It stirs my world of the Past like a summons to Resurrection ... When I left Ostend on a mild February Morning and found myself on the road to Brussels, nothing could look vapid to me. My sense of enjoyment possessed an edge whetted to the finest, untouched, keen, exquisite ... Liberty I clasped in my arms for the first time and the influence of her smile and embrace revived my life like the sun and the west-wind.[20]

Charlotte herself had at first found new and satisfying life in Belgium—satisfying because, like William, she was equipping herself for independence. She had found joy, too, in becoming a pupil again; M. Heger was an exacting but inspiring master. In her second, and lonely, year in Brussels, he became the dominant figure in her mind and, as her letters show, in her feelings. Increasingly distrustful of both fellow-teachers and pupils, alien to her in their religion and further alienated by her own proud reserve, she concentrated her affection and admiration on the 'master' who alone showed any understanding.

This relation between master and pupil becomes the major theme in *The Professor*. Chapters VII to XII are concerned with William's first impressions of Belgium, his disillusionment with the 'young lady pupils', and the greater disillusion caused by the selfish coquetry of Zoraïde Reuter. The rest of the novel deals with his growing interest in his Anglo-Swiss pupil, Frances Henri, her affection for him, their separation, reunion and marriage. Thus baldly stated, the plot seems thin—a transcript of the author's experience rather pathetically brought

[20] *The Professor*, pp. 49–50.

to a happy conclusion by a piece of wish-fulfilment. Some early reviewers, their hopes raised by the fiery passions of *Jane Eyre* and the sombre splendours of *Villette*, certainly found *The Professor* tame and attenuated: *Villette* especially seems almost miraculously more powerful in its transformation of the Brussels scenes. Yet *The Professor* at its best has the attractiveness of a clear, quiet voice, touched with grace and occasional humour. In *Villette* comedy and tragedy are in tension, overshadowed by the grief of Charlotte after the deaths of her sisters; *The Professor* still looks forward to life and happiness, to be attained through a master–pupil relationship leading to marriage.

Such a relationship between hero and heroine was not uncommon in eighteenth- and nineteenth-century novels, though it was rarely more than episodic. Thus, though personal experience accounts for the choice of theme in *The Professor*, the shaping of it may have been influenced by literary antecedents. Charlotte had Richardson much in her mind in the early 1840s. She makes repeated reference to his novels, and especially to *Sir Charles Grandison*; for example, in her long letter to Hartley Coleridge about her story 'Mr. Percy and Mr. West,'[21] in its fuller version *Ashworth*,[22] in her Brussels cahier dated May 1843,[23] and in Chapter XXIV of *The Professor*. Remembering Charlotte's feelings for her 'master', and her desperate need for self-control as her correspondence with him came to an end, one wonders whether certain chapters of *Sir Charles Grandison* had a special significance for her, in spite of her conscious rejection of 'Richardsonian Multiplication' of characters. Richardson portrays a tense conflict of love and duty, especially the conflict of Clementina's love for Sir Charles with her devotion to her religion and her duty to her parents. As his pupil, Clementina responds like Frances with a growing pleasure in working for him, and is sad and quiet in his absence. Harriet Byron thinks Clementina's parents should not have

[21] See Fran Carlock Stephens, 'Hartley Coleridge and the Brontës', *TLS* (14 May 1970) 544.

[22] See for example two references in ch. 1 of *Ashworth*.

[23] BPM MS Bonnell 118.

allowed her to attend the lessons: 'Teach her English! Very discreet . . . In every case, the teacher is the obliger. He is called *master*, you know: and where there is a *master*, a *servant* is implied.'[24] Charlotte Brontë does not, at least in *The Professor*, touch the deeper emotions that Richardson analyses with such delicate minuteness. Nevertheless she endows her heroine, who is in many ways her own *alter ego*, with qualities she felt herself to lack. Frances's charm, her grace, and the independence which removes from her love of her master any hint of slavish adoration, all recall the lovely, dignified, and self-controlled Clementina.

Charlotte may also have read George Sand's *Consuelo* before writing *The Professor*. It appeared in 1842–3, and she told G. H. Lewes in 1848 that it was the best of Sand's novels that she had read, coupling 'strange extravagance with wondrous excellence'. She deeply respected the 'sagacious and profound' Sand in contrast to Jane Austen, who was 'only shrewd and observant'.[25] The singer Consuelo is introduced as a quiet, studious child, both poor and plain, in contrast to the showy beauty of the other pupils in her class; her music master Porpora must have vividly reminded Charlotte Brontë of M. Heger. He addresses his pupils dramatically:

Il n'en est pas moins vrai, ajouta-t-il en mettant ses lunettes dans leur étui et sa tabatière dans sa poche . . . que cette sage, cette docile, cette studieuse, cette attentive, cette bonne enfant, ce n'est pas vous, Signora Clorinda; ni vous, Signora Costanza . . . il alla se poser . . . en face d'une petite personne accroupie sur un gradin. Elle, les coudes sur les genoux, les doigts dans les oreilles pour n'être pas distraite par le bruit, étudiait sa leçon à demi-voix.[26] ('It is none the less true,' he added, as he put his spectacles in their case and his snuff-box in his pocket . . . 'that this well-behaved, docile, studious, attentive, good child is not you, Signora Clorinda, nor you, Signora Costanza . . .' he went over to stand in front of a little girl sitting crouched on a bench. Elbows on knees, fingers in her ears so as not to be distracted by the noise, she was studying her lesson in an undertone.)

[24] Samuel Richardson, *Sir Charles Grandison* (1754) iii. letter XXII.
[25] Letter to G. H. Lewes, 12 Jan. 1848; British Library Add. MS 39763.
[26] George Sand, *Consuelo* (1844 edn.) ch. i.

When he approaches her, Consuelo is 'non confuse, mais un peu effrayée' ('not embarrassed, but rather frightened'); but when he asks her to sing, she does so 'sans faire une seule faute de mémoire, sans hasarder un son qui ne fût complètement juste' ('without forgetting a note, without venturing a sound that was not absolutely accurate'). The other girls are astonished and jealous. Consuelo works hard, but they say spitefully that she is both poor and ugly. Nor is her master easy to please, yet he delights to foster genuine talent, and Consuelo, like Frances, responds willingly. She loves to work, for she is 'une de ces rares et bienheureuses organisations pour lesquelles le travail est une jouissance' ('one of those rare and fortunate characters for whom work is a delight').[27] Porpora is amazed by her ability:

> je vois bien que je ne puis plus être ton maître.
> —Vous serez toujours mon maître respecté et bien-aimé, s'écria-t-elle en se jetant à son cou et en le serrant à l'étouffer.
> ('I see clearly that I can no longer be your master.'
> 'You will always be my respected and dearly loved master,' she exclaimed, throwing her arms round his neck and hugging him so tightly as almost to choke him.')[28]

George Sand stresses her purity and innocence. Like Frances she has a 'conventual' appearance, but a warmth and fire of spirit which transforms her. Though Consuelo never loves Porpora in the romantic sense, their master–pupil relationship is an essential and unifying element in the novel. One need not look for specific borrowings in Charlotte Brontë's work: the fact that she had seen such a relationship described, and that the pupil happened to be a character she understood and appreciated, might well have encouraged her to develop it in her own terms in *The Professor*.

Once Charlotte moves her hero to Belgium to begin his career as a master, she moves away from her harsh and uncertain presentation of him. His odd, ungracious response to the substantial help given by Hunsden gives place to a more natural eager gratitude for 'Mr Brown's' recommendations, and a

[27] Ibid. ch. vii. [28] Ibid. ch. xii.

sensible appreciation of the civilized régime of his new employer. There is an attractive youthful zest about him; he knows that the 'sun will face him', he is 'sustained by energy', drawn on by 'hopes as bright as vague', he gazes with delight on the new landscape, lyrically described though realistically flat and dirty—'all was beautiful, all was more than picturesque.' In *Villette*, Lucy Snowe starts out with elation, and drinks in a 'divine' delight as she journeys to Belgium; but it is characteristic of the later novel that the new land is belittled by its name of 'Labassecour', and that Lucy's dreamland of a 'long coast one line of gold' beneath a rainbow arch of hope is immediately negated: 'Cancel the whole of that, if you please, reader—or rather let it stand, and draw thence a moral . . . "Day-dreams are delusions of the demon." '[29] Lucy the older narrator looks back on her young self with the controlled despair which is the dominant note of the novel.

Certainly the removal of delusions is a main theme in *The Professor*, but the tone is different. William as narrator laughs without bitterness at his younger self: he knows that the hotel housemaid is stupid, but joyfully finds her charming; he knows he must find work but still rejoices in the 'cheerful and fine' buildings with a sense of exhilaration. We are of course meant to predict disillusion for his naïve eagerness, but no very sombre shadows are cast: unlike Nicholas Nickleby, a recent schoolteacher hero, he finds no tyrannical Squeers for a headmaster, but a liberal, intelligent, and prepossessing M. Pelet. There is a light irony, an indulgent amusement, in William's recollection of his delight at the prospect of entering the charming secret garden of Mlle Reuter's school and seeing the schoolgirls—the 'angels and their Eden', and we are meant to smile at his 'air rayonnant' and the 'exquisite pleasure' of his anticipation. All this is comfortably in the tradition of the *Bildungsroman*; we expect progress through the disillusion to wisdom and fulfilment. William is youthful in his resilience: 'I cannot say I was chagrined or downcast by the contrast which the reality of a

[29] *Villette*, ch. vi, 76.

Pensionnat de demoiselles presented to my vague ideal of the same community; I was only enlightened and amused.'[30] Having achieved mastery of both boy and girl pupils with a somewhat unrealistic speed, William moves on to the more subtle challenge of Mlle Reuter's adroit manœuvring for power.

It is here that the contrast with *Villette* is most noticeable: Mlle Reuter has youth, freshness, and charm enough to be attractive, at first sight, to the young Crimsworth. William's amused appraisal of her tactics yields to a romantic attraction, then to sharp disillusion and finally contemptuous hostility. Mme Beck in *Villette* is older and far more formidable; Lucy Snowe's initial amusement at her spying and manipulation does not last long, and by the end it has changed into intense loathing of her evil dominance. Images of warfare are used in both novels to convey these antagonisms, but in *The Professor* the battle is a game to be won, in *Villette* a mortal combat. After a penetrating analysis of the 'windings' of talk by which Mlle Reuter seeks to become 'Mistress' of his nature, William, who has been watching her as keenly as she watches him, notes his own positive relish for the contest: 'I enjoyed the game much . . .', 'I delighted to turn round . . . it was a regular drawn battle.' If he has something 'feverish and fiery' in his veins after her betrayal, he is capable of 'masking' his visage, 'locking' his heart, and retaining his mastery over himself and her. Nor is this victory so unrealistically simple as his class-room mastery. Charlotte Brontë presents his complex emotional response with some acuteness: 'There was at once a sort of low gratification in receiving this luscious incense from an attractive and still young worshipper and an irritating sense of degradation in the very experience of the pleasure . . . I felt at once barbarous and sensual as a pasha.'[31] This disturbing and corrupting master–slave relationship contrasts with and helps to evaluate the creative and enabling master–pupil relationship of William and Frances, which leaves intact their respect for each other's identity. The contrast and the use made of it anticipate the

[30] *The Professor*, p. 79. [31] Ibid. 170–1.

emotional crux in *Jane Eyre*, where Rochester seeks to impose a pasha-like and therefore degrading mastery on the defiant Jane.

Charlotte Brontë distinguishes between tyranny and the kind of despotism assumed by William Crimsworth in his dealings with Frances: this is used at first as a challenge to her withdrawn personality, and later as a comforting formality to set his shy pupil at her ease. It helps him to discover and develop her ardour for work, her ambition, and her 'Judgment and Imagination', as Charlotte's master M. Heger had discovered and fostered those of his foreign pupil. In transforming her life into her art, Charlotte to some extent controlled its pain by making herself—or at any rate her first person narrator—the master. She attributes to William the inward qualities she had looked for in M. Heger. He delights in the 'wakening to life' of his pupil, watching her change to 'vivacity and alertness . . . much as a gardener watches the growth of a precious plant'. We are allowed to share his 'resentment, disappointment and grief' when Frances is dismissed, and his joy in finding her. His love for her is expressed with some of the freedom and directness which were to startle and delight the readers of *Jane Eyre*:

> I hate boldness—that boldness which is of the brassy brow and insensate nerves, but I love the courage of the strong heart, the fervour of the generous blood; I loved with passion the light of Frances Evans' clear hazel eye when it did not fear to look straight into mine; I loved the tones with which she uttered the words:
>
> 'Mon maître! Mon Maître!'
>
> I loved the movement with which she confided her hand to my hand; I loved her, as she stood there, pennyless and parentless, for a sensualist—charmless, for me a treasure . . . silent possessor of a well of tenderness, of a flame as genial as still, as pure as quenchless, of natural feeling, natural passion.[32]

The balance of power is engagingly reversed in the following scene in Frances's room, where the master admits that 'a certain glance, sweetened with gaiety, and pointed with defiance . . . thrilled me as nothing had ever done; and made me, in a fashion

[32] Ibid. 156.

(though happily she did not know it) her subject, if not her slave.' Later Frances accepts William's proposal in a way that seems to promise a conventional Victorian marriage—'Master, I consent to pass my life with you,' so that William's 'fathomless' content is mingled with the flattering notion that he will become the 'providence of what he loves'; but he is quickly disabused: 'Think of my marrying you to be kept by you, Monsieur! I could not do it—and how dull my days would be!' If the subsequent picture of marriage as a working partnership, helped by the miraculously smooth attainment of the 'most popular' school in Brussels, is far too good to be true, it is at least in intention (like William's practical challenge to the class-structure in marrying a lace-mender), innovative. Charlotte Brontë goes out of her way to stress the contrast with the unmarried state of the theoretical radical, Hunsden, who advocates democracy and revolution but has failed to marry the actress he loved.

In other respects Hunsden makes an important contribution to the theme of mastery. An early 'Byronic' hero oddly mingled with traits of the real-life Yorkshire manufacturer Joshua Taylor and his son Joe Taylor, he sometimes appears inconsistent and unconvincing; but his activities widen the novel's social relevance. 'We are reformers born, radical reformers,' he says of his family. His attempts to goad 'the oppressed into rebellion against the oppressor' and his taunts against William's 'rotten order' of aristocratic connections reflect the social unrest of the 1830s, and especially the outcry against factory conditions in the West Riding of Yorkshire. This was the period when Richard Oastler reported on local meetings in the stirring rhetoric of his *White Slavery* pamphlets: 'At Bradford the battle was waged against the strength of the Factory System. And Leeds has nobly responded, and secured the triumph of JUSTICE and HUMANITY by a victory more glorious than the deeds of heroes.'[33] The *British Labourer's Protector, and Factory Child's Friend* was begun in 1832 to bring the facts of 'white slavery' in the factories to public notice. The avarice and cruelty of many

[33] Richard Oastler, Reports and Pamphlets collected under the title *White Slavery*, vol. iv, report of Leeds meeting on Sadler's 10 Hour Bill, 9 Jan. 1831.

mill-owners were exposed: 'Lady Avarice has been stripped of her stage dress and her *blood-stained* garments are now discovered. No longer able to play her part she now flourishes her straps, and billy-rollers, and horse-whips, on high, and is determined to *die hard*.'[34] Edward's threatened use of his horse-whip was not merely a figment of Charlotte Brontë's imagination: a footnote to the passage quoted above notes that 'In a certain Worsted Mill, within ten miles of Leeds, a horse-whip was used a few weeks ago.' William's personal and instinctive rebellion against tyranny is placed in a public context by Hunsden's intervention; at a meeting in the Town Hall Hunsden stirs up the anger of the 'mob' against Edward 'for whom personally I care nothing, I only consider the brutal injustice with which he violated your natural claim to equality'.

Later in the novel Hunsden reappears to widen the contemporary relevance still further. In his spirited verbal battle with Frances he attributes the social evils of England—rhetorically condemned as Famine, Disease, Infamy, Ignorance coexisting with wanton Luxury—to a corrupt system of government: 'Examine the foot-prints of our august aristocracy—see how they walk in blood.' Frances argues hotly against his sweeping generalizations, but has an equal concern for liberty and resistance against unjust mastery. Hunsden's reference to her as a 'sort of Swiss Sybil'[35] suggests that Charlotte Brontë was alert to the appeals to social conscience made in Disraeli's 'Condition of England' novels. His *Coningsby* appeared in 1844, and *Sybil* in May 1845, when *The Professor* was being written. In the last chapter of the novel William and Frances enjoy the 'exciting and strange' conversations of Hunsden and his guests, concerned not just with English freedoms, but 'European progress—the spread of liberal sentiments over the continent; on their mental tablets, the names of Russia, Austria and the Pope are inscribed in red ink.' No other of Charlotte Brontë's novels was so strikingly up to date.

Other characters are presented with some skill—even with a

[34] Ibid., Sept. 1832, 3.
[35] *The Professor*, p. 218.

modest brilliance. Mrs Gaskell thought there were 'one or two remarkable portraits—the most charming *woman* she ever drew, and a glimpse of that woman as a mother—very lovely'.[36] With unobtrusive art, Charlotte mingles description, action, and dialogue to show the gradual shy unfolding of Frances Henri's nature, with its piquant interplay of proud independence and gentle modesty, firmness and delicacy. M. Pelet and Mlle Reuter are slight but integrated and original sketches. For Mlle Reuter especially, Charlotte has employed a series of effective images and associations—of predatory animals, of hardness and enclosure—which influence our attitude to her, and strengthen the contrast with Frances, whose associations are of soft glowing light and natural growth. Patterns of imagery are also sensitively used to mark William's development from frustrated to fulfilled life. Characteristic of Charlotte Brontë's style in all her work, they are a successful and influential element in this early novel where techniques, diction, and rhetoric vary markedly in their nature and in the degree of control with which they are deployed.

Often Charlotte seems to be making a conscious effort to match her style to the modernity of her theme and the masculinity of her narrator. She chooses a forthright, energetic, even slangy mode: 'My God! how he did snuffle, snort and wheeze!' William comments on one of his pupils—though 'when it came to shrieking, the girls indisputably beat the boys hollow'. Priests are no better: 'How the repeater of the prayer did cackle and splutter! I never before or since heard language enounced with such steam-engine haste.' William's revulsion from some of the girl-pupils is conveyed with vivid, tactile force—Aurelia has 'large feet tortured into small bottines . . . hair smoothed, braided, oiled and gummed to perfection . . . glossy with gum and grease'. Attempts at 'fine writing' are less successful. In the unfortunate 'Alfred' essay perpetrated by Frances, the results can be risible: 'Fate—thou hast done thy worst . . . aye! I see thine eye confront mine . . .' William's

[36] E. C. Gaskell to Emily Shaen [7 and 8 Sept. 1856], CP 308.

comment that her style 'stood in great need of polish' seems an understatement. Happily such purple passages are the exception, and the norm is an unforced, clear, agreeable prose. The brief descriptions of natural background are all the more effective for their unpretentious simplicity and for being in keeping with the youthful sensibility of the narrator. William recalls the 'clear, icy blue' of a January sky undimmed by the frost-mist rising from the river near the town of X——; in contrast, his first impression of Brussels is of lights shining 'through streaming and starless darkness'. A 'cloudless night-sky', where 'splendid moonlight subdued the tremulous sparkle of the stars' ironically reveals Mlle Reuter's treachery, and her garden, full of scented flowers and a 'soft and sweet south wind', is also the 'amphitheatre' where she seeks to recapture him. Settings and the style in which they are conveyed are far from the clichés of the romantic novel. The setting for William's reunion with Frances is the 'warm, breathless gloom' of the Protestant cemetery, described in phrases echoing Emily Brontë's poems, for the 'fitful, wandering airs' have 'fallen asleep', and the tombs lie 'impassible to sun or shadow, to rain or drought'.[37] Later, the background to the 'bridal snow' of Frances's wedding is a chilly winter scene: 'It was snowing fast out-of-doors; the afternoon had turned out wild and cold—the leaden sky seemed full of drifts and the street was already ankle-deep in the white down-fall. Our fire burned bright . . .'[38]

Charlotte Brontë was a shrewd critic of her own work. The narrative, she said, was 'deficient in incident and in general attractiveness; yet the middle and latter portions of the work, all that relates to Brussels, the Belgian school, &c. is as good as I can write; it contains more pith, more substance, more reality, in my judgment, than much of "Jane Eyre".'[39]

[37] *The Professor*, p. 154.
[38] Ibid. 227.
[39] Letter to W. S. Williams, 14 Dec. 1847; Princeton University Library MS.

NOTE ON THE TEXT

The manuscript of *The Professor* in the Pierpont Morgan library, on which this edition is based, reflects two stages of composition, several layers of authorial revision, and a final censorship by Charlotte Brontë's husband A. B. Nicholls and her father Patrick Brontë. It is a fair copy, dated on the last page '27th June 1846'. The first chapter is old material, both in content and in physical form, for apart from the recopied first and last leaves, it is written on yellowed, much-folded paper in the strongly sloping handwriting Charlotte Brontë had used in about 1840 rather than 1846. The recopied leaves link the old with the new material, from folio 13 to the end, written on whiter paper in her normal fair-copy hand (resembling that used in *Jane Eyre*, which she completed in 1847). The first leaf also shows a change in the title of the novel, for Charlotte has pasted a slip of paper over its original name, 'The Master'.

In her efforts to improve and resurrect *The Professor* after it had been rejected by Smith, Elder as well as six other publishers, Charlotte made corrections and additions, most of them in ink. There are also pencilled revisions—some, especially the deletions, being confirmed by overwriting in dark ink by A. B. Nicholls. While several of the pencilled revisions are routine improvements in phrasing, others show a common concern for removing oaths, references to physical contact, or 'passion'—all features which had led Miss Rigby to accuse Charlotte Brontë of coarseness in her review of *Jane Eyre* in the *Quarterly* for December 1848. For example 'God damn your insolence' becomes 'Confound your insolence' (p. 36), a 'warm, cherishing touch' becomes a 'cordial and gentle word' (p. 137), and a passage which probably read 'I can only say that the face and countenance of Hunsden Yorke Hunsden Esqre resembled more the result of a ?cross between Oliver Cromwell and a French grisette, than anything else in Heaven above or in the Earth beneath' has been heavily deleted (p. 186, after the word 'indescribable'). A very few other short passages or phrases have been obliterated beyond retrieval, or literally cut out. Late 1849 or early 1850 would seem a likely date for the pencilled revisions, for Charlotte wrote at about that time her second 'Preface', 'This little book . . .', 'with a view to the publication of "The Professor" shortly after the appearance of "Shirley" ', as Mr Nicholls explained in a foreword to the first edition. Authorial revisions would not be later than 5 February 1851, when *The Professor*, rejected for a ninth time, was 'locked up in a cupboard by himself', and some of the Brussels episodes were reused, much altered and indeed transformed, in *Villette*.

The final censorship by Mr Nicholls, after discussion with Mr Brontë, was not exhaustive; some of the rare dark ink deletions may originate from him (not simply confirming an authorial revision), but he was remarkably restrained. Mrs Gaskell wished he had altered more, for he had left intact some of the 'blasphemous' expressions which embarrassed her as she made out her case for Charlotte's 'essential purity of mind' in the *Life*. On the whole, therefore, the manuscript must very fairly represent the author's final intentions as regards the presentation of her cherished first novel. The Clarendon edition of the novel (1987), on which the present edition is based, followed the manuscript, with minimal emendations only where the original was misleading or unacceptably eccentric. The first edition, the posthumous production by Smith, Elder of 1857, departs from the manuscript in its more formal punctuation, in its inconsistent use of Charlotte Brontë's capitalization, and in almost a hundred misreadings, misprints, or omissions. We give here a list of some of the more significant manuscript readings compared with the erroneous text of the first edition. For fuller details of the text, see the Clarendon edition introduction and footnotes.

We are grateful to the Pierpont Morgan Library in New York for permission to use and quote from the manuscript of *The Professor*, MA32.

The page and line numbers on the left are those of the present edition.

Page	*Line*	*Pierpont Morgan draft MS (Preface)*		*First Edition, vol. i*
1	20	beautiful nor a rich wife, nor	vi	beautiful girl or
1	22	doom—Labour throughout life and a	vi	doom, and drain throughout life a
		Pierpont Morgan fair copy (Main text)		
6	32	the dank, gloomy mists	9	the dark gloomy mists
30	26	never talk about change	64	never take change
47	27	envy any king in	100	envy any being in
48	1	from a side-table, he	101	from a sideboard, he
62	17	the fat, dull soil	132	the flat, dull soil
67	27	Ah the world	144	All the world
68	2	Mesdames—infinitely obliged	145	mesdames –I am infinitely obliged
77	34	Simi-collong? Ah	168	Semi-collong? Ah
79	25	dazzled my perspicacity	172	dazzled my perspicuity
81	8	this little real woman!	175	this little woman;
91	36	coarse, worky-day sort	199	coarse, work-day sort
98	1	longer "inconvenanant" for	213	longer "inconvenient" for
99	1	heart? She must have—what kindness and affection were in her manner to me to-day! What a good,	215	heart? What a good,
105	2	she but glanced down	228	she had glanced down
		MS		*First Edition, vol. ii*
152	12	the chairs of the Chapel royal	40	the choirs of the chapel-royal,
154	21	and a human being,	45	and a human thing;
160	27	a tiny silver cream-ewer,	60	a tidy silver cream-ewer,
165	24	I left the West	71	I felt the West

170	25	some insinuating inquiry	82	some interesting inquiry
228	21	given Mimie	215	given Minnie"
228	34	Mimie having	215	Minnie having

SELECT BIBLIOGRAPHY

Editions of The Professor

First edition, 2 vols. (Smith, Elder & Co., 1857).

Collins edition (1954). Includes 'Emma' and selected tales from Angria, edited with an introduction and biography by Phyllis Bentley.

Clarendon edition (Oxford University Press, 1987). Based on the manuscript; introduction, textual and explanatory notes by Margaret Smith and Herbert Rosengarten. Includes 'Emma', based on the manuscript, and indexes of quotations and allusions in the novels of Charlotte Brontë.

Penguin edition (1989). Edited with an introduction by Heather Glen.

Bibliography

T. J. Wise, *A Bibliography of the Writings in Prose and Verse of the Members of the Brontë Family* (1917, repr. 1965).

Lionel Stevenson (ed.), *Victorian Fiction: a Guide to Research* (1964). Section on the Brontës by M. G. Christian.

G. H. Ford (ed.), *Victorian Fiction: a second Guide to Research* (1978). Section on the Brontës by Herbert Rosengarten.

G. A. Yablon and J. R. Turner, *A Brontë Bibliography* (1978).

Christine Alexander, *A Bibliography of the Manuscripts of Charlotte Brontë* (1982).

Biography and Letters

Elizabeth C. Gaskell, *The Life of Charlotte Brontë* (Smith, Elder & Co., 1857). Edited by Alan Shelston for Penguin (1975), giving the text of the 'libellous' first edition, but recording also the revisions of the third edition.

T. J. Wise and J. A. Symington, *The Brontës: their Lives, Friendships and Correspondence* (1932, reprinted 1980). The text of the letters is unreliable, but the collection is the most extensive so far published.

Winifred Gérin, *Charlotte Brontë: the Evolution of Genius* (1967, reprinted with corrections 1968).

Rebecca Fraser, *Charlotte Brontë* (1988).

Juvenilia

T. J. Wise and J. A. Symington (eds.), *Miscellaneous and Unpublished Writings of Charlotte and Patrick Branwell Brontë*, 2 vols. (1936).

F. E. Ratchford, *The Brontës' Web of Childhood* (1941).

Winifred Gérin (ed.), *Five Novelettes* by Charlotte Brontë (1971).

Christine Alexander, *The Early Writings of Charlotte Brontë* (1983).

—— *An Edition of the Early Writings of Charlotte Brontë 1826–1832* (1987).

Background and Criticism

Herbert Wroot, *Sources of the Brontë Novels: Persons and Places*, a Supplement to the *Brontë Society Transactions* for 1935.

R. B. Martin, *The Accents of Persuasion: Charlotte Brontë's Novels* (1966).

Margot Peters, *Charlotte Brontë: Style in the Novel* (1973).

Miriam Allott, *The Brontës: the Critical Heritage* (1974).

Enid L. Duthie, *The Foreign Vision of Charlotte Brontë* (1975).

F. B. Pinion, *A Brontë Companion: Literary Assessment, Background, and Reference* (1975).

C. A. Linder, *Romantic Imagery in the Novels of Charlotte Brontë* (1978).

John Maynard, *Charlotte Brontë and Sexuality* (1984).

Enid L. Duthie, *The Brontës and Nature* (1986).

Periodicals

The *Transactions* of the Brontë Society include bibliographies, catalogues, transcripts of juvenilia, letters, and essays, biographical and topographical material, and critical commentary. A subject and author index by A. G. Foster was published in 1968, covering vol. 1 (1895) to vol. 15 (1967).

Articles in this and other periodicals include:

J. A. Falconer, '*The Professor* and *Villette*: a Study of Development', *English Studies* (Apr. 1927).

M. M. Brammer, 'The Manuscript of *The Professor*', *Review of English Studies* (May 1960).

M. D. Wheeler, 'Literary and Biblical Allusions in "The Professor" ', *Brontë Society Transactions* (1976).

Melodie Monahan, '*Ashworth*: an unfinished novel by Charlotte Brontë', *Studies in Philology: Texts and Studies* (1983).

Margaret Smith, 'The Manuscripts of Charlotte Brontë's Novels', *Brontë Society Transactions* (1983).

Sue Ann Betsinger, 'Charlotte Brontë's Archetypal Heroine', *Brontë Society Transactions* (1989, part 7).

A CHRONOLOGY OF CHARLOTTE BRONTË

		Age
1816	(21 Apr.) Born at Thornton, Bradford, Yorkshire, third child of Patrick and Maria Brontë	
1817	(26 June) Patrick Branwell Brontë born	
1818	(30 July) Emily Jane Brontë born	
1820	(17 Jan.) Anne Brontë born	
	(20 Apr.) The Brontës move to Haworth, near Keighley, Yorkshire	3
1821	(15 Sept.) Mrs Brontë dies	5
1824	(10 Aug.) Charlotte arrives at Cowan Bridge school, Lancashire	8
	(25 Nov.) joined by Emily	
1825	(6 May) Charlotte's elder sister Maria dies	9
	(1 June) Charlotte and Emily return to Haworth	
	(15 June) Elizabeth Brontë dies	
1825–30	Brontë children at home under supervision of their aunt, Elizabeth Branwell	9–14
1831	(17 Jan.) Charlotte arrives at Miss Wooler's school, Roe Head, near Mirfield, Yorkshire	14
1832	(May) Charlotte leaves Roe Head	16
1835	(29 July) Charlotte returns to Roe Head as teacher	19
1837	(May) Miss Wooler's school moves to Dewsbury Moor	21
1838	(23 May) Charlotte leaves Dewsbury Moor	22
1839	(5 Mar.) Refuses Henry Nussey's proposal of marriage	22
	(May) Governess at Mrs Sidgwick's at Stonegappe, Lothersdale	23

1839 (*cont.*) (19 July) Leaves Stonegappe
(July) Refuses Mr Bryce's proposal
(Aug.–Sept.) Holiday with Ellen Nussey at Easton and Bridlington

1840 With Emily at Haworth 23–4

1841 (2 Mar.) Governess at Mrs White's, Upperwood House, Rawdon, near Bradford 24
(24 Dec.) Leaves Upperwood House 25

1842 (12 Feb.) Goes with Emily to Mme Heger's school in Brussels 25
(29 Oct.) Miss Branwell dies at Haworth 26
(8 Nov.) Charlotte and Emily return to Haworth

1843 (28 Jan.) Charlotte returns alone to Brussels 26

1844 (1 Jan.) Charlotte leaves Brussels for Haworth 27
(July) Occupied with project of school at Haworth Parsonage 28

1844–5 Letters from Charlotte to M. Heger written 28–9

1845 (17 July) Branwell receives dismissal from his post as tutor 29

1846 (May) Publication of *Poems* by Currer, Ellis, and Acton Bell (Charlotte, Emily, and Anne) 30–1
(Apr. 1846–July 1847) *The Professor* offered, without success, to various publishers
(Aug.) *Jane Eyre* begun

1847 (19 Oct.) *Jane Eyre* published 31
(Dec.) *Wuthering Heights* (by Emily Brontë) and *Agnes Grey* (by Anne Brontë) published

1848 (June) Anne's *The Tenant of Wildfell Hall* published
(July) Charlotte and Anne visit their publishers in London to prove the separate identity of the 'Bells' 32
(24 Sept.) Branwell dies
(19 Dec.) Emily dies

1849 (28 May) Anne dies
(26 Oct.) *Shirley* published 33

	(Nov.–Dec.) Charlotte visits London; meets Thackeray	
1850	(May–June) Visits London, sits for portrait to Richmond	34
	(3–6 July) Visits Edinburgh	
	(Aug.) Meets Mrs Gaskell during visit to Kay-Shuttleworth	
1851	(April) Refuses James Taylor's proposal of marriage	34
	(May–June) Visits London for the Exhibition	35
	Begins writing *Villette*	
1852	*Villette* completed	35–6
1853	(Jan.) Last visit to London	36
	(28 Jan.) *Villette* published	
	(Apr.) Visits Mrs Gaskell in Manchester	37
	(Nov.) Writes 'Emma'	37
1854	(29 June) Marries Revd A. B. Nicholls	38
1855	(31 Mar.) Dies at Haworth	38

THE PROFESSOR

Preface

THIS little book was written before either "Jane Eyre" or "Shirley" and yet no indulgence can be solicited for it on the plea of a first attempt. A first attempt it certainly was not as the pen which wrote it had been previously worn down a good deal in a practice of some years. I had not indeed published anything before I commenced "The Professor"—but in many a crude effort destroyed almost as soon as composed I had got over any such taste as I might once have had for the ornamented and redundant in composition—and had come to prefer what was plain and homely. At the same time I had adopted a set of principles on the subject of incident &c. such as would be generally approved in theory, but the results of which when carried out into practise often procure for an author more surprise than pleasure. I said to myself that my hero should work his way through life as I had seen real living men work theirs—that he should never get a shilling he had not earned—that no sudden turns should lift him in a moment to wealth and high station—that whatever small competency he might gain should be won by the sweat of his brow—that before he could find so much as an arbour to sit down in—he should master at least half the ascent of the hill of Difficulty—that he should not even marry a beautiful nor a rich wife, nor a lady of rank—As Adam's Son he should share Adam's doom—Labour throughout life and a mixed and moderate cup of enjoyment.

In the sequel, however, I found that Publishers, in general—scarcely approved this system, but would have liked something more imaginative and poetical—something more consonant with a highly wrought fancy, with a native taste for pathos—with sentiments more tender—elevated—unworldly—indeed until an author has tried to dispose of a M.S. of this kind he can never know what stores of romance and sensibility lie hidden in breasts he would not have suspected of casketing such treasures. Men in business are usually thought to prefer the real—on trial this idea will be often found fallacious: a passionate preference for the wild wonderful and thrilling—the strange, startling and harrowing agitates divers souls that shew a calm and sober surface.

Such being the case—the reader will comprehend that to have reached him in the form of a printed book—this brief narrative must have gone through some struggles—which indeed it has—and after all its worst struggle and strongest ordeal is yet to come—but it takes comfort—subdues fear—leans on the staff of a moderate expectation—and mutters under its breath—while lifting its eye to that of the Public,

"He that is low need fear no fall."

THE PROFESSOR

a Tale

by

CURRER BELL

CHAPTER I

INTRODUCTORY

THE other day, in looking over my papers, I found in my desk the following copy of a letter, sent by me a year since to an old school-acquaintance.

"Dear Charles—

I think when you and I were at Eton together, we were neither of us what could be called—popular characters—; you were a sarcastic, observant, shrewd, cold-blooded creature; my own portrait—I will not attempt to draw—but I cannot recollect that it was a strikingly attractive one—can you? What animal magnetism drew thee and me together—I know not; certainly I never experienced anything of the Pylades and Orestes sentiment for you, and I have reason to believe that you, on your part, were equally free from all romantic regard to me. Still, out of school-hours, we walked and talked continually together; when the theme of conversation was our companions or our masters, we understood each other, and when I recurred to some sentiment of affection, some vague love of an excellent or beautiful object, whether in animate or inanimate nature—your sardonic coldness did not move me—I felt myself superior to that check *then* as I do *now*.

It is a long time since I wrote to you and a still longer time since I saw you—chancing to take up a newspaper of your County, the other day, my eye fell upon your name—I began to think of old times; to run over the events which have transpired since we separated—and I sat down and commenced this letter; what you have been doing I know not, but you shall hear, if you choose to listen, how the world has wagged with me.

First, after leaving Eton, I had an interview with my maternal uncles, Lord Tynedale and the Hon. John Seacombe. They asked me if I would enter the church and my uncle the nobleman offered me the living of Seacombe, which is in his gift, if I would; then my other uncle, Mr. Seacombe, hinted that when I became Rector of Seacombe-cum-Scaife—I might perhaps be allowed to take, as mistress of my house and head of my parish, one of my six cousins, his daughters, all of whom I greatly dislike.

I declined both the church and matrimony—a good clergyman is a good thing—but I should have made a very bad one—as to the wife—Oh how like a nightmare is the thought of being bound for life to one of my Cousins! No doubt they are accomplished and pretty, but not an accomplishment, not a charm of theirs, touches a chord in my bosom. To think of passing the winter-evenings by the parlour-fireside of Seacombe Rectory—alone—with one of them, for instance the large and well-modelled statue, Sarah—no, I should be a bad husband, under such circumstances, as well as a bad clergyman.

When I had declined my Uncles' offers, they asked me "what I intended to do." I said—I should reflect; they reminded me that I had no fortune and no expectations of any, and, after a considerable pause, Lord Tynedale demanded sternly "Whether I had thoughts of following my father's steps and engaging in trade?" Now I had had no thoughts of the sort; I do not think that my turn of mind qualifies me to make a good tradesman—my taste, my ambition does not lie that way, but such was the scorn expressed in Lord Tynedale's countenance as he pronounced the word *Trade*, such the contemptuous sarcasm of his tone, that I was instantly decided. My father was but a name to me—yet that name I did not like to hear mentioned with a sneer to my very face; I answered then, with haste and warmth, "I cannot do better than follow in my father's steps—yes—I will be a tradesman." My uncles did not remonstrate—they and I parted with mutual disgust. In reviewing this transaction I find that I was quite right to shake off the burden of Tynedale's patronage—but a fool to offer my shoulders instantly for the reception of another burden which might be more intolerable and which certainly was yet untried.

I wrote instantly to Edward—you know Edward—my only brother—ten years my senior—married to a rich millowner's daughter and now possessor of the Mill and business which was my father's before he failed. You are aware that my father—once reckoned a Crœsus of wealth, became bankrupt a short time previous to his death—and that my mother lived in destitution for some six months after him, unhelped by her aristocratical brothers, whom she had mortally offended by her union with Crimsworth the ——shire Manufacturer. At the end of the six months she brought me into the world and then herself left it without, I should think, much regret—as it contained little hope or comfort for her.

My father's relations took charge of Edward—as they did of me, till I was nine years old. At that period it chanced that the representation of an important borough in our County, fell vacant; Mr. Seacombe stood for it: my Uncle Crimsworth, an astute, mercantile man, took the opportunity of writing a fierce letter to the Candidate, stating, that if he and Lord Tynedale did not consent to do something towards the support of their sister's orphan children—he would expose their relentless and malignant conduct towards that sister and do his best to turn the circumstances against Mr. Seacombe's election. That Gentleman and Lord T—— knew well enough that the Crimsworths were an unscrupulous and determined race—they knew also that they had influence in the borough of X—— and making a virtue of necessity they consented to defray the expenses of my education. I was sent to Eton—where I remained ten years, during which space of time, Edward and I never met. He, when he grew up, entered into trade and pursued his calling with such diligence, ability and success that now, in his thirtieth year, he was fast making a fortune. Of this I was apprised by the occasional short letters I received from him, some three or four times a year; which said letters, never concluded without some expression of determined enmity against the house of Seacombe and some reproach to me for living, as he said, on the bounty of that house. At first, while still in boyhood, I could not understand why, as I had no parents, I should not be indebted to my uncles Tynedale and Seacombe for my education—but as I grew up and heard by degrees of the persevering hostility, the hatred till death evinced by them against my father—of the sufferings of my mother, of all the wrongs, in short, of our house, then did I conceive shame of the dependence in which I lived and form a resolution no more to take bread from hands, which had refused to minister to the necessities of my dying mother. It was by these feelings I was influenced when I refused the Rectory of Seacombe and the union with one of my patrician Cousins.

An irreparable breach thus being effected between my uncles and myself, I wrote to Edward, told him what had occurred and informed him of my intention to follow his steps and be a tradesman—I asked, moreover, if he could give me employment. His answer expressed no approbation of my conduct—but he said I might come down to ——shire if I liked and he would "see what could be done in the way of furnishing me with work." I repressed all—even *mental* comment on his note—packed my trunk and carpet-bag and started for the North directly.

After two days' travelling (railroads were not then in existence) I arrived, one wet October afternoon, in the town of X——. I had always understood that Edward lived in this town but on enquiry I found that it was only Mr. Crimsworth's Mill and Warehouse which were situated in the smoky atmosphere of Bigben Close—his *residence* lay four miles out, in the Country.

It was late in the evening when I alighted at the gates of the habitation designated to me as my brother's. As I advanced up the avenue, I could see through the shades of twilight, and the dank, gloomy mists which deepened those shades, that the house was large and the grounds surrounding it, sufficiently spacious. I paused a moment on the lawn in front—and leaning my back against a tall tree which rose in the centre—I gazed with interest on the exterior of Crimsworth Hall.

"Edward is rich," thought I to myself. "I believed him to be doing well—but I did not know he was master of a mansion like this." Cutting short all marvelling, speculation, conjecture &c.—I advanced to the front door and rang. A man-servant opened it—I announced myself—he relieved me of my wet cloak and carpet-bag and ushered me into a room, furnished as a library, where there was a bright fire, and candles burning on the table: he informed me that his master was not yet returned from X—— market but that he would certainly be at home in the course of half an hour.

Being left to myself, I took the stuffed easy chair, covered with red morocco, which stood by the fireside, and while my eyes watched the flames dart from the glowing coals, and the cinders fall at intervals on the hearth—my mind busied itself in conjectures concerning the meeting about to take place. Amidst much that was doubtful in the subject of these conjectures, there was one thing tolerably certain—I was in no danger of encountering severe disappointment—from this, the moderation of my expectations guaranteed me—I anticipated no overflowings of fraternal tenderness—Edward's letters had always been such as to prevent the engendering or harbouring of delusions of this sort. Still as I sat awaiting his arrival—I felt eager—very eager—I cannot tell you why; my hand, so utterly a stranger to the grasp of a kindred hand, clenched itself to repress the tremor with which impatience would fain have shaken it.

I thought of my uncles—and as I was engaged in wondering whether Edward's indifference would equal the cold disdain I had always experienced from them—I heard the avenue gates open: wheels approached the house, Mr. Crimsworth was arrived and after the lapse of some minutes and a brief dialogue between himself and his servant in the hall, his tread drew near the library-door—that tread alone announced the master of the house.

I still retained some confused recollection of Edward as he was ten years ago—a tall, wiry, raw youth—*now*—as I rose from my seat and turned towards the library-door—I saw a fine-looking and powerful man—light-complexioned, well-made and of athletic proportions. The first glance made me aware of an air of promptitude and sharpness, shewn as well in his movements as in his port, his eye, and the general expression of his face. He greeted me with brevity and, in the moment of shaking hands, scanned me from head to foot; he took his seat in the morocco-covered arm-chair and motioned me to another seat.

"I expected you would have called at the counting-house in the Close," said he—and his voice, I noticed, had an abrupt accent, probably habitual to him, he spoke also with a guttural northern tone, which sounded harsh in my ears, accustomed to the silvery utterance of the South.

"The landlord of the Inn where the coach stopped, directed me here," said I—"I doubted at first the accuracy of his information, not being aware that you had such a residence as this."

"Oh it is all right!" he replied. "Only I was kept half an hour behind time, waiting for you—that is all—I thought you must be coming by the eight o'clock coach."

I expressed regret that he had had to wait—he made no answer but stirred the fire as if to cover a movement of impatience—then he scanned me again.

I felt an inward satisfaction that I had not, in the first moment of meeting, betrayed any warmth, any enthusiasm, that I had saluted this man with a quiet and steady phlegm.

"Have you quite broken with Tynedale and Seacombe?" he asked hastily.

"I do not think I shall have any further communication with them; my refusal of their proposals will I fancy operate as a barrier against all future intercourse."

"Why," said he, "I may as well remind you at the very outset of our connection that 'no man can serve two masters.' Acquaintance with Lord Tynedale will be incompatible with assistance from me." There was a kind of gratuitous menace in his eye as he looked at me in finishing this observation.

Feeling no disposition to reply to him—I contented myself with an inward speculation on the differences which exist in the constitution of men's minds. I do not know what inference Mr. Crimsworth drew from my silence—whether he considered it a symptom of contumacity or an evidence of my being cowed by his peremptory manner. After a long and hard stare at me, he rose sharply from his seat.

"To-morrow," said he, "I shall call your attention to some other points—but now it is supper-time and Mrs. Crimsworth is probably waiting; will you come?"

He strode from the room and I followed. In crossing the hall I wondered what Mrs. Crimsworth might be. "Is she," thought I, "as alien to what I like as Tynedale, Seacombe, the Misses Seacombe —as the affectionate relative now striding before me? or is she better than these? Shall I, in conversing with her, feel free to shew something of my real nature—or—" Further conjectures were arrested by my entrance into the dining-room. A lamp, burning under a shade of ground-glass, shewed a handsome apartment, wainscotted with oak; supper was laid on the table; by the fire-place, standing as if waiting our entrance, appeared a lady; she was young, tall and well-shaped—her dress was handsome and fashionable—so much my first glance sufficed to ascertain. A gay salutation passed between her and Mr. Crimsworth; she chid him, half-playfully, half poutingly, for being late; her voice—(I always take voices into the account in judging of character) was lively—it indicated, I thought, good animal spirits. Mr. Crimsworth soon checked her animated scolding with a kiss—a kiss that still told of the bridegroom (they had not yet been married a year)—she took her seat at the supper-table in first-rate spirits. Perceiving me—she begged my pardon for not noticing me before and then shook hands with me as ladies do when a flow of good-humour disposes them to be cheerful to all, even the most indifferent of their acquaintance. It was now further obvious to me that she had a good complexion and features sufficiently marked but agreeable; her hair was red—quite red. She and Edward talked much—always in a vein of playful contention; she was vexed, or pretended to be vexed, that he had that day driven a vicious horse in the gig and he made light of her fears. Sometimes she appealed to me—

"Now, Mr. William, isn't it absurd in Edward to talk so? He says he will drive Jack and no other horse and the brute has thrown him twice already."

She spoke with a kind of lisp not disagreeable but childish,—I soon saw also that there was a more than girlish—a somewhat infantine expression in her, by-no-means small, features; this lisp and expression were, I have no doubt, a charm in Edward's eyes, and would be so to those of most men—but they were not to mine. I sought her eye, desirous to read there the intelligence which I could not discern in her face or hear in her conversation; it was merry, rather small; by turns I saw vivacity, vanity—coquetry, look out through its irid, but I watched in vain for a glimpse of soul. I am no Oriental, white necks—carmine lips and cheeks, clusters of bright curls do not suffice for me without that Promethean spark which will live after the roses and lilies are faded, the burnished hair grown grey. In sunshine, in prosperity the flowers are very well—but how many wet days are there in life—November seasons of disaster—when a man's hearth and home would be cold indeed, without the clear, cheering gleam of intellect.

Having perused the fair page of Mrs. Crimsworth's face—a deep, involuntary sigh announced my disappointment—she took it as a homage to her beauty—and Edward, who was evidently proud of his rich and handsome young wife—threw on me a glance—half-ridicule, half-ire.

I turned from them both—and gazing wearily round the room, I saw two pictures set in the oak-panelling, one on each side the mantelpiece—ceasing to take part in the bantering conversation that flowed on between Mr. and Mrs. Crimsworth—I bent my thoughts to the examination of these pictures. They were portraits—a lady and a gentleman, both costumed in the fashion of twenty years ago. The gentleman was in the shade—I could not see him well—the lady had the benefit of a full beam from the softly shaded lamp—I presently recognized her; I had seen this picture before, in childhood; it was my mother; that and the companion picture being the only heir-looms saved out of the sale of my father's property.

The face, I remembered, had pleased me as a boy, but *then* I did not understand it; *now* I knew how rare that class of face is in the world, and I appreciated keenly its thoughtful yet gentle expression. The serious grey eye possessed for me a strong charm, as did certain lines in the features indicative of most true and tender feeling. I was sorry it was only a picture.

I soon left Mr. and Mrs. Crimsworth to themselves; a servant conducted me to my bed-room; in closing my chamber-door I shut out all intruders, you, Charles, as well as the rest.

Good bye for the present.
William Crimsworth."

To this letter I never got an answer—before my old friend received it, he had accepted a government appointment in one of the colonies, and was already on his way to the scene of his official labours. What has become of him since I know not.

The leisure time I have at command, and which I intended to employ for his private benefit—I shall now dedicate to that of the public at large. My narrative is not exciting and, above all, not marvellous—but it may interest some individuals, who, having toiled in the same vocation as myself, will find in my experience, frequent reflections of their own. The above letter will serve as introduction—I now proceed.

CHAPTER II

A FINE October Morning succeeded to the foggy evening that had witnessed my first introduction to Crimsworth-Hall. I was early up and walking in the large, park-like meadow surrounding the house. The autumn sun, rising over the ——shire hills, disclosed a pleasant country; woods brown and mellow varied the fields from which the harvest had been lately carried, a river, gliding between the woods, caught on its surface the somewhat cold gleam of the October sun and sky: at frequent intervals along the banks of the river—tall, cylindrical chimnies, almost like slender, round towers, indicated the factories which the trees half concealed; here and there mansions, similar to Crimsworth-Hall, occupied agreeable sites on the hill-side; the country wore, on the whole, a cheerful, active, fertile look—Steam, Trade, Machinery had long banished from it all romance and seclusion. At a distance of five miles—a valley, opening between the low hills, held in its cup the great town of X——; a dense, permanent vapour brooded over this locality—there lay Edward's "Concern".

I forced my eye to scrutinize this prospect, I forced my mind to dwell on it for a time, and when I found that it communicated no pleasurable emotion to my heart—that it stirred in me none of the hopes a man ought to feel when he sees laid before him the scene of his life's career—I said to myself, "William—you are a rebel against circumstances; you are a fool and know not what you want—you have chosen trade and you shall be a tradesman; look!" I continued mentally, "Look at the sooty smoke in that hollow and know that there is your post! There you cannot dream, you cannot speculate and theorize—there you shall out and work!"

Thus self-schooled, I returned to the house. My brother was in the breakfast-room—I met him collectedly—I could not meet him cheerfully; he was standing on the rug—his back to the fire—how much did I read in the expression of his eye as my glance encountered his, when I advanced to bid him good-morning—how much that was contradictory to my nature! He said "Good-morning" abruptly and nodded, and then he snatched, rather than took, a newspaper from the table, and began to read it with the air of a master who seizes a pretext to escape the bore of conversing with an underling. It was well I had taken a resolution to endure for a time or his manner would have gone far to render insupportable the disgust I had just been endeavouring to subdue. I looked at him—I measured his robust frame and powerful proportions—I saw my own reflection in the mirror over the mantel-piece; I amused myself with comparing the two pictures. In face I resembled him, though I was not so handsome—my features were less regular—I had a darker eye and a broader brow—in form I was greatly inferior—thinner, slighter, not so tall. As an animal, Edward excelled me far—should he prove as paramount in mind as in person I must be his slave—for I must expect from him no lion-like generosity to one weaker than himself; his cold, avaricious eye, his stern, forbidding manner told me he would not spare. Had I then force of mind to cope with him? I did not know—I had never been tried.

Mrs. Crimsworth's entrance diverted my thoughts for a moment. She looked well—dressed in white—her face and her attire shining in Morning and bridal freshness. I addressed her with the degree of ease her last night's careless gaiety seemed to warrant, but she replied with coolness and restraint—her husband had tutored her—she was not to be too familiar with his clerk.

As soon as breakfast was over—Mr. Crimsworth intimated to me that they were bringing the gig round to the door and that in five minutes he should expect me to be ready to go down with him to X——. I did not keep him waiting; we were soon dashing at a rapid rate along the road. The horse he drove was the same vicious animal about which Mrs. Crimsworth had expressed her fears the night before; once or twice Jack seemed disposed to turn restive, but a vigorous and determined application of the whip from the ruthless hand of his master soon compelled him to submission, and

Edward's dilated nostril expressed his triumph in the result of the contest; he scarcely spoke to me during the whole of the brief drive, only opening his lips at intervals to damn his horse.

X—— was all stir and bustle when we entered it; we left the clean streets where there were dwelling-houses and shops, churches and public-buildings, we left all these, and turned down to a region of mills and warehouses, thence we passed through two massive gates into a great paved yard, and we were in Bigben Close, and the Mill was before us, vomiting soot from its long chimney and quivering through its thick brick walls with the commotion of its iron bowels. Work-people were passing to and fro, a waggon was being laden with pieces. Mr. Crimsworth looked from side to side and seemed at one glance to comprehend all that was going on; he alighted and leaving his horse and gig to the care of a man who hastened to take the reins from his hand—he bid me follow him to the counting-house. We entered it; a very different place from the parlours of Crimsworth-hall, a place for business, with a bare, planked floor, a safe, two high desks and stools, and some chairs. A person was seated at one of the desks, who took off his square cap when Mr. Crimsworth entered, and in an instant was again absorbed in his occupation of writing or calculating—I know not which.

Mr. Crimsworth having removed his mackintosh sat down by the fire, I remained standing near the hearth; he said presently:

"Steighton, you may leave the room; I have some business to transact with this gentleman. Come back when you hear the bell."

The individual at the desk rose and departed, closing the door as he went out. Mr. Crimsworth stirred the fire, then folded his arms and sat a moment thinking, his lips compressed, his brow knit; I had nothing to do but to watch him—how well his features were cut! What a handsome man he was! Whence then came that air of contraction—that narrow and hard aspect on his forehead, in all his lineaments?

Turning to me he began abruptly:

"You are come down to ——shire to learn to be a tradesman?"

"Yes I am."

"Have you made up your mind on the point? Let me know that at once."

"Yes."

"Well, I am not bound to help you, but I have a place here vacant—if you are qualified for it—I will take you on trial. What can you do? Do you know anything besides that useless trash of college learning, Greek, Latin and so forth?"

"I have studied Mathematics."

"Stuff! I daresay you have."

"I can read and write French and German."

"Hum!" He reflected a moment, then—opening a drawer in a desk near him took out a letter and gave it to me.

"Can you read that?" he asked.

It was a German commercial letter; I translated it; I could not tell whether he was gratified or not—his countenance remained fixed.

"It is well," he said after a pause, "that you are acquainted with something useful, something that may enable you to earn your board and lodging: since you know French and German I will take you as second clerk to manage the foreign correspondence of the House—I shall give you a good salary—£90 a year—and now," he continued, raising his voice, "hear once for all what I have to say about our relationship and all that sort of humbug! I must have no nonsense on that point, it would never suit me—I shall excuse you nothing on the plea of being my brother; if I find you stupid, negligent, dissipated, idle or possessed of any faults detrimental to the interests of the House—I shall dismiss you as I would any other clerk. £90 a year are good wages and I expect to have the full value of my money out of you; remember too that things are on a practical footing in my establishment, business-like habits, feelings and ideas suit me best—do you understand?"

"Partly," I replied. "I suppose you mean that I am to do my work for my wages, not to expect favour from you and not to depend on you for any help but what I earn—that suits me exactly and on these terms I will consent to be your clerk."

I turned on my heel and walked to the window; this time I did not consult his face to learn his opinion; what it was I do not know, nor did I then care. After a silence of some minutes, he recommenced:

"You perhaps expect to be accommodated with apartments at Crimsworth-Hall and to go and come with me in the gig, I wish you however to be aware that such an arrangement would be quite inconvenient to me; I like to have the seat in my gig at liberty for any gentleman whom for business reasons, I may wish to take down to the Hall for a night or so. You will seek out lodgings in X——."

Quitting the window, I walked back to the hearth:

"Of course I shall seek out lodgings in X——," I answered. "It would not suit me either to lodge at Crimsworth-Hall."

My tone was quiet—I always speak quietly—yet Mr. Crimsworth's blue eye became incensed—he took his revenge rather oddly. Turning to me—he said bluntly,

"You are poor enough, I suppose; how do you expect to live till your quarter's salary becomes due?"

"I shall get on," said I.

"How do you expect to live?" he repeated in a louder voice.

"As I can, Mr. Crimsworth."

"Get into debt at your peril!—that's all," he answered, "for aught I know you may have extravagant aristocratic habits; if you have, drop them; I tolerate nothing of the sort here, and I will never give you a shilling extra, whatever liabilities you may incur; mind that—"

"Yes, Mr. Crimsworth, you will find I have a good memory."

I said no more—I did not think the time was come for much parley; I had an instinctive feeling that it would be folly to let one's temper effervesce often with such a man as Edward. I said to myself, "I will place my cup under this continual dropping—it shall stand there still and steady; when full it will run over of itself—meantime—patience—two things are certain—I am capable of performing the work Mr. Crimsworth has set me; I can earn my wages conscientiously and those wages are sufficient to enable me to live; as to the fact of my brother assuming towards me the bearing of a proud, harsh master—the fault is his, not mine; and shall his injustice, his bad feeling turn me at once aside from the path I have chosen? No—at least, ere I deviate, I will advance far enough to see whither my career tends. As yet I am only pressing in at the entrance—a strait gate enough—it ought to have a good terminus." While I thus reasoned Mr. Crimsworth rang a bell; his first clerk, the individual dismissed previously to our conference, re-entered.

"Mr. Steighton," said he, "shew Mr. William the letters from Voss, brothers—and give him English copies of the answers, he will translate them."

Mr. Steighton, a man of about thirty-five, with a face at once sly and heavy, hastened to execute this order; he laid the letters on the desk, and I was soon seated at it, and engaged in rendering the English answers into German. A sentiment of keen pleasure accompanied this first effort to earn my own living—a sentiment neither poisoned nor weakened by the presence of the taskmaster who stood and watched me for some time as I wrote. I thought he was trying to read my character but I felt as secure against his scrutiny as if I had had on a casque with the visor down—or rather I shewed him my countenance with the confidence that one would shew an unlearned man a letter written in Greek—he might see lines, and trace characters, but he could make nothing of them—my nature was not his nature, and its signs were to him like the words of an unknown tongue; erelong he turned away abruptly, as if baffled, and left the counting-house; he returned to it but twice in the course of that day—each time he mixed and swallowed a glass of brandy and water—the materials for making which, he extracted from a cupboard on one side of the fire-place; having glanced at my translations—he could read both French and German—he went out again in silence.

CHAPTER III

I SERVED Edward as his second clerk faithfully, punctually, diligently. What was given me to do, I had the power and the determination to do well. Mr. Crimsworth watched sharply for defects but found none; he set Timothy Steighton, his favourite and head-man, to watch also, Tim was baffled; I was as exact as himself, and quicker: Mr. Crimsworth made enquiries as to how I lived, whether I got into debt—no—my accounts with my landlady were always straight; I had hired small lodgings which I contrived to pay for out of a slender fund—the accumulated savings of my Eton pocket-money; for as it had ever been abhorrent to my nature to ask pecuniary assistance, I had early acquired habits of self-denying economy; husbanding my monthly allowance with anxious care; in order to obviate the danger of being forced, in some moment of future exigency, to beg additional aid. I remember many called me Miser at the time, and I used to couple the reproach with this consolation—better to be misunderstood now than repulsed hereafter. At this day I had my reward; I had had it before, when on parting with my irritated uncles, one of them threw down on the table before me a £5 note which I was able to leave there—saying that my travelling expenses were already provided for. Mr. Crimsworth employed Tim to find out whether my landlady had any complaint to make on the score of my morals; she answered that she believed I was a very religious man, and asked Tim, in her turn, if he thought I had any intention of going into the church some day, for—she said—she had had young curates to lodge in her house who were nothing equal to me for steadiness and quietness. Tim was "a religious man" himself—indeed he was "a joined Methodist" which did not (be it understood) prevent him from being at the same time an engrained rascal—and he came away much posed at hearing this account of my piety. Having imparted it to Mr. Crimsworth—that gentleman who himself frequented no place of worship and owned no God but Mammon, turned the information into a weapon of attack against the equability of my temper. He commenced a series of covert sneers, of which I did not at first perceive the drift, till my landlady happened to relate the conversation she had had with Mr. Steighton —this enlightened me; afterwards I came to the counting-house prepared, and managed to receive the Millowner's blasphemous sarcasms, when next levelled at me, on a buckler of impenetrable indifference. Erelong he tired of wasting his ammunition on a statue—but he did not throw away the shafts—he only kept them quiet in his quiver.

Once during my Clerkship I had an invitation to Crimsworth-Hall—it was on the occasion of a large party given in honour of the Master's birthday; he had always been accustomed to invite his clerks on similar anniversaries and could not well pass me over; I was however kept strictly in the background. Mrs. Crimsworth elegantly dressed in satin and lace—blooming in youth and health—vouchsafed me no more notice than was expressed by a distant move; Crimsworth, of course, never spoke to me; I was introduced to none of the band of young ladies who, enveloped in silvery clouds of white gauze and muslin sat in array against me on the opposite side of a long and large room—in fact I was fairly isolated, and could but contemplate the shining ones from afar, and when weary of such dazzling scene, turn for a change to the consideration of the carpet pattern. Mr. Crimsworth, standing on the rug, his elbow supported by the marble mantel-piece and about him a group of very pretty girls with whom he conversed gaily—Mr. Crimsworth, thus placed, glanced at me, I looked weary, solitary, kept-down—like some desolate tutor or governess—he was satisfied.

Dancing began—I should have liked well enough to be introduced to some pleasing and intelligent girl and to have freedom and opportunity to shew that I could both feel and communicate the pleasure of social intercourse—that I was not in short a block, or a piece of furniture but an acting, thinking, sentient man. Many smiling faces and graceful figures glided past me—but the smiles were lavished on other eyes—the figures sustained by other hands than mine—I turned away tantalized, left the dancers and wandered into the oak-panelled dining-room. No fibre of sympathy united me to any living thing in this house, I looked for and found my Mother's picture. I took a wax taper from a stand and held it up—I gazed long, earnestly; my heart grew to the image. My Mother, I perceived, had bequeathed to me much of her features and countenance—her forehead, her eyes, her complexion; no regular beauty pleases egotistical human beings so much as a softened and refined likeness of themselves; for this reason, fathers regard with complacency the lineaments of their daughters' faces, where frequently their own similitude is found flatteringly associated with softness of hue and delicacy of outline. I was just wondering how that picture, to me so interesting, would strike an impartial spectator, when a voice close behind me pronounced the words:

"Humph! there's some sense in that face."

I turned; at my elbow stood a tall man, young, though probably five or six years older than I, in other respects of an appearance the opposite to common-place, though just now, as I am not disposed to paint his portrait in detail, the reader must be content with the silhouette I have just thrown off; it was all I myself saw of him for the moment; I did not investigate the colour of his eye-brows, nor of his eyes either—I saw his stature and the outline of his shape, I saw too his fastidious-looking retroussé nose; these observations few in number, and general in character (the last excepted) sufficed, for they enabled me to recognize him.

"Good evening, Mr. Hunsden," muttered I with a bow and then, like a shy noodle as I was, I began moving away. And why? Simply because Mr. Hunsden was a manufacturer and a millowner and I was only a clerk, and my instinct propelled me from my superior. I had frequently seen Hunsden in Bigben Close, where he came almost weekly to transact business with Mr. Crimsworth, but I had never spoken to him, nor he to me, and I owed him a sort of involuntary grudge because he had more than once been the tacit witness of insults offered by Edward to me. I had the conviction that he could only regard me as a poor-spirited slave; wherefore I now went about to shun his presence and eschew his conversation.

"Where are you going?" asked he, as I edged off sideways—I had already noticed that Mr. Hunsden indulged in abrupt forms of speech and I perversely said to myself:

"He thinks he may speak as he likes to a poor clerk; but my mood is not perhaps so supple as he deems it, and his rough freedom pleases me not at all."

I made some slight reply, rather indifferent than courteous; and continued to move away. He coolly planted himself in my path:

"Stay here awhile;" said he. "It is so hot in the dancing-room; besides you don't dance; you have not had a partner to-night."

He was right, and as he spoke neither his look, tone, nor manner displeased me—my amour-propre was propitiated; he had not addressed me out of condescension, but because, having repaired to the cool dining-room for refreshment, he now wanted someone to talk to, by way of temporary amusement. I hate to be condescended to—but I like well enough to oblige—I stayed.

"That is a good picture," he continued, recurring to the portrait.

"Do you consider the face pretty?" I asked.

"Pretty! no—how can it be pretty with sunk eyes and hollow cheeks? but it is peculiar; it seems to think. You could have a talk with that woman, if she were alive, on other subjects than dress, visiting and compliments."

I agreed with him—but did not say so—he went on:

"Not that I admire a head of that sort—it wants character and force; there's too much of the sen-si-tive (so he articulated it, curling his lip at the same time,) in that mouth, besides there is Aristocrat written on the brow and defined in the figure—I hate your Aristocrats."

"You think then, Mr. Hunsden, that patrician descent may be read in a distinctive cast of form and features?"

"Patrician descent be hanged! Who doubts that your lordlings may have their 'distinctive cast of form and features' as much as we ——shire tradesmen have ours? But which is the best? Not theirs assuredly. As to their women—it is a little different—they cultivate beauty from childhood upwards, and may by care and training attain to a certain degree of excellence in that point—just like the oriental odalisques. Yet even this superiority is doubtful; compare the figure in that frame with Mrs. Edward Crimsworth—which is the finer animal?"

I replied quietly:

"Compare yourself and Mr. Edward Crimsworth, Mr. Hunsden."

"Oh Crimsworth is better filled up than I am—I know; besides he has a straight nose, arched eyebrows and all that—but these advantages—if they are advantages—he did not inherit from his mother, the patrician, but from his father, old Crimsworth—who, *my* father says, was as veritable a ——shire blue-dyer as ever put indigo in a vat, yet withal the handsomest man in the three Ridings. It is you, William, who are the aristocrat of your family and you are not as fine a fellow as your plebeian brother by a long chalk."

There was something in Mr. Hunsden's point-blank mode of speech which rather pleased me than otherwise, because it set me at my ease; I continued the conversation with a degree of interest:

"How do you happen to know that I am Mr. Crimsworth's brother? I thought you and every body else looked upon me only in the light of a poor clerk."

"Well—and so we do—and what are you but a poor clerk? You do Crimsworth's work and he gives you wages—shabby wages they are too—"

I was silent—Hunsden's language now bordered on the impertinent, still his manner did not offend me in the least—it only piqued my curiosity; I wanted him to go on, which he did in a little while.

"This world is an absurd one," said he.

"Why so, Mr. Hunsden?"

"I wonder you should ask—you are yourself a strong proof of the absurdity I allude to."

I was determined he should explain himself of his own accord, without my pressing him so to do—so I resumed my silence.

"Is it your intention to become a tradesman?" he enquired presently.

"It was my serious intention three months ago."

"Humph! the more fool you—you look like a tradesman! What a practical business-like face you have!"

"My face is as the Lord made it, Mr. Hunsden."

"The Lord never made either your face or head for X——. What good can your bumps of ideality, comparison, self-esteem, conscientiousness, do you here? But if you like Bigben Close—stay there; it's your own affair—not mine."

"Perhaps I have no choice."

"Well I care naught about it—it will make little difference to me what you do or where you go; but I'm cool now—I want to dance again—and I see such a fine girl sitting in the corner of the sofa there by her Mamma; see if I don't get her for a partner in a jiffy. There's Waddy—Sam Waddy making up to her—won't I cut him out?"

And Mr. Hunsden strode away; I watched him through the open folding-doors—he outstripped Waddy, applied for the hand of the fine girl, and led her off triumphant. She was a tall, well-made, full-formed, dashingly-dressed young woman, much in the style of Mrs. E. Crimsworth; Hunsden whirled her through the waltz with spirit; he kept at her side during the remainder of the evening, and I read in her animated and gratified countenance that he succeeded in making himself perfectly agreeable. The Mamma too (a stout person in a turban—Mrs. Lupton by name) looked well pleased; prophetic visions probably flattered her inward eye. The Hunsdens were of an old stem—and scornful as Yorke (such was my late interlocutor's name) professed to be of the advantages of birth, in his secret heart he well knew and fully appreciated the distinction his ancient, if not high lineage conferred on him in a mushroom place like X——, concerning whose inhabitants it was proverbially said, that not one in a thousand knew his own grandfather. Moreover the Hunsdens—once rich—were still independent and report affirmed that Yorke bade fair by his success in business to restore to pristine prosperity the partially decayed fortunes of his house. These circumstances considered, Mrs. Lupton's broad face might well wear a smile of complacency as she contemplated the heir of Hunsden-Wood occupied in paying assiduous court to her darling Sarah-Martha: I however, whose observations being less anxious, were likely to be more accurate, soon saw that the grounds for maternal self-congratulation were slight indeed; the gentleman appeared to me much more desirous of making—than susceptible of receiving an impression. I know not what it was in Mr. Hunsden that, as I watched him, (I had nothing better to do) suggested to me, every now and then, the idea of a foreigner. In form and features he might be pronounced English—though even there one caught a dash of something Gallic—but he had no English shyness; he had learnt somewhere—somehow, the art of setting himself quite at his ease, and of allowing no insular timidity to intervene as a barrier between him and his convenience, or pleasure. Refinement, he did not affect, yet vulgar, he could not be called; he was not odd—no quiz—yet he resembled no one else I had ever seen before; his general bearing intimated complete, sovereign satisfaction with himself, yet, at times, an indescribable shade passed like an eclipse over his countenance, and seemed to me like the sign of a sudden and strong inward doubt of himself, his words and actions; an energetic discontent at his life or his social position, his future prospects or his mental attainments, I know not which—perhaps after all it might only be a bilious caprice.

CHAPTER IV

No man likes to acknowledge that he has made a mistake in the choice of his profession, and every man, worthy of the name, will row long against wind and tide before he allows himself to cry out "I am baffled!" and submits to be floated passively back to land. From the first week of my residence in X—— I felt my occupation irksome. The thing itself—the work of copying and translating business-letters—was a dry and tedious task enough, but had that been all, I should long have borne with the nuisance; I am not of an impatient nature, and influenced by the double desire of getting my living and justifying to myself and others the resolution I had taken to become a tradesman, I should have endured in silence the rust and cramp of my best faculties; I should not have whispered, even inwardly, that I longed for liberty; I should have pent in every sigh by which my heart might have ventured to intimate its distress under the closeness, smoke, monotony and joyless tumult of Bigben Close, and its panting desire for freer and fresher scenes; I should have set up the image of Duty, the fetish of Perseverance in my small bed-room at Mrs. King's lodgings, and they two should have been my household gods, from which my Darling, my Cherished-in-secret, Imagination, the tender and the mighty, should never, either by softness or strength, have severed me. But this was not all; the Antipathy, which had sprung up between myself and my Employer, striking deeper root and spreading denser shade daily, excluded me from every glimpse of the sunshine of life; and I began to feel like a plant growing in humid darkness out of the slimy walls of a well.

Antipathy is the only word which can express the feeling Edward Crimsworth had for me; a feeling, in a great measure, involuntary, and which was liable to be excited by every, the most trifling movement, look or word of mine. My southern accent annoyed him, the degree of education evinced in my language irritated him, my punctuality, industry and accuracy fixed his dislike and gave it the high flavour and poignant relish of envy; he feared that I too should one day make a successful tradesman. Had I been in anything inferior to him, he would not have hated me so thoroughly, but I knew all that he knew and, what was worse, he suspected that I kept the padlock of silence on mental wealth in which he was no sharer. If he could have once placed me in a ridiculous or mortifying position, he would have forgiven me much, but I was guarded by three faculties; Caution, Tact, Observation; and prowling and prying as was Edward's malignity, it could never baffle the lynx-eyes of these—my natural Sentinels. Day by day did his Malice watch my Tact, hoping it would sleep, and prepared to steal snake-like on its slumber, but Tact—if it be genuine—never sleeps.

I had received my first quarter's wages and was returning to my lodgings, possessed heart and soul with the pleasant feeling that the master, who had paid me, grudged every penny of that hard-earned pittance—(I had long ceased to regard Mr. Crimsworth as my brother—he was a hard, grinding Master, he wished to be an inexorable tyrant—that was all.) Thoughts—not varied but strong—occupied my mind; two voices spoke within me; again and again they uttered the same monotonous phrases: one said: "William, your life is intolerable." The other: "What can you do to alter it?" I walked fast—for it was a cold, frosty night in January; as I approached my lodgings I turned from a general view of my affairs, to the particular speculation as to whether my fire would be out; looking towards the window of my sitting-room—I saw no cheering red gleam.

"That slut of a servant has neglected it as usual," said I, "and I shall see nothing but pale ashes if I go in; it is a fine starlight night—I will walk a little farther."

It *was* a fine night—and the streets were dry and even clean for X——; there was a crescent curve of moonlight to be seen by the Parish-Church tower and hundreds of stars shone keenly bright in all quarters of the sky.

Unconsciously I steered my course towards the country; I had got into Grove-Street and began to feel the pleasure of seeing dim trees at the extremity—round a suburban house, when a person leaning over the iron gate of one of the small gardens which front the neat dwelling-houses in this street, addressed me as I was hurrying with quick stride past.

"What the deuce is the hurry? Just so must Lot have left Sodom, when he expected fire to pour down upon it, out of burning brass clouds."

I stopped short and looked towards the speaker—I smelt the fragrance, and saw the red spark of a cigar, the dusk outline of a man too, bent towards me over the wicket.

"You see I am meditating in the field at eventide," continued this shade. "God knows it's cool work! especially as instead of Rebecca on a camel's hump, with bracelets on her arms and a ring in her nose, Fate sends me only a Counting-house clerk in a grey Tweed wrapper."

The voice was familiar to me—its second utterance enabled me to seize the speaker's identity.

"Mr. Hunsden! good-evening."

"Good-evening indeed! Yes, but you would have passed me without recognition if I had not been so civil as to speak first."

"I did not know you."

"A famous excuse! You ought to have known me; I knew you, though you were going ahead like a steam-engine. Are the police after you?"

"It wouldn't be worth their while; I'm not of consequence enough to attract them."

"Alas poor Shepherd! Alack and well-a-day! What a theme for regret, and how down in the mouth you must be, judging from the sound of your voice! But since you're not running from the police from whom are you running? the devil?"

"On the contrary, I'm going post to him."

"That is well—you're just in luck. This is Tuesday evening; there are scores of Market gigs and carts returning to Dinneford to-night and he or some of his have a seat in all regularly; so if you'll step in and sit half an hour in my bachelor's parlour, you may catch him as he passes without much trouble. I think though you'd better let him alone to-night—he'll have so many customers to serve; Tuesday is his busy day in X—— and Dinneford; come in at all events."

He swung the wicket open as he spoke.

"Do you really wish me to go in?" I asked.

"As you please—I'm alone, your company for an hour or two would be agreeable to me, but if you don't choose to favour me so far, I'll not press the point. I hate to bore any one."

It suited me to accept the invitation as it suited Hunsden to give it; I passed through the gate and followed him to the front door, which he opened; thence we traversed a passage and entered his parlour; the door being shut, he pointed me to an arm-chair by the hearth, I sat down and glanced round me.

It was a comfortable room, at once snug and handsome; the bright grate was filled with a genuine ——shire fire, red, clear and generous, no penurious South-of-England ember happed in the corner of a grate. On the table a shaded lamp diffused around a soft, pleasant and equal light; the furniture was almost luxurious for a young bachelor, comprising a couch and two very easy chairs; bookshelves filled the recesses on each side of the mantel-piece; they were well-furnished and arranged with perfect order. The neatness of the room suited my taste; I hate irregular and slovenly habits; from what I saw, I concluded that Hunsden's ideas on that point corresponded with my own. While he removed from the centre-table to the side-board a few pamphlets and periodicals, I ran my eye along the shelves of the book-case nearest me. French and German works predominated; the old French dramatists, sundry modern authors, Thiers, Villemain, Paul de Kock, George Sand, Eugène Sue; in German, Goethe, Schiller, Zschokke, Jean Paul Richter; in English there were works on Political Economy—I examined no further for Mr. Hunsden himself recalled my attention.

"You shall have something," said he, "for you ought to feel disposed for refreshment after walking nobody knows how far on such a Canadian night as this—but it shall not be brandy-and-water and it shall not be a bottle of Port nor ditto of Sherry—I keep no such poison—I have Rhein-wein for my own drinking and you may choose between that and coffee."

Here again Hunsden suited me; if there was one generally received practice I abhorred more than another, it was the habitual imbibing of spirits and strong wines. I had however no fancy for his acid German nectar, but I liked coffee, so I responded:

"Give me some coffee, Mr. Hunsden."

I perceived my answer pleased him; he had doubtless expected to see a chilling effect produced by his steady announcement that he would give me neither wine nor spirits; he just shot one searching glance at my face to ascertain whether my cordiality was genuine or a mere feint of politeness—I smiled because I quite understood him, and while I honoured his conscientious firmness, I was amused at his mistrust; he seemed satisfied, rang the bell and ordered coffee, which was presently brought; for himself a bunch of grapes and half a pint of something sour sufficed. My coffee was excellent, I told him so and expressed the shuddering pity with which his anchorite fare inspired me. He did not answer and, I scarcely think, heard, my remark; at that moment one of those momentary eclipses I before alluded to, had come over his face, extinguishing his smile and replacing by an abstracted and alienated look the customarily shrewd, bantering glance of his eye. I employed the interval of silence in a rapid scrutiny of his physiognomy. I had never observed him closely before and, as my sight is very short, I had gathered only a vague, general idea of his appearance; I was surprised now, on examination, to perceive how small and even feminine were his lineaments; his tall figure, long and dark locks, his voice and general bearing had impressed me with the notion of something powerful and massive; not at all—my own features were cast in a harsher and squarer mould than his. I discerned that there would be contrasts between his inward and outward man, contentions too, for I suspected his soul had more of will and ambition, than his body had of fibre and muscle. Perhaps in these incompatibilities of the "physique" with the "morale" lay the secret of that fitful gloom; he *would* but *could* not and the athletic mind scowled scorn on its more fragile companion. As to his good looks, I should have liked to have a woman's opinion on that subject; it seemed to me that his face might produce the same effect on a lady that a very piquant and interesting, though scarcely pretty, female face would on a man. I have mentioned his dark locks, they were brushed sideways above a white and sufficiently expansive forehead—his cheek had a rather hectic freshness—his features might have done well on canvass but indifferently in marble—they were plastic; character had set a stamp upon each, expression re-cast them at her pleasure—and strange metamorphoses she wrought, giving him now the mien of a morose bull and anon that of an arch and mischievous girl; more frequently the two semblances were blent, and a queer, composite countenance they made.

Starting from his silent fit, he began:

"William! what a fool you are to live in those dismal lodgings of Mrs. King's, when you might take rooms here in Grove Street and have a garden like me!"

"I should be too far from the Mill."

"What of that? It would do you good to walk there and back two or three times a day; besides, are you such a fossil that you never wish to see a flower or a green leaf?"

"I am no fossil."

"What are you then? You sit at that desk in Crimsworth's Counting-house day by day and week by week; scraping with a pen on paper, just like an automaton; you never get up, you never say you are tired, you never ask for a holiday, you never talk about change or relaxation, you give way to no excess of an evening, you neither keep wild company nor indulge in strong drink."

"Do you, Mr. Hunsden?"

"Don't think to pose me with short questions; your case and mine are diametrically different, and it is nonsense attempting to draw a parallel. I say that when a man endures patiently what ought to be unendurable, he is a fossil."

"Whence do you acquire the knowledge of my patience?"

"Why man, do you suppose you are a mystery? The other night you seemed surprised at my knowing to what family you belonged;

now you find subject for wonderment in my calling you patient. What do you think I do with my eyes and ears? I've been in your Counting-house more than once when Crimsworth has treated you like a dog; called for a book, for instance, and when you gave him the wrong one, or what he chose to consider the wrong one, flung it back almost in your face; desired you to shut or open the door as if you had been his flunkey, to say nothing of your position at the party about a month ago, where you had neither place nor partner but hovered about like a poor, shabby hanger-on, and how patient you were under each and all of these circumstances!"

"Well, Mr. Hunsden—what then?"

"I can hardly tell you what then; the conclusion to be drawn as to your character depends upon the nature of the motives which guide your conduct; if you are patient because you expect to make something eventually out of Crimsworth, notwithstanding his tyranny, or perhaps by means of it, you are what the world calls an interested and mercenary, but may be a very wise fellow; if you are patient because you think it a duty to meet insult with submission, you are an essential sap and in no shape the man for my money; if you are patient because your nature is phlegmatic, flat, unexcitable and that you cannot get up to the pitch of resistance; why God made you to be crushed; and lie down by all means, and lie flat, and let Juggernaut ride well over you."

Mr. Hunsden's eloquence was not, it will be perceived, of the smooth and oily order; as he spoke he pleased me ill; I seemed to recognize in him one of those characters who, sensitive enough themselves, are selfishly relentless towards the sensitiveness of others. Moreover though he was neither like Crimsworth nor Lord Tynedale yet he was acrid, and, I suspected, overbearing in his way; there was a tone of despotism in the urgency of the very reproaches, by which he aimed at goading the oppressed into rebellion against the oppressor; looking at him still more fixedly than I had yet done, I saw written in his eye and mien, a resolution to arrogate to himself a freedom so unlimited that it might often trench on the just liberty of his neighbours. I rapidly ran over these thoughts and then I laughed, a low and involuntary laugh; moved thereto by a slight, inward revelation of the inconsistency of man. It was as I thought, Hunsden had expected me to take with calm his incorrect and offensive surmises, his bitter and haughty taunts, and himself was chafed by a laugh, scarce louder than a whisper.

His brow darkened, his thin nostril dilated a little:

"Yes," he began. "I told you that you were an Aristocrat, and who but an Aristocrat would laugh such a laugh as that and look such a look? A laugh frigidly jeering; a look lazily mutinous; gentlemanlike irony, patrician resentment. What a nobleman you would have made, William Crimsworth! You are cut out for one; pity Fortune has balked Nature!—Look at the features, figure, even to the hands—distinction all over—ugly distinction! Now if you'd only an estate and a mansion and a park and a title, how you could play the exclusive, maintain the rights of your class, train your tenantry in habits of respect to the peerage, oppose at every step the advancing power of the people, support your rotten order and be ready for its sake to wade knee-deep in churls' blood. As it is you've no power; you can do nothing; you're wrecked and stranded on the shores of Commerce; forced into collision with practical Men, with whom you cannot cope, for *you'll never be a tradesman.*"

The first part of Hunsden's speech moved me not at all, or if it did, it was only to wonder at the perversion into which prejudice had twisted his judgment of my character; the concluding sentence however not only moved but shook me; the blow it gave was a severe one, because Truth wielded the weapon. If I smiled now it was only in disdain of myself.

Hunsden saw his advantage; he followed it up.

"You'll make nothing by trade," continued he, "nothing more than the crust of dry bread and the draught of fair water on which you now live; your only chance of getting a competency lies in marrying a rich widow or running away with an heiress."

"I leave such shifts to be put in practice by those who devise them," said I, rising.

"And even that is hopeless," he went on coolly. "What widow would have you? Much less what heiress? You're not bold and venturesome enough for the one, nor handsome and fascinating enough for the other; you think perhaps you look intelligent and polished—carry your intellect and refinement to market and tell me in a private note what price is bid for them."

Mr. Hunsden had taken his tone for the night—the string he struck was out of tune, he would finger no other—averse to discord, of which I had enough every day and all day long—I concluded at last that silence and solitude were preferable to jarring converse; I bade him good-night.

"What! Are you going, lad? Well, good-night, you'll find the door."

And he sat still in front of the fire, while I left the room and the house. I had got a good way on my return to my lodgings, before I found out that I was walking very fast and breathing very hard, and that my nails were almost stuck into the palms of my clenched hands, and that my teeth were set fast; on making this discovery I relaxed both my pace, fists and jaws, but I could not so soon cause the regrets rushing rapidly through my mind to slacken their tide. Why did I make myself a tradesman? Why did I enter Hunsden's house this evening? Why, at dawn to-morrow, must I repair to Crimsworth's Mill? All that night did I ask myself these questions and all that night fiercely demanded of my soul an answer. I got no sleep, my head burned, my feet froze; at last the factory-bells rang and I sprung from my bed with other slaves.

CHAPTER V

THERE is a climax to everything, to every state of feeling as well as to every position in life. I turned this truism over in my mind as, in the frosty dawn of a January Morning, I hurried down the steep and now icy street which descended from Mrs. King's to the Close. The factory work-people had preceded me by nearly an hour and the Mill was all lighted up and in full operation when I reached it; I repaired to my post in the Counting-house as usual; the fire there, but just lit, as yet only smoked, Steighton was not yet arrived. I shut the door and sat down at the desk; my hands, recently washed in half-frozen water, were still numb, I could not write till they had regained vitality, so I went on thinking; and still the theme of my thoughts was "The Climax". Self-dissatisfaction troubled exceedingly the current of my meditations.

"Come, William Crimsworth," said my Conscience or whatever it is that within ourselves, takes ourselves to task, "come, get a clear notion of what you would have, or what you would not have; you talk of a Climax; pray has your endurance reached its climax? It is not four months old. What a fine resolute fellow you imagined yourself to be when you told Tynedale you would tread in your Father's steps—and a pretty treading you are likely to make of it! How well you like X——! Just at this moment—how redolent of pleasant associations are its streets, its shops, its warehouses, its factories! How the prospect of this day cheers you! Letter-copying till noon, solitary dinner at your lodgings; letter-copying till evening, solitude; for you neither find pleasure in Brown's nor Smith's nor Nicholl's nor Eccles' company, and as to Hunsden—you fancied there was pleasure to be derived from his society—he! —he! how did you like the taste you had of him last night? was it sweet? Yet he is a talented, an original-minded man and even he does not like you; your self-respect defies you to like him; he has always seen you to disadvantage; he always will see you to disadvantage; your positions are unequal, and were they on the same level your minds could not assimilate; never hope then to gather the honey of friendship out of that thorn-guarded plant—Hollo Crimsworth! where are your thoughts tending?—you leave the recollection of Hunsden as a bee would a rock—as a bird, a desert, and your aspirations spread eager wings towards a land of visions where, now in advancing day-light, in X—— daylight, you dare to dream of Congeniality, Repose, Union. Those three you will never meet in this world; they are angels; the souls of just men made perfect may encounter them in heaven—but your soul will never be made perfect. Eight o'clock strikes! your hands are thawed, get to work!"

"Work? why should I work?" said I sullenly. "I cannot please though I toil like a slave." "Work—work!" reiterated the inward voice.

"I may work—it will do no good," I growled, but nevertheless I drew out a packet of letters and commenced my task; task thankless and bitter as that of the Israelite crawling over the sun-baked fields of Egypt in search of straw and stubble wherewith to accomplish his tale of bricks.

About ten o'clock I heard Mr. Crimsworth's gig turn into the yard and in a minute or two he entered the counting-house. It was his custom to glance his eye at Steighton and myself, to hang up his mackintosh, stand a minute with his back to the fire and then walk out. To-day he did not deviate from his usual habits; the only difference was that when he looked at me, his brow, instead of being merely hard, was surly—his eye, instead of being cold, was fierce. He studied me a minute or two longer than usual but went out in silence.

Twelve o'clock arrived, the bell rang for a suspension of labour, the work-people went off to their dinners; Steighton too departed, desiring me to lock the Counting-house door and take the key with me. I was tying up a bundle of papers and putting them in their place, preparatory to closing my desk, when Crimsworth re-appeared at the door and entering, closed it behind him.

"You'll stay here a minute," said he in a deep, brutal voice, while his nostrils distended and his eye shot a spark of sinister fire. Alone with Edward, I remembered our relationship and remembering that, forgot the difference of position, I put away deference and careful forms of speech, I answered him with simple brevity.

"It is time to go home," I said turning the key in my desk.

"You'll stay here!" he reiterated. "And take your hand off that key! leave it in the lock!"

"Why?" asked I. "What cause is there for changing my usual plans?"

"Do as I order," was the answer. "And no questions!—you are my servant—obey me! What have you been about—?" he was going on in the same breath, when an abrupt pause announced that rage had for the moment got the better of articulation.

"You may look—if you wish to know," I replied. "There is the open desk—there are the papers—"

"Confound your insolence! What have you been about?"

"Your work—and have done it well."

"Hypocrite and Twaddler! Smooth-faced, snivelling Greasehorn!" (This last term is—I believe—purely ——shire and alludes to the horn of black, rancid whale-oil, usually to be seen suspended to cart-wheels and employed for greasing the same.)

"Come, Edward Crimsworth, enough of this. It is time you and I wound up accounts. I have now given your service three months' trial and I find it the most nauseous slavery under the sun. Seek another clerk—I stay no longer."

"What! Do you dare to give me notice? Stop at least for your wages." He took down the heavy gig-whip hanging beside his Mackintosh.

I permitted myself to laugh with a degree of scorn I took no pains to temper or hide; his fury boiled up and when he had sworn half-a-dozen vulgar, impious oaths, without however venturing to lift the whip, he continued:

"I've found you out and know you thoroughly; you mean, whining lickspittle! What have you been saying all over X—— about me? Answer me that!"

"You? I have neither inclination nor temptation to talk about you."

"You lie—it is your practice to talk about me, it is your constant habit to make public complaint of the treatment you receive at my hands. You have gone and told it far and near that I give you low wages and knock you about like a dog. I wish you were a dog! I'd set to this minute and never stir from the spot till I'd cut every strip of flesh from your bones, with this whip."

He flourished his tool—the end of the lash just touched my forehead. A warm excited thrill ran through my veins, my blood seemed to give a bound, and then raced fast and hot along its channels; I got up nimbly, came round to where he stood and faced him.

"Down with your whip!" said I, "and explain this instant what you mean."

"Sirrah! to whom are you speaking?"

"To you—there is no one else present—I think: you say I have been calumniating you, complaining of your low wages and bad treatment, give your grounds for these assertions."

Crimsworth had no dignity, and when I sternly demanded an explanation—he gave one in a loud, scolding voice.

"Grounds! you shall have them—and turn to the light that I may see your brazen face blush black, when you hear yourself proved to be a liar and a hypocrite. At a public meeting in the Town-hall yesterday I had the pleasure of hearing myself insulted by the speaker opposed to me in the question under discussion, by allusions to my private affairs; by cant about monsters without natural affection, family despots and such trash—and when I rose to answer, I was met by a shout from the filthy mob, where the mention of your name enabled me at once to detect the quarter in which this base attack had originated; when I looked round, I saw that treacherous villain, Hunsden, acting as fugleman—I detected you in close conversation with Hunsden at my house a month ago and I know that you were at Hunsden's rooms last night. Deny it if you dare."

"Oh I shall not deny it! and if Hunsden hounded on the people to hiss you, he did quite right—you deserve popular execration for a worse man, a harder master, a more brutal brother than you are has seldom existed."

"Sirrah! Sirrah!" reiterated Crimsworth, and to complete his apostrophe, he cracked the whip straight over my head.

A minute sufficed to wrest it from him, break it in two pieces and throw it under the grate; he made a headlong rush at me which I evaded and said:

"Touch me and I'll have you up before the nearest magistrate."

Men like Crimsworth, if firmly and calmly resisted, always abate something of their exorbitant insolence; he had no mind to be brought before a magistrate, and I suppose he saw I meant what I said. After an odd and long stare at me, at once bull-like and amazed, he seemed to bethink himself that after all, his money gave him sufficient superiority over a beggar like me, and that he had in his hands a surer and more dignified mode of revenge than the somewhat hazardous one of personal chastisement.

"Take your hat," said he. "Take what belongs to you, and go out at that door; get away to your parish, you pauper—beg, steal, starve, get transported, do what you like—but at your peril venture again into my sight! If ever I hear of your setting foot on an inch of ground belonging to me, I'll hire a man to cane you."

"It is not likely you'll have the chance; once off your premises, what temptation can I have to return to them—I leave a prison, I leave a tyrant; I leave what is worse than the worst that can lie before me, so no fear of my coming back—"

"Go or I'll make you!" exclaimed Crimsworth. I walked deliberately to my desk, took out such of its contents as were my own property, put them in my pocket, locked the desk and placed the key on the top.

"What are you abstracting from that desk?" demanded the Millowner. "Leave all behind in its place or I'll send for a policeman to search you."

"Look sharp about it then," said I, and I took down my hat, drew on my gloves and walked leisurely out of the Counting-house; walked out of it to enter it no more.

I recollect that when the Mill-bell rang the dinner hour, before Mr. Crimsworth entered, and the scene above related took place, I had had rather a sharp appetite, and had been waiting somewhat impatiently to hear the signal of feeding-time; I forgot it now however; the images of potatoes and roast mutton were effaced from my mind by the stir and tumult which the transaction of the last half hour had there excited; I only thought of walking that the action of my muscles might harmonize with the action of my nerves; and walk I did, fast and far; how could I do otherwise? A load was lifted off my heart, I felt light and liberated. I had got away from Bigben Close without a breach of resolution; without injury to my self-respect: I had not forced Circumstances, Circumstances had freed me; Life was again open to me; no longer was its horizon limited by the high, black wall surrounding Crimsworth's Mill. Two hours had elapsed before my sensations had so far subsided as to leave me calm enough to remark for what wider and clearer boundaries I had exchanged that sooty girdle. When I did look up—lo! straight before me lay Grovetown, a village of villas about five miles out of X——. The short winter day, as I perceived from the far-declined sun, was already approaching its close; a chill frost-mist was rising from the river on which X—— stands and along whose banks the road I had taken lay, it dimmed the earth but did not obscure the clear, icy blue of the January sky. There was a great stillness near and far; the time of the day favoured tranquillity as the people were all employed within doors, the hour of evening release from the factories not being yet arrived. A sound of full-flowing water alone pervaded the air, for the river was deep and abundant, swelled by the melting of a late snow—I stood awhile, leaning over a wall, and looking down at the current, I watched the rapid rush of its waves. I desired Memory to take a clear and permanent impression of the scene and treasure it for future years. Grovetown Church clock struck four; looking up I beheld the last of that day's sun, glinting red through the leafless boughs of some very old oak-trees surrounding the Church—its light coloured and characterized the picture as I wished—I paused yet a moment—till the sweet, slow sound of the bell had quite died out of the air, then ear, eye and feeling satisfied I quitted the wall and once more turned my face towards X——.

CHAPTER VI

I RE-ENTERED the town, a hungry man; the dinner I had forgotten recurred seductively to my recollection, and it was with a quick step and sharp appetite I ascended the narrow street leading to my lodgings. It was dark when I opened the front door and walked into the house; I wondered how my fire would be; the night was cold and I shuddered at the prospect of a grate full of sparkless cinders. To my joyful surprise, I found, on entering my sitting room, a good fire and a clean hearth. I had hardly noticed this phenomenon, when I became aware of another subject for wonderment; the chair I usually occupied near the hearth was already filled, a person sat there with his arms folded on his chest and his legs stretched out on the rug. Short-sighted as I am, doubtful as was the gleam of the firelight, a moment's examination enabled me to recognize in this person my acquaintance, Mr. Hunsden. I could not of course be much pleased to see him, considering the manner in which I had parted from him the night before, and as I walked to the hearth, stirred the fire and said coolly, "Good evening," my demeanour evinced as little cordiality as I felt; yet I wondered in my own mind what had brought him there, and I wondered, also, what motives had induced him to interfere so actively between me and Edward; it was to him, it appeared, that I owed my welcome dismissal; still I could not bring myself to ask him questions, to shew any eagerness of curiosity; if he chose to explain, he might, but the explanation should be a perfectly voluntary one on his part; I thought he was entering upon it.

"You owe me a debt of gratitude," were his first words.

"Do I?" said I. "I hope it is not a large one, for I am much too poor to charge myself with heavy liabilities of any kind."

"Then declare yourself bankrupt, at once—for this liability is a ton weight at least. When I came in I found your fire out and I had it lit again and made that sulky drab of a servant stay and blow at it with the bellows till it had burnt up properly—now, say thank you."

"Not till I have had something to eat, I can thank nobody while I am so famished."

I rang the bell and ordered tea and some cold meat.

"Cold meat!" exclaimed Hunsden, as the servant closed the door. "What a glutton you are, man! Meat with tea! you'll die of eating too much."

"No, Mr. Hunsden, I shall not." I felt a necessity for contradicting him; I was irritated with hunger and irritated at seeing him there, and irritated at the continued roughness of his manner.

"It is over-eating that makes you so ill-tempered," said he.

"How do you know?" I demanded. "It is like you to give a pragmatical opinion without being acquainted with any of the circumstances of the case—I have had no dinner."

What I said was petulant and snappish enough, and Hunsden only replied by looking in my face and laughing.

"Poor thing!" he whined after a pause. "It has had no dinner has it? What! I suppose its Master would not let it come home. Did Crimsworth order you to fast by way of punishment, William?"

"No, Mr. Hunsden." Fortunately, at this sulky juncture, tea was brought in and I fell to upon some bread and butter and cold beef directly. Having cleared a plateful, I became so far humanized as to intimate to Mr. Hunsden, "That he need not sit there staring, but might come to the table and do as I did, if he liked."

"But I don't like in the least," said he, and therewith he summoned the servant by a fresh pull of the bell-rope and intimated a desire to have a glass of toast and water. "And some more coal," he added, "Mr. Crimsworth shall keep a good fire while I stay."

His orders being executed, he wheeled his chair round to the table so as to be opposite me.

"Well," he proceeded. "You are out of work I suppose."

"Yes," said I and, not disposed to shew the satisfaction I felt on this point, I, yielding to the whim of the moment, took up the subject as though I considered myself aggrieved rather than benefited by what had been done. "Yes—thanks to you, I am. Crimsworth turned me off at a minute's notice owing to some interference of yours at a public meeting, I understand."

"Ah! What! he mentioned that? He observed me signalling the lads, did he? What had he to say about his friend Hunsden—anything sweet?"

"He called you a treacherous villain."

"Oh he hardly knows me yet! I'm one of those shy people who don't come out all at once and he is only just beginning to make my acquaintance—but he'll find I've some good qualities, excellent ones! The Hunsdens were always unrivalled at tracking a rascal; a downright, dishonourable villain is their natural prey, they could not keep off him wherever they met him; you used the word pragmatical just now, that word is the property of our family, it has been applied to us from generation to generation; we have fine noses for abuses, we scent a scoundrel a mile off, we are reformers born, radical reformers, and it was impossible for me to live in the same town with Crimsworth, to come into weekly contact with him, to witness some of his conduct to you (for whom personally I care nothing, I only consider the brutal injustice with which he violated your natural claim to equality). I say it was impossible for me to be thus situated and not feel the angel or the demon of my race at work within me—I followed my instinct, opposed a tyrant and broke a chain."

Now this speech interested me much, both because it brought out Hunsden's character and because it explained his motives—it interested me so much that I forgot to reply to it and sat silent, pondering over a throng of ideas it had suggested.

"Are you grateful to me?" he asked presently.

In fact I was grateful, or almost so, and I believe I half liked him at the moment, notwithstanding his proviso that what he had done was not out of regard for me; but human nature is perverse; impossible to answer his blunt question in the affirmative, so I disclaimed all tendency to gratitude and advised him if he expected any reward for his championship to look for it in a better world, as he was not likely to meet with it here. In reply he termed me "a dry-hearted aristocratic scamp;" whereupon I again charged him with having taken the bread out of my mouth.

"Your bread was dirty, man!" cried Hunsden. "Dirty and unwholesome! It came through the hands of a tyrant, for I tell you Crimsworth is a tyrant, a tyrant to his workpeople, a tyrant to his clerks, and will some day be a tyrant to his wife."

"Nonsense! Bread is bread; and a salary is a salary; I've lost mine and through your means."

"There's sense in what you say after all," rejoined Hunsden. "I must say I am rather agreeably surprised to hear you make so practical an observation as that last. I had imagined now, from my previous observation of your character, that the sentimental delight you would have taken in your newly regained liberty would, for a while at least, have effaced all ideas of forethought and prudence; I think better of you for looking steadily to the needful."

"Looking steadily to the needful! How can I do otherwise? I must live, and to live, I must have what you call 'the needful', which I can only get by working; I repeat it, you have taken my work from me."

"What do you mean to do?" pursued Hunsden coolly. "You have influential relations, I suppose they'll soon provide you with another place."

"Influential relations? who? I should like to know their names."

"The Seacombes."

"Stuff! I have cut them."

Hunsden looked at me incredulously.

"I have," said I, "and that definitively."

"You must mean they have cut you, William."

"As you please; they offered me their patronage on condition of my entering the church; I declined both the terms and the recompense; I withdrew from my cold uncles and preferred throwing myself into my elder brother's arms, from whose affectionate embrace I am now torn by the cruel intermeddling of a stranger—of yourself in short."

I could not repress a half-smile as I said this; a similar demi-manifestation of feeling appeared at the same moment on Hunsden's lips:

"Oh I see!" said he, looking into my eyes, and it was evident he *did* see right down to my heart; having sat a minute or two with his chin resting on his hand, diligently occupied in the continued perusal of my countenance, he went on:

"Seriously, have you then nothing to expect from the Seacombes?"

"Yes; Rejection and Repulsion. Why do you ask me twice? How can hands, stained with the ink of a counting-house, soiled with the grease of a wool-warehouse, ever again be permitted to come into contact with aristocratic palms?"

"There would be a difficulty, no doubt; still you are such a complete Seacombe in appearance, feature, language, almost manner, I wonder they should disown you."

"They have disowned me, so talk no more about it—"

"Do you regret it, William?"

"No."

"Why not, lad?"

"Because they are not people with whom I could ever have had any sympathy."

"I say you are one of them."

"That merely proves that you know nothing at all about it; I am my mother's son, but not my Uncles' nephew."

"Still—one of your Uncles is a lord, though rather an obscure and not a very wealthy one, and the other a right honourable—you should consider worldly interest."

"Nonsense, Mr. Hunsden—you know or may know that even had I desired to be submissive to my Uncles, I could not have stooped with a good enough grace ever to have won their favour. I should have sacrificed my own comfort and not have gained their patronage in return."

"Very likely. So you calculated your wisest plan was to follow your own devices at once?"

"Exactly—I must follow my own devices—I must till the day of my death—because I can neither comprehend, adopt nor work out those of other people."

Hunsden yawned—"Well," said he, "in all this, I see but one thing clearly—that is, that the whole affair is no business of mine."

He stretched himself and again yawned. "I wonder what time it is," he went on, "I have an appointment for seven o'clock."

"Three quarters past six by my watch."

"Well then I'll go." He got up. "You'll not meddle with trade again?" said he, leaning his elbow on the mantel-piece.

"No—I think not."

"You would be a fool if you did. Probably, after all, you'll think better of your Uncle's proposal and go into the Church?"

"A singular regeneration must take place in my whole inner and outer man before I do that. A good clergyman is one of the best of men—"

"Indeed! Do you think so?" interrupted Hunsden scoffingly—

"I do—and no mistake. But I have not the peculiar points which go to make a good clergyman, and rather than adopt a profession for which I have no vocation, I would endure extremities of hardship from poverty."

"You're a mighty difficult customer to suit. You won't be a tradesman or a parson, you can't be a lawyer or a doctor or a gentleman, because you've no money—I'd recommend you to travel."

"What—without money?"

"You must travel in search of money, man. You can speak French—with a vile English accent—no doubt—still, you can speak it; go on to the Continent and see what will turn up for you there."

"God knows I should like to go!" exclaimed I with involuntary ardour.

"Go—what the deuce hinders you? You may get to Brussels, for instance, for five or six pounds—if you know how to manage with economy."

"Necessity would teach me if I didn't."

"Go then—and let your wits make a way for you when you get there. I know Brussels almost as well as I know X—— and I am sure it would suit such a one as you better than London."

"But occupation, Mr. Hunsden! I must go where occupation is to be had—and how could I get a recommendation or introduction or employment at Brussels?"

"There speaks the organ of Caution. You hate to advance a step before you know every inch of the way. You haven't a sheet of paper and a pen and ink?"

"I hope so," and I produced writing materials with alacrity; for I guessed what he was going to do. He sat down, wrote a few lines, folded, sealed and addressed a letter and held it out to me:

"There Prudence—there's a pioneer to hew down the first rough difficulties of your path—I know well enough, lad, you are not one of those who will run their neck into a noose without seeing how they are to get it out again, and you're right there. A reckless man is my aversion and nothing should ever persuade me to meddle with the concerns of such a one. Those who are reckless for themselves are generally ten times more so for their friends."

"This is a letter of introduction, I suppose?" said I, taking the epistle.

"Yes—with that in your pocket you will run no risk of finding yourself in a state of absolute destitution which, I know, you would regard as a degradation, so should I for that matter; the person, to whom you will present it, generally has two or three respectable places depending upon his recommendation."

"That will just suit me," said I.

"Well—and where's your gratitude?" demanded Mr. Hunsden: "don't you know how to say thank you?"

"I've fifteen pounds and a watch, which my godmother, whom I never saw, gave me eighteen years ago," was my rather irrelevant answer, and I further avowed myself a happy man and professed that I did not envy any king in Christendom.

"And your gratitude?"

"I shall be off presently, Mr. Hunsden—to-morrow if all be well—I'll not stay a day longer in X—— than I am obliged."

"Very good—but it will be decent to make due acknowledgement for the assistance you have received—be quick! It is just going to strike seven; I'm waiting to be thanked."

"Just stand out of the way will you, Mr. Hunsden, I want a key there is on the corner of the mantel-piece—I'll pack my portmanteau before I go to bed."

The house-clock struck seven.

"The lad is a heathen," said Hunsden, and taking his hat from a side-table, he left the room laughing to himself. I had half an inclination to follow him, I really intended to leave X—— the next morning and should certainly not have another opportunity of bidding him good-bye. The front-door banged to—"Let him go," said I. "We shall meet again some day."

CHAPTER VII

READER—perhaps you were never in Belgium? Haply you don't know the physiognomy of the country? You have not its lineaments defined upon your memory as I have them on mine?

Three—nay four pictures line the four-walled cell where are stored for me the Records of the Past. First, Eton. All in that picture is in far perspective, receding, diminutive; but freshly coloured, green, dewy; with a spring-sky, piled with glittering yet showery clouds—for my childhood was not all sunshine—it had its overcast, its cold, its stormy hours. Second, X——; huge, dingy; the canvass cracked and smoked; a yellow sky, sooty clouds; no sun, no azure; the verdure of the suburbs blighted and sullied—a very dreary scene.

Third—Belgium; and I will pause before this landscape. As to the fourth, a curtain covers it, which I may hereafter withdraw, or may not, as suits my convenience and capacity. At any rate for the present it must hang undisturbed. Belgium! name unromantic and unpoetic, yet name that whenever uttered, has in my ear a sound, in my heart an echo such as no other assemblage of syllables, however sweet or classic, can produce. Belgium! I repeat the word, now as I sit alone near midnight. It stirs my world of the Past like a summons to Resurrection; the graves unclose, the dead are raised; Thoughts, Feelings, Memories that slept, are seen by me ascending from the clods—haloed most of them—but while I gaze on their vapoury forms and strive to ascertain definitely their outline, the sound which wakened them dies and they sink, each and all, like a light wreath of mist, absorbed in the mould, recalled to urns, resealed in monuments. Farewell luminous phantoms!

This is Belgium, Reader—look! Don't call the picture a flat or a dull one—it was neither flat nor dull to me when I first beheld it. When I left Ostend on a mild February Morning and found myself on the road to Brussels, nothing could look vapid to me. My sense of enjoyment possessed an edge whetted to the finest, untouched, keen, exquisite—I was young; I had good health; Pleasure and I had never met; no indulgence of hers had enervated or sated one faculty of my nature—Liberty I clasped in my arms for the first time and the influence of her smile and embrace revived my life like the sun and the west-wind. Yes, at that epoch, I felt like a morning traveller who doubts not that from the hill he is ascending he shall behold a glorious sunrise; what if the track be strait, steep and stony? he sees it not—his eyes are fixed on that summit, flushed already, flushed and gilded, and having gained it he is certain of the scene beyond. He knows that the sun will face him, that his chariot is even now coming over the eastern horizon and that the herald-breeze, he feels on his cheek, is opening for the God's career a clear, vast path of azure, amidst clouds, soft as pearl and warm as flame. Difficulty and toil were to be my lot but sustained by energy, drawn on by hopes as bright as vague, I deemed such a lot no hardship—I mounted now the hill in shade, there were pebbles, inequalities, briars on my path, but my eyes were fixed on the crimson peak above, my imagination was with the refulgent firmament beyond, and I thought nothing of the stones turning under my feet or of the thorns scratching my face and hands.

I gazed often, and always with delight from the window of the diligence (these, be it remembered, were not the days of trains and railroads). Well! and what did I see? I will tell you faithfully. Green, reedy swamps, fields fertile but flat, cultivated in patches that made them look like magnified kitchen-gardens; belts of cut trees, formal as pollard willows, skirting the horizon; narrow canals, gliding slow by the roadside, painted Flemish farm-houses, some very dirty hovels, a grey, dead sky, wet road, wet fields, wet house-tops; not a beautiful, scarcely a picturesque object met my eye along the whole route, yet to me, all was beautiful, all was more than picturesque. It continued fair so long as daylight lasted, though the moisture of many preceding damp days had sodden the whole country; as it grew dark, however, the rain re-commenced, and it was through streaming and starless darkness my eye caught the first gleam of the lights of Brussels. I saw little of the city but its lights, that night. Having alighted from the diligence, a fiacre conveyed me to the

Hotel de —— where I had been advised by a fellow-traveller to put up; having eaten a traveller's supper, I retired to bed, and slept a traveller's sleep.

Next morning I awoke from prolonged and sound repose with the impression that I was yet in X—— and perceiving it to be broad daylight, I started up, imagining that I had overslept myself and should be behind time at the Counting-house. The momentary and painful sense of restraint vanished before the revived and reviving consciousness of freedom, as, throwing back the white curtains of my bed, I looked forth into a wide, lofty foreign chamber—how different from the small and dingy, though not uncomfortable apartment, I had occupied for a night or two at a respectable inn in London, while waiting for the sailing of the packet! Yet far be it from me to profane the memory of that little dingy room! It too is dear to my soul, for there, as I lay in quiet and darkness, I first heard the great bell of St. Paul's telling London it was midnight, and well do I recall the deep deliberate tones, so full charged with colossal phlegm and force. From the small, narrow window of that room, I first saw *the* Dome, looming through a London Mist. I suppose the sensations stirred by those first sounds, first sights are felt but once; treasure them, Memory! seal them in urns and keep them in safe niches! Well—I rose. Travellers talk of the apartments in foreign dwellings being bare and uncomfortable, I thought my chamber looked stately and cheerful. It had such large windows—croisées that opened like doors, with such broad, clear panes of glass; such a great looking-glass stood on my dressing-table—such a fine mirror glittered over the mantel-piece, the painted floor looked so clean and glossy; when I had dressed and was descending the stairs, the broad marble steps almost awed me and so did the lofty hall into which they conducted. On the first landing I met a Flemish housemaid, she had wooden shoes, a short red petticoat, a printed cotton bed-gown, her face was broad, her physiognomy eminently stupid; when I spoke to her in French, she answered me in Flemish, with an air the reverse of civil, yet I thought her charming; if she was not pretty or polite, she was, I conceived, very picturesque; she reminded me of the female figures in certain

Dutch paintings I had seen in other years at Seacombe-Hall.

I repaired to the public room; that too was very large and very lofty and warmed by a stove; the floor was black and the stove was black and most of the furniture was black; yet I never experienced a freer sense of exhilaration than when I sat down at a very long black table (covered however in part by a white cloth), and, having ordered breakfast, began to pour out my coffee from a little black coffee-pot. The stove might be dismal looking to some eyes, not to mine, but it was indisputably very warm, and there were two gentlemen seated by it, talking in French; impossible to follow their rapid utterance or comprehend much of the purport of what they said—yet French, in the mouths of Frenchmen, or Belgians (I was not then sensible of the horrors of the Belgian accent)—was as music to my ears. One of these gentlemen presently discerned me to be an Englishman—no doubt from the fashion in which I addressed the waiter, for I would persist in speaking French in my execrable South-of-England style though the man understood English. The gentleman, after looking towards me once or twice, politely accosted me in very good English—I remember I wished to God that I could speak French as well; his fluency and correct pronunciation impressed me for the first time with a due notion of the cosmopolitan character of the capital I was in; it was my first experience of that skill in living languages, I afterwards found to be so general in Brussels.

I lingered over my breakfast as long as I could, while it was there on the table and while that stranger continued talking to me, I was a free, independent traveller; but at last the things were removed, the two gentlemen left the room, suddenly the illusion ceased; reality and business came back. I, a bondsman just released from the yoke, freed for one week, from twenty-one years of constraint, must, of necessity, resume the fetters of dependency; hardly had I tasted the delight of being without a master, when duty issued her stern mandate: "Go forth and seek another service." I never linger over a painful and necessary task, I never take pleasure before business, it is not in my nature to do so; impossible to enjoy a leisurely walk over the city, though I perceived the morning was very fine, until I had first presented Mr. Hunsden's letter of introduction and got fairly on to the track of a new situation. Wrenching my mind from Liberty and delight, I seized my hat, and forced my reluctant body out of the Hotel de —— into the foreign street.

It was a fine day but I would not look at the blue sky nor at the stately houses round me; my mind was bent on one thing, finding out "Mr. Brown—Numéro —— Rue Royale", for so my letter was addressed. By dint of enquiry, I succeeded, I stood, at last, at the desired door, knocked, asked for Mr. Brown and was admitted.

Being shewn into a small breakfast-room, I found myself in the presence of an elderly gentleman, very grave, business-like and respectable looking—I presented Mr. Hunsden's letter, he received me very civilly; after a little desultory conversation he asked me if there was anything in which his advice or experience could be of use; I said "Yes" and then proceeded to tell him that I was not a gentleman of fortune, travelling for pleasure—but an ex-counting-house clerk who wanted employment of some kind and that immediately too. He replied that as a friend of Mr. Hunsden's he would be willing to assist me as well as he could. After some meditation he named a place in a mercantile house at Liège and another in a bookseller's shop at Louvain.

"Clerk and shopman!" murmured I to myself. "No—" I shook my head, I had tried the high stool—I hated it, I believed there were other occupations that would suit me better—besides I did not wish to leave Brussels.

"I know of no place in Brussels," answered Mr. Brown, "unless indeed you were disposed to turn your attention to teaching—I am acquainted with the Director of a large establishment who is in want of a Professor of English and Latin."

I thought two minutes—then I seized the idea eagerly—

"The very thing, Sir!" said I.

"But," asked he, "do you understand French well enough to teach Belgian boys English?"

Fortunately I could answer this question in the affirmative;

having studied French under a Frenchman, I could speak the language intelligibly though not fluently, I could also read it well, and write it decently.

"Then," pursued Mr. Brown, "I think I can promise you the place, for Monsieur Pelet will not refuse a professor recommended by me, but come here again at five o'clock this afternoon and I will introduce you to him."

The word professor struck me. "I am not a professor," said I.

"Oh," returned Mr. Brown—"Professor, here in Belgium, means a teacher—that is all."

My conscience thus quieted—I thanked Mr. Brown, and, for the present, withdrew. This time I stepped out into the street with a relieved heart; the task I had imposed on myself, for that day, was executed, I might now take some hours of holiday. I felt free to look up; for the first time I remarked the sparkling clearness of the air, the deep blue of the sky; the gay, clean aspect of the white-washed or painted houses; I saw what a fine street was the Rue Royale and, walking leisurely along its broad pavement, I continued to survey its stately hotels, till the palisades, the gates and trees of the park, appearing in sight, offered to my eye a new attraction. I remember, before entering the park, I stood awhile to contemplate the statue of General Belliard and then I advanced to the top of the great staircase just beyond and I looked down into a narrow back-street which, I afterwards learnt, was called the Rue d'Isabelle. I well recollect that my eye rested on the green door of a rather large house opposite, where, on a brass plate, was inscribed "Pensionnat de demoiselles". Pensionnat! The word excited an uneasy sensation in my mind—it seemed to speak of restraint. Some of the demoiselles, externats no doubt, were at that moment issuing from the door—I looked for a pretty face amongst them, but their close, little French bonnets hid their features—in a moment they were gone.

I had traversed a good deal of Brussels before five o'clock arrived, but punctually as that hour struck, I was again in the Rue Royale. Re-admitted to Mr. Brown's breakfast-room, I found him, as before, seated at the table and he was not alone, a gentleman stood by the hearth; two words of introduction designated him as my future master—M. Pelet Mr. Crimsworth—Mr. Crimsworth M. Pelet—a bow on each side finished the ceremony. I don't know what sort of a bow I made, an ordinary one I suppose, for I was in a tranquil, common-place frame of mind, I felt none of the agitation which had troubled my first interview with Edward Crimsworth; M. Pelet's bow was extremely polite yet not theatrical, scarcely French; he and I were presently seated opposite to each other. In a pleasing voice, low, and, out of consideration to my foreign ears, very distinct and deliberate, M. Pelet intimated that he had just been receiving from "le respectable M. Brown" an account of my attainments and character which relieved him from all scruple as to the propriety of engaging me as professor of English and Latin in his establishment; nevertheless, for form's sake, he would put a few questions to test my powers; he did and expressed in flattering terms his satisfaction at my answers. The subject of salary next came on—it was fixed at 1000 francs per annum besides board and lodging: "And in addition," suggested M. Pelet, "as there will be some hours in each day during which your services will not be required in my establishment, you may, in time, obtain employment in other seminaries and thus turn your vacant moments to profitable account."

I thought this very kind, and indeed I found afterwards that the terms on which M. Pelet had engaged me were really liberal for Brussels; instruction being extremely cheap there on account of the number of teachers; it was further arranged that I should be installed in my new post the very next day, after which M. Pelet and I parted.

Well—and what was he like? and what were my impressions concerning him? He was a man of about forty years of age, of middle size and rather emaciated figure, his face was pale, his cheeks were sunk and his eyes hollow; his features were pleasing and regular, they had a French turn (for M. Pelet was no Fleming, but a Frenchman both by birth and parentage) yet the degree of harshness inseparable from Gallic lineaments was, in his case, softened by a mild blue eye and a melancholy, almost suffering expression of countenance; his physiognomy was "fine et spirituelle"—I use two French words because they define better than any English terms the species of intelligence with which his features were embued. He was altogether an interesting and prepossessing personage—I wondered only at the utter absence of all the ordinary characteristics of his profession, and almost feared he could not be stern and resolute enough for a schoolmaster. Externally—at least—M. Pelet presented an absolute contrast to my late Master—Edward Crimsworth.

Influenced by the impression I had received of his gentleness—I was a good deal surprised when, on arriving the next day at my new employer's house and being admitted to a first view of what was to be the sphere of my future labours, namely—the large, lofty and well-lighted school-rooms, I beheld a numerous assemblage of pupils, boys of course, whose collective appearance shewed all the signs of a full, flourishing and well-disciplined seminary. As I traversed the classes in company with M. Pelet, a profound silence reigned on all sides and if by chance a murmur or a whisper arose, one glance from the pensive eye of this most gentle pedagogue stilled it instantly. It was astonishing, I thought, how so mild a check could prove so effectual. When I had perambulated the length and breadth of the classes, M. Pelet turned and said to me:

"Would you object to taking the boys as they are and testing their proficiency in English?"

The proposal was unexpected—I had thought I should have been allowed at least a day to prepare, but it is a bad omen to commence any career by hesitation, so I just stepped to the professor's desk near which we stood and faced the circle of my pupils. I took a moment to collect my thoughts and likewise to frame in French the sentence by which I proposed to open business—I made it as short as possible—

"Messieurs, prenez vos livres de lecture."

"Anglais ou Français, Monsieur?" demanded a thick-set, moon-faced young Flamand in a blouse. The answer was fortunately easy:

"Anglais."

I determined to give myself as little trouble as possible in this lesson; it would not do yet to trust my unpractised tongue with the delivery of explanations; my accent and idiom would be too open to the criticisms of the young gentlemen before me, relative to whom I felt already it would be necessary at once to take up an advantageous position, and I proceeded to employ means accordingly.

"Commencez!" cried I, when they had all produced their books; the moon-faced youth (by name Jules Vanderkelkov—as I afterwards learnt) took the first sentence. The "livre de lecture" was the "Vicar of Wakefield", much used in foreign schools because it is supposed to contain prime samples of conversational English, it might, however, have been a Runic scroll for any resemblance the words, as enunciated by Jules, bore to the language in ordinary use amongst the natives of Great Britain. My God! how he did snuffle, snort and wheeze! All he said was said in his throat and nose, for it is thus the Flamands speak; but I heard him to the end of his paragraph without proffering a word of correction, whereat he looked vastly self-complacent, convinced, no doubt, that he had acquitted himself like a real born and bred "Anglais". In the same unmoved silence I listened to a dozen in rotation, and when the twelfth had concluded with splutter, hiss and mumble, I solemnly laid down the book.

"Arrêtez!" said I—there was a pause—during which I regarded them all with a steady and somewhat stern gaze; a dog, if stared at hard enough and long enough, will shew symptoms of embarrassment, and so at length did my bench of Belgians; perceiving that some of the faces before me were beginning to look sullen and others ashamed, I slowly joined my hands and ejaculated in a deep "voix de poitrine":

"Comme c'est affreux!"

They looked at each other, pouted, coloured, swung their heels; they were not pleased, I saw, but they were impressed, and in the way I wished them to be. Having thus taken them down a peg in their self-conceit, the next step was to raise myself in their estimation; not a very easy thing, considering that I hardly dared to speak for fear of betraying my own deficiencies.

"Écoutez, Messieurs!" said I, and I endeavoured to throw into my accents the compassionate tone of a superior being, who, touched by the extremity of the helplessness, which at first only excited his scorn, deigns at length to bestow aid. I then began at the very beginning of the "Vicar of Wakefield" and read, in a slow, distinct voice, some twenty pages; they, all the while, sitting mute and listening with fixed attention; by the time I had done, nearly an hour had elapsed, I then rose and said:

"C'est assez pour aujourd'hui, Messieurs, demain nous recommencerons et j'espère que tout ira bien."

With this oracular sentence, I bowed, and in company with M. Pelet, quitted the school-room.

"C'est bien! c'est très bien!" said my principal as we entered his parlour. "Je vois que Monsieur a de l'adresse, cela me plaît, car, dans l'instruction, l'adresse fait tout autant que le savoir."

From the parlour, M. Pelet conducted me to my apartment, my "Chambre", as Monsieur said with a certain air of complacency: it was a very small room, with an excessively small bed, but M. Pelet gave me to understand that I was to occupy it quite alone, which was of course a great comfort. Yet, though so limited in dimensions, it had two windows; light not being taxed in Belgium, the people never grudge its admission into their houses; just here, however, this observation is not very apropos—for one of these windows was boarded up; the open window looked into the boys' playground—I glanced at the other, as wondering what aspect it would present if disencumbered of the boards—M. Pelet read, I suppose, the expression of my eye—he explained—

"La fenêtre fermée donne sur un jardin appartenant à un pensionnat de demoiselles," said he, "et les convenances exigent—enfin, vous comprenez—n'est-ce pas, Monsieur?"

"Oui, oui," was my reply—and I looked—of course—quite satisfied but when M. Pelet had retired and closed the door after him, the first thing I did was to scrutinize closely the nailed boards, hoping to find some chink or crevice which I might enlarge and so get a peep at the consecrated ground; my researches were vain—for the boards were well joined and strongly nailed; it is astonishing how disappointed I felt—I thought it would have been so pleasant to have looked out upon a garden planted with flowers and trees, so amusing to have watched the demoiselles at their play—to have studied female character in a variety of phases, myself the while, sheltered from view by a modest muslin curtain; whereas, owing doubtless to the absurd scruples of some old duenna of a Directress, I had now only the option of looking at a bare, gravelled court with an enormous "pas de géant" in the middle and the monotonous walls and windows of a boys' school-house round. Not only then, but many a time after, especially in moments of weariness and low spirits did I look with dissatisfied eyes on that most tantalizing board, longing to tear it away and get a glimpse of the green region which I imagined to lie beyond. I knew a tree grew close up to the window, for though there were, as yet, no leaves to rustle, I often heard, at night, the tapping of branches against the panes. In the day-time, when I listened attentively I could hear, even through the boards, the voices of the demoiselles in their hours of recreation and, to speak the honest truth, my sentimental reflections were occasionally a trifle disarranged by the not quite silvery, in fact—the too-often brazen sounds which rising from the unseen Paradise below, penetrated clamorously into my solitude. Not to mince matters—it really seemed to me a doubtful case whether the lungs of Mdlle. Reuter's girls or those of M. Pelet's boys were the strongest and, when it came to shrieking, the girls indisputably beat the boys hollow. I forgot to say, by the by—that Reuter was the name of the old lady who had had my window boarded up—I say old, for such I, of course, concluded her to be, judging from her cautious, chaperon-like proceedings; besides nobody ever spoke of her as young. I remember I was very much amused when I first heard her christian name—it was Zoraïde—Mademoiselle Zoraïde Reuter—but the continental nations do allow themselves vagaries in the choice of names, such as we sober English never run into—I think indeed we have too limited a list to choose from.

Meantime my path was gradually growing smooth before me. I, in a few weeks, conquered the teasing difficulties inseparable from the commencement of almost every career. Erelong I had acquired as much facility in speaking French as set me at my ease with my pupils, and as I had encountered them on a right footing at the very beginning and continued tenaciously to retain the advantage I had early gained, they never attempted mutiny, which circumstance all, who are in any degree acquainted with the ongoings of Belgian schools, and who know the relation in which professors and pupils too frequently stand towards each other in those establishments, will consider an important and uncommon one. Before concluding this chapter I will say a word on the system I pursued with regard to my classes, my experience may possibly be of use to others.

It did not require very keen observation to detect the character of the youth of Brabant, but it needed a certain degree of tact to adapt one's measures to their capacity. Their intellectual faculties were generally weak, their animal propensities strong; thus there was at once an impotence and a kind of inert force in their natures; they were dull, but they were also singularly stubborn, heavy as lead and like lead, most difficult to move. Such being the case it would have been truly absurd to exact from them much in the way of mental exertion; having short memories, dense intelligence, feeble reflective powers—they recoiled with repugnance from any occupation that demanded close study or deep thought; had the abhorred effort been extorted from them by injudicious and arbitrary measures on the part of the professor, they would have resisted as obstinately, as clamorously as desperate swine; and though not brave, singly, they were relentless, acting en masse. I understood that before my arrival in M. Pelet's establishment, the combined insubordination of the pupils had effected the dismissal of more than one English Master. It was necessary then to exact only the most moderate application from natures so little qualified to apply; to assist, in every practicable way, understandings so opaque and contracted; to be ever gentle, considerate, yielding even, to a certain point, with dispositions so irrationally perverse;—but, having reached that culminating point of indulgence—you must fix your foot, plant it, root it in rock—become immutable as the towers of Ste. Gudule, for a step—but half a step further, and you would plunge headlong into the gulph of imbecility—there lodged, you would speedily receive proofs of Flemish gratitude and magnanimity in showers of Brabant saliva and handfuls of Low-Country mud. You might smooth to the utmost the path of learning, remove every pebble from the track, but then you must finally insist with decision on the pupil taking your arm and allowing himself to be led quietly along the prepared road. When I had brought down my lesson to the lowest level of my dullest pupil's capacity, when I had shewn myself the mildest, the most tolerant of masters, a word of impertinence, a movement of disobedience changed me at once into a despot—I offered then but one alternative; submission and acknowledgement of error or ignominious expulsion. This system answered—and my influence, by degrees, became established on a firm basis. "The boy is father to the Man," it is said, and so I often thought when I looked at my boys and remembered the political history of their ancestors: Pelet's school was merely an epitome of the Belgian Nation.

CHAPTER VIII

AND Pelet himself? How did I continue to like him? Oh extremely well! Nothing could be more smooth, gentlemanlike and even friendly than his demeanour to me. I had to endure from him neither cold neglect, irritating interference nor pretentious assumption of superiority—I fear, however, two poor, hard-worked Belgian ushers in the establishment could not have said as much—to them the Director's manner was invariably dry, stern and cool: I believe he perceived once or twice that I was a little shocked at the difference he made between them and me and accounted for it by saying with a quiet, sarcastic smile:

"Ce ne sont que des Flamands—allez!"

And then he took his cigar gently from his lips and spat on the painted floor of the room in which we were sitting. Flamands certainly they were, and both had the true Flamand physiognomy, where intellectual inferiority is marked in lines none can mistake; still they were men and in the main, honest men, and I could not see why their being aboriginals of the fat, dull soil should serve as a pretext for treating them with perpetual severity and contempt. This idea of injustice somewhat poisoned the pleasure I might otherwise have derived from Pelet's soft, affable manner to myself. Certainly it was agreeable, when the day's work was over, to find in one's employer an intelligent and cheerful companion, and if he was sometimes a little sarcastic and sometimes a little too insinuating, and if I did discover that his mildness was more a matter of appearance than of reality, if I did occasionally suspect the existence of flint or steel under an external covering of velvet, still we are none of us perfect, and weary as I was of the atmosphere of brutality and insolence, in which I had constantly lived at X——, I had no inclination now, on casting anchor in calmer regions, to institute at once a prying search after defects that were scrupulously withdrawn, and carefully veiled from my view—I was willing to take Pelet for what he seemed—to believe him benevolent and friendly until some untoward event should prove him otherwise. He was not married and I soon perceived he had all a Frenchman's, all a Parisian's notions about matrimony and women; I suspected a degree of laxity in his code of morals, there was something so cold and blasé in his tone whenever he alluded to, what he called, "le beau sexe"; but he was too gentleman-like to intrude topics I did not invite, and as he was really intelligent and really fond of intellectual subjects of discourse, he and I always found enough to talk about, without seeking themes in the mire—I hated his fashion of mentioning Love, I abhorred, from my soul, mere Licentiousness, he felt the difference of our notions and, by mutual consent, we kept off ground debateable.

Pelet's house was kept and his kitchen managed by his Mother, a real old Frenchwoman; she had been handsome, at least she told me so and I strove to believe her; she was now ugly, as only continental old women can be; perhaps though, her style of dress made her look uglier than she really was. In doors she would go about without cap, her gray hair strangely dishevelled; then, when at home, she seldom wore a gown, only a shabby cotton camisole, shoes too, were strangers to her feet and in lieu of them she sported roomy slippers, trodden down at the heels. On the other hand, whenever it was her pleasure to appear abroad, as on Sundays and fête-days, she would put on some very brilliant coloured dress, usually of thin texture, a silk bonnet with a wreath of flowers and a very fine shawl. She was not, in the main, an ill-natured old woman but an incessant and most indiscreet talker; she kept chiefly in and about the kitchen and seemed rather to avoid her son's august presence, of him indeed she evidently stood in awe; when he reproved her, his reproofs were bitter and unsparing, but he seldom gave himself that trouble.

Madame Pelet had her own society, her own circle of chosen visitors whom, however, I seldom saw as she generally entertained them in what she called her "Cabinet", a small den of a place adjoining the kitchen and descending into it by one or two steps. On these steps, by the by, I have not unfrequently seen Mde. Pelet seated with a trencher on her knee, engaged in the threefold employment of eating her dinner, gossiping with her favourite servant, the housemaid, and scolding her antagonist, the cook; she never dined, and seldom indeed took any meal with her son, and as to shewing her face at the boys' table, that was quite out of the question. These details will sound very odd in English ears, but Belgium is not England, and its ways are not our ways.

Mde. Pelet's habits of life then, being taken into consideration, I was a good deal surprised when, one Thursday evening (Thursday was always a half holiday), as I was sitting all alone in my apartment, correcting a huge pile of English and Latin exercises, a servant tapped at the door and, on its being opened, presented Mde. Pelet's compliments and she would be happy to see me to take my "goûter" (a meal which answers to our English "Tea") with her in the dining-room.

"Plaît-il?" said I—for I thought I must have misunderstood, the message and invitation were so unusual; the same words were repeated. I accepted, of course, and as I descended the stairs, I wondered what whim had entered the old lady's brain; her son was out, gone to pass the evening at the salle of the Grande Harmonie or some other club of which he was a member. Just as I laid my hand on the handle of the dining-room door—a queer idea glanced across my mind:

"Surely she's not going to make love to me," said I. "I've heard of old Frenchwomen doing odd things in that line—and the goûter? They generally begin such affairs with eating and drinking, I believe."

There was a fearful dismay in this suggestion of my excited imagination and if I had allowed myself time to dwell upon it, I should no doubt have cut there and then, rushed back to my chamber and bolted myself in; but whenever a danger or a horror is veiled with uncertainty, the primary wish of the mind is to ascertain first the naked truth, reserving the expedient of flight for the moment when its dread anticipations shall be realized. I turned the door-handle and in an instant had crossed the fatal threshold, closed the door behind me and stood in the presence of Mde. Pelet.

Gracious heavens! The first view of her seemed to confirm my worst apprehensions. There she sat—dressed out in a light green muslin gown, on her head a lace cap with flourishing red roses in the frill; her table was carefully spread—there were fruit, cakes and coffee with a bottle of something, I did not know what. Already the cold sweat started on my brow—already I glanced back over my shoulder at the closed door when, to my unspeakable relief, my eye, wandering wildly in the direction of the stove, rested upon a second figure, seated in a large fauteuil beside it. This was a woman too, and moreover an old woman and as fat and as rubicund as Mde. Pelet was meagre and yellow; her attire was likewise very fine, and spring-flowers of different hues circled in a bright wreath the crown of her violet-coloured velvet bonnet.

I had only time to make these general observations when Mde. Pelet, coming forward with, what she intended should be, a graceful and elastic step, thus accosted me:

"Monsieur is indeed most obliging to quit his books, his studies, at the request of an insignificant person like me—will Monsieur complete his kindness by allowing me to present him to my dear friend Mde. Reuter who resides in the neighbouring house—the young ladies' school."

"Ah!" thought I, "I knew she was old." And I bowed and took my seat; Mde. Reuter placed herself at the table opposite to me.

"How do you like Belgium, Monsieur?" asked she in an accent of the broadest Bruxellois—I could now well distinguish the difference between the fine and pure Parisian utterance of M. Pelet, for instance, and the guttural enunciation of the Flamands. I answered politely and then wondered how so coarse and clumsy an old woman as the one before me, should be at the head of a ladies' seminary which I had always heard spoken of in terms of high commendation. In truth there was something to wonder at; Mde. Reuter looked more like a joyous, free-living old Flemish fermière or even a maîtresse d'auberge than a staid, grave, rigid directrice de pensionnat. In general, the continental, or at least the Belgian old women permit themselves a licence of manners, speech and aspect such as our venerable grand-dames would recoil from as absolutely disreputable, and Mde. Reuter's jolly face bore evidence that she was no exception to the rule of her country; there was a twinkle and leer in her left eye—her right she kept habitually half-shut, which I thought very odd indeed. After several vain attempts to comprehend the motives of these two droll old creatures for inviting me to join them at their goûter I, at last, fairly gave it up and resigning myself to inevitable mystification I sat and looked first at one, then at the other, taking care meantime to do justice to the confitures, cakes and coffee with which they amply supplied me. They too ate, and that with no delicate appetite and having demolished a large portion of the solids—they proposed a "petit verre"; I declined—not so Mesdames Pelet and Reuter; each mixed herself, what I thought, rather a stiff tumbler of punch and placing it on a stand near the stove, they drew up their chairs to that convenience and invited me to do the same; I obeyed and being seated fairly between them, I was thus addressed first by Mde. Pelet—then by Mde. Reuter:

"We will now speak of business," said Mde. Pelet and she went on to make an elaborate speech which, being interpreted, was to the effect that she had asked for the pleasure of my company that evening in order to give her friend Mde. Reuter an opportunity of broaching an important proposal which might turn out greatly to my advantage.

"Pourvu que vous soyez sage," said Mde. Reuter, "et, à vrai dire, vous en avez bien l'air. Take one drop of the punch (or ponche as she pronounced it)—it is an agreeable and wholesome beverage after a full meal."

I bowed, but again declined it—she went on:

"I feel," said she, after a solemn sip, "I feel profoundly the importance of the commission with which my dear daughter has entrusted me, for you are aware, Monsieur, that it is my daughter who directs the establishment in the next house?"

"Ah! I thought it was yourself, Madame." Though indeed, at that moment, I recollected that it was called Mademoiselle—not Madame Reuter's pensionnat.

"I? Oh no! I manage the house and look after the servants, as my friend Mde. Pelet does for Monsieur, her son—nothing more. Ah! you thought I gave lessons in class—did you?" And she laughed, loud and long, as though the idea tickled her fancy amazingly.

"Madame is in the wrong to laugh," I observed, "if she does not give lessons, I am sure it is not because she cannot." And I whipped out a white pocket-handkerchief and wafted it, with a French grace, past my nose, bowing at the same time.

"Quel charmant jeune homme!" murmured Mde. Pelet in a low voice; Mde. Reuter, being less sentimental, as she was Flamand and not French—only laughed again.

"You are a dangerous person I fear," said she; "if you can forge compliments at that rate Zoraïde will positively be afraid of you, but if you are good, I will keep your secret and not tell her how well you can flatter. Now listen what sort of a proposal she makes to you. She has heard that you are an excellent professor and as she wishes to get the very best masters for her school (car Zoraïde fait tout comme une reine, c'est une véritable maîtresse-femme), she has commissioned me to step over this afternoon and sound Mde. Pelet as to the possibility of engaging you: Zoraïde is a wary general, she never advances without first examining well her ground; I don't think she would be pleased if she knew I had already disclosed her intentions to you—she did not order me to go so far—but I thought there would be no harm in letting you into the secret and Mde. Pelet was of the same opinion. Take care however you don't betray either of us to Zoraïde—to my daughter, I mean, she is so discreet and circumspect herself—she cannot understand that one should find a pleasure in gossiping a little—"

"C'est absolument comme mon fils!" cried Mde. Pelet.

"Ah the world is so changed since our girlhood!" rejoined the other. "Young people have such old heads now—but to return, Monsieur; Mde. Pelet will mention the subject of your giving lessons in my daughter's establishment to her son, and he will speak to you, and then, to-morrow, you will step over to our house and ask to see my daughter, and you will introduce the subject as if the first intimation of it had reached you from M. Pelet himself, and be sure you never mention my name, for I would not displease Zoraïde on any account."

"Bien! bien!" interrupted I—for all this chatter and circumlocution began to bore me very much; "I will consult M. Pelet and the thing shall be settled as you desire. Good-evening Mesdames—infinitely obliged to you."

"Comment! vous vous en allez déjà?" exclaimed Mde. Pelet—"Prenez encore quelquechose Monsieur—une pomme cuite, des biscuits, encore une tasse de café?"

"Merci—merci Madame—au revoir—" and I backed at last out of the apartment.

Having regained my own room, I set myself to turn over in my mind the incident of the evening. It seemed a queer affair altogether, and queerly managed—the two old women had made quite a little intricate mess of it—still—I found that the uppermost feeling in my mind on the subject was one of satisfaction. In the first place it would be a change to give lessons in another seminary, and then to teach young ladies would be an occupation so interesting—to be admitted at all into a ladies' boarding-school would be an incident so new in my life. "Besides," thought I, as I glanced at the boarded window, "I shall now at last see the mysterious garden, I shall gaze both on the angels and their Eden."

CHAPTER IX

M. PELET could not of course object to the proposal made by Mdlle. Reuter; permission to accept such additional employment, should it offer, having formed an article of the terms on which he had engaged me. It was therefore arranged in the course of next day that I should be at liberty to give lessons in Mdlle. Reuter's establishment, four afternoons in every week.

When evening came, I prepared to step over in order to seek a conference with Mademoiselle herself on the subject. I had not had time to pay the visit before, having been all day closely occupied in class. I remember very well that before quitting my chamber—I held a brief debate with myself as to whether I should change my ordinary attire for something smarter; at last I concluded it would be a waste of labour; "Doubtless," thought I, "she is some stiff old maid, for though the daughter of Mde. Reuter, she may well number upwards of forty winters—besides if it were otherwise, if she be both young and pretty—I am not handsome, and no dressing can make me so—therefore, I'll go as I am." And off I started, cursorily glancing sideways as I passed the toilet-table, surmounted by a looking-glass; a thin irregular face I saw, with sunk, dark eyes under a large, square forehead, complexion destitute of bloom or attraction, something young but not youthful, no object to win a lady's love, no butt for the shafts of Cupid.

I was soon at the entrance of the Pensionnat, in a moment I had pulled the bell—in another moment the door was opened and within appeared a passage, paved alternately with black and white marble; the walls were painted in imitation of marble also, and at the far-end opened a glass-door, through which I saw shrubs and a grass-plat, looking pleasant in the sunshine of the mild, spring evening, for it was now the middle of April. This then was my first glimpse of *The* Garden—but I had not time to look long, the porteress, after having answered in the affirmative my question as to whether her mistress was at home, opened the folding-doors of a room to the left and having ushered me in, closed them behind me. I found myself in a salon with a very well painted, highly varnished floor; chairs and sofas covered with white draperies, a green porcelain stove, walls hung with pictures in gilt frames, a gilt pendule and other ornaments on the mantel-piece, a large lustre pendent from the centre of the ceiling, mirrors, consoles, muslin-curtains and a handsome centre table completed the inventory of furniture; all looked extremely clean and glittering but the general effect would have been somewhat chilling, had not a second large pair of folding-doors, standing wide open, and disclosing another and smaller salon—more snugly furnished—offered some relief to the eye. This room was carpeted, and therein was a piano, a couch, a chiffonnière; above all it contained a lofty window with a crimson curtain, which being undrawn—afforded another glimpse of the garden, through the large, clear panes, round which some leaves of ivy, some tendrils of a vine were trained.

"Monsieur Creemsvort—n'est-ce pas?" said a voice behind me and starting involuntarily, I turned; I had been so taken up with the contemplation of the pretty little salon that I had not noticed the entrance of a person into the larger room. It was however Mademoiselle Reuter, who now addressed me and stood close beside me; and when I had bowed with instantaneously recovered sang-froid—for I am not easily embarrassed—I commenced the conversation by remarking on the pleasant aspect of her little cabinet and the advantage she had over M. Pelet in possessing a garden.

"Yes," she said, "she often thought so," and added, "it is my garden, Monsieur, which makes me retain this house—otherwise I should probably have removed to larger and more commodious premises long since—but you see I could not take my garden with me and I should scarcely find one so large and pleasant anywhere else in town."

I approved her judgment.

"But you have not seen it yet," said she rising. "Come to the window and take a better view." I followed her, she opened the sash and leaning out, I saw in full the enclosed demesne which had hitherto been to me an unknown region. It was a long, not very broad strip of cultured ground with an alley bordered by enormous old fruit trees down the middle; there was a sort of lawn, a parterre of rose-trees, some flower-borders and, on the far-side, a thickly planted copse of lilacs, laburnams and acacias. It looked pleasant, to me—very pleasant, so long a time had elapsed since I had seen a garden of any sort. But it was not only on Mdlle. Reuter's garden that my eyes dwelt; when I had taken a view of her well trimmed beds and budding shrubberies, I allowed my glance to come back to herself, nor did I hastily withdraw it.

I had thought to see a tall, meagre, yellow, conventual image in black, with a close white cap, bandaged under the chin like a nun's head-gear; whereas, there stood by me a little and roundly formed woman, who might indeed be older than I, but was still young, she could not, I thought, be more than six or seven and twenty; she was as fair as a fair Englishwoman, she had no cap, her hair was nut-brown and she wore it in curls; pretty her features were not, nor very soft, nor very regular, but neither were they in any degree plain and I already saw cause to deem them expressive. What was their predominant cast? Was it sagacity? sense? Yes—I thought so, but I could scarcely as yet be sure; I discovered however that there was a certain serenity of eye and freshness of complexion, most pleasing to behold. The colour on her cheek was like the bloom on a good apple, which is as sound at the core as it is red on the rind.

Mademoiselle Reuter and I entered upon business. She said she was not absolutely certain of the wisdom of the step she was about to take because I was so young and parents might possibly object to a professor like me for their daughters: "But it is often well to act on one's own judgment," said she, "and to lead parents, rather than to be led by them; the fitness of a professor is not a matter of age and from what I have heard and from what I observe myself, I would much rather trust you than M. Ledru the music-master who is a married man of near fifty."

I remarked that I hoped she would find me worthy of her good opinion, that, if I knew myself, I was incapable of betraying any confidence reposed in me. "Du reste," said she, "the surveillance will be strictly attended to." And then she proceeded to discuss the subject of terms. She was very cautious, quite on her guard, she did not absolutely bargain, but she warily sounded me to find out what my expectations might be, and when she could not get me to name a sum, she reasoned and reasoned with a fluent yet quiet circumlocution of speech, and at last nailed me down to 500 francs per annum: not too much, but I agreed. Before the negociation was completed, it began to grow a little dusk—I did not hasten it, for I liked well enough to sit and hear her talk; I was amused with the sort of business-talent she displayed; Edward could not have shewn himself more practical, though he might have evinced more coarseness and urgency; and then she had so many reasons, so many explanations and after all she succeeded in proving herself quite disinterested and even liberal. At last she concluded, she could say no more, because, as I acquiesced in all things, there was no further ground for the exercise of her parts of speech—I was obliged to rise—I would rather have sat a little longer; what had I to return to but my small, empty room? And my eyes had a pleasure in looking at Mdlle. Reuter, especially now, when the twilight softened her features a little and, in the doubtful dusk, I could fancy her forehead as open as it was really elevated, her mouth touched with turns of sweetness as well as defined in lines of sense. When I rose to go I held out my hand, on purpose, though I knew it was contrary to the etiquette of foreign habits, she smiled and said:

"Ah! c'est comme tous les Anglais," but gave me her hand very kindly.

"It is the privilege of my country, Mademoiselle," said I, "and remember, I shall always claim it."

She laughed a little, quite good naturedly and with the sort of tranquillity obvious in all she did—a tranquillity which soothed and suited me singularly, at least I thought so that evening. Brussels seemed a very pleasant place to me when I got out again into the street, and it appeared as if some cheerful, eventful, upward-tending career were even then opening to me, on that self-same mild, still April night. So impressionable a being is man—or at least such a man as I was—in those days.

CHAPTER X

NEXT day the Morning hours seemed to pass very slowly at M. Pelet's; I wanted the afternoon to come that I might go again to the neighbouring Pensionnat and give my first lesson within its pleasant precincts, for pleasant they appeared to me. At noon the hour of recreation arrived; at one o'clock we had lunch; this got on the time and at last Ste. Gudule's deep bell, tolling slowly two, marked the moment for which I had been waiting.

At the foot of the narrow back-stairs that descended from my room, I met M. Pelet.

"Comme vous avez l'air rayonnant!" said he. "Je ne vous ai jamais vu aussi gai. Que s'est-il donc passé?"

"Apparemment que j'aime les changements," replied I.

"Ah! je comprends—c'est cela—soyez sage seulement. Vous êtes bien jeune—trop jeune pour le rôle que vous allez jouer—il faut prendre garde—savez-vous?"

"Mais quel danger y-a-t-il?"

"Je n'en sais rien—ne vous laissez pas aller à de vives impressions—voilà tout."

I laughed—a sentiment of exquisite pleasure played over my nerves at the thought that "vives impressions" were likely to be created; it was the deadness, the sameness of life's daily ongoings that had hitherto been my bane; my blouse-clad élèves in the boys' seminary never stirred in me any "vives impressions" except it might be occasionally some of anger. I broke from M. Pelet and as I strode down the passage he followed me with one of his laughs—a very French, rakish, mocking sound.

Again I stood at the neighbouring door and soon was re-admitted into the cheerful passage with its clear, dove-colour, imitation marble walls. I followed the portress and descending a step and making a turn, I found myself in a sort of corridor; a side-door opened, Mdlle. Reuter's little figure, as graceful as it was plump, appeared. I could now see her dress in full daylight; a neat, simple mousseline-laine gown fitted her compact, round shape to perfection—delicate little collar and manchettes of lace, trim Parisian brodequins showed her neck, wrists and feet to complete advantage; but how grave was her face as she came suddenly upon me! Solicitude and business were in her eye—on her forehead, she looked almost stern. Her "bon-jour Monsieur" was quite polite, but so orderly, so common-place; it spread directly a cool, damp towel over my "vives impressions". The servant turned back when her mistress appeared and I walked slowly along the corridor side by side with Mdlle. Reuter.

"Monsieur will give a lesson in the first class to-day," said she. "Dictation or Reading will perhaps be the best thing to begin with, for those are the easiest forms of communicating instruction in a foreign language, and at the first, a master naturally feels a little unsettled."

She was quite right as I had found from experience, it only remained for me to acquiesce. We proceeded now in silence. The corridor terminated in a hall, large, lofty and square; a glass door on one side shewed within a long, narrow refectory—with tables, an armoire and two lamps; it was empty; large glass doors, in front, opened on the play-ground and garden; a broad staircase ascended spirally on the opposite side; the remaining wall shewed a pair of great folding-doors, now closed and admitting, doubtless, to the classes.

Mdlle. Reuter turned her eye laterally on me, to ascertain probably whether I was collected enough to be ushered into her sanctum sanctorum. I suppose she judged me to be in a tolerable state of self-government, for she opened the door and I followed her through. A rustling sound of uprising greeted our entrance; without looking to the right or left, I walked straight up the lane between two sets of benches and desks and took possession of the empty chair and isolated desk raised on an estrade of one step high, so as to command one division; the other division being under the surveillance of a Maîtresse, similarly elevated. At the back of the estrade and attached to a moveable partition dividing this school-room from another beyond, was a large tableau of wood painted black and varnished; a thick crayon of white chalk lay on my desk for the convenience of elucidating any grammatical or verbal obscurity which might occur in my lessons by writing it upon the tableau, a wet spunge appeared beside the chalk to enable me to efface the marks when they had served the purpose intended.

I carefully and deliberately made these observations before allowing myself to take one glance at the benches before me; having handled the crayon, looked back at the tableau, fingered the spunge in order to ascertain that it was in a right state of moisture—I found myself cool enough to admit of looking calmly up and gazing deliberately round me.

And first I observed that Mdlle. Reuter had already glided away, she was nowhere visible; a maîtresse or teacher, the one who occupied the corresponding estrade to my own, alone remained to keep guard over me; she was a little in the shade and, with my short sight, I could only see that she was of a thin, bony figure and rather tallowy complexion and that her attitude, as she sat, partook equally of listlessness and affectation. More obvious, more prominent, shone on by the full light of the large window, were the occupants of the benches just before me, of whom some were girls of fourteen, fifteen, sixteen, some young women from eighteen (as it appeared to me) up to twenty; the most modest attire, the simplest fashion of wearing the hair were apparent in all and good features, ruddy, blooming complexions, large and brilliant eyes, forms full even to solidity seemed to abound. I did not bear the first view like a stoic, I was dazzled, my eyes fell, and in a voice somewhat too low, I murmured:

"Prenez vos cahiers de dictée, Mesdemoiselles."

Not so had I bid the boys at Pelet's take their reading-books. A rustle followed and an opening of desks; behind the lifted lids which momentarily screened the heads bent down to search for exercise-books, I heard tittering and whispers.

"Eulalie—je suis prête à pâmer de rire," observed one.

"Comme il a rougi en parlant!"

"Oui, c'est un véritable blanc-bec."

"Tais-toi, Hortense—il nous écoute."

And now the lids sank and the heads reappeared; I had marked three, the whisperers, and I did not scruple to take a very steady look at them as they emerged from their temporary eclipse. It is astonishing what ease and courage their little phrases of flippancy had given me; the idea by which I had been awed was that the youthful beings before me, with their dark nun-like robes and softly braided hair, were a kind of half-angels. The light titter, the giddy whisper had already in some measure relieved my mind of that fond and oppressive fancy.

The three I allude to were just in front, within half a yard of my estrade and were among the most womanly-looking present. Their names I knew afterwards and may as well mention now; they were Eulalie, Hortense, Caroline. Eulalie was tall and very finely shaped, she was fair and her features were those of a Low-Country Madonna; many a "figure de vierge" have I seen in Dutch pictures, exactly resembling hers; there were no angles in her shape or in her face, all was curve and roundness—neither thought, sentiment nor passion disturbed by line or flush the equality of her pale, clear skin; her noble bust heaved with her regular breathing, her eyes moved a little—by these evidences of life alone, could I have distinguished her from some large handsome figure, moulded in wax. Hortense was of middle size and stout, her form was ungraceful, her face striking, more alive and brilliant than Eulalie's, her hair was dark brown, her complexion richly coloured; there were frolic and mischief in her eye; consistency and good sense she might possess—but none of her features betokened those qualities.

Caroline was little, though evidently full-grown; raven-black hair, very dark eyes, absolutely regular features, with a colourless olive complexion, clear as to the face and sallow about the neck, formed in her that assemblage of points whose union many persons regard as the perfection of beauty. How, with the tintless pallor of her skin and the classic straightness of her lineaments, she managed to look sensual—I don't know—I think her lips and eyes contrived the affair between them and the result left no uncertainty on the beholder's mind. She was sensual now, and in ten years' time she would be coarse—promise plain was written in her face of much future folly.

If I looked at these girls with little scruple—they looked at me with still less. Eulalie raised her unmoved eye to mine and seemed to expect, passively but securely, an impromptu tribute to her majestic charms. Hortense regarded me boldly and giggled at the same time, while she said with an air of impudent freedom:

"Dictez-nous quelquechose de facile pour commencer, Monsieur."

Caroline shook her loose ringlets of abundant but somewhat coarse hair over her rolling black eyes, parting her lips, as full as those of a hot-blooded Maroon, she shewed her well-set teeth sparkling between them and treated me at the same time to a smile "de sa façon". Beautiful as Pauline Borghese, she looked at the moment scarcely purer than Lucrèce de Borgia. Caroline was of noble family—I heard her lady-mother's character afterwards, and then I ceased to wonder at the precocious accomplishments of the daughter.

These three, I at once saw, deemed themselves the queens of the school and conceived that by their splendour they threw all the rest into the shade. In less than five minutes they had thus revealed to me their characters and in less than five minutes I had buckled on a breast-plate of steely indifference and let down a visor of impassible austerity.

"Take your pens and commence writing," said I in as dry and trite a voice as if I had been addressing only Jules Vanderkelkov and Co.

The dictée now commenced—my three belles interrupted me perpetually with little, silly questions and uncalled-for remarks, to some of which I made no answer and to others replied very quietly and briefly.

"Comment dit-on point et virgule en Anglais, Monsieur?"

"Semi-colon, Mademoiselle."

"Simi-collong? Ah comme c'est drôle!" (giggle)

"J'ai une si mauvaise plume—impossible d'écrire!"

"Mais Monsieur—je ne sais pas suivre—vous allez si vite."

"Je n'ai rien compris, moi!"

Here a general murmur arose and the teacher, opening her lips for the first time—ejaculated:

"Silence, Mesdemoiselles!"

No silence followed—on the contrary—the three ladies in front began to talk more loudly.

"C'est si difficile—l'Anglais!"

"Je déteste la dictée."

"Quel ennui d'écrire quelquechose que l'on ne comprend pas!" Some of those behind laughed; a degree of confusion began to pervade the class; it was necessary to take prompt measures.

"Donnez-moi votre cahier," said I to Eulalie in an abrupt tone and bending over, I took it before she had time to give it.

"Et vous Mademoiselle—donnez-moi le vôtre," continued I, more mildly, addressing a little pale, plain-looking girl who sat in the first row of the other division and whom I had remarked as being at once the ugliest and the most attentive in the room; she rose up, walked over to me and delivered her book with a grave, modest curtsey—I glanced over the two dictations; Eulalie's was slurred, blotted and full of silly mistakes; Sylvie's (such was the name of the ugly little girl) was cleanly written, it contained no error against sense and but few faults of orthography. I coolly read aloud both exercises, marking the faults—then I looked at Eulalie:

"C'est honteux," said I and I deliberately tore her dictation in four parts and presented her with the fragments. I returned Sylvie her book with a smile, saying,

"C'est bien—je suis content de vous."

Sylvie looked calmly pleased; Eulalie swelled like an incensed Turkey, but the mutiny was quelled: the conceited coquetry and futile flirtation of the first bench were exchanged for a taciturn sullenness, much more convenient to me, and the rest of my lesson passed without interruption.

A bell clanging out in the yard announced the moment for the cessation of school labours—I heard our own bell at the same time and that of a certain public college immediately after. Order dissolved instantly, up started every pupil, I hastened to seize my hat, bow to the maîtresse and quit the room before the tide of externats should pour from the inner class, where I knew near a hundred were prisoned and whose rising tumult I already heard.

I had scarcely crossed the hall and gained the corridor when Mdlle. Reuter came again upon me:

"Step in here a moment," said she and she held open the door of the side-room from whence she had issued on my arrival; it was a salle à manger as appeared from the beaufet and the armoire vitrée, filled with glass and china, which formed part of its furniture. Ere she had closed the door on me and herself—the corridor was already filled with day-pupils, tearing down their cloaks, bonnets and cabas from the wooden pegs on which they were suspended; the shrill voice of a maîtresse was heard at intervals vainly endeavouring to enforce some sort of order; vainly, I say, discipline there was none in these rough ranks and yet this was considered one of the best conducted schools in Brussels.

"Well—you have given your first lesson," began Mdlle. Reuter in the most calm, equable voice, as though quite unconscious of the chaos from which we were separated only by a single wall.

"Were you satisfied with your pupils, or did any circumstance in their conduct give you cause for complaint? Conceal nothing from me, repose in me entire confidence."

Happily I felt in myself, complete power to manage my pupils without aid; the enchantment, the golden haze which had dazzled my perspicacity at first, had been a good deal dissipated—I cannot say I was chagrined or downcast by the contrast which the reality of a Pensionnat de demoiselles presented to my vague ideal of the same community; I was only enlightened and amused; consequently I felt in no disposition to complain to Mdlle. Reuter and I received her considerate invitation to confidence with a smile.

"A thousand thanks Mademoiselle—all has gone very smoothly."

She looked more than doubtful:

"Et les trois demoiselles du premier banc?" said she.

"Ah! tout va au mieux!" was my answer, and Mdlle. Reuter ceased to question me, but her eye—not large, not brilliant, not melting or kindling, but astute, penetrating, practical, shewed she was even with me; it let out a momentary gleam which said plainly "Be as close as you like—I am not dependent on your candour—what you would conceal—I already know."

By a transition so quiet as to be scarcely perceptible, the Directress's manner changed; the anxious, business-air passed from her face, and she began chatting about the weather and the town and asking in neighbourly wise after M. and Mde. Pelet. I answered all her little questions; she prolonged her talk, I went on following its many little windings; she sat so long, said so much, varied so often the topics of discourse that it was not difficult to perceive she had a particular aim in thus detaining me. Her mere words could have afforded no clue to this aim, but her countenance aided; while her lips uttered only affable common-places, her eyes reverted continually to my face. Her glances were not given in full but out of the corners, so quietly, so stealthily, yet I think I lost not one. I watched her as keenly as she watched me; I perceived soon that she was feeling after my real character, she was searching for salient points and weak points and eccentric points; she was applying now this test, now that, hoping in the end to find some chink, some niche where she could put in her little firm foot and stand up on my neck—Mistress of my nature. Do not mistake me, reader, it was no amorous influence she wished to gain—at that time it was only the power of the politician to which she aspired; I was now installed as a professor in her establishment, and she wanted to know where her mind was superior to mine—by what feeling or opinion she could lead me.

I enjoyed the game much and did not hasten its conclusion; sometimes I gave her hopes, beginning a sentence rather weakly, when her shrewd eye would light up—she thought she had me—having led her a little way, I delighted to turn round and finish with sound, hard sense—whereat her countenance would fall. At last a servant entered to announce dinner, the conflict being thus necessarily terminated, we parted without having gained any advantage on either side: Mademoiselle Reuter had not even given me an opportunity of attacking her with feeling and I had managed to baffle her little schemes of craft. It was a regular drawn battle. I again held out my hand when I left the room, she gave me hers; it was a small and white hand but how cool! I met her eye too in full—obliging her to give me a straight-forward look; this last test went against me, it left her as it found her, moderate, temperate, tranquil; me, it disappointed.

"I am growing wiser," thought I as I walked back to M. Pelet's. "Look at this little real woman! is she like the women of novelists and romancers? To read of female character as depicted in Poetry and Fiction, one would think it was made up of sentiment, either for good or bad—here is a specimen, and a most sensible and respectable specimen too, whose staple ingredient is abstract reason. No Talleyrand was ever more passionless than Zoraïde Reuter!"—So I thought then—I found afterwards that blunt susceptibilities are very consistent with strong propensities.

CHAPTER XI

I HAD indeed had a very long talk with the crafty little politician and on regaining my quarters I found that dinner was half over. To be late at meals was against a standing rule of the establishment and had it been one of the Flemish Ushers who thus entered after the removal of the soup and the commencement of the first course—M. Pelet would probably have greeted him with a public rebuke and would certainly have mulcted him both of soup and fish; as it was, that polite though partial gentleman only shook his head and as I took my place, unrolled my napkin and said my heretical grace to myself, he civilly despatched a servant to the kitchen to bring me a plate of "purée aux carottes" (for this was a maigre-day) and before sending away the first course, reserved for me a portion of the stock-fish of which it consisted. Dinner being over, the boys rushed out for their evening play; Kint and Vandam (the two ushers) of course followed them. Poor fellows! if they had not looked so very heavy, so very soulless, so very indifferent to all things in heaven above or in the earth beneath, I could have pitied them greatly for the obligation they were under to trail after those rough lads everywhere and at all times; even as it was I felt disposed to scout myself as a privileged prig when I turned to ascend to my chamber, sure to find there, if not enjoyment, at least liberty; but this evening (as had often happened before) I was to be still further distinguished.

"Eh bien mauvais sujet!" said the voice of M. Pelet behind me, as I set my foot on the first step of the stair. "Où allez-vous? Venez à la salle à manger—que je vous gronde un peu."

"I beg pardon, Monsieur," said I as I followed him to his private sitting-room, "for having returned so late—it was not my fault."

"That is just what I want to know," rejoined M. Pelet, as he ushered me into the comfortable parlour with a good wood-fire—for the stove had now been removed for the season. Having rung the bell he ordered "Coffee for two" and presently he and I were seated, almost in English comfort, one on each side of the hearth, a little round table between us with a coffee-pot, a sugar basin and two large white china cups. While M. Pelet employed himself in choosing a cigar from a box, my thoughts reverted to the two outcast ushers whose voices I could hear even now crying hoarsely for order in the play-ground.

"C'est une grande responsabilité, que la surveillance," observed I.

"Plaît-il?" fit M. Pelet.

I remarked that I thought Messieurs Vandam and Kint must sometimes be a little fatigued with their labours.

"Des bêtes de somme—des bêtes de somme," murmured scornfully the Director. Meantime I offered him his cup of coffee.

"Servez-vous mon garçon," said he blandly when I had put a couple of huge lumps of continental sugar into his cup. "And now tell me why you stayed so long at Mdlle. Reuter's—I know that lessons conclude, in her establishment as in mine, at four o'clock and when you returned, it was past five."

"Mademoiselle wished to speak with me, Monsieur."

"Indeed! on what subject? if one may ask."

"Mademoiselle talked about nothing, Monsieur."

"A fertile topic! And did she discourse thereon in the school-room, before the pupils?"

"No—like you, Monsieur—she asked me to walk into her parlour."

"And Mde. Reuter—the old duenna—my Mother's gossip was there of course?"

"No, Monsieur—I had the honour of being quite alone with Mademoiselle."

"C'est joli—cela—" observed M. Pelet and he smiled and looked into the fire.

"Honi soit qui mal y pense," murmured I significantly.

"Je connais un peu ma petite voisine—voyez-vous."

"In that case Monsieur will be able to aid me in finding out what was Mademoiselle's reason for making me sit before her sofa, one mortal hour, listening to the most copious and fluent dissertation on the merest frivolities."

"She was sounding your character."

"I thought so, Monsieur."

"Did she find out your weak point?"

"What is my weak point?"

"Why the sentimental. Any woman, sinking her shaft deep enough, will at last reach a fathomless spring of sensibility in thy breast, Crimsworth."

I felt the blood stir about my heart and rise warm to my cheek.

"Some women might, Monsieur."

"Is Mademoiselle Reuter of the number? Come, speak frankly, mon fils; elle est encore jeune, plus âgée que toi peut-être, mais juste assez pour unir la tendresse d'une petite maman à l'amour d'une épouse dévouée; n'est-ce pas que cela t'irait supérieurement?"

"No, Monsieur—I should like my wife to be my wife, and not half my mother."

"She is then a little too old for you?"

"No, Monsieur—not a day too old if she suited me in other things."

"In what does she not suit you, William? She is personally agreeable is she not?"

"Very—her hair and complexion are just what I admire, and her turn of form, though quite Belgian, is full of grace."

"Bravo! and her face? her features? How do you like them?"

"A little harsh—especially her mouth."

"Ah, yes! her mouth—" said M. Pelet and he chuckled inwardly. "There is character about her mouth—firmness—but she has a very pleasant smile—don't you think so?"

"Rather crafty."

"True—but that expression of craft is owing to her eye-brows—have you remarked her eyebrows?"

I answered that I had not.

"You have not seen her looking down then?" said he.

"No."

"It is a treat notwithstanding. Observe her when she has some knitting or some other woman's work in hand and sits the image of peace, calmly intent on her needles and her silk, some discussion meantime going on around her, in the course of which peculiarities of character are being developed or important interests canvassed; she takes no part in it, her humble, feminine mind is wholly with her knitting; none of her features move; she neither presumes to smile approval nor frown disapprobation; her little hands assiduously ply their unpretending task, if she can only get this purse finished or this bonnet grec completed—it is enough for her. If gentlemen approach her chair, a deeper quiescence, a meeker modesty settles on her features and clothes her general mien; observe then her eye-brows, et dites-moi s'il n'y a pas du chat dans l'un et du renard dans l'autre."

"I will take careful notice the first opportunity," said I.

"And then," continued M. Pelet, "the eye-lid will flicker, the light-coloured lashes be lifted a second, and a blue eye, glancing out from under the screen, will take its brief, sly, searching survey and retreat again."

I smiled and so did Pelet and after a few minutes' silence I asked, "Will she ever marry—do you think?"

"Marry! Will birds pair? Of course it is both her intention and resolution to marry when she finds a suitable match and no one is better aware than herself of the sort of impression she is capable of producing; no one likes better to captivate in a quiet way. I am mistaken if she will not yet leave the print of her stealing steps on thy heart, Crimsworth."

"Of her steps? Confound it—no! My heart is not a plank to be walked on."

"But the soft touch of a patte de velours will do it no harm?"

"She offers me no patte de velours; she is all form and reserve with me."

"That to begin with; let Respect be the foundation, Affection the first floor, Love the superstructure; Mdlle. Reuter is a skilful architect."

"And Interest, Monsieur Pelet—Interest—Will not Mademoiselle consider that point?"

"Yes—yes—no doubt, it will be the cement between every stone. And now we have discussed the Directress—what of the pupils? N'y-a-t-il pas de belles études parmi ces jeunes têtes?"

"Studies of character? Yes—curious ones, at least, I imagine, but one cannot divine much from a first interview."

"Ah—you affect discretion—but tell me now—were you not a little abashed before those blooming young creatures?"

"At first—yes—but I rallied and got through with all due sang-froid."

"I don't believe you."

"It is true notwithstanding; at first I thought them angels but they did not leave me long under that delusion; three of the eldest and handsomest undertook the task of setting me right and they managed so cleverly that in five minutes, I knew *them*, at least, for what they were; three arrant coquettes."

"Je les connais!" exclaimed M. Pelet. "Elles sont toujours au premier rang à l'église et à la promenade; une blonde superbe, une jolie espiègle, une belle brune."

"Exactly."

"Lovely creatures all of them—heads for artists—what a group they would make, taken together! Eulalie (I know their names) with her smooth, braided hair and calm, ivory brow, Hortense with her rich chesnut locks so luxuriantly knotted, plaited, twisted, as if she did not know how to dispose of all their abundance, with her vermillion lips, damask cheek and roguish, laughing eye—and Caroline de Blémont! Ah there is beauty! beauty in perfection—what a cloud of sable curls about the face of a houri! What fascinating lips! What glorious black eyes! Your Byron would have worshipped her and you—you cold frigid Islander! you played the austere, the insensible in the presence of an Aphrodite so exquisite?"

I might have laughed at the Director's enthusiasm had I believed it real—but there was something in his tone which indicated got-up raptures—I felt he was only affecting fervor in order to put me off my guard, to induce me to come out in return—so I scarcely even smiled—he went on:

"Confess, William, do not the mere good-looks of Zoraïde Reuter appear dowdyish and common-place, compared with the splendid charms of some of her pupils?"

The question discomposed me, but I now felt plainly that my principal was endeavouring (for reasons best known to himself—at that time I could not fathom them) to excite ideas and wishes in my mind alien to what was right and honourable. The iniquity of the instigation proved its antidote and when he further added:

"Each of those three beautiful girls will have a handsome fortune, and with a little address, a gentlemanlike, intelligent young fellow like you might make himself master of the hand, heart and purse of any one of the trio," I replied by a look and an interrogative "Monsieur?" which startled him.

He laughed a forced laugh, affirmed that he had only been joking and demanded whether I could possibly have thought him in earnest. Just then the bell rang—the play hour was over—it was an evening on which M. Pelet was accustomed to read passages from the drama and the belles lettres to his pupils—he did not wait for my answer but rising left the room, humming as he went some gay strain of Béranger's.

CHAPTER XII

DAILY, as I continued my attendance at the seminary of Mdlle. Reuter, did I find fresh occasions to compare the ideal with the real. What had I known of female character previously to my arrival at Brussels? Precious little. And what was my notion of it? Something vague, slight, gauzy, glittering; now when I came in contact with it I found it to be a palpable substance enough; very hard too sometimes and often heavy—there was metal in it, both lead and iron.

Let the idealists—the dreamers about earthly angels and human flowers, just look here, while I open my portfolio and shew them a sketch or two, pencilled after nature. I took these sketches in the second class school-room of Mdlle. Reuter's establishment where about a hundred specimens of the genus "jeune fille," collected together, offered a fertile variety of subject. A miscellaneous assortment they were, differing both in caste and country; as I sat on my estrade and glanced over the long range of desks, I had under my eye French, English, Belgians, Austrians and Prussians. The majority belonged to the class bourgeois, but there were many Comtesses, there were the daughters of two generals and of several colonels, captains and government employés; these ladies sat side by side with young females destined to be demoiselles de magasins and with some Flamandes, genuine aborigines of the Country. In dress all were nearly similar and in manners there was small difference; exceptions there were to the general rule but the majority gave the tone to the establishment, and that tone was rough, boisterous, marked by a point-blank disregard of all forbearance towards each other or their teachers; an eager pursuit by each individual of her own interest and convenience, and a coarse indifference to the interest and convenience of every one else. Most of them could lie with audacity when it appeared advantageous to do so. All understood the art of speaking fair when a point was to be gained and could with consummate skill and at a moment's notice turn the cold shoulder the instant civility ceased to be profitable. Very little open quarrelling ever took place amongst them, but back-biting and tale-bearing were universal; close friendships were forbidden by the rules of the school, and no one girl seemed to cultivate more regard for another than was just necessary to secure a companion when solitude would have been irksome. They were each and all supposed to have been reared in utter unconsciousness of vice—the precautions used to keep them ignorant, if not innocent, were innumerable; how was it then that scarcely one of those girls having attained the age of fourteen could look a man in the face with modesty and propriety? An air of bold, impudent flirtation or a loose, silly leer was sure to answer the most ordinary glance from a masculine eye. I know nothing of the arcana of the Roman-Catholic religion and I am not a bigot in matters of theology, but I suspect the root of this precocious impurity, so obvious, so general in popish Countries, is to be found in the discipline, if not the doctrines of the Church of Rome. I record what I have seen—these girls belonged to, what are called, the respectable ranks of society, they had all been carefully brought up, yet was the mass of them mentally depraved. So much for a general view, now for one or two selected specimens.

The first picture is a full-length of Aurelia Koslow, a German fräulein, or rather a half-breed between German and Russian. She is eighteen years of age and has been sent to Brussels to finish her education; she is of middle size, stiffly made, body long, legs short, bust much developed but not compactly moulded, waist disproportionately compressed by an inhumanly braced corset, dress carefully arranged, large feet tortured into small bottines, head small, hair smoothed, braided, oiled and gummed to perfection, very low forehead, very diminutive and vindictive grey eyes, somewhat Tartar features, rather flat nose, rather high cheek-bones yet the ensemble not positively ugly, tolerably good complexion. So much for person. As to mind deplorably ignorant and ill-informed, incapable of writing or speaking correctly even German, her native tongue, a dunce in French and her attempts at learning English a mere farce, yet she has been at school twelve years, but as she invariably gets her exercises, of every description, done by a fellow-pupil, and reads her lessons off a book concealed in her lap, it is not wonderful that her progress has been so snail-like. I do not know what Aurelia's daily habits of life are—because I have not the opportunity of observing her at all times, but from what I see of the state of her desk, books and papers, I should say she is slovenly and even dirty; her outward dress, as I have said, is well attended to, but in passing behind her bench, I have remarked that her neck is grey for want of washing, and her hair, so glossy with gum and grease, is not such as one feels tempted to pass the hand over, much less to run the fingers through. Aurelia's conduct in class, at least when I am present, is something extraordinary, considered as an index of girlish innocence. The moment I enter the room, she nudges her next neighbour and indulges in a half-suppressed laugh; as I take my seat on the estrade, she fixes her eye on me, she seems resolved to attract and, if possible, monopolize my notice; to this end, she launches at me all sorts of looks, languishing, provoking, leering, laughing; as I am found quite proof against this sort of artillery—for we scorn what, unasked, is lavishly offered—she has recourse to the expedient of making noises; sometimes she sighs, sometimes groans, sometimes utters inarticulate sounds for which language has no name; if, in walking up the school-room, I pass near her, she puts out her foot that it may touch mine, if I do not happen to observe the manœuvre and my boot comes in contact with her brodequin, she affects to fall into convulsions of suppressed laughter; if I notice the snare and avoid it, she expresses her mortification in sullen muttering, where I hear myself abused in bad French, pronounced with an intolerable, low-German accent.

Not far from Mdlle. Koslow sits another young lady, by name Adèle Dronsart; this is a Belgian, rather low of stature, in form heavy, with broad waist, short neck and limbs, good red and white complexion, features well-chiselled and regular, well-cut eyes of a clear brown colour, light brown hair, good teeth, age not much above fifteen but as full-grown as a stout young Englishwoman of twenty. This portrait gives the idea of a somewhat dumpy but good-looking damsel, does it not? Well—when I looked along the row of young heads—my eye generally stopped at this of Adèle's; her gaze was ever waiting for mine and it frequently succeeded in arresting it. She was an unnatural-looking being, so young, fresh, blooming, yet so Gorgon-like. Suspicion, sullen ill-temper were on her forehead, vicious propensities in her eye, envy and panther-like deceit about her mouth. In general she sat very still, her massive shape looked as if it could not bend much, nor did her large head, so broad at the base, so narrow towards the top, seem made to turn readily on her short neck. She had but two varieties of expression; the prevalent one a forbidding, dissatisfied scowl, varied sometimes by a most pernicious and perfidious smile. She was shunned by her fellow-pupils, for, bad as many of them were, few were as bad as she.

Aurelia and Adèle were in the first division of the second Class, the second division was headed by a pensionnaire named Juanna Trista; this girl was of mixed Belgian and Spanish origin, her Flemish Mother was dead, her Catalonian father was a merchant, residing in the —— Isles where Juanna had been born and whence she was sent to Europe to be educated. I wonder that any one, looking at that girl's head and countenance, would have received her under their roof. She had precisely the same shape of skull as Pope Alexander the sixth; her organs of benevolence, veneration, conscientiousness, adhesiveness were singularly small, those of self-esteem, firmness, destructiveness, combativeness preposterously large; her head sloped up in the penthouse shape, was contracted about the forehead and prominent behind; she had rather good, though large and marked features; her temperament was fibrous and bilious, her complexion pale and dark, hair and eyes black, form angular and rigid but proportionate, age fifteen. Juanna was not very thin but she had a gaunt visage and her "regard" was fierce and hungry; narrow as was her brow it presented space enough for the legible graving of two words, Mutiny and Hate; in some one of her other lineaments—I think the eye—Cowardice had also its distinct cipher. Mdlle. Trista thought fit to trouble my first lessons with a coarse, worky-day sort of turbulence; she made noises with her mouth like a horse, she ejected her saliva, she uttered brutal expressions; behind and below her were seated a band of very vulgar, inferior-looking Flamandes, including two or three examples of that deformity of person and imbecility of intellect whose frequency in the Low Countries would seem to furnish proof that the climate is such as to induce degeneracy of the human mind and body; these, I soon found, were completely under her influence and with their aid she got up and sustained a swinish tumult which I was constrained at last to quell by ordering her and two of her tools to rise from their seats and, having kept them standing five minutes, turning them bodily out of the school-room, the accomplices into a large place adjoining called the grande salle—the principal into a cabinet of which I closed the door and pocketed the key. This judgment I executed in the presence of Mdlle. Reuter who looked much aghast at beholding so decided a proceeding, the most severe that had ever been ventured on in her establishment. Her look of affright I answered with one of composure and finally with a smile which perhaps flattered, and certainly soothed her. Juanna Trista remained in Europe long enough to repay by malevolence and ingratitude all who had ever done her a good turn, and she then went to join her father in the —— Isles, exulting in the thought that she should there have slaves whom, as she said, she could kick and strike at will.

These three pictures are from the life—I possess others as marked and as little agreeable but I will spare my readers the exhibition of them.

Doubtless it will be thought that I ought now, by way of contrast, to shew something charming; some gentle virgin head, circled with a halo, some sweet personification of Innocence, clasping the dove of peace to her bosom. No—I saw nothing of the sort and therefore cannot portray it. The pupil in the school possessing the happiest disposition was a young girl from the country, Louise Path; she was sufficiently benevolent and obliging but not well-taught nor well mannered, moreover the plague-spot of dissimulation was in her also; Honour and Principle were unknown to her, she had scarcely heard their names. The least exceptionable pupil was the poor little

Sylvie I have mentioned once before; Sylvie was gentle in manners, intelligent in mind, she was even sincere, as far as her religion would permit her to be so, but her physical organisation was defective; weak health stunted her growth and chilled her spirits, and then, destined as she was for the cloister, her whole soul was warped to a conventual bias, and, in the tame, trained subjection of her manner, one read that she had already prepared herself for her future course of life by giving up her independence of thought and action into the hands of some despotic confessor. She permitted herself no original opinion, no preference of companion or employment, in everything she was guided by another. With a pale, passive automaton-air she went about all day long doing what she was bid, never what she liked or what, from innate conviction, she thought it right to do; the poor little future religieuse had been early taught to make the dictates of her own reason and conscience quite subordinate to the will of her spiritual Director. She was the model pupil of Mdlle. Reuter's establishment; pale, blighted image where life lingered feebly but whence the soul had been conjured by Romish wizard-craft!

A few English pupils there were in this school and these might be divided into two classes. First the continental English—the daughters chiefly of broken adventurers whom debt or dishonour had driven from their own country; these poor girls had never known the advantages of settled homes, decorous example, or honest protestant education; resident a few months now in one Catholic school—now in another, as their parents wandered from land to land, from France to Germany, from Germany to Belgium, they had picked up some scanty instruction, many bad habits, losing every notion even of the first elements of religion and morals, and acquiring an imbecile indifference to every sentiment that can elevate humanity—they were distinguishable by an habitual look of sullen dejection—the result of crushed self-respect and constant brow-beating from their popish fellow-pupils who hated them as English and scorned them as heretics.

The second class were British English, of these I did not encounter half a dozen during the whole time of my attendance at the seminary; their characteristics were, clean but careless dress, ill-arranged hair (compared with the tight and trim foreigners) erect carriage, flexible figures, white and taper hands, features more irregular but also more intellectual than those of the Belgians, grave and modest countenances, a general air of native propriety and decency; by this last circumstance alone I could at a glance distinguish the daughter of Albion and nursling of Protestantism from the foster-child of Rome, the protégée of Jesuitry: proud too was the aspect of these British girls—at once envied and ridiculed by their continental associates, they warded off insult with austere civility and met hate with mute disdain; they eschewed company-keeping and in the midst of numbers seemed to dwell isolated.

The teachers presiding over this mixed multitude were three in number, all French, their names Mesdemoiselles Zéphyrine, Pélagie and Suzette; the two last were common-place personages enough; their look was ordinary, their manner was ordinary, their temper was ordinary, their thoughts, feelings and views were all ordinary—were I to write a chapter on the subject I could not elucidate it further. Zéphyrine was somewhat more distinguished in appearance and deportment than Pélagie and Suzette, but in character, a genuine Parisian coquette, perfidious, mercenary and dry-hearted; a fourth maîtresse I sometimes saw who seemed to come daily to teach needle-work or netting or lace-mending or some such flimsy art, but of her I never had more than a passing glimpse, as she sat in the carré with her frames and some dozen of the elder pupils about her, consequently I had no opportunity of studying her character or even of observing her person much—the latter, I remarked had a very girlish air for a maîtresse, otherwise it was not striking, of character, I should think she possessed but little, as her pupils seemed constantly "en révolte" against her authority. She did not reside in the house, her name I think was Mdlle. Henri.

Amidst this assemblage of all that was insignificant and defective, much that was vicious and repulsive, (by that last epithet many would have described the two or three stiff, silent, decently behaved, ill-dressed British girls) the sensible, sagacious affable

Directress shone like a steady star over a marsh-full of Jack o'lanthorns; profoundly aware of her superiority she derived an inward bliss from that consciousness which sustained her under all the care and responsibility inseparable from her position, it kept her temper calm, her brow smooth, her manner tranquil. She liked, as who would not? on entering the school-room, to feel that her sole presence sufficed to diffuse that order and quiet which all the remonstrances and even commands of her underlings frequently failed to enforce; she liked to stand in comparison or rather contrast with those who surrounded her, and to know that in personal as well as mental advantages, she bore away the undisputed palm of preference—(the three teachers were all plain). Her pupils she managed with such indulgence and address, taking always on herself the office of Recompenser and Eulogist—and abandoning to her subalterns every invidious task of blame and punishment, that they all regarded her with deference if not with affection; her teachers did not love her, but they submitted because they were her inferiors in everything; the various masters who attended her school were each and all in some way or other under her influence; over one she had acquired power by her skilful management of his bad temper, over another by little attentions to his petty caprices, a third she had subdued by flattery, a fourth—a timid man, she kept in awe by a sort of austere decision of mien. Me, she still watched, still tried by the most ingenious tests, she roved round me, baffled yet persevering; I believe she thought I was like a smooth and bare precipice which offered neither jutting stone nor tree-root, nor tuft of grass to aid the climber. Now she flattered with exquisite tact, now she moralized, now she tried how far I was accessible to mercenary motives, then she disported on the brink of affectation—knowing that some men are won by weakness, anon she talked excellent sense, aware that others have the folly to admire judgment. I found it at once pleasant and easy to evade all these efforts; it was sweet, when she thought me nearly won—to turn round and to smile in her very eyes, half scornfully, and then to witness her scarcely-veiled though mute mortification. Still she persevered and at last—I am bound to confess it, her finger, essaying, proving every atom of the casket—touched its secret spring and for a moment—the lid sprung open, she laid her hand on the jewel within; whether she stole and broke it, or whether the lid shut again with a snap on her fingers—read on—and you shall know.

It happened that I came one day to give a lesson when I was indisposed, I had a bad cold and a cough; two hours' incessant talking left me very hoarse and tired; as I quitted the school-room and was passing along the corridor, I met Mdlle. Reuter, she remarked with an anxious air that I looked very pale and tired: "Yes," I said—"I was fatigued;" and then with increased interest she rejoined, "You shall not go away till you have had some refreshment." She persuaded me to step into the parlour and was very kind and gentle while I stayed. The next day she was kinder still, she came herself into the class to see that the windows were closed and that there was no draught, she exhorted me with friendly earnestness not to over-exert myself, when I went away she gave me her hand unasked and I could not but mark by a respectful and gentle pressure that I was sensible of the favour and grateful for it; my modest demonstration kindled a little merry smile on her countenance; I thought her almost charming. During the remainder of the evening, my mind was full of impatience for the afternoon of the next day to arrive that I might see her again.

I was not disappointed, for she sat in the class during the whole of my subsequent lesson, and often looked at me almost with affection. At four o'clock she accompanied me out of the school-room, asking with solicitude after my health, then scolding me sweetly because I spoke too loud and gave myself too much trouble; I stopped at the glass-door which led into the garden, to hear her lecture to the end; the door was open, it was a very fine day, and while I listened to the soothing reprimand, I looked at the sunshine and flowers and felt very happy. The day-scholars began to pour from the school-rooms into the passage. "Will you go into the garden a minute or two," asked she, "till they are gone?" I descended the steps without answering, but I looked back as much as to say:

"You will come with me?"

In another minute I and the Directress were walking side by side down the alley bordered with fruit-trees whose white blossoms were then in full blow as well as their tender green leaves. The sky was blue, the air still, the May afternoon was full of brightness and fragrance; released from the stifling Class, surrounded with flowers and foliage, with a pleasing, smiling, affable woman at my side—how did I feel? Why—very enviably. It seemed as if the romantic visions my imagination had suggested of this garden, while it was yet hidden from me by the jealous boards, were more than realized, and when a turn in the alley shut out the view of the house and some tall shrubs excluded M. Pelet's mansion and screened us momentarily from the other houses, rising amphitheatre-like round this green spot, I gave my arm to Mdlle. Reuter and led her to a garden-chair, nestled under some lilacs near. She sat down, I took my place at her side; she went on talking to me with that ease which communicates ease and, as I listened, a revelation dawned in my mind that I was on the brink of falling in love. The dinner-bell rang, both at her house and M. Pelet's; we were obliged to part; I detained her a moment as she was moving away:

"I want something," said I.

"What?" asked Zoraïde naïvely.

"Only a flower."

"Gather it then, or two or twenty—if you like."

"No—one will do—but you must gather it and give it to me."

"What a caprice!" she exclaimed, but she raised herself on her tip-toes and plucking a beautiful branch of lilac, offered it to me with grace. I took it and went away, satisfied for the present and hopeful for the future.

Certainly that May-day was a lovely one and it closed in a moonlight night of summer warmth and serenity. I remember this well; for having sat up late that evening, correcting devoirs, and feeling weary and a little oppressed with the closeness of my small room—I opened the often-mentioned, boarded window, whose boards however I had persuaded old Mde. Pelet to have removed since I had filled the post of professor in the Pensionnat de demoiselles, as from that time it was no longer "inconvenant" for me to overlook my own pupils at their sports. I sat down in the window-seat, rested my arm on the sill and leaned out; above me was the clear-obscure of a cloudless night-sky; splendid moonlight subdued the tremulous sparkle of the stars; below lay the garden, varied with silvery lustre and deep shade and all fresh with dew; a grateful perfume exhaled from the closed blossoms of the fruit-trees; not a leaf stirred, the night was breezeless. My window looked directly down upon a certain walk of Mdlle. Reuter's garden, called "l'allée défendue", so named because the pupils were forbidden to enter it on account of its proximity to the boys' school; it was here that the lilacs and laburnams grew especially thick, this was the most sheltered nook in the enclosure, its shrubs screened the garden-chair where that afternoon I had sat with the young Directress. I need not say that my thoughts were chiefly with her, as I leaned from the lattice and let my eye roam, now over the walks and borders of the garden, now along the many-windowed front of the house which rose white beyond the masses of foliage. I wondered in what part of the building was situated her apartment, and a single light, shining through the persiennes of one croisée, seemed to direct me to it.

"She watches late," thought I, "for it must be now near midnight. She is a fascinating little woman," I continued in voiceless soliloquy; "her image forms a pleasant picture in memory; I know she is not what the world calls pretty, no matter, there is harmony in her aspect and I like it; her brown hair, her blue eye, the freshness of her cheek, the whiteness of her neck, all suit my taste. Then I respect her talent; the idea of marrying a doll or a fool was always abhorrent to me; I know that a pretty doll, a fair fool might do well enough for the honey-moon—but when passion cooled, how dreadful to find a lump of wax and wood laid in my bosom, a half idiot clasped in my arms, and to remember that I had made of this my equal—nay my idol, to know that I must pass the rest of my dreary life with a creature incapable of understanding what I said, of appreciating what I thought or of sympathising with what I felt! Now Zoraïde Reuter—" thought I—"has tact, 'caractère', judgment, discretion; has she heart? She must have—what kindness and affection were in her manner to me to-day! What a good, simple little smile played about her lips when she gave me the branch of lilacs! I have thought her crafty, dissembling, interested sometimes, it is true, but may not much that looks like cunning and dissimulation in her conduct be only the efforts made by a bland temper to traverse quietly perplexing difficulties? And as to interest —she wishes to make her way in the world no doubt—and who can blame her? Even if she be truly deficient in sound principle—is it not rather her misfortune than her fault? She has been brought up a Catholic—had she been born an Englishwoman and reared a Protestant—might she not have added straight integrity to all her other excellencies? Supposing she were to marry an English and protestant husband, would she not, rational, sensible as she is, quickly acknowledge the superiority of right over expediency, honesty over policy? It would be worth a man's while to try the experiment; to-morrow I will renew my observations. She knows that I watch her; how calm she is under scrutiny! it seems rather to gratify than annoy her." Here a strain of music stole in upon my monologue and suspended it; it was a bugle, very skilfully played—in the neighbourhood of the Park—I thought—or on the Place Royale. So sweet were the tones, so subduing their effect at that hour, in the midst of silence and under the quiet reign of moonlight, I ceased to think, that I might listen more intently. The strain retreated, its sound waxed fainter and was soon gone; my ear prepared to repose on the absolute hush of midnight once more—No—What murmur was that which, low and yet near and approaching nearer, frustrated the expectation of total silence? It was some one conversing—yes, evidently—an audible though subdued voice spoke in the garden immediately below me. Another answered; the first voice was that of a man, the second that of a woman, and a man and a woman I saw, coming slowly down the alley. Their forms were at first in shade, I could but discern a dusk outline of each, but a ray of moonlight met them at the termination of the walk, when they were under my very nose, and revealed very plainly, very unequivocally, Mdlle. Zoraïde Reuter, arm in arm, or hand in hand (I forget which) with my principal, confidant and counsellor Monsieur François Pelet. And M. Pelet was saying:

"À quand donc le jour des noces, ma bien-aimée?"

And Mdlle. Reuter answered, "Mais François, tu sais bien qu'il me serait impossible de me marier avant les vacances."

"June, July, August, a whole quarter!" exclaimed the Director. "How can I wait so long—I who am ready, even now, to expire at your feet with impatience!"

"Ah! if you die, the whole affair will be settled without any trouble about notaries and contracts; I shall only have to order a slight mourning dress, which will be much sooner prepared than the nuptial trousseau."

"Cruel Zoraïde! you laugh at the distress of one who loves you so devotedly as I do, my torment is your sport; you scruple not to stretch my soul on the rack of jealousy for, deny it as you will, I am certain you have cast encouraging glances on that school-boy, Crimsworth; he has presumed to fall in love, which he dared not have done unless you had given him room to hope."

"What do you say François? Do you say Crimsworth is in love with me?"

"Over head and ears."

"Has he told you so?"

"No—but I see it in his face—he blushes whenever your name is mentioned."

A little laugh of exulting coquetry announced Mdlle. Reuter's gratification at this piece of intelligence (which was a lie, by the bye, I had never been so far gone as that, after all). M. Pelet proceeded to ask what she intended to do with me, intimating pretty plainly and not very gallantly that it was nonsense for her to think of taking such a "blanc-bec" as a husband, since she must be at least ten years older than I; (was she then thirty-two? I should not have thought it). I heard her disclaim any intentions on the subject—the Director however still pressed her to give a definite answer.

"François," said she, "you are jealous," and still she laughed; then, as if suddenly recollecting that this coquetry was not consistent with the character for modest dignity she wished to establish, she proceeded in a demure voice:

"Truly, my dear François, I will not deny that this young Englishman may have made some attempts to ingratiate himself with me; but, so far from giving him any encouragement, I have always treated him with as much reserve as it was possible to combine with civility; affianced as I am to you, I would give no man false hopes; believe me, dear friend."

Still Pelet uttered murmurs of distrust—so I judged, at least, from her reply:

"What folly! How could I prefer an unknown foreigner to you? And then—not to flatter your vanity—Crimsworth could not bear comparison with you either physically or mentally; he is not a handsome man at all; some may call him gentleman-like and intelligent-looking, but for my part—"

The rest of the sentence was lost in the distance as the pair, rising from the chair in which they had been seated, moved away. I waited their return but soon, the opening and shutting of a door informed me that they had re-entered the house; I listened a little longer, all was perfectly still—I listened more than an hour—at last I heard M. Pelet come in and ascend to his chamber. Glancing once more towards the long front of the garden-house, I perceived that its solitary light was at length extinguished, so, for a time, was my faith in love and friendship; I went to bed—but something feverish and fiery had got into my veins which prevented me from sleeping much that night.

CHAPTER XIII

NEXT morning I rose with the dawn and having dressed myself and stood half an hour, my elbow leaning on the chest of drawers, considering what means I should adopt to restore my spirits, fagged with sleeplessness, to their ordinary tone—for I had no intention of getting up a scene with M. Pelet, reproaching him with perfidy, sending him a challenge or performing other gambadoes of the sort—I hit at last on the expedient of walking out in the cool of the morning to a neighbouring establishment of baths and treating myself to a bracing plunge. The remedy produced the desired effect—I came back at seven o'clock steadied and invigorated and was able to greet M. Pelet, when he entered to breakfast, with an unchanged and tranquil countenance; even a cordial offering of the hand and the flattering appellation of "Mon fils" pronounced in that caressing tone with which Monsieur had, of late days especially, been accustomed to address me, did not elicit any external sign of the feeling which, though subdued, still glowed at my heart. Not that I nursed vengeance—no—but the sense of insult and treachery lived in me like a kindling though as yet smothered coal. God knows I am not by nature vindictive; I would not hurt a man because I can no longer trust or like him; but neither my reason nor feelings are of the vacillating order; they are not of that sand-like sort where impressions, if soon made, are as soon effaced. Once convinced that my friend's disposition is incompatible with my own, once assured that he is indelibly stained with certain defects obnoxious to my principles and I dissolve the connection. I did so with Edward—as to Pelet—the discovery was yet new—should I act thus with him? It was the question I placed before my mind as I stirred my cup of coffee with a half-pistolet (we never had spoons) Pelet meantime being seated opposite—his pallid face looking as knowing and more haggard than usual—his blue eye turned, now sternly on his boys and ushers and now graciously on me. "Circumstances must guide me," said I, and meeting Pelet's false glance and insinuating smile, I thanked Heaven that I had last night opened my window and read by the light of a full moon the true meaning of that guileful countenance; I felt half his master, because the reality of his nature was now known to me; smile and flatter as he would, I saw his soul lurk behind his smile and heard in every one of his smooth phrases, a voice interpreting their treacherous import.

But Zoraïde Reuter? Of course her defection had cut me to the quick? That sting must have gone too deep for any Consolations of Philosophy to be available in curing its smart? Not at all. The night-fever over—I looked about for balm to that wound also, and found some nearer home than at Gilead. Reason was my physician; she began by proving that the prize I had missed was of little value—she admitted that, physically, Zoraïde might have suited me but affirmed that our souls were not in harmony and that discord must have resulted from the union of her mind with mine; she then insisted on the suppression of all repining and commanded me rather to rejoice that I had escaped a snare. Her medicament did me good—I felt its strengthening effect when I met the Directress next day; its stringent operation on the nerves suffered no trembling, no faltering—it enabled me to face her with firmness, to pass her with ease—she had held out her hand to me—that I did not choose to see—she had greeted me with a charming smile—it fell on my heart like light on stone; I passed on to the estrade, she followed me, her eye, fastened on my face demanded of every feature the meaning of my changed and careless manner. "I will give her an answer," thought I, and meeting her gaze full; arresting, fixing her glance, I shot into her eyes from my own a look where there was no respect, no love, no tenderness, no gallantry, where the strictest analysis could detect nothing but scorn, hardihood, irony; I made her bear it and feel it; her steady countenance did not change but her colour rose and she approached me as if fascinated. She stepped on to the estrade and stood close by my side; she had nothing to say, I would not relieve her embarrassment, but negligently turned over the leaves of a book.

"I hope you feel quite recovered to-day," at last she said in a low tone.

"And I, Mademoiselle, hope that you took no cold last night in consequence of your late walk in the garden."

Quick enough of comprehension, she understood me directly; her face became a little blanched—a very little, but no muscle in her rather marked features moved, and calm and self-possessed, she retired from the estrade, taking her seat quietly at a little distance and occupying herself with netting a purse. I proceeded to give my lesson; it was a "Composition": i.e. I dictated certain general questions, of which the pupils were to compose the answers from memory, access to books being forbidden. While Mesdemoiselles Eulalie, Hortense, Caroline &c. were pondering over the string of rather abstruse grammatical interrogatories I had propounded, I was at liberty to employ the vacant half hour in further observing the Directress herself. The green silk purse was progressing fast in her hands; her eyes were bent upon it; her attitude, as she sat netting within two yards of me, was still yet guarded, in her whole person were expressed at once, and with equal clearness, vigilance and repose—a rare union! Looking at her, I was forced, as I had often been before, to offer her good sense, her wondrous self-control the tribute of involuntary admiration. She had felt that I had withdrawn from her my esteem, she had seen contempt and coldness in my eye, and to her, who coveted the approbation of all around her, who thirsted after universal good opinion, such discovery must have been an acute wound; I had witnessed its effect in the momentary pallor of her cheek—cheek unused to vary—yet how quickly, by dint of self-control, had she recovered her composure! With what quiet dignity she now sat, almost at my side, sustained by her sound and vigorous sense; no trembling in her somewhat lengthened, though shrewd upper lip, no coward shame on her austere forehead:

"There is metal there," I said as I gazed. "Would that there were fire also, living ardour to make the steel glow, then I could love her."

Presently I discovered that she knew I was watching her, for she stirred not, she lifted not her crafty eyelid; she but glanced down from her netting to her small foot, peeping from the soft folds of her purple merino gown, thence her eye reverted to her hand, ivory white, with a bright garnet ring on the fore-finger and a light frill of lace round the wrist; with a scarcely perceptible movement she turned her head, causing her nut-brown curls to wave gracefully; in these slight signs I read that the wish of her heart, the design of her brain was to lure back the game she had scared. A little incident gave her the opportunity of addressing me again.

While all was silence in the class—silence but for the rustling of copy-books and the travelling of pens over their pages, a leaf of the large folding-door, opening from the hall, unclosed, admitting a pupil who, after making a hasty obeisance, ensconced herself with some appearance of trepidation—probably occasioned by her entering so late, in a vacant seat at the desk nearest the door. Being seated, she proceeded, still with an air of hurry and embarrassment to open her cabas, to take out her books and while I was waiting for her to look up in order to make out her identity—for, short-sighted as I was, I had not recognised her at her entrance, Mdlle. Reuter, leaving her chair, approached the estrade.

"Monsieur Creemsvort," she said in a whisper, for when the school-rooms were silent, the Directress always moved with velvet tread and spoke in the most subdued key, enforcing order and stillness fully as much by example as precept. "M. Creemsvort, that young person who has just entered wishes to have the advantage of taking lessons with you in English—she is not a pupil of the house—she is indeed, in one sense, a teacher, for she gives instruction in lace-mending and in little varieties of ornamental needle-work; she very properly proposes to qualify herself for a higher department of education and has asked permission to attend your lessons in order to perfect her knowledge of English, in which language she has, I believe, already made some progress; of course it is my wish to aid her in an effort so praise-worthy; you will permit her then to benefit by your instructions—n'est-ce pas Monsieur?"

And Mademoiselle Reuter's eyes were raised to mine with a look at once naïve, benign and beseeching. I replied "Of course," very laconically, almost abruptly.

"Another word," she said with softness, "Mdlle. Henri has not received a regular education; perhaps her natural talents are not of the highest order; but I can assure you of the excellence of her intentions, and even of the amiability of her disposition—Monsieur will then, I am sure, have the goodness to be considerate with her at first, and not expose her backwardness, her inevitable deficiencies before the young ladies—who—in a sense, are her pupils; will M. Creemsvort favour me by attending to this hint?" I nodded—she continued with subdued earnestness:

"Pardon me, Monsieur, if I venture to add that what I have just said is of importance to the poor girl; she already experiences great difficulty in impressing these giddy young things with a due degree of deference for her authority, and should that difficulty be increased by new discoveries of her incapacity, she might find her position in my establishment too painful to be retained; a circumstance I should much regret for her sake, as she can ill afford to lose the profits of her occupation here."

Mdlle. Reuter possessed marvellous tact, but tact the most exquisite, unsupported by sincerity, will sometimes fail of its effect; thus—on this occasion, the longer she preached about the necessity of being indulgent to the governess-pupil, the more impatient I felt as I listened, I discerned so clearly that while her professed motive was a wish to aid the dull, though well-meaning Mdlle. Henri, her real one was no other than a design to impress me with an idea of her own exalted goodness and tender considerateness; so having again hastily nodded assent to her remarks, I obviated their renewal by suddenly demanding the compositions in a sharp accent and, stepping from the estrade, I proceeded to collect them; as I passed the governess-pupil I said to her:

"You have come in too late to receive a lesson to-day; try to be more punctual next time."

I was behind her and could not read in her face the effect of my, not very civil speech; probably I should not have troubled myself to do so, had I been full in front, but I observed that she immediately began to slip her books into her cabas again, and presently after I had returned to the estrade, while I was arranging the mass of compositions, I heard the folding-door again open and close and, on looking up, I perceived her place vacant; I thought to myself "She will consider her first attempt at taking a lesson in English something of a failure," and I wondered whether she had departed in the sulks, or whether stupidity had induced her to take my words too literally or, finally, whether my irritable tone had wounded her feelings. The last notion I dismissed almost as soon as I had conceived it, for not having seen any appearance of sensitiveness in any human face since my arrival in Belgium, I had begun to regard it almost as a fabulous quality; whether her physiognomy announced it I could not tell for her speedy exit had allowed me no time to ascertain the circumstance. I had indeed on two or three previous occasions caught a passing view of her (as I believe has been mentioned before) but I had never stopped to scrutinize either her face or person, and had but the most vague idea of her general appearance. Just as I had finished rolling up the compositions, the four o'clock bell rang; with my accustomed alertness in obeying that signal, I grasped my hat and evacuated the premises.

CHAPTER XIV

If I was punctual in quitting Mdlle. Reuter's domicile, I was at least equally punctual in arriving there; I came the next day at five minutes before two, and on reaching the school-room door, before I opened it, I heard a rapid, gabbling sound—which warned me that the "prière du midi" was not yet concluded—I waited the termination thereof—it would have been impious to intrude my heretical presence during its progress. How the repeater of the prayer did cackle and splutter! I never before or since heard language enounced with such steam-engine haste. "Notre père qui êtes au ciel" went off like a shot; then followed an address to Marie, "vierge céleste, reine des anges, maison d'or, tour d'ivoire!!" and then an invocation to the saint of the day, and then down they all sat, and the solemn (?) rite was over; and I entered, flinging the door wide and striding in fast, as it was my wont to do now, for I had found that in entering with aplomb and mounting the estrade with emphasis consisted the grand secret of ensuring immediate silence. The folding-doors between the two classes, opened for the prayer, were instantly closed; a Maîtresse, work-box in hand, took her seat at her appropriate desk, the pupils sat still with their pens and books before them, my three beauties in the van, now well-humbled by a demeanour of consistent coolness, sat erect with their hands folded quietly on their knees, they had given up giggling and whispering to each other and no longer ventured to utter pert speeches in my presence; they now only talked to me occasionally with their eyes, by means of which organs they could still however say very audacious and coquettish things. Had affection, goodness, modesty, real talent ever employed those bright orbs as interpreters, I do not think I could have refrained from giving a kind and encouraging, perhaps an ardent reply now and then, but as it was I found pleasure in answering the glance of vanity with the gaze of stoicism; youthful, fair, brilliant as were many of my pupils, I can truly say that in me they never saw any other bearing than such as an austere though just guardian might have observed towards them. If any doubt the accuracy of this assertion, as inferring more conscientious self-denial or Scipio-like self-control than they feel disposed to give me credit for, let them take into consideration the following circumstances, which, while detracting from my merit, justify my veracity.

Know, O incredulous Reader! that a master stands in a somewhat different relation towards a pretty, light-headed, probably ignorant girl to that occupied by a partner at a ball or a gallant on the promenade. A professor does not meet his pupil to see her dressed in satin and muslin, with hair perfumed and curled, neck scarcely shaded by aerial lace, round, white arms circled with bracelets, feet dressed for the gliding dance; it is not his business to whirl her through the waltz, to feed her with compliments, to heighten her beauty by the flush of gratified vanity. Neither does he encounter her on the smooth-rolled, tree-shaded Boulevard, in the green and sunny Park, whither she repairs clad in her becoming walking dress—her scarf thrown with grace over her shoulders, her little bonnet scarcely screening her curls, the red rose under its brim adding a new tint to the softer rose on her cheek, her face and eyes too illumined with smiles, perhaps as transient as the sunshine of the gala-day, but also quite as brilliant; it is not his office to walk by her side, to listen to her lively chat, to carry her parasol, scarcely larger than a broad green leaf, to lead in a ribbon her Blenheim spaniel or Italian grey-hound. No—he finds her in the schoolroom, plainly dressed, with books before her; owing to her education or her nature books are to her a nuisance and she opens them with aversion, yet her teacher must instil into her mind the contents of these books—that mind resists the admission of grave information, it recoils, it grows restive; sullen tempers are shewn, disfiguring frowns spoil the symmetry of the face, sometimes coarse gestures banish grace from the deportment while muttered expressions, redolent of native and ineradicable vulgarity, desecrate the sweetness of the voice. Where the temperament is serene though the intellect sluggish, an unconquerable dullness opposes every effort to instruct. Where there is cunning but not energy, dissimulation, falsehood, a thousand schemes and tricks are put in play to evade the necessity of application; in short, to the tutor, female youth, female charms are like tapestry hangings of which the wrong side is continually turned towards him, and even when he sees the smooth, neat, external surface, he so well knows what knots, long stitches and jagged ends are behind that he has scarce a temptation to admire too fondly the seemly forms and bright colours exposed to general view.

Our likings are regulated by our circumstances; the artist prefers a hilly country because it is picturesque, the engineer a flat one because it is convenient; the man of pleasure likes what he calls "a fine woman"; she suits him; the fashionable young gentleman admires the fashionable young lady; she is of his kind; the toil-worn, fagged, probably irritable tutor, blind almost to beauty, insensible to airs and graces, glories chiefly in certain mental qualities; application, love of knowledge, natural capacity, docility, truthfulness, gratefulness are the charms that attract his notice and win his regard. These he seeks but seldom meets; these if by chance he finds he would fain retain for ever, and when Separation deprives him of them, he feels as if some ruthless hand had snatched from him his only ewe-lamb. Such being the case, and the case it is, my readers will agree with me that there was nothing either very meritorious or very marvellous in the integrity and moderation of my conduct at Mdlle. Reuter's Pensionnat de demoiselles.

My first business this afternoon consisted in reading the list of places for the month, determined by the relative correctness of the compositions, given the preceding day. The list was headed, as usual, by the name of Sylvie, that plain, quiet little girl I have described before as being at once the best and ugliest pupil in the establishment; the second place had fallen to the lot of a certain Léonie Ledru, a diminutive, sharp-featured and parchment-skinned creature of quick wits, frail conscience, and indurated feelings; a lawyer-like thing of whom I used to say that had she been a boy, she would have made a model of an unprincipled, clever attorney. Then came Eulalie, the proud beauty, the Juno of the school, whom six long years of drilling in the simple grammar of the English language had compelled, despite the stiff phlegm of her intellect, to acquire a mechanical acquaintance with most of its rules. No smile, no trace of pleasure or satisfaction appeared in Sylvie's nun-like and passive face as she heard her name read first; I always felt saddened by the sight of that poor girl's absolute quiescence on all occasions and it was my custom to look at her, to address her as seldom as possible; her extreme docility, her assiduous perseverance would have recommended her warmly to my good opinion; her modesty, her intelligence would have induced me to feel most kindly—most affectionately towards her, notwithstanding the almost ghastly plainness of her features, the disproportion of her form, the corpse-like lack of animation in her countenance, had I not been aware that every friendly word, every kindly action would be reported by her to her confessor and by him misinterpreted and poisoned—once I laid my hand on her head in token of approbation; I thought Sylvie was going to smile, her dim eye almost kindled—but presently she shrunk from me; I was a man and a heretic; she—poor child!—a destined nun and devoted Catholic—thus a fourfold wall of separation divided her mind from mine. A pert smirk and a hard glance of triumph was Léonie's method of testifying her gratification; Eulalie looked sullen and envious, she had hoped to be first; Hortense and Caroline exchanged a reckless grimace on hearing their names read out somewhere near the bottom of the list; the brand of mental inferiority was considered by them as no disgrace; their hopes for the future being based solely on their personal attractions.

This affair arranged, the regular lesson followed; during a brief interval, employed by the pupils in ruling their books, my eye, ranging carelessly over the benches, observed for the first time that the farthest seat in the farthest row—a seat usually vacant, was again filled by the new scholar, the Mdlle. Henri, so ostentatiously recommended to me by the Directress; to-day I had on my spectacles, her appearance therefore was clear to me at the first glance, I had not to puzzle over it; she looked young, yet had I been required to name her exact age I should have been somewhat nonplussed; the slightness of her figure might have suited seventeen, a certain anxious and preoccupied expression of face seemed the indication of riper years; she was dressed, like all the rest, in a dark stuff gown and a white collar; her features were dissimilar to any there, not so rounded, more defined yet scarcely regular. The shape of her head too was different, the superior part more developed, the base considerably less—I felt assured at first sight that she was not a Belgian, her complexion, her countenance, her lineaments, her figure were all distinct from theirs and evidently the type of another race—of a race less gifted with fulness of flesh and plenitude of blood, less jocund, material, unthinking. When I first cast my eyes on her, she sat looking fixedly down, her chin resting on her hand and she did not change her attitude till I commenced the lesson—none of the Belgian girls would have retained one position and that a reflective one for the same length of time. Yet having intimated that her appearance was peculiar, as being unlike that of her Flemish companions, I have little more to say respecting it; I can pronounce no encomiums on her beauty for she was not beautiful, nor offer condolence on her plainness for neither was she plain; a care-worn character of forehead and a corresponding moulding of the mouth struck me with a sentiment resembling surprise, but these traits would probably have passed unnoticed by any less crotchetty observer.

Now Reader—though I have spent a page and a half in describing Mdlle. Henri, I know well enough that I have left on your mind's eye no distinct picture of her; I have not painted her complexion, nor her eyes, nor her hair, nor even drawn the outline of her shape. You cannot tell whether her nose was aquiline or retroussé, whether her chin was long or short, her face square or oval, nor could I the first day and it is not my intention to communicate to you at once, a knowledge I myself gained by little and little.

I gave a short exercise which they all wrote down; I saw the new pupil was puzzled at first with the novelty of the form and language; once or twice she looked at me with a sort of painful solicitude, as not comprehending at all what I meant; then she was not ready when the others were, she could not write her phrases so fast as they did; I would not help her, I went on relentless, she looked at me, her eye said most plainly, "I cannot follow you." I disregarded the appeal and carelessly leaning back in my chair, glancing from time to time with a nonchalant air out at the window, I dictated a little faster. On looking towards her again, I perceived her face clouded with embarrassment but she was still writing on most diligently; I paused a few seconds, she employed the interval in hurriedly reperusing what she had written, and shame and discomfiture were apparent in her countenance, she evidently found she had made great nonsense of it. In ten minutes more, the dictation was complete and, having allowed a brief space in which to correct it, I took their books; it was with a reluctant hand Mdlle. Henri gave up hers, but having once yielded it to my possession, she composed her anxious face as if, for the present, she had resolved to dismiss regret and had made up her mind to be thought unprecedentedly stupid. Glancing over her exercise, I found that several lines had been omitted, but what was written contained very few faults; I instantly inscribed "Bon" at the bottom of the page, and returned it to her; she smiled, at first incredulously, then as if reassured, but did not lift her eyes; she could look at me, it seemed, when perplexed and bewildered, but not when gratified; I thought that scarcely fair.

CHAPTER XV

SOME time elapsed before I again gave a lesson in the first Class; the holiday of Whitsuntide occupied three days, and on the fourth it was the turn of the second Division to receive my instructions. As I made the transit of the carré, I observed, as usual, the band of sewers surrounding Mdlle. Henri; there were only about a dozen of them but they made as much noise as might have sufficed for fifty; they seemed very little under her control; three or four at once assailed her with importunate requirements; she looked harrassed, she demanded silence, but in vain. She saw me and I read in her eye pain that a stranger should witness the insubordination of her pupils; she seemed to entreat order, her prayers were useless; then I remarked that she compressed her lips and contracted her brow, and her countenance, if I read it correctly, said, "I have done my best; I seem to merit blame notwithstanding; blame me then, who will." I passed on, as I closed the school-room door, I heard her say suddenly and sharply, addressing one of the eldest and most turbulent of the lot:

"Amélie Müllenberg—ask me no question and request of me no assistance for a week to come; during that space of time I will neither speak to you nor help you."

The words were uttered with emphasis, nay with vehemence, and a comparative silence followed; whether the calm was permanent I know not, two doors now closed between me and the carré.

Next day was appropriated to the first class; on my arrival, I found the Directress seated, as usual, in a chair between the two estrades and before her was standing Mdlle. Henri in an attitude (as it seemed to me) of somewhat reluctant attention. The Directress was knitting and talking at the same time. Amidst the hum of a large school-room it was easy so to speak in the ear of one person, as to be heard by that person alone, and it was thus Mdlle.

Reuter parleyed with her teacher. The face of the latter was a little flushed, not a little troubled; there was vexation in it, whence resulting I know not, for the Directress looked very placid indeed; she could not be scolding in such gentle whispers and with so equable a mien—no—it was presently proved that her discourse had been of the most friendly tendency for I heard the closing words:

"C'est assez, ma bonne amie, à présent je ne veux pas vous retenir davantage."

Without reply Mdlle. Henri turned away; dissatisfaction was plainly evinced in her face, and a smile, slight and brief, but bitter, distrustful and, I thought, scornful, curled her lip as she took her place in the class; it was a secret, involuntary smile which lasted but a second, an air of depression succeeded, chased away presently by one of attention and interest when I gave the word for all the pupils to take their reading-books. In general I hated the reading-lesson, it was such a torture to the ear to listen to their uncouth mouthing of my native tongue, and no effort of example or precept on my part, ever seemed to effect the slightest improvement in their accent. To-day, each in her appropriate key, lisped, stuttered, mumbled and jabbered as usual; about fifteen had racked me in turn, and my auricular nerve was expecting with resignation the discords of the sixteenth, when a full though low voice read out, in clear correct English:

"On his way to Perth, the King was met by a Highland woman calling herself a prophetess; she stood at the side of the ferry by which he was about to travel to the North, and cried with a loud voice, 'My lord the king—if you pass this water you will never return again alive'!" (Vide, the history of Scotland.)

I looked up in amazement; the voice was a voice of Albion; the accent was pure and silvery, it only wanted firmness and assurance to be the counterpart of what any well-educated lady in Essex or Middlesex might have enounced, yet the speaker or reader was no other than Mdlle. Henri, in whose grave, joyless face I saw no mark of consciousness that she had performed any extraordinary feat. No one else evinced surprise either; Mdlle. Reuter knitted away assiduously; I was aware however that at the conclusion of the paragraph, she had lifted her eyelid and honoured me with a glance sideways; she did not know the full excellency of the teacher's style of reading, but she perceived that her accent was not that of the others and wanted to discover what I thought; I masked my visage with indifference, and ordered the next girl to proceed.

When the lesson was over, I took advantage of the confusion caused by breaking up, to approach Mdlle. Henri; she was standing near the window and retired as I advanced; she thought I wanted to look out, and did not imagine that I could have anything to say to her; I took her exercise-book out of her hand, as I turned over the leaves I addressed her:

"You have had lessons in English before?" I asked.

"No, Sir."

"No! you read it well; you have been in England?"

"Oh no!" with some animation.

"You have lived in English families?"

Still the answer was "no". Here my eye, resting on the fly-leaf of the book, saw written: "Frances Evans Henri."

"Your name?" I asked.

"Yes, Sir."

My interrogations were cut short, I heard a little rustling behind me and close at my back was the Directress, professing to be examining the interior of a desk.

"Mademoiselle," said she, looking up and addressing the teacher, "will you have the goodness to go and stand in the corridor, while the young ladies are putting on their things, and try to keep some order." Mdlle. Henri obeyed.

"What splendid weather!" observed the Directress cheerfully, glancing at the same time from the window, I assented and was withdrawing—"What of your new pupil, Monsieur?" continued she, following my retreating steps. "Is she likely to make progress in English?"

"Indeed I can hardly judge; she possesses a pretty good accent;

of her real knowledge of the language I have as yet had no opportunity of forming an opinion."

"And her natural capacity, Monsieur? I have had my fears about that—can you relieve me by an assurance at least of its average power?"

"I see no reason to doubt its average power, Mademoiselle, but really I scarcely know her and have not had time to study the calibre of her capacity—I wish you a very good afternoon."

She still pursued me; "You will observe, Monsieur, and tell me what you think; I could so much better rely on your opinion than on my own; women cannot judge of these things as men can, and, excuse my pertinacity, Monsieur, but it is natural I should feel interested about this poor little girl (pauvre petite) she has scarcely any relations, her own efforts are all she has to look to, her acquirements must be her sole fortune; her present position has once been mine, or nearly so, it is then but natural I should sympathize with her; and sometimes, when I see the difficulty she has in managing pupils, I feel quite chagrined; I doubt not she does her best, her intentions are excellent, but, monsieur, she wants tact and firmness—I have talked to her on the subject—but—I am not fluent and probably did not express myself with clearness; she never appears to comprehend me; now would you occasionally, when you see an opportunity, slip in a word of advice to her on the subject? Men have so much more influence than women have, they argue so much more logically than we do, and you, Monsieur, in particular, have so paramount a power of making yourself obeyed; a word of advice from you could not but do her good, even if she were sullen and headstrong (which I hope she is not)—she would scarcely refuse to listen to you: for my own part, I can truly say that I never attend one of your lessons without deriving benefit from witnessing your management of the pupils—the other masters are a constant source of anxiety to me; they cannot impress the young ladies with sentiments of respect, nor restrain the levity natural to youth; in you, Monsieur, I feel the most absolute confidence; try then to put this poor child into the way of controlling our giddy, high-spirited Brabantoises. But, Monsieur—I would add one word more; don't alarm her amour-propre; beware of inflicting a wound there; I reluctantly admit that in that particular she is blameably—some would say, ridiculously, susceptible; I fear I have touched this sore point inadvertently and she cannot get over it."

During the greater part of this harangue my hand was on the lock of the outer door, I now turned it:

"Au revoir, Mademoiselle," said I, and I escaped; I saw the Directress's stock of words was yet far from exhausted; she looked after me, she would fain have detained me longer. Her manner towards me had been altered ever since I had begun to treat her with hardness and indifference; she almost cringed to me on every occasion, she consulted my countenance incessantly and beset me with innumerable little officious attentions. Servility creates despotism. This slavish homage, instead of softening my heart, only pampered whatever was stern and exacting in its mood. The very circumstance of her hovering round me like a fascinated bird, seemed to transform me into a rigid pillar of stone; her flatteries irritated my scorn, her blandishments confirmed my reserve. At times I wondered what she meant by giving herself such trouble to win me, when the more profitable Pelet was already in her nets, and when too she was aware that I possessed her secret, for I had not scrupled to tell her as much; but the fact is that as it was her nature to doubt the reality and undervalue the worth of Modesty, Affection, Disinterestedness; to regard these qualities as foibles of character; so it was equally her tendency to consider Pride, Hardness, Selfishness as proofs of strength. She would trample on the neck of Humility, she would kneel at the feet of Disdain; she would meet Tenderness with secret contempt, Indifference she would woo with ceaseless assiduities; Benevolence, Devotedness, Enthusiasm were her Antipathies; for Dissimulation and Self-Interest she had a preference—they were real wisdom in her eyes; Moral and physical Degradation, Mental and bodily Inferiority she regarded with indulgence, they were foils capable of being turned to good account as set-offs for her own endowments; to Violence, Injustice, Tyranny she succumbed, they were her natural masters

—she had no propensity to hate, no impulse to resist them; the indignation their behests awake in some hearts was unknown in hers. From all this it resulted that the False and Selfish called her wise, the Vulgar and Debased termed her charitable, the Insolent and Unjust dubbed her amiable, the Conscientious and Benevolent generally at first accepted as valid her claim to be considered one of themselves, but erelong the plating of pretention wore off, the real material appeared below and they laid her aside as a deception.

CHAPTER XVI

In the course of another fortnight I had seen sufficient of Frances Evans Henri to enable me to form a more definite opinion of her character. I found her possessed in a somewhat remarkable degree of at least two good points, viz. Perseverance and a Sense of duty; I found she was really capable of applying to study, of contending with difficulties. At first I offered her the same help which I had always found it necessary to confer on the others; I began with unloosing for her each knotty point but I soon discovered that such help was regarded by my new pupil as degrading; she recoiled from it with a certain proud impatience. Thereupon I appointed her long lessons and left her to solve alone any perplexities they might present. She set to the task with serious ardour and having quickly accomplished one labour, eagerly demanded more. So much for her Perseverance—as to her Sense of duty, it evinced itself thus; she liked to learn, but hated to teach; her progress as a pupil depended upon herself, and I saw that on herself she could calculate with certainty; her success as a teacher rested partly, perhaps chiefly, upon the will of others; it cost her a most painful effort to enter into conflict with this foreign will, to endeavour to bend it into subjection to her own; for in what regarded people in general the action of her will was impeded by many scruples; it was as unembarrassed as strong where her own affairs were concerned, and to it she could at any time subject her inclination, if that inclination went counter to her convictions of right; yet when called upon to wrestle with the propensities, the habits, the faults of others, of children especially, who are deaf to reason and, for the most part, insensate to persuasion, her will sometimes almost refused to act; then came in the Sense of duty and forced the reluctant Will into operation. A wasteful expense of energy and labour was frequently the consequence; Frances toiled for and with her pupils like a drudge, but it was long ere her conscientious exertions were rewarded by anything like docility on their part;

because they saw that they had power over her, inasmuch as by resisting her painful attempts to convince, persuade, control; by forcing her to the employment of coercive measures, they could inflict upon her exquisite suffering. Human beings—human children especially, seldom deny themselves the pleasure of exercising a power which they are conscious of possessing, even though that power consist only in a capacity to make others wretched; a pupil whose sensations are duller than those of his instructor, while his nerves are tougher and his bodily strength perhaps greater, has an immense advantage over that instructor and he will generally use it relentlessly, because the very young, very healthy, very thoughtless know neither how to sympathize nor how to spare. Frances, I fear, suffered much; a continual weight seemed to oppress her spirits; I have said she did not live in the house and whether in her own abode—wherever that might be—she wore the same preoccupied, unsmiling, sorrowfully resolved air that always shaded her features under the roof of Mdlle. Reuter, I could not tell.

One day, I gave as a devoir the trite little anecdote of Alfred tending cakes in the herdsman's hut, to be related with amplifications. A singular affair most of the pupils made of it; brevity was what they had chiefly studied; the majority of the narratives were perfectly unintelligible; those of Sylvie and Léonie Ledru alone pretended to anything like sense and connection. Eulalie, indeed, had hit upon a clever expedient for at once ensuring accuracy and saving trouble; she had obtained access somehow to an abridged history of England, and had copied the anecdote out fair; I wrote on the margin of her production "Stupid and deceitful" and then tore it down the middle. Last in the pile of single-leaved devoirs, I found one of several sheets, neatly written out and stitched together; I knew the hand and scarcely needed the evidence of the signature, "Frances Evans Henri" to confirm my conjecture as to the writer's identity.

Night was my usual time for correcting devoirs and my own room the usual scene of such task—task most onerous hitherto, and it seemed strange to me to feel rising within me an incipient sense of interest, as I snuffed the candle and addressed myself to the perusal of the poor teacher's manuscript.

"Now," thought I, "I shall see a glimpse of what she really is; I shall get an idea of the nature and extent of her powers; not that she can be expected to express herself well in a foreign tongue, but still, if she has any mind, here will be a reflection of it."

The narrative commenced by a description of a Saxon peasant's hut, situated within the confines of a great, leafless, winter forest; it represented an evening in December, flakes of snow were falling and the herdsman foretold a heavy storm; he summoned his wife to aid him in collecting their flock, roaming far away on the pastoral banks of the Thone; he warns her that it will be late ere they return. The good woman is reluctant to quit her occupation of baking cakes for the evening-meal, but acknowledging the primary importance of securing the herds and flocks, she puts on her sheep-skin mantle and addressing a stranger who rests half reclined on a bed of rushes near the hearth, bids him mind the bread till her return:

"Take care young man," she continues, "that you fasten the door well after us; and, above all, open to none in our absence; whatever sound you hear, stir not and look not out. The night will soon fall, this forest is most wild and lonely, strange noises are often heard therein after sunset, wolves haunt these glades and Danish warriors infest the country; worse things are talked of; you might chance to hear, as it were, a child cry, and on opening the door to afford it succour, a great, black bull or a shadowy goblin dog might rush over the threshold; or, more awful still, if something flapped as with wings against the lattice and then a raven or a white dove flew in and settled on the hearth, such a visitor would be a sure sign of misfortune to the house; therefore heed my advice and lift the latchet for nothing."

Her husband calls her away, both depart. The stranger, left alone, listens awhile to the muffled snow-wind, the remote, swollen sound of the river and then he speaks.

"It is Christmas-Eve," says he, "I mark the date; here I sit alone on a rude couch of rushes, sheltered by the thatch of a herdsman's hut; I, whose inheritance was a kingdom, owe my night's harbourage to a poor serf. My throne is usurped, my crown presses the brow of an invader; I have no friends; my troops wander broken in the hills of Wales; reckless robbers spoil my country; my subjects lie prostrate, their breasts crushed by the heel of the brutal Dane. Fate—thou hast done thy worst and now thou standest before me resting thy hand on thy blunted blade; aye! I see thine eye confront mine and demand why I still live, why I still hope. Pagan demon! I credit not thine omnipotence and so cannot succumb to thy power. My God, whose Son, as on this night, took on him the form of man and for man vouchsafed to suffer and bleed, controls thy hand, and without his behest thou canst not strike a stroke. My God is sinless, eternal, all-wise, in him is my trust, and though stripped and crushed by thee; though naked, desolate, void of resource, I do not despair, I cannot despair, were the lance of Guthrum now wet with my blood, I should not despair. I watch, I toil, I hope, I pray; Jehovah, in his own time, will aid." I need not continue the quotation; the whole devoir was in the same strain. There were errors of orthography, there were foreign idioms, there were some faults of construction, there were verbs irregular transformed into verbs regular; it was mostly made up, as the above example shews, of short and somewhat rude sentences, and the style stood in great need of polish and sustained dignity; yet such as it was, I had hitherto seen nothing like it in the course of my professoral experience. The girl's mind had conceived a picture of the hut, of the two peasants, of the crownless king; she had imagined the wintry forest, she had recalled the old Saxon ghost-legends, she had appreciated Alfred's courage under calamity, she had remembered his christian education and had shewn him, with the rooted confidence of those primitive days, relying on the scriptural Jehovah for aid against the mythological Destiny. This she had done without a hint from me, I had given the subject, but not said a word about the manner of treating it.

"I will find or make an opportunity of speaking to her," I said to myself as I rolled the devoir up; "I will learn what she has of English in her besides the name of Frances Evans; she is no novice in the language—that is evident—yet she told me she had neither been in England, nor taken lessons in English, nor lived in English families."

In the course of my next lesson, I made a report of the other devoirs, dealing out praise and blame in very small retail parcels, according to my custom, for there was no use in blaming severely, and high encomiums were rarely merited. I said nothing of Mdlle. Henri's exercise and, spectacles on nose, I endeavoured to decipher in her countenance, her sentiments at the omission; I wanted to find out whether in her existed a consciousness of her own talents. "If she thinks she did a clever thing in composing that devoir, she will now look mortified," thought I. Grave as usual, almost sombre was her face, as usual her eyes were fastened on the cahier open before her; there was something, I thought, of expectation in her attitude as I concluded a brief review of the last devoir, and when, casting it from me and rubbing my hands, I bade them take their grammars, some slight change did pass over her air and mien, as though she now relinquished a faint prospect of pleasant excitement; she had been waiting for something to be discussed in which she had a degree of interest, the discussion was not to come on, so Expectation sank back, shrunk and sad, but Attention, promptly filling up the void, repaired in a moment the transient collapse of feature; still, I felt, rather than saw, during the whole course of the lesson, that a hope had been wrenched from her, and that if she did not shew distress, it was because she would not.

At four o'clock when the bell rang and the room was in immediate tumult, instead of taking my hat and starting from the estrade, I sat still a moment; I looked at Frances, she was putting her books into her cabas; having fastened the button, she raised her head, encountering my eye, she made a quiet, respectful obeisance, as bidding good afternoon and was turning to depart.

"Come here," said I, lifting my finger at the same time. She hesitated, she could not hear the words amidst the uproar now pervading both school-rooms; I repeated the sign, she approached, again she paused, within half a yard of the estrade and looked shy and still doubtful whether she had mistaken my meaning.

"Step up," I said, speaking with decision; it is the only way of dealing with diffident, easily embarrassed characters, and with some slight manual aid, I presently got her placed just where I wanted her to be; that is between my desk and the window, where she was screened from the rush of the second Division, and where no one could sneak behind her to listen.

"Take a seat," I said, placing a tabouret and I made her sit down; I knew what I was doing would be considered a very strange thing and, what was more, I did not care; Frances knew it also and, I fear, by an appearance of agitation and trembling, that she cared much. I drew from my pocket the rolled-up devoir:

"This is yours I suppose?" said I, addressing her in English, for I now felt sure she could speak English.

"Yes," she answered distinctly and as I unrolled it and laid it out flat on the desk before her with my hand upon it and a pencil in that hand, I saw her moved, and, as it were, kindled; her depression beamed as a cloud might, behind which the sun is burning.

"This devoir has numerous faults," said I. "It will take you some years of careful study before you are in a condition to write English with absolute correctness. Attend; I will point out some principal defects." And I went through it carefully, noting every error and demonstrating why they were errors and how the words or phrases ought to have been written. In the course of this sobering process she became calm. I now went on:

"As to the substance of your devoir, Mademoiselle Henri, it has surprised me; I perused it with pleasure because I saw in it some proofs of taste and fancy. Taste and fancy are not the highest gifts of the human mind but such as they are you possess them—not probably in a paramount degree, but in a degree beyond what the majority can boast. You may then take courage; cultivate the faculties that God and Nature have bestowed on you, and do not fear in any crisis of suffering, under any pressure of injustice to derive free and full consolation from the consciousness of their strength and rarity."

"Strength and Rarity!" I repeated to myself. "Aye, the words are probably true," for on looking up, I saw the sun had dissevered its screening cloud, her countenance was transfigured, a smile shone in her eyes—a smile almost triumphant, it seemed to say:

"I am glad you have been forced to discover so much of my nature; you need not so carefully moderate your language. Do you think I am myself a stranger to myself? What you tell me in terms so qualified, I have known fully from a child."

She did say this as plainly as a frank and flashing glance could, but in a moment the glow of her complexion, the radiance of her aspect had subsided; if strongly conscious of her talents, she was equally conscious of her harassing defects and the remembrance of these, obliterated for a single second, now reviving with sudden force, at once subdued the too vivid characters in which her sense of her powers had been expressed. So quick was the revulsion of feeling I had not time to check her triumph by reproof; ere I could contract my brows to a frown she had become serious and almost mournful-looking.

"Thank you, sir," said she rising; there was gratitude both in her voice and in the look with which she accompanied it. It was time indeed for our conference to terminate, for, when I glanced around, behold all the boarders (the day-scholars had departed) were congregated within a yard or two of my desk and stood staring with eyes and mouths wide open; the three maîtresses formed a whispering knot in one corner, and, close at my elbow, was the Directress, sitting on a low chair, calmly clipping the tassels of her finished purse.

CHAPTER XVII

AFTER all I had profited but imperfectly by the opportunity I had so boldly achieved of speaking to Mdlle. Henri; it was my intention to ask her how she came to be possessed of two English baptismal names, Frances and Evans, in addition to her French surname, also whence she derived her good accent; I had forgotten both points, or rather, our colloquy had been so brief that I had not had time to bring them forward; moreover I had not half tested her powers of speaking English; all I had drawn from her in that language were the words "Yes" and "Thank you, Sir." "No matter," I reflected. "What has been left incomplete now, shall be finished another day." Nor did I fail to keep the promise thus made to myself. It was difficult to get even a few words of particular conversation with one pupil among so many, but, according to the old proverb, "Where there is a will, there is a way," and again and again I managed to find an opportunity for exchanging a few words with Mdlle. Henri; regardless that Envy stared and Detraction whispered whenever I approached her.

"Your book an instant"—such was the mode in which I often began these brief dialogues, the time was always just at the conclusion of the lesson—and motioning to her to rise, I installed myself in her place, allowing her to stand deferentially at my side, for I esteemed it wise and right in her case to enforce strictly all forms ordinarily in use between master and pupil; the rather because I perceived that in proportion as my manner grew austere and magisterial, hers became easy and self-possessed; an odd contradiction doubtless to the ordinary effect in such cases—but so it was.

"A pencil—" said I—holding out my hand without looking at her—(I am now about to sketch a brief report of the first of these conferences). She gave me one and while I underlined some errors in a grammatical exercise she had written, I observed:

"You are not a native of Belgium?"

"No."

"Nor of France?"

"No."

"Where then is your birth-place?"

"I was born at Geneva."

"You don't call Frances and Evans Swiss names I presume?"

"No, Sir—they are English names."

"Just so—and is it the custom of the Genevese to give their children English appellatives?"

"Non, monsieur, mais—"

"Speak English, if you please—"

"Mais—"

"English—"

"But—" (slowly and with embarrassment) "my parents were not all the two Genevese."

"Say *both*—instead of 'all the two', mademoiselle."

"Not *both* Swiss—my Mother was English."

"Ah! and of English extraction?"

"Yes—her ancestors were all English."

"And your father?"

"He was Swiss."

"What besides? What was his profession?"

"Ecclesiastic—pastor—he had a church."

"Since your Mother is an Englishwoman—why do you not speak English with more facility?"

"Maman est morte—il y a dix ans."

"And you do homage to her memory by forgetting her language? Have the goodness to put French out of your mind so long as I converse with you—keep to English."

"C'est si difficile, Monsieur, quand on n'en a plus l'habitude."

"You had the habitude formerly I suppose—? Now answer me in your mother-tongue."

"Yes, Sir—I spoke the English more than the French when I was a child."

"Why do you not speak it now?"

"Because I have no English friends."

"You live with your father I suppose?"

"My father is dead."

"You have brothers and sisters?"

"Not one."

"Do you live alone?"

"No—I have an Aunt—ma tante Julienne."

"Your father's sister?"

"Justement, monsieur."

"Is that English?"

"No—but I forget—"

"For which, Mademoiselle, if you were a child I should certainly devise some slight punishment—at your age—you must be two or three and twenty—I should think?"

"Pas encore, monsieur—en un mois j'aurai dix-neuf ans."

"Well nineteen is a mature age, and having attained it, you ought to be so solicitous for your own improvement that it should not be needful for a master to remind you twice of the expediency of your speaking English whenever practicable."

To this wise speech, I received no answer, and when I looked up, my pupil was smiling to herself, a much-meaning though not very gay smile— it seemed to say "He talks of he knows not what." It said this so plainly, that I determined to request information on the point concerning which my ignorance seemed to be thus tacitly affirmed.

"Are you solicitous for your own improvement?"

"Rather."

"How do you prove it, Mademoiselle?"

An odd question and bluntly put—it excited a second smile.

"Why, monsieur, I am not inattentive—am I? I learn my lessons well—"

"Oh a child can do that! and what more do you do?"

"What more can I do?"

"Oh certainly not much—but you are a teacher are you not as well as a pupil?"

"Yes."

"You teach lace-mending?"

"Yes."

"A dull—stupid occupation—do you like it?"

"No—it is tedious."

"Why do you pursue it? Why do you not rather teach history, geography, grammar—even arithmetic?"

"Is Monsieur certain that I am myself thoroughly acquainted with these studies?"

"I don't know—you ought to be at your age."

"But I never was at school, Monsieur—"

"Indeed! What then were your friends—what was your Aunt about? She is very much to blame."

"No, Monsieur, no—my Aunt is good—she is not to blame. She does what she can, she lodges and nourishes me." (I report Mdlle. Henri's phrases literally and it was thus she translated from the French.) "She is not rich—she has only an annuity of twelve hundred francs and it would be impossible for her to send me to school."

"Rather," thought I to myself on hearing this—but I continued in the dogmatical tone I had adopted:

"It is sad however that you should be brought up in ignorance of the most ordinary branches of education; had you known something of history and grammar you might, by degrees, have relinquished your lace-mending drudgery, and risen in the world."

"It is what I mean to do."

"How? By a knowledge of English alone? That will not suffice; no respectable family will receive a governess whose whole stock of knowledge consists in a familiarity with one foreign language."

"Monsieur—I know other things."

"Yes—yes—you can work with Berlin wools, and embroider handkerchiefs and collars—that will do little for you—"

Mdlle. Henri's lips were unclosed to answer, but she checked herself as thinking the discussion had been sufficiently pursued and remained silent.

"Speak—" I continued impatiently, "I never like the appearance of acquiescence when the reality is not there—and you had a contradiction at your tongue's end."

"Monsieur, I have had many lessons both in grammar, history, geography and arithmetic—I have gone through a course of each study."

"Bravo! but how did you manage it—since your Aunt could not afford to send you to school?"

"By lace-mending, by the thing Monsieur despises so much."

"Truly! And now Mademoiselle, it will be a good exercise for you to explain to me in English how such a result was produced by such means."

"Monsieur—I begged my Aunt to have me taught lace-mending soon after we came to Brussels, because I knew it was a métier—a trade which was easily learnt and by which I could earn some money very soon—I learnt it in a few days and I quickly got work, for all the Brussels ladies have old lace—very precious—which must be mended all the times it is washed; I earned money, a little, and this money I gave for lessons in the studies I have mentioned, some of it I spent in buying books, English books especially; soon I shall try to find a place of governess, or school-teacher when I can write and speak English well—but it will be difficult, because those who know I have been a lace-mender will despise me, as the pupils here despise me; pourtant j'ai mon projet," she added in a lower tone.

"What is it?"

"I will go and live in England—I will teach French there."

The words were pronounced emphatically—she said "England" as you might suppose an Israelite of Moses' days would have said Canaan.

"Have you a wish to see England?"

"Yes—and an intention."

And here a voice—the voice of the Directress—interposed:

"Mademoiselle Henri, je crois qu'il va pleuvoir; vous feriez bien, ma bonne amie, de retourner chez vous tout de suite."

In silence, without a word of thanks for this officious warning, Mdlle. Henri collected her books; she moved to me respectfully, endeavoured to move to her superior, though the endeavour was almost a failure, for her head seemed as if it would not bend, and thus departed.

Where there is one grain of perseverance or wilfulness in the composition, trifling obstacles are ever known rather to stimulate than discourage; Mdlle. Reuter might as well have spared herself the trouble of giving that intimation about the weather (by the by her prediction was falsified by the event—it did not rain that evening). At the close of the next lesson, I was again at Mdlle. Henri's desk; thus did I accost her:

"What is your idea of England, Mademoiselle? Why do you wish to go there?"

Accustomed by this time to the calculated abruptness of my manner, it no longer discomposed or surprised her, and she answered with only so much of hesitation as was rendered inevitable by the difficulty she experienced in improvising the translation of her thoughts from French to English:

"England is something unique as I have heard and read; my idea of it is vague and I want to go there to render my idea clear, definite."

"Hum! How much of England do you suppose you could see if you went there in the capacity of a teacher? A strange notion you must have of getting a clear and definite idea of a country! All you could see of Great Britain would be the interior of a school or at most of one or two private dwellings."

"It would be an English school—they would be English dwellings."

"Indisputably—but what then? What would be the value of observations made on a scale so narrow?"

"Monsieur, might not one learn something by analogy? An—échantillon—a—a sample often serves to give an idea of the whole; besides narrow and wide are words comparative—are they not? All my life would perhaps seem narrow in your eyes—all the life of a—that little animal subterranean—une taupe—comment dit-on?"

"Mole."

"Yes—a mole, which lives underground, would seem narrow even to me."

"Well, mademoiselle—what then? proceed—"

"Mais, Monsieur, vous me comprenez—"

"Not in the least; have the goodness to explain."

"Why, monsieur, it is just so. In Switzerland I have done but little, learnt but little, and seen but little; my life there was in a circle; I walked the same round every day; I could not get out of it; had I rested—remained there even till my death, I should never have enlarged it because I am poor and not skilful, I have not great acquirements; when I was quite tired of this round, I begged my Aunt to go to Brussels; my existence is no larger here because I am no richer or higher—I walk in as narrow a limit, but the scene is changed, it would change again if I went to England. I knew something of the bourgeois of Geneva, now I know something of the bourgeois of Brussels, if I went to London I should know something of the bourgeois of London. Can you make any sense out of what I say Monsieur or is it all obscure?"

"I see, I see—now let us advert to another subject; you propose to devote your life to teaching, and you are a most unsuccessful teacher, you cannot keep your pupils in order."

A flush of painful confusion was the result of this harsh remark; she bent her head to the desk, but soon raising it, replied:

"Monsieur, I am not a skilful teacher—it is true, but practice improves; besides I work under difficulties; here I only teach sewing, I can shew no power in sewing, no superiority—it is a subordinate art; then I have no associates in this house, I am isolated; I am too a heretic, which deprives me of influence."

"And in England you would be a foreigner; that too would deprive you of influence, would effectually separate you from all round you; in England you would have as few connexions, as little importance as you have here."

"But I should be learning something—for the rest, there are probably difficulties for such as I, everywhere, and if I must contend and perhaps be conquered, I would rather submit to English pride than to Flemish coarseness; besides, Monsieur—" She stopped—not evidently from any difficulty in finding words to express herself, but because Discretion seemed to say "You have said enough."

"Finish your phrase," I urged.

"Besides, Monsieur, I long to live once more among Protestants, they are more honest than Catholics; a Romish school is a building with porous walls, a hollow floor, a false ceiling; every room in this house, Monsieur, has eye-holes and ear-holes, and what the house is, the inhabitants are, very treacherous; they all think it lawful to tell lies, they all call it politeness to profess friendship where they feel hatred."

"All?" said I. "You mean the pupils—the mere children—inexperienced, giddy things who have not learnt to distinguish the difference between right and wrong?"

"On the contrary, Monsieur—the children are the most sincere; they have not yet had time to become accomplished in duplicity; they will tell lies, but they do it inartificially, and you know they are lying; but the grown-up people are very false; they deceive strangers, they deceive each other—" A servant here entered:

"Mdlle. Henri—Mdlle. Reuter vous prie de vouloir bien conduire la petite de Dorlodot chez elle, elle vous attend dans le cabinet de Rosalie la portière—c'est que sa bonne n'est pas venue la chercher—voyez-vous."

"Eh bien! est-ce que je suis sa bonne—moi?" demanded Mdlle. Henri—then smiling, with that same bitter, derisive smile I had seen on her lips once before—she hastily rose and made her exit.

CHAPTER XVIII

THE young Anglo-Swiss evidently derived both pleasure and profit from the study of her Mother-tongue; in teaching her I did not of course confine myself to the ordinary school-routine; I made instruction in English a channel for instruction in literature. I prescribed to her a course of reading; she had a little selection of English classics, a few of which had been left her by her mother, and the others she had purchased with her own penny-fee; I lent her some more modern works; all these she read with avidity; giving me, in writing, a clear summary of each work when she had perused it; composition too, she delighted in—such occupation seemed the very breath of her nostrils, and soon her improved productions wrung from me the avowal that those qualities in her I had termed Taste and Fancy ought rather to have been denominated Judgment and Imagination. When I intimated so much, which I did as usual in dry and stinted phrase, I looked for the radiant and exulting smile my one word of eulogy had elicited before; but Frances coloured—if she did smile, it was very softly and shyly, and instead of looking up to me with a conquering glance, her eyes rested on my hand which, stretched over her shoulder, was writing some directions with a pencil on the margin of her book.

"Well, are you pleased that I am satisfied with your progress?" I asked. "Yes," said she slowly, gently, the blush that had half subsided, returning.

"But I do not say enough, I suppose?" I continued. "My praises are too cool?"

She made no answer and, I thought looked a little sad; I divined her thoughts and should much have liked to have responded to them, had it been expedient so to do. She was not now very ambitious of my admiration; not eagerly desirous of dazzling me—a little affection, ever so little, pleased her better than all the panegyrics in the world. Feeling this, I stood a good while behind her, writing on the margin of her book; I could hardly quit my station or relinquish my occupation, something retained me bending there, my head very near hers, and my hand near hers too; but the margin of a copy-book is not an illimitable space—so, doubtless, the Directress thought, and she took occasion to walk past in order to ascertain by what art I prolonged so disproportionately the period necessary for filling it—I was obliged to go—distasteful effort—to leave what we most prefer!

Frances did not become pale or feeble in consequence of her sedentary employment—perhaps the stimulus it communicated to her mind counterbalanced the inaction it imposed on her body. She changed indeed, changed obviously and rapidly—but it was for the better. When I first saw her, her countenance was sunless, her complexion colourless—she looked like one who had no source of enjoyment, no store of bliss anywhere in the world; now the cloud had passed from her mien, leaving space for the dawn of hope and interest, and those feelings rose like a clear morning, animating what had been depressed, tinting what had been pale. Her eyes whose colour I had not at first known, so dim were they with repressed tears, so shadowed with ceaseless dejection, now, lit by a ray of the sunshine that cheered her heart, revealed irids of bright hazel; irids large and full, screened with long lashes; and pupils instinct with fire. That look of wan emaciation which anxiety or low-spirits often communicates to a thoughtful, thin face, rather long than round—having vanished from hers, a clearness of skin, almost bloom—and a plumpness almost embonpoint softened the decided lines of her features. Her figure shared in this beneficial change—it became rounder and as the harmony of her form was complete and her stature of the graceful middle height, one did not regret (or at least *I* did not regret) the absence of confirmed fulness, in contours, still slight, though compact, elegant, flexible—the exquisite turning of waist, wrist, hand, foot and ancle satisfied completely my notions of symmetry, and allowed a lightness and freedom of movement which corresponded with my ideas of grace. Thus improved, thus wakened to life, Mdlle. Henri began to take a new footing in the school; her mental power, manifested gradually but steadily, erelong extorted recognition even from the envious, and when the Young and Healthy saw that she could smile brightly, converse gaily, move with vivacity and alertness they acknowledged in her a Sisterhood of Youth and Health and tolerated her as of their kind accordingly.

To speak truth, I watched this change much as a gardener watches the growth of a precious plant and I contributed to it too, even as the said gardener contributes to the development of his favourite. To me it was not difficult to discover how I could best foster my pupil, cherish her starved feelings and induce the outward manifestation of that inward vigour which sunless drought and blighting blast had hitherto forbidden to expand. Constancy of Attention—a kindness as mute as watchful, always standing by her, cloaked in the rough garb of austerity and making its real nature known only by a rare glance of interest, or a cordial and gentle word; real respect masked with seeming imperiousness, directing, urging her actions—yet helping her too and that with devoted care. These were the means I used, for these means best suited Frances' feelings as susceptible as deep-vibrating, her nature, at once proud and shy.

The benefits of my system became apparent also in her altered demeanour as a teacher; she now took her place amongst her pupils with an air of spirit and firmness which assured them at once that she meant to be obeyed—and obeyed she was; they felt they had lost their power over her; if any girl had rebelled, she would no longer have taken her rebellion to heart; she possessed a source of comfort they could not drain, a pillar of support they could not overthrow; formerly when insulted, she wept; now she only smiled.

The public reading of one of her devoirs achieved the revelation of her talents to all and sundry; I remember the subject—it was an emigrant's letter to his friends at home. It opened with simplicity; some natural and graphic touches disclosed to the reader the scene of virgin forest and great, new-world river, barren of sail and flag—amidst which the epistle was supposed to be indited; the difficulties and dangers that attend a settler's life were hinted at and in the few words said on that subject, Mdlle. Henri failed not to render audible the voice of resolve, patience, endeavour. The disasters which had driven him from his native country were alluded to; stainless honour, inflexible independence, indestructible self-respect there took the word. Past days were spoken of; the grief of parting, the regrets of absence were touched upon; feeling, forcible and fine, breathed eloquent in every period. At the close, consolation was suggested—religious Faith became there the speaker and she spoke well.

The devoir was powerfully written in language at once chaste and choice, in a style nerved with vigour and graced with harmony.

Mdlle. Reuter was quite sufficiently acquainted with English to understand it when read or spoken in her presence, though she could neither speak nor write it herself; during the perusal of this devoir she sat placidly busy, her eyes and fingers occupied with the formation of a "rivière", or open-work hem round a cambric-handkerchief; she said nothing and her face and forehead, clothed with a mask of purely negative expression, were as blank of comment as her lips. As neither surprise, pleasure, approbation nor interest were evinced in her countenance, so no more were disdain, envy, annoyance, weariness; if that inscrutable mien said anything it was simply this:

"The matter is too trite to excite an emotion or call forth an opinion." As soon as I had done, a hum rose, several of the pupils, pressing round Mdlle. Henri, began to beset her with compliments; the composed voice of the Directress was now heard:

"Young ladies, such of you as have cloaks and umbrellas will hasten to return home before the shower becomes heavier (it was raining a little), the remainder will wait till their respective servants arrive to fetch them." And the school dispersed for it was four o'clock.

"Monsieur, a word—" said Mdlle. Reuter stepping on to the estrade and signifying by a movement of the hand that she wished me to relinquish for an instant, the castor I had clutched.

"Mademoiselle, I am at your service."

"Monsieur, it is of course an excellent plan to encourage effort in young people by making conspicuous the progress of any particularly industrious pupil, but do you not think that in the present instance,

Mdlle. Henri can hardly be considered as a concurrent with the other pupils? She is older than most of them and has advantages of an exclusive nature for acquiring a knowledge of English; on the other hand, her sphere of life is somewhat beneath theirs; under these circumstances—a public distinction, conferred upon Mdlle. Henri, may be the means of suggesting comparisons and exciting feelings such as would be far from advantageous to the individual forming their object. The interest I take in Mdlle. Henri's real welfare makes me desirous of screening her from annoyances of this sort; besides, Monsieur, as I have before hinted to you, the sentiment of amour-propre has a somewhat marked preponderance in her character, celebrity has a tendency to foster this sentiment and in her it should be rather repressed; she rather needs keeping down than bringing forward; and then I think, Monsieur—it appears to me that ambition—*literary* ambition especially, is not a feeling to be cherished in the mind of a woman; would not Mdlle. Henri be much safer and happier if taught to believe that in the quiet discharge of social duties consists her real vocation, than if stimulated to aspire after applause and publicity? She may never marry; scanty as are her resources, obscure as are her connections, uncertain as is her health (for I think her consumptive, her mother died of that complaint) it is more than probable she never will; I do not see how she can rise to a position whence such a step would be possible—but even in celibacy it would be better for her to retain the character and habits of a respectable, decorous female."

"Indisputably, Mademoiselle," was my answer. "Your opinion admits of no doubt," and, fearful of the harangue being renewed, I retreated under cover of that cordial sentence of assent.

At the date of a fortnight after the little incident noted above I find it recorded in my diary that a hiatus occurred in Mdlle. Henri's usually regular attendance in class. The first day or two I wondered at her absence but did not like to ask an explanation of it; I thought indeed some chance word might be dropped which would afford me the information I wished to obtain, without my running the risk of exciting silly smiles and gossiping whispers by demanding it—but when a week passed and the seat at the desk near the door still remained vacant and when no allusion was made to the circumstance by any individual of the class, when on the contrary I found that all observed a marked silence on the point, I determined, coûte que coûte, to break the ice of this silly reserve. I selected Sylvie as my informant because from her I knew that I should at least get a sensible answer, unaccompanied by wriggle, titter or other flourish of folly.

"Où donc est Mdlle. Henri?" I said one day as I returned an exercise-book I had been examining.

"Elle est partie, Monsieur."

"Partie! et pour combien de temps? Quand reviendra-t-elle?"

"Elle est partie pour toujours, Monsieur—elle ne reviendra plus."

"Ah!" was my involuntary exclamation, then—after a pause,

"En êtes-vous bien sûre, Sylvie?"

"Oui, oui, Monsieur, Mademoiselle la Directrice nous l'a dit elle-même il y a deux ou trois jours."

And I could pursue my inquiries no further, time, place and circumstances forbade my adding another word; I could neither comment on what had been said nor demand further particulars—a question as to the reason of the teacher's departure, as to whether it had been voluntary or otherwise, was indeed on my lips, but I suppressed it—there were listeners all round. An hour after—in passing Sylvie in the corridor as she was putting on her bonnet—I stopped short and asked:

"Sylvie, do you know Mdlle. Henri's address? I have some books of hers—" I added carelessly, "and I should wish to send them to her."

"No, Monsieur," replied Sylvie, "but perhaps Rosalie the portress will be able to give it you."

Rosalie's cabinet was just at hand, I stepped in and repeated the inquiry. Rosalie—a smart French grisette—looked up from her work with a knowing smile—precisely the sort of smile I had been so desirous to avoid exciting. Her answer was prepared, she knew nothing whatever of Mdlle. Henri's address, had never known it. Turning from her with impatience—for I believed she lied and was hired to lie—I almost knocked down some one who had been standing at my back; it was the Directress—my abrupt movement made her recoil two or three steps—I was obliged to apologize, which I did more concisely than politely. No man likes to be dogged and in the very irritable mood in which I then was—the sight of Mdlle. Reuter thoroughly incensed me. At the moment I turned, her countenance looked hard, dark and inquisitive, her eyes were bent upon me with an expression of almost hungry curiosity; I had scarce caught this phase of physiognomy ere it had vanished; a bland smile played on her features, my harsh apology was received with good-humoured facility.

"Oh don't mention it, Monsieur—you only touched my hair with your elbow—it is no worse—only a little dishevelled—" She shook it back and passing her fingers through her curls—loosened them into more numerous and flowing ringlets; then she went on with vivacity:

"Rosalie, I was coming to tell you to go instantly and close the windows of the salon, the wind is rising and the muslin curtains will be covered with dust."

Rosalie departed. "Now," thought I, "this will not do; Mdlle. Reuter thinks her meanness in eaves-dropping is screened by her art in devising a pretext, whereas the muslin curtains she speaks of are not more transparent than this same pretext." An impulse came over me to thrust the flimsy screen aside and confront her craft boldly with a word or two of plain truth. "The rough-shod foot treads most firmly on slippery ground," thought I, so I began:

"Mdlle. Henri has left your establishment; been dismissed I presume?"

"Ah, I wished to have a little conversation with you, Monsieur," replied the Directress with the most natural and affable air in the world; "but we cannot talk quietly here; will Monsieur step into the garden a minute?" And she preceded me, stepping out through the glass-door I have before mentioned.

"There," said she—when we had reached the centre of the middle alley and when the foliage of shrubs and trees, now in their summer pride, closing behind and around us, shut out the view of the house and thus imparted a sense of seclusion even to this little plot of ground in the very core of a capital:

"There—one feels quiet and free when there are only pear-trees and rose-bushes about one; I daresay you, like me, monsieur, are sometimes tired of being eternally in the midst of life; of having human faces always round you, human eyes always upon you, human voices always in your ear—I am sure I often wish intensely for liberty to spend a whole month in the country at some little farm house, bien gentille, bien propre, tout entourée de champs et de bois; quelle vie charmante que la vie champêtre! N'est-ce pas, Monsieur?"

"Cela dépend, Mademoiselle."

"Que le vent est bon et frais!" continued the Directress, and she was right there—for it was a south wind, soft and sweet—I carried my hat in my hand and this gentle breeze, passing through my hair, soothed my temples like balm. Its refreshing effect however penetrated no deeper than the mere surface of the frame, for as I walked by the side of Mdlle. Reuter, my heart was still hot within me, and while I was musing the fire burned, then spake I with my tongue:

"I understand Mdlle. Henri is gone from hence and will not return?"

"Ah, true! I meant to have named the subject to you some days ago but my time is so completely taken up—I cannot do half the things I wish—have you never experienced what it is, Monsieur, to find the day too short by twelve hours for your numerous duties?"

"Not often—Mdlle. Henri's departure was not voluntary—I presume? If it had been she would certainly have given me some intimation of it, being my pupil."

"Oh—did she not tell you? that was strange—for my part I never thought of adverting to the subject; when one has so many things to attend to, one is apt to forget little incidents that are not of primary importance."

"You consider Mdlle. Henri's dismission then as a very insignificant event?"

"Dismission? Ah! she was not dismissed; I can say with truth,

Monsieur—that since I became the head of this establishment no master or teacher has ever been *dismissed* from it."

"Yet some have left it, Mademoiselle?"

"Many—I have found it necessary to change frequently—a change of instructors is often beneficial to the interests of a school; it gives life and variety to the proceedings; it amuses the pupils and suggests to the parents the idea of exertion and progress."

"Yet when you are tired of a professor or maîtresse you scruple to dismiss them?"

"No need to have recourse to such extreme measures, I assure you. Allons, Monsieur le professeur—asseyons-nous—je vais vous donner une petite leçon dans votre état d'instituteur." (I wish I might write all she said to me in French—it loses sadly by being translated into English.) We had now reached *the* garden-chair; the Directress sat down and signed to me to sit by her, but I only rested my knee on the seat and stood leaning my head and arm against the embowering branch of a huge laburnam whose golden flowers, blent with the dusky green leaves of a lilac-bush, formed a mixed arch of shade and sunshine over the retreat. Mdlle. Reuter sat silent a moment; some novel movements were evidently working in her mind and they shewed their nature on her astute brow; she was meditating some chef-d'œuvre of policy. Convinced by several months' experience that the affectation of virtues she did not possess was unavailing to ensnare me; aware that I had read her real nature and would believe nothing of the character she gave out as being hers, she had determined at last to try a new key, and see if the lock of my heart would yield to that; a little audacity—a word of truth, a glimpse of the real. "Yes—I will try," was her inward resolve, and then her blue eye glittered upon me—it did not flash—nothing of flame ever kindled in its temperate gleam.

"Monsieur fears to sit by me?" she inquired playfully.

"I have no wish to usurp Pelet's place," I answered, for I had got the habit of speaking to her bluntly—a habit begun in anger—but continued because I saw that instead of offending—it fascinated her. She cast down her eyes and drooped her eye-lids—she sighed uneasily—she turned with an anxious gesture as if she would give me the idea of a bird that flutters in its cage and would fain fly from its jail and jailor, and seek its natural mate and pleasant nest.

"Well—and your lesson?" I demanded briefly.

"Ah!" she exclaimed, recovering herself, "you are so young, so frank and fearless—so talented, so impatient of imbecility, so disdainful of vulgarity—you need a lesson; here it is then: far more is to be done in this world by Dexterity than by Strength—but perhaps you knew that before, for there is delicacy as well as power in your character—policy as well as pride?"

"Go on," said I, and I could hardly help smiling—the flattery was so piquant, so finely-seasoned. She caught the prohibited smile though I passed my hand over my mouth to conceal it—and again she made room for me to sit beside her—I shook my head—though temptation penetrated to my senses at the moment and once more I told her to go on.

"Well then—if ever you are at the head of a large establishment, dismiss nobody.—To speak truth, monsieur, (and to you I will speak truth) I despise people who are always making rows, blustering, sending off one to the right and another to the left, urging and hurrying circumstances. I'll tell you what I like best to do, monsieur, shall I?" She looked up again; she had compounded her glance well this time, much archness, more deference, a spicy dash of coquetry, an unveiled consciousness of capacity; I nodded—she treated me like the great Mogul so I became the great Mogul as far as she was concerned.

"I like, monsieur, to take my knitting in my hands and to sit quietly down in my chair; circumstances defile past me, I watch their march—so long as they follow the course I wish, I say nothing and do nothing; I don't clap my hands and cry out bravo! How lucky I am! to attract the attention and envy of my neighbours; I am merely passive; but when events fall out ill—when circumstances become adverse, I watch very vigilantly; I knit on still, and still I hold my tongue, but every now and then, monsieur, I just put my toe out—so—and give the rebellious circumstance a little secret push without noise, which sends it the way I wish, and I am successful after all and nobody has seen my expedient. So, when teachers or masters become troublesome and inefficient—when, in short, the interests of the school would suffer from their retaining their places, I mind my knitting, events progress, circumstances glide past, I see one which if pushed ever so little awry will render untenable the post I wish to have vacated, the deed is done—the stumbling block removed—and no one saw me—I have not made an enemy, I am rid of an incumbrance."

A moment since and I thought her alluring—this speech concluded—I looked on her with distaste: "Just like you," was my cold answer. "And in this way you have ousted Mdlle. Henri? you wanted her office, therefore you rendered it intolerable to her?"

"Not at all, monsieur—I was merely anxious about Mdlle Henri's health—no—your moral sight is clear and piercing, but there you have failed to discover the truth—I took—I have always taken a real interest in Mdlle. Henri's welfare—I did not like her going out in all weathers—I thought it would be more advantageous for her to obtain a permanent situation—besides I considered her now qualified to do something more than teach sewing—I reasoned with her—left the decision to herself—she saw the correctness of my views and adopted them."

"Excellent! and now Mademoiselle you will have the goodness to give me her address."

"Her address!" and a sombre and stony change came over the mien of the Directress. "Her address? ah!—well—I wish I could oblige you, Monsieur, but I cannot, and I will tell you why; whenever I myself asked her for her address—she always evaded the inquiry—I thought—I may be wrong—but I *thought* her motive for doing so, was a natural though mistaken reluctance to introduce me to some probably very poor abode; her means were narrow, her origin obscure—she lives somewhere doubtless in the 'basse ville'."

"I'll not lose sight of my best pupil yet," said I, "though she were born of beggars and lodged in a cellar—for the rest it is absurd to make a bugbear of her origin to me—I happen to know that she was a Swiss pastor's daughter, neither more nor less—and as to her narrow means—I care nothing for the poverty of her purse so long as her heart overflows with affluence."

"Your sentiments are perfectly noble, monsieur," said the Directress—affecting to suppress a yawn—her sprightliness was now extinct, her temporary candour shut up—the little, red-coloured, piratical-looking pennon of audacity she had allowed to float a minute in the air was furled, and the broad, sober-hued flag of dissimulation again hung low over the citadel; I did not like her thus—so I cut short the tête à tête and departed.

CHAPTER XIX

NOVELISTS should never allow themselves to weary of the study of real Life—if they observed this duty conscientiously, they would give us fewer pictures checquered with vivid contrasts of light and shade; they would seldom elevate their heros and heroines to the heights of rapture—still seldomer sink them to the depths of despair; for if we rarely taste the fulness of joy in this life, we yet more rarely savour the acrid bitterness of hopeless anguish; unless indeed, we have plunged like beasts into sensual indulgence, abused, strained, stimulated, again overstrained and at last destroyed our faculties for enjoyment; then truly, we may find ourselves without support, robbed of hope. Our agony is great and how can it end? We have broken the spring of our powers; life must be all suffering—too feeble to conceive faith—death must be darkness—God, spirits, religion can have no place in our collapsed minds where linger only hideous and polluting recollections of vice; and Time brings us on to the brink of the grave and Dissolution flings us in—a rag eaten through and through with disease, wrung together with pain, stamped into the churchyard sod by the inexorable heel of Despair.

But the man of regular life and rational mind never despairs. He loses his property—it is a blow—he staggers a moment; then, his energies, roused by the smart, are at work to seek a remedy; activity soon mitigates regret. Sickness affects him, he takes patience, endures what he cannot cure. Acute pain racks him, his writhing limbs know not where to find rest, he leans on Hope's anchor. Death takes from him what he loves, roots up and tears violently away the stem round which his affections were twined—a dark, dismal time, a frightful wrench—but some morning—Religion looks into his desolate house with sunrise, and says that in another world, another life, he shall meet his kindred again. She speaks of that world as a place unsullied by sin—of that life, as an era unembittered by suffering; she mightily strengthens her consolation by connecting with it two ideas—which mortals cannot comprehend but on which they love to repose—Eternity, Immortality; and the mind of the mourner, being filled with an image, faint yet glorious, of heavenly hills all light and peace, of a spirit resting there in bliss, of a day when his spirit shall also alight there, free and disembodied, of a re-union perfected by love purified from fear, he takes courage—goes out to encounter the necessities and discharge the duties of life, and though Sadness may never lift her burden from his mind, Hope will enable him to support it.

Well—and what suggested all this? and what is the inference to be drawn therefrom? What suggested it is the circumstance of my best pupil—my treasure, being snatched from my hands and put away out of my reach—the inference to be drawn from it is—that being a steady, reasonable man I did not allow the resentment, disappointment and grief, engendered in my mind by this evil chance, to grow there to any monstrous size, nor did I allow them to monopolize the whole space of my heart—I pent them on the contrary in one strait and secret nook. In the day-time too—when I was about my duties—I put them on the silent system and it was only after I had closed the door of my chamber at night that I somewhat relaxed my severity towards these morose nurslings and allowed vent to their language of murmurs—then in revenge—they sat on my pillow, haunted my bed and kept me awake with their long, midnight cry.

A week passed—I had said nothing more to Mdlle. Reuter, I had been calm in my demeanour to her though, stony cold and hard; when I looked at her, it was with the glance fitting to be bestowed on one who I knew had consulted Jealousy as an adviser and employed Treachery as an instrument; the glance of quiet disdain and rooted distrust. On Saturday evening, ere I left the house—I stept into the salle à manger where she was sitting alone and placing myself before her—I asked with the same tranquil tone and manner that I should have used, had I put the question for the first time:

"Mademoiselle, will you have the goodness to give me the address of Frances Evans Henri?"

A little surprised but not disconcerted—she smilingly disclaimed any knowledge of that address adding, "Monsieur has perhaps forgotten that I explained all about that circumstance before—a week ago?"

"Mademoiselle—" I continued, "you would greatly oblige me by directing me to that young person's abode."

She seemed somewhat puzzled and at last looking up with an admirably counterfeited air of naïveté—she demanded "Does monsieur think I am telling an untruth?"

Still avoiding to give her a direct answer, I said "It is not then your intention, Mademoiselle, to oblige me in this particular?"

"But, monsieur, how can I tell you what I do not know?"

"Very well—I understand you perfectly, mademoiselle—and now I have only two or three words more to say. This is the last week in July—in another month the vacation will commence; have the goodness to avail yourself of the leisure it will afford you to look out for another English master, at the close of August I shall be under the necessity of resigning my post in your establishment."

I did not wait for her comments on this announcement, but bowed and immediately withdrew.

That same evening—soon after dinner—a servant brought me a small packet—it was directed in a hand I knew but had not hoped so soon to see again; being in my own apartment and alone, there was nothing to prevent my immediately opening it; it contained four five-franc pieces and a note in English.

"Monsieur—I came to Mdlle. Reuter's house yesterday, at the time when I knew you would be just about finishing your lesson, and I asked if I might go into the school-room and speak to you. Mdlle. Reuter came out and said you were already gone, it had not yet struck four—so I thought she must be mistaken, but concluded it would be vain to call another day on the same errand. In one sense a note will do as well—it will wrap up the 20frs.—the price of the lessons I have received from you; and if it will not fully express the thanks I owe you in addition, if it will not bid you good-bye as I could wish to have done—if it will not tell you, as I long to do, how sorry I am that I shall probably never see you more—why—spoken words would hardly be more adequate to the task. Had I seen you, I should probably have stammered out something feeble and unsatisfactory, something belying my feelings rather than explaining them—so it is perhaps as well that I was denied admission to your presence. You often remarked, monsieur, that my devoirs dwelt a great deal on fortitude in bearing grief—you said I introduced that theme too often—I find indeed that it is much easier to write about a severe duty than to perform it, for I am oppressed when I see and feel to what a reverse fate has condemned me; you were kind to me, Monsieur—very kind—I am afflicted—I am heart-broken to be quite separated from you—soon I shall have no friend on earth—but it is useless troubling you with my distresses. What claim have I on your sympathy? None; I will then say no more.

Farewell, Monsieur—F.E.Henri.

I put up the note in my pocket-book—I slipped the five franc pieces into my purse—then I took a turn through my narrow chamber.

"Mdlle. Reuter talked about her poverty," said I, "and she is poor, yet she pays her debts and more—I have not yet given her a quarter's lessons and she has sent me a quarter's due. I wonder of what she deprived herself to scrape together the twenty francs—I wonder what sort of a place she has to live in, and what sort of a woman her aunt is—and whether she is likely to get employment to supply the place she has lost. No doubt she will have to trudge about long enough from school to school—to inquire here and apply there—be rejected in this place, disappointed in that. Many an evening she'll go to her bed tired and unsuccessful. And the Directress would not let her in to bid me good-bye? I might not have the chance of standing with her for a few minutes at a window in the school-room and exchanging some half dozen of sentences—getting to know where she lived—putting matters in train for having all things arranged to my mind? No address on the note—" I continued, drawing it again from the pocket-book and examining it on each side of the two leaves. "Women are women—that is certain, and always do business like women; men mechanically put a date and address to their communications. And these five-franc pieces?" (I hauled them forth from my purse—) "if she had offered me them herself instead of tying them up with a thread of green silk in a kind of Lilliputian packet—I could have thrust them back again into her little hand and shut up the small, taper fingers over them—so—and compelled her Shame, her pride, her shyness all to yield to a little bit of determined Will—now, where is she? How can I get at her?"

Opening my chamber-door I walked down into the kitchen.

"Who brought the packet?" I asked of the servant who had delivered it to me.

"Un petit commissionaire, Monsieur."

"Did he say anything?"

"Rien."

And I wended my way up the back-stairs, wondrously the wiser for my enquiries.

"No matter," said I to myself as I again closed the door. "No matter—I'll seek her through Brussels."

And I did. I sought her day by day whenever I had a moment's leisure, for four weeks; I sought her on Sundays all day long; I sought her on the Boulevards, in the Allée verte, in the Park; I sought her in Ste. Gudule and St. Jacques, I sought her in the two protestant chapels; I attended these latter at the German, French and English services, not doubting that I should meet her at one of them. All my researches were absolutely fruitless, my security on the last point was proved by the event to be equally groundless with my other calculations; I stood at the door of each chapel after the service and waited till every individual had come out, scrutinizing every gown, draping a slender form, peering under every bonnet covering a young head; in vain—I saw girlish figures pass me, drawing their black scarves over their sloping shoulders, but none of them had the exact turn and air of Mdlle. Henri's; I saw pale and thoughtful faces "encadrées" in bands of brown hair but I never found her forehead, her eyes, her eyebrows. All the features of all the faces I met seemed frittered away, because my eye failed to recognize the peculiarities it was bent upon; an ample space of brow and a large, dark and serious eye with a fine but decided line of eye-brow traced above.

"She has probably left Brussels—perhaps is gone to England as she said she would," muttered I inwardly, as on the afternoon of the fourth Sunday I turned from the door of the chapel royal which the door-keeper had just closed and locked, and followed in the wake of the last of the congregation, now dispersed and dispersing over the square. I had soon outwalked the couples of English gentlemen and ladies—(gracious Goodness! why don't they dress better? My eye is yet filled with visions of the high-flounced, slovenly and tumbled dresses in costly silk and satin, of the large, unbecoming collars in expensive lace, of the ill-cut coats and strangely-fashioned pantaloons which every Sunday, at the English service, filled the chairs of the Chapel royal and after it, issuing forth into the square, came into disadvantageous contrast with freshly and trimly attired foreign figures, hastening to attend salut at the church of Coburg.) I had passed these pairs of Britons and the groups of pretty British children and the British footmen and waiting-maids, I had crossed the Place royale and got into the Rue Royale, thence I had diverged into the rue de Louvain—an old and quiet street; I remember that feeling a little hungry and not desiring to go back and take my share of the "goûter" now on the refectory-table at Pelet's, to wit, pistolets and water—I stepped into a baker's and refreshed myself on a couc? (it is a Flemish word—I don't know how to spell it) à Corinthe—anglice—a currant bun—and a cup of coffee, and then I strolled on towards the porte de Louvain. Very soon I was out of the city and slowly mounting the hill, which ascends from the gate, I took my time; for the afternoon though cloudy, was very sultry and not a breeze stirred to refresh the atmosphere. No inhabitant of Brussels need wander far to search for Solitude; let him but move half a league from his own city and he will find her brooding still and blank over the wide fields, so drear though so fertile, spread out treeless and trackless round the capital of Brabant. Having gained the summit of the hill and having stood and looked long over the cultured but lifeless campaign, I felt a wish to quit the high-road, which I had hitherto followed, and get in among those tilled grounds—fertile as the beds of a Brobdingnagian kitchen-garden, spreading far and wide even to the boundaries of the horizon, where, from a dusk green, distance changed them to a sullen blue and confused their tints with those of the livid and thunderous-looking sky. Accordingly I turned up a by-path to the right, I had not followed it far ere it brought me, as I expected, into the fields, amidst which, just before me, stretched a long and lofty white wall enclosing, as it seemed from the foliage shewing above, some thickly planted nursery of yew and cypress, for of that species were the branches resting on the pale parapets and crowding gloomily about a massive cross, planted doubtless on a central eminence and extending its arms, which seemed of black marble, over the summits of those sinister trees. I approached, wondering to what house this well-protected garden appertained; I turned the angle of the wall, thinking to see some stately residence; I was close upon great iron gates; there was a hut serving for a lodge near—but I had no occasion to apply for the key, the gates were open; I pushed one leaf back, rain had rusted its hinges, for it groaned dolefully as they revolved. Thick planting embowered the entrance; passing up the avenue, I saw objects on each hand which, in their own mute language of inscription and sign, explained clearly to what abode I had made my way. This was the house appointed for all living; crosses, monuments, and garlands of everlastings announced "The protestant Cemetery, outside the gate of Louvain."

The place was large enough to afford half an hour's strolling without the monotony of treading continually the same path and, for those who love to peruse the annals of grave-yards, here was variety of inscription enough to occupy the attention for double or treble that space of time. Hither people of many kindreds, tongues and nations had brought their dead for interment, and here, on pages of stone, of marble and of brass, were written names, dates, last tributes of pomp or love in English, in French, in German and Latin. Here the Englishman had erected a marble monument over the remains of his Mary Smith or Jane Brown and inscribed it only with her name; there the French widower had shaded the grave of his Elmire or Célestine with a brilliant thicket of roses, amidst which a little tablet rising, bore an equally bright testimony to her countless virtues. Every nation, tribe and kindred mourned after its own fashion and how soundless was the mourning of all! My own tread though slow and upon smooth-rolled paths seemed to startle because it formed the sole break to a silence—otherwise—total. Not only the winds—but the very fitful, wandering airs were that afternoon, as by common consent, all fallen asleep in their various quarters—the North was hushed, the South silent, the East sobbed not, nor did the West whisper. The clouds in heaven were condensed and dull but apparently quite motionless; under the trees of this cemetery nestled a warm, breathless gloom, out of which the cypresses stood up straight and mute, above which the willows hung low and still, where the flowers, as languid as fair, waited listless for night-dew or thunder-shower, where the tombs and those they hid, lay impassible to sun or shadow, to rain or drought.

Importuned by the sound of my own footsteps, I turned off upon the turf and slowly advanced to a grove of yews; I saw something stir among the stems, I thought it might be a broken branch swinging, my short-sighted vision had caught no form, only a sense of motion, but the dusky shade passed on, appearing and disappearing at the openings in the avenue. I soon discerned it was a living thing and a human being, and drawing nearer, I perceived it was a woman, pacing slowly to and fro and evidently deeming herself alone as I had deemed myself alone, and meditating as I had been meditating. Erelong she returned to a seat which I fancy she had but just quitted or I should have caught sight of her before—it was in a nook, screened by a clump of trees—there was the white wall before her and a little stone set up against the wall and, at the foot of the stone was an allotment of turf freshly turned up, a new-made grave. I put on my spectacles and passed softly close behind her; glancing at the inscription on the stone—I read "Julienne Henri, died at Brussels aged sixty. Augst. 10th. 18——." Having perused this inscription I looked down at the form sitting bent and thoughtful just under my eyes, unconscious of the vicinity of any living thing; it was a slim, youthful figure in mourning apparel of the plainest black stuff, with a little simple black crape bonnet; I felt, as well as saw, who it was, and moving neither hand nor foot,

I stood some moments enjoying the security of conviction. I had sought her for a month and had never discovered one of her traces, never met a hope or seized a chance of encountering her anywhere; I had been forced to loosen my grasp on expectation and, but an hour ago, had sunk slackly under the discouraging thought that the current of life and the impulse of destiny had swept her forever from my reach; and behold—while bending sullenly earthward beneath the pressure of despondency, while following with my eyes the track of sorrow on the turf of a grave-yard, here was my lost jewel dropped on the tear-fed herbage, nestling in the mossy and mouldy roots of yew-trees!

Frances sat very quiet, her elbow on her knee and her head on her hand; I knew she could retain a thinking attitude a long time without change; at last a tear fell, she had been looking at the name on the stone before her and her heart had no doubt endured one of those constrictions with which the desolate living, regretting the dead, are at times so sorely oppressed. Many tears rolled down, which she wiped away again and again with her handkerchief, some distressed sobs escaped her and then, the paroxysm over, she sat quiet as before. I put my hand gently on her shoulder, no need further to prepare her, for she was neither hysterical nor liable to fainting-fits; a sudden push indeed might have startled her, but the contact of my quiet touch merely woke attention as I wished and, though she turned quickly, yet so lightning-swift is thought—in some minds especially—I believe the wonder of what—the consciousness of who it was that thus stole unawares on her solitude, had passed through her brain and flashed into her heart even before she had effected that hasty movement; at least, Amazement had hardly opened her eyes and raised them to mine, ere Recognition informed their irids with most speaking brightness; Nervous Surprise had hardly discomposed her features, ere a sentiment of most vivid joy shone clear and warm on her whole countenance—I had hardly time to observe that she was wasted and pale, ere called to feel a responsive inward pleasure by the sense of most full and exquisite pleasure glowing in the animated flush and shining in the expansive light, now diffused over my pupil's face. It was the summer sun flashing out after the heavy summer shower, and what fertilizes more rapidly than that beam, burning almost like fire in its ardour?

I hate boldness—that boldness which is of the brassy brow and insensate nerves, but I love the courage of the strong heart, the fervour of the generous blood; I loved with passion the light of Frances Evans' clear hazel eye when it did not fear to look straight into mine; I loved the tones with which she uttered the words: "Mon maître! Mon Maître!"

I loved the movement with which she confided her hand to my hand; I loved her, as she stood there, pennyless and parentless, for a sensualist—charmless, for me a treasure, my best object of sympathy on earth, thinking such thoughts as I thought, feeling such feelings as I felt, my ideal of the shrine in which to seal my stores of love; personification of discretion and forethought, of diligence and perseverance, of self-denial and self-control—those guardians, those trusty keepers of the gift I longed to confer on her—the gift of all my affections; Model of truth and honour, of independence and conscientiousness, those refiners and sustainers of an honest life; silent possessor of a well of tenderness, of a flame as genial as still, as pure as quenchless, of natural feeling, natural passion, those sources of refreshment and comfort to the sanctuary of home. I knew how quietly and how deeply the well bubbled in her heart; I knew how the more dangerous flame burned safely under the eye of reason; I had seen when the fire shot up a moment high and vivid, when the accelerated heat troubled life's current in its channels, I had seen Reason reduce the rebel and humble its blaze to embers. I had confidence in Frances Evans, I had respect for her, and as I drew her arm through mine and led her out of the cemetery, I felt I had another sentiment, as strong as confidence, as firm as respect, more fervid than either—that of love.

"Well, my pupil," said I, as the ominous-sounding gate swung to behind us, "well—I have found you again: a month's search has seemed long and I little thought to have discovered my lost sheep, straying amongst graves."

Never had I addressed her but as Mademoiselle before, and to speak thus, was to take up a tone new to both her and me. Her answer apprised me that this language ruffled none of her feelings, woke no discord in her heart:

"Mon Maître," she said, "have you troubled yourself to seek me? I little imagined you would think much of my absence—but I grieved bitterly to be taken away from you—I was sorry for that circumstance when heavier troubles ought to have made me forget it."

"Your Aunt is dead?"

"Yes, a fortnight since and she died full of regret which I could not chase from her mind; she kept repeating even during the last night of her existence, "Frances, you will be so lonely when I am gone, so friendless: she wished too, that she could have been buried in Switzerland and it was I who persuaded her in her old age to leave the banks of Lake Leman and to come, only as it seems, to die, in this flat region of Flanders: willingly would I have observed her last wish and taken her remains back to our own country, but that was impossible; I was forced to lay her here."

"She was ill but a short time, I presume?"

"But three weeks; when she began to sink, I asked Mdlle. Reuter's leave to stay with her and wait on her; I readily got leave."

"Do you return to the Pensionnat?" I demanded hastily.

"Monsieur, when I had been at home a week, Mdlle. Reuter called one evening, just after I had got my aunt to bed; she went into her room to speak to her and was extremely civil and affable, as she always is; afterwards she came and sat with me a long time and, just as she rose to go away, she said: 'Mademoiselle, I shall not soon cease to regret your departure from my establishment, though indeed it is true that you have taught your class of pupils so well that they are all quite accomplished in the little works you manage so skilfully, and have not the slightest need of further instruction; my second teacher must in future supply your place, with regard to the younger pupils, as well as she can, though she is indeed an inferior artiste to you, and doubtless it will be your part now to assume a higher position in your calling; I am sure you will everywhere find schools and families willing to profit by your talents.' And then she paid me my last quarter's salary. I asked, as Mademoiselle would no doubt think, very bluntly, if she designed to discharge me from her establishment. She smiled at my inelegance of speech and answered that 'our connexion as employer and employed was certainly dissolved but that she hoped still to retain the pleasure of my acquaintance, she should always be happy to see me as a friend;' and then she said something about the excellent condition of the streets and the long continuance of fine weather and went away quite cheerful."

I laughed inwardly; all this was so like the Directress, so like what I had expected and guessed of her conduct; and then the exposure and proof of her lie, unconsciously afforded by Frances: "She had frequently applied for Mdlle. Henri's address, forsooth; Mdlle. Henri had always evaded giving it &c. &c.;" and here I found her a visitor at the very house of whose locality she had professed absolute ignorance!

Any comments I might have intended to make on my pupil's communication, were checked by the plashing of large rain-drops on our faces and on the path, and by the muttering of a distant, but coming storm. The warning obvious in stagnant air and leaden sky had already induced me to take the road leading back to Brussels, and now I hastened my own steps and those of my companion, and as our way lay down-hill, we got on rapidly. There was an interval after the fall of the first broad drops before heavy rain came on, in the meantime we had passed through the porte de Louvain and were again in the city.

"Where do you live?" I asked. "I will see you safe home."

"Rue Notre Dame aux Neiges," answered Frances—it was not far from the rue de Louvain and we stood on the door-steps of the house we sought, ere the clouds, severing with loud peal and shattered cataract of lightning, emptied their livid folds in a torrent heavy, prone and broad.

"Come in! Come in!" said Frances as, after putting her into the house, I paused ere I followed: the word decided me; I stepped across the threshold, shut the door on the rushing, flashing, whitening storm and followed her up-stairs to her apartments. Neither she nor I were wet; a projection over the door had warded off the straight-descending flood; none but the first, large drops had touched our garments; one minute more and we should not have had a dry thread on us.

Stepping over a little mat of green wool, I found myself in a small room with a painted floor and a square of green carpet in the middle; the articles of furniture were few, but all bright and exquisitely clean: order reigned through its narrow limits; such order as it soothed my punctilious soul to behold—and I had hesitated to enter the abode because I apprehended after all that Mdlle. Reuter's hint about its extreme poverty might be too well-founded and I feared to embarrass the lace-mender by entering her lodgings unawares! Poor the place might be; poor truly it was, but its neatness was better than elegance and, had but a bright little fire shone on that clean hearth, I should have deemed it more attractive than a palace. No fire was there however, and no fuel laid ready to light; the lace-mender was unable to allow herself that indulgence, especially now when, deprived by death of her sole relative, she had only her own unaided exertions to rely on. Frances went into an inner room to take off her bonnet and she came out, a model of frugal neatness, with her well-fitting black stuff dress, so accurately defining her elegant bust and taper waist, with her spotless white collar turned back from a fair and shapely neck, with her plenteous brown hair arranged in smooth bands on her temples and in a large Grecian plat behind: ornaments she had none, neither broach, ring nor ribbon; she did well enough without them; perfection of fit, proportion of form, grace of carriage agreeably supplied their place. Her eye, as she re-entered the small-sitting-room, instantly sought mine, which was just then lingering on the hearth; I knew she read at once the sort of inward ruth and pitying pain which the chill vacancy of that hearth stirred in my soul: quick to penetrate, quick to determine and quicker to put in practice, she had in a moment tied a holland apron round her waist; then she disappeared and reappeared with a basket; it had a cover; she opened it, and produced wood and coal; deftly and compactly she arranged them in the grate. "It is her whole stock and she will exhaust it out of hospitality," thought I.

"What are you going to do?" I asked. "Not surely to light a fire this hot evening? I shall be smothered."

"Indeed, Monsieur, I feel it very chilly since the rain began, besides I must boil the water for my tea—for I take tea on Sundays, so you will be obliged to try and bear the heat."

She had struck a light; the wood was already in a blaze, and truly, when contrasted with the darkness, the wild tumult of the tempest without, that peaceful glow which began to beam on the now animated hearth, seemed very cheering. A low, purring sound from some quarter announced that another being, besides myself, was pleased with the change; a black cat, roused by the light from its sleep on a little cushioned foot-stool, came and rubbed its head against Frances' gown, as she knelt; she caressed it saying it had been a favourite with her "pauvre tante Julienne."

The fire being lit, the hearth swept, and a small kettle of a very antique pattern, such as I thought I remembered to have seen in old farm-houses in England, placed over the now ruddy flame, Frances' hands were washed and her apron removed in an instant; then she opened a cupboard and took out a tea-tray, on which she had soon arranged a china tea-equipage whose pattern, shape and size denoted a remote antiquity; a little, old-fashioned silver spoon was deposited in each saucer, and a pair of silver tongs, equally old-fashioned were laid on the sugar-bason; from the cupboard too, was produced a tiny silver cream-ewer, not larger than an egg-shell. While making these preparations, she chanced to look up, and reading curiosity in my eyes, she smiled and asked:

"Is this like England, Monsieur?"

"Like the England of a hundred years ago," I replied.

"Is it truly? Well, everything on this tray is at least a hundred years old: these cups, these spoons, this ewer are all heir-looms; my great-grandmother left them to my grandmother, she to my mother, and my mother brought them with her from England to

Switzerland and left them to me; and ever since I was a little girl, I have thought I should like to carry them back to England, whence they came."

She put some pistolets on the table; she made the tea, as foreigners do make tea; i.e. at the rate of a tea-spoonful to half a dozen cups; she placed me a chair and, as I took it, she asked with a sort of exultation:

"Will it make you think yourself at home for a moment?"

"If I had a home in England, I believe it would recall it," I answered, and in truth there was a sort of illusion in seeing the fair-complexioned, English-looking girl presiding at the English meal and speaking the English language.

"You have then no home?" was her remark.

"None—nor ever have had; if ever I possess a home, it must be of my own making, and the task is yet to begin." And as I spoke, a pang, new to me, shot across my heart: it was a pang of mortification at the humility of my position and the inadequacy of my means; while with that pang was born a strong desire to do more, earn more, be more, possess more; and in the increased possessions, my roused and eager spirit panted to include the home I had never had, the wife I inwardly vowed to win.

Frances' tea was little better than hot water, sugar and milk; but I liked it and it cheered me; and her pistolets, with which she could not offer me butter, were sweet to my palate as manna. The repast over, and the treasured plate and porcelain being washed and put by; the bright table rubbed still brighter, "le chat de ma tante Julienne" also being fed with provisions brought forth on a plate for its special use, a few stray cinders and a scattering of ashes too, being swept from the hearth, Frances at last sat down; and then, as she took a chair opposite to me, she betrayed, for the first time, a little embarrassment; and no wonder, for indeed I had unconsciously watched her rather too closely; followed all her steps and all her movements a little too perseveringly with my eyes; for she mesmerized me by the grace and alertness of her action; by the deft, cleanly, and even decorative effect resulting from each touch of her slight and fine fingers; and when, at last, she subsided to stillness, the intelligence of her face seemed beauty to me, and I dwelt on it accordingly. Her colour however rising, rather than settling with repose and her eyes remaining downcast, though I kept waiting for the lids to be raised that I might drink a ray of the light I loved; a light where fire dissolved in softness, where affection tempered penetration, where just now at least, pleasure played with thought: this expectation not being gratified, I began at last to suspect that I had probably myself to blame for the disappointment; I must cease gazing and begin talking if I wished to break the spell under which she now sat motionless; so recollecting the composing effect which an authoritative tone and manner had ever been wont to produce on her, I said,

"Get one of your English books, Mademoiselle, for the rain yet falls heavily, and will probably detain me half an hour longer."

Released and set at ease, up she rose, got her book and accepted at once the chair I placed for her at my side. She had selected "Paradise Lost" from her shelf of classics—thinking, I suppose, the religious character of the book best adapted it to Sunday—I told her to begin at the beginning, and while she read Milton's invocation to that heavenly Muse who on the "secret top of Oreb or Sinai" had taught the Hebrew Shepherd how in the womb of chaos, the conception of a world had originated and ripened—I enjoyed undisturbed the treble pleasure of having her near me, hearing the sound of her voice, a sound sweet and satisfying in my ear, and looking, by intervals, at her face: of this last privilege I chiefly availed myself when I found fault with an intonation, a pause, or an emphasis; as long as I dogmatized I might also gaze, without exciting too warm a flush.

"Enough;" said I when she had gone through some half dozen pages, (a work of time with her—for she read slowly and paused often to ask and receive information) "enough; and now the rain is ceasing and I must soon go." For indeed at that moment, looking towards the window, I saw it all blue; the thunder-clouds were broken and scattered, and the setting August sun sent a gleam like the reflection of rubies through the lattice. I got up; I drew on my gloves.

"You have not yet found another situation to supply the place of that from which you were dismissed by Mdlle. Reuter?"

"No, Monsieur; I have made inquiries everywhere, but they all ask me for references and to speak truth I do not like to apply to the Directress, because I consider she acted neither justly nor honourably towards me—she used underhand means to set my pupils against me, and thereby render me unhappy while I held my place in her establishment and she eventually deprived me of it by a masked and hypocritical manœuvre—pretending that she was acting for my good, but really snatching from me my chief means of subsistence at a crisis when not only my own life but that of another, depended on my exertions; of her, I will never more ask a favour."

"How then do you propose to get on? How do you live now?"

"I have still my lace-mending trade; with care it will keep me from starvation, and I doubt not by dint of exertion to get better employment yet; it is only a fortnight since I began to try; my courage or hopes are by no means worn out yet."

"And if you get what you wish—what then? what are your ultimate views?"

"To save enough to cross the Channel—I always look to England as my Canaan."

"Well—well—erelong I shall pay you another visit, good evening now," and I left her rather abruptly—I had much ado to resist a strong inward impulse, urging me to take a warmer, a more expressive leave: what so natural as to fold her for a moment in a close embrace, to imprint one kiss on her cheek or forehead? I was not unreasonable—that was all I wanted; satisfied in that point, I could go away content—and Reason denied me even this, she ordered me to turn my eyes from her face and my steps from her apartment, to quit her as dryly and coldly as I would have quitted old Mde. Pelet. I obeyed but I swore rancorously to be avenged one day. "I'll earn a right to do as I please in this matter or I'll die in the contest. I have one object before me now—to get that Genevese girl for my wife; and my wife she shall be—that is, provided she has as much—or half as much regard for her master as he has for her. And would she be so docile, so smiling, so happy under my instructions if she had not? Would she sit at my side when I dictate or correct, with such a still, contented, halcyon mien?" For I had ever remarked that however sad or harrassed her countenance might be when I entered a room; yet after I had been near her, spoken to her a few words, given her some directions, uttered perhaps some reproofs, she would, all at once, nestle into a nook of happiness and look up serene and revived. The reproofs suited her best of all: while I scolded she would chip away with her pen-knife at a pencil or a pen; fidgetting a little, pouting a little, defending herself by monosyllables, and when I deprived her of the pen or pencil, fearing it would be all cut away, and when I interdicted even the monosyllabic defence, for the purpose of working up the subdued excitement a little higher, she would at last raise her eyes and give me a certain glance, sweetened with gaiety, and pointed with defiance, which, to speak truth, thrilled me as nothing had ever done; and made me, in a fashion (though happily she did not know it), her subject, if not her slave. After such little scenes, her spirits would maintain their flow, often, for some hours, and as I remarked before, her health therefrom took a sustenance and vigour which, previously to the event of her Aunt's death and her dismissal, had almost recreated her whole frame.

It has taken me several minutes to write these last sentences; but I had thought all their purport during the brief interval of descending the stairs from Frances' room; just as I was opening the outer door, I remembered the twenty francs which I had not restored; I paused: impossible to carry them away with me; difficult to force them back on their original owner; I had now seen her in her own humble abode, witnessed the dignity of her poverty, the pride of order, the fastidious care of conservatism, obvious in the arrangement and economy of her little home; I was sure she would not suffer herself to be excused paying her debts; I was certain the favour of indemnity would be accepted from no hand—perhaps least of all from mine: yet these four five-franc pieces were a burden to my self-respect, and I must get rid of them. An expedient—a clumsy one no doubt, but the best I could devise, suggested itself to me. I darted up the stairs, knocked, re-entered the room as if in haste:

"Mademoiselle—I have forgotten one of my gloves; I must have left it here."

She instantly rose to seek it; as she turned her back, I—being now at the hearth—noiselessly lifted a little vase, one of a set of china ornaments, as old-fashioned as the tea-cups—slipped the money under it, then saying:

"Oh here is my glove! I had dropped it within the fender; good evening, Mademoiselle," I made my second exit. Brief as my impromptu return had been, it had afforded me time to pick up a heart-ache; I remarked that Frances had already removed the red embers of her cheerful little fire from the grate: forced to calculate every item, to save in every detail, she had instantly on my departure, retrenched a luxury, too expensive to be enjoyed alone.

"I am glad it is not yet winter," thought I; "but in two months more come the winds and rains of November; would to God that before then I could earn the right and the power to shovel coals into that grate ad libitum!"

Already the pavement was drying; a balmy and fresh breeze stirred the air, purified by lightning: I left the West behind me, where spread a sky like opal; azure immingled with crimson: the enlarged sun, glorious in Tyrian tints, dipped his brim already; stepping, as I was, eastward, I faced a vast bank of clouds, but also, I had before me the arch of an evening rainbow; a perfect rainbow, high, wide, vivid. I looked long; my eye drank in the scene and I suppose my brain must have absorbed it, for that night, after lying awake in pleasant fever a long time; watching the silent sheet-lightning which still played among the retreating clouds, and flashed silvery over the stars, I at last fell asleep; and then in a dream were re-produced the setting-sun, the bank of clouds, the mighty rainbow. I stood, methought, on a terrace, I leaned over a parapeted wall; there was space below me, depth I could not fathom, but hearing an endless dash of waves, I believed it to be the sea; sea spread to the horizon; sea of changeful green and intense blue: all was soft in the distance; all vapour-veiled. A spark of gold glistened on the line between water and air, floated up, approached, enlarged, changed; the object hung midway between heaven and earth, under the arch of the rainbow; the soft but dusk clouds diffused behind. It hovered as on wings; pearly, fleecy, gleaming air streamed like raiment round it; light, tinted with carnation, coloured what seemed face and limbs; a large star shone with still lustre on an angel's forehead; an upraised arm and hand, glancing like a ray, pointed to the bow overhead, and a voice in my heart whispered:

"Hope smiles on Effort!"

CHAPTER XX

A COMPETENCY was what I wanted; a competency it was now my aim and resolve to secure; but never had I been farther from the mark. With August the school-year (l'année scolaire) closed, the examinations concluded, the prizes were adjudged, the schools dispersed, the gates of all Colleges, the doors of all Pensionnats shut, not to be reopened till the beginning or middle of October. The last day of August was at hand, and what was my position? Had I advanced a step since the commencement of the past quarter? On the contrary, I had receded one: by renouncing my engagement as English Master in Mdlle. Reuter's establishment, I had voluntary cut off £20 from my yearly income; I had diminished my £60 per ann. to £40, and even that sum I now held by a very precarious tenure.

It is some time since I made any reference to M. Pelet; the moonlight walk is, I think, the last incident recorded in this narrative where that gentleman cuts any conspicuous figure: the fact is, since that event, a change had come over the spirit of our intercourse. He indeed, ignorant that the still hour, a cloudless moon and an open lattice had revealed to me the secret of his selfish love and false friendship, would have continued smooth and complaisant as ever; but I grew spiny as a porcupine and inflexible as a blackthorn cudgel—I never had a smile for his raillery, never a moment for his society; his invitations to take coffee with him in his parlour were invariably rejected, and very stiffly and sternly rejected too; his jesting allusions to the Directress (which he still continued) were heard with a grim calm very different from the petulant pleasure they were formerly wont to excite. For a long time Pelet bore with my frigid demeanour very patiently; he even increased his attentions—but finding that even a cringing politeness failed to thaw or move me, he at last altered too; in his turn he cooled; his invitations ceased; his countenance became suspicious and overcast, and I read in the perplexed yet brooding aspect of his brow, a constant examination and comparison of premises, and an anxious endeavour to draw thence some explanatory inference. Erelong, I fancy, he succeeded, for he was not without penetration, perhaps too Mdlle. Zoraïde might have aided him in the solution of the enigma; at any rate I soon found that the uncertainty of doubt had vanished from his manner: renouncing all pretence of friendship and cordiality, he adopted a reserved, formal, but still scrupulously polite deportment. This was the point to which I had wished to bring him and I was now again comparatively at my ease. I did not, it is true, like my position in his house, but being freed from the annoyance of false professions and double-dealing I could endure it, especially as no heroic sentiments of hatred or jealousy of the Director distracted my philosophical soul—he had not I found wounded me in a very tender point, the wound was so soon and so radically healed, leaving only a sense of contempt for the treacherous fashion in which it had been inflicted and a lasting mistrust of the hand which I had detected attempting to stab in the dark.

This state of things continued till about the middle of July and then there was a little change; Pelet came home one night, an hour after his usual time, in a state of unequivocal intoxication; a thing anomalous with him, for if he had some of the worst faults of his countrymen, he had also one at least of their virtues, i.e. sobriety: so drunk however was he upon this occasion that after having roused the whole establishment (except the pupils whose dormitory, being over the classes in a building apart from the dwelling-house, was consequently out of the reach of disturbance), by violently ringing the hall-bell and ordering lunch to be brought in immediately—for he imagined it was noon, whereas the city-bells had just tolled midnight; after having furiously rated the servants for their want of punctuality and gone near to chastise his poor old mother who advised him to go to bed, he began raving dreadfully about "le maudit Anglais, Creemsvort." I had not yet retired; some German books I had got hold of had kept me up late; I heard the uproar below and could distinguish the Director's voice exalted in a manner as appalling as it was unusual. Opening my door a little, I became aware of a demand on his part for "Creemsvort" to be brought down to him that he might cut his throat on the hall-table and wash his honour, which he affirmed to be in a dirty condition, in infernal British blood—"He is either mad or drunk," thought I, "and in either case the old woman and the servants will be the better of a man's assistance;" so I descended straight to the hall. I found him staggering about, his eyes in a fine frenzy rolling; a pretty sight he was—a just medium between the fool and the lunatic.

"Come, M. Pelet," said I, "you had better go to bed," and I took hold of his arm. His excitement of course increased greatly at sight and touch of the individual for whose blood he had been making application: he struggled and struck with fury—but a drunken man is no match for a sober one—and even in his normal state, Pelet's worn-out frame could not have stood against my sound one; I got him up-stairs and, in process of time, to bed. During the operation he did not fail to utter comminations which, though broken, had a sense in them; while stigmatizing me as the treacherous spawn of a perfidious country, he, in the same breath, anathematized Zoraïde Reuter; he termed her "femme sotte et vicieuse" who in a fit of lewd caprice had thrown herself away on an unprincipled adventurer, directing the point of the last appellation by a furious blow, obliquely aimed at me—I left him in the act of bounding elastically out of the bed into which I had tucked him—but as I took the precaution of turning the key in the door behind me, I retired to my own room, assured of his safe custody till the morning, and free to draw undistorted conclusions from the scene I had just witnessed.

Now it was precisely about this time that the Directress, stung by my coldness, bewitched by my scorn, and excited by the preference she suspected me of cherishing for another, had fallen into a snare of her own laying, was herself caught in the meshes of the very passion with which she wished to entangle me: conscious of the state of things in that quarter, I gathered from the condition in which I saw my employer that his ladye-love had betrayed the alienation of her affections—inclinations rather I would say;

affection is a word at once too warm and too pure for the subject—had let him see that the cavity of her hollow heart emptied of his image, was now occupied by that of his usher. It was not without some surprise that I found myself obliged to entertain this view of the case; Pelet, with his old-established school was so convenient, so profitable a match; Zoraïde was so calculating, so interested a woman, I wondered mere personal preference could, in her mind, have prevailed for a moment over worldly advantage: yet it was evident, from what Pelet said, that not only had she repulsed him but had even let slip expressions of partiality for me. One of his drunken exclamations was "And the jade doats on your youth, you raw blockhead! and talks of your noble deportment as she calls your accursed English formality—and your pure morals forsooth! des mœurs de Caton a-t-elle dit—Sotte!" Hers I thought must be a curious soul where in spite of a strong, natural tendency to estimate unduly advantages of wealth and station, the sardonic disdain of a fortuneless subordinate had wrought a deeper impression than could be imprinted by the most flattering assiduities of a prosperous chef-d'institution. I smiled inwardly, and strange to say, though my amour-propre was excited not disagreeably by the conquest, my better feelings remained untouched. Next day when I saw the Directress and when she made an excuse to meet me in the corridor and besought my notice by a demeanour and look, subdued to Helot humility, I could not love, I could scarcely pity her. To answer briefly and dryly some insinuating inquiry about my health; to pass her by with a stern bow, was all I could; her presence and manner had then, and for some time previously and subsequently, a singular effect on me: they sealed up all that was good, elicited all that was noxious in my nature; sometimes they enervated my senses, but they always hardened my heart. I was aware of the detriment done, and quarrelled with myself for the change. I had ever hated a tyrant, and behold the possession of a slave, self-given, went near to transform me into what I abhorred! There was at once a sort of low gratification in receiving this luscious incense from an attractive and still young worshipper and an irritating sense of degradation in the very experience of the pleasure. When she stole about me with the soft step of a slave—I felt at once barbarous and sensual as a pasha—I endured her homage sometimes, sometimes I rebuked it—my indifference or harshness served equally to increase the evil I desired to check—

"Que le dédain lui sied bien!" I once overheard her say to her mother. "Il est beau commme Apollon quand il sourit de son air hautain."

And the jolly old dame laughed and said, she thought her daughter was bewitched for I had no point of a handsome man about me, except being straight and without deformity. "Pour moi," she continued, "il me fait tout l'effet d'un chat-huant, avec ses besicles."

Worthy old girl! I could have gone and kissed her, had she not been a little too old, too fat and too red-faced; her sensible, truthful words seemed so wholesome, contrasted with the morbid illusions of her daughter.

When Pelet awoke on the morning after his frenzy-fit, he retained no recollection of what had happened the previous night, and his mother fortunately had the discretion to refrain from informing him that I had been a witness of his degradation. He did not again have recourse to wine for curing his griefs, but even in his sober mood he soon shewed that the iron of jealousy had entered into his soul. A thorough Frenchman, the national characteristic of ferocity had not been omitted by Nature in compounding the ingredients of his character; it had appeared first in his access of drunken wrath, when some of his demonstrations of hatred to my person were of a truly fiendish character, and now it was more covertly betrayed by momentary contractions of the features, and flashes of fierceness in his light, blue eyes, when their glance chanced to encounter mine. He absolutely avoided speaking to me; I was now spared even the falsehood of his politeness. In this state of our mutual relations, my soul rebelled, sometimes almost ungovernably, against living in the house and discharging the service of such a man; but who is free from the constraint of circumstances? At that time, I was not: I used to rise each morning eager to shake off his yoke, and go out with my portmanteau under my arm, if a beggar at least a freeman; and in the evening when I came back from the Pensionnat de demoiselles, a certain pleasant voice in my ear; a certain face, so intelligent yet so docile, so reflective yet so soft in my eye; a certain cast of character, at once proud and pliant, sensitive and sagacious, serious and ardent, in my head; a certain tone of feeling, fervid and modest, refined and practical, pure and powerful, delighting and troubling my memory—visions of new ties, I longed to contract, of new duties I longed to undertake, had taken the rover and the rebel out of me, and had shewn endurance of my hated lot in the light of a Spartan virtue.

But Pelet's fury subsided; a fortnight sufficed for its rise, progress and extinction: in that space of time the dismissal of the obnoxious teacher had been effected in the neighbouring house, and in the same interval I had declared my resolution to follow and find out my pupil, and upon my application for her address being refused, I had summarily resigned my own post. This last act seemed at once to restore Mdlle. Reuter to her senses; her sagacity, her judgment so long misled by a fascinating delusion, struck again into the right track the moment that delusion vanished. By the right track, I do not mean the steep and difficult path of principle, in that path she never trod—but the plain high-way of Common Sense from which she had of late widely diverged—when there, she carefully sought, and having found, industriously pursued the trail of her old suitor, M. Pelet. She soon overtook him. What arts she employed to soothe and blind him, I know not, but she succeeded both in allaying his wrath and hoodwinking his discernment, as was soon proved by the alteration in his mien and manner; she must have managed to convince him that I neither was, nor ever had been a rival of his, for the fortnight of fury against me terminated in a fit of exceeding graciousness and amenity; not unmixed with a dash of exulting self-complacency, more ludicrous than irritating. Pelet's bachelor's life had been passed in proper French style with due disregard to moral restraint—and I thought his married life promised to be very French also. He often boasted to me what a terror he had been to certain husbands of his acquaintance, I perceived it would not now be difficult to pay him back in his own coin.

The crisis drew on. No sooner had the holidays commenced than note of preparation for some momentous event sounded all through the premises of Pelet: painters, polishers and upholsterers were immediately set to work and there was talk of "la chambre de Madame", "le salon de Madame". Not deeming it probable that the old duenna at present graced with that title in our house, had inspired her son with such enthusiasm of filial piety, as to induce him to fit up apartments expressly for her use, I concluded in common with the cook, the two house-maids and the kitchen-scullion, that a new and more juvenile Madame was destined to be the tenant of these gay chambers. Presently official announcement of the coming event was put forth—in another week's time M. François Pelet, Directeur and Mdlle. Zoraïde Reuter, directrice, were to be joined together in the bands of matrimony. Monsieur, in person, heralded the fact to me, terminating his communication by an obliging expression of his desire that I should continue, as heretofore, his ablest assistant and most trusted friend, and a proposition to raise my salary by an additional 200 francs per annum. I thanked him, gave no conclusive answer at the time, and when he had left me, threw off my blouse, put on my coat, and set out on a long walk outside the porte de Flandre, in order, as I thought, to cool my blood, calm my nerves, and shake my disarranged ideas into some order. In fact I had just received what was virtually my dismissal. I could not conceal, I did not desire to conceal from myself the conviction that being now certain Mdlle. Reuter was destined to become Mde. Pelet—it would not do for me to remain a dependent dweller in the house which was soon to be hers. Her present demeanour towards me was deficient neither in dignity nor propriety—but I knew her former feeling was unchanged. Decorum now repressed, and Policy masked it, but Opportunity would be too strong for either of these—Temptation would shiver their restraints.

I was no pope—I could not boast infallibility—in short—if I stayed, the probability was that in three months' time, a practical

Modern French novel would be in full process of concoction under the roof of the unsuspecting Pelet. Now modern French novels are not to my taste either practically or theoretically. Limited as had yet been my experience of life, I had once had the opportunity of contemplating near at hand an example of the results produced by a course of interesting and romantic domestic treachery. No golden halo of fiction was about this example, I saw it bare and real and it was very loathsome. I saw a mind degraded by the practice of mean subterfuge, by the habit of perfidious deception, and a body depraved by the infectious influence of the vice-polluted soul. I had suffered much from the forced and prolonged view of this spectacle; those sufferings I did not now regret, for their simple recollection acted as a most wholesome antidote to temptation. They had inscribed on my reason the conviction that unlawful pleasure, trenching on another's rights, is delusive and envenomed pleasure—its hollowness disappoints at the time, its poison cruelly tortures afterwards, its effects deprave for ever.

From all this resulted the conclusion that I must leave Pelet's and that instantly; "But," said Prudence, "you know not where to go nor how to live;" and then the dream of True Love came over me: Frances Henri seemed to stand at my side; her slender waist to invite my arm; her hand to court my hand; I felt it was made to nestle in mine; I could not relinquish my right to it, nor could I withdraw my eyes for ever from hers, where I saw so much happiness, such a correspondence of heart with heart; over whose expression I had such influence; where I could kindle bliss, infuse awe, stir deep delight, rouse sparkling spirit, and sometimes waken pleasurable dread. My hopes to win and possess, my resolutions to work and rise, rose in array against me; and here I was about to plunge into the gulph of absolute destitution; "And all this," suggested an inward voice, "because you fear an evil which may never happen!" "It will happen; you *know* it will;" answered that stubborn monitor, conscience. "Do what you feel is right; obey me and even in the sloughs of want I will plant for you firm footing." And then, as I walked fast along the road, there rose upon me a strange, inly-felt idea of some Great Being, unseen but all-present, who in his beneficence desired only my welfare and now watched the struggle of good and evil in my heart, and waited to see whether I should obey his voice, heard in the whispers of my Conscience; or lend an ear to the sophisms by which his enemy and mine, the Spirit of evil, sought to lead me astray. Rough and steep was the path indicated by divine Suggestion; mossy and declining the green way along which Temptation strewed flowers; but whereas, methought, the Deity of love, the Friend of all that exists would smile well-pleased were I to gird up my loins and address myself to the rude ascent, so, on the other hand, each inclination to the velvet declivity seemed to kindle a gleam of triumph on the brow of the man-hating, God-defying Demon. Sharp and short I turned round; fast I retraced my steps; in half an hour I was again at M. Pelet's: I sought him in his study; brief parley, concise explanation sufficed; my manner proved that I was resolved; he perhaps at heart approved my decision. After twenty minutes' conversation I re-entered my own room, self-deprived of the means of living, self-sentenced to leave my present home, with the short notice of a week in which to provide another.

CHAPTER XXI

DIRECTLY as I closed the door, I saw laid on the table two letters; my thought was that they were notes of invitation from the friends of some of my pupils; I had received such marks of attention occasionally, and with me, who had no friends, correspondence of more interest was out of the question; the postman's arrival had never yet been an event of interest to me since I came to Brussels. I laid my hand carelessly on the documents, and coldly and slowly glancing at them, I prepared to break the seals; my eye was arrested and my hand too; I saw what excited me as if I had found a vivid picture where I expected to discover only a blank page: on one cover was an English post-mark; on the other a lady's clear, fine autograph; the last, I opened first.

"Monsieur, I found out what you had done the very morning after your visit to me; you might be sure I should dust the china every day, and as no one but you had been in my room for a week and as fairy-money is not current in Brussels, I could not doubt who left the twenty francs on the chimney-piece. I thought I heard you stir the vase when I was stooping to look for your glove under the table, and I wondered you should imagine it had got into such a little cup. Now, Monsieur, the money is not mine and I shall not keep it; I will not send it in this note because it might be lost, besides it is heavy, but I will restore it to you the first time I see you, and you must make no difficulties about taking it; because in the first place I am sure, Monsieur, you can understand that one likes to pay one's debts; that it is satisfactory to owe no man anything; and in the second place I can now very well afford to be honest as I am provided with a situation. This last circumstance is indeed the reason of my writing to you, for it is pleasant to communicate good news and in these days I have only my master to whom I can tell anything.

A week ago, Monsieur, I was sent for by a Mrs. Wharton, an English lady; her eldest daughter was going to be married and some rich relation having made her a present of a veil and dress in costly old lace, as precious, they said, almost as jewels, but a little damaged by time, I was commissioned to put them in repair. I had to do it at the house, they gave me besides some embroidery to complete and nearly a week elapsed before I had finished everything. While I worked, Miss Wharton often came into the room and sat with me, and so did Mrs. Wharton; they made me talk English, asked how I had learned to speak it so well; then they enquired what I knew besides—what books I had read; soon they seemed to make a sort of wonder of me, considering me no doubt as a learned grisette. One afternoon, Mrs. Wharton brought in a Parisian lady to test the accuracy of my knowledge of French; the result of it was that, owing probably in a great degree to the Mother's and daughter's good humour about the marriage, which inclined them to do beneficent deeds; and partly, I think, because they are naturally benevolent people, they decided that the wish I had expressed to do something more than mend lace, was a very legitimate one, and the same day they took me in their carriage to Mrs. D——'s who is the Directress of the first English school in Brussels. It seems she happened to be in want of a French lady to give lessons in Geography, History, Grammar and Composition, in the French language; Mrs. Wharton recommended me very warmly, and as two of her younger daughters are pupils in the house, her patronage availed to get me the place. It was settled that I am to attend six hours daily (for happily it was not required that I should live in the house, I should have been sorry to leave my lodgings) and for this Mrs. D. will give me twelve hundred francs per annum. You see therefore, Monsieur, that I am now rich; richer almost than I ever hoped to be: I feel thankful for it, especially as my sight was beginning to be injured by constant working at fine lace; and I was getting too, very weary of sitting up late at nights and yet not being able to find time for reading or study. I began to fear that I should fall ill and be unable to pay my way; this fear is now in a great measure removed, and in truth, Monsieur, I am very grateful to God for the relief, and I feel it necessary almost to speak of my happiness to some one who is kind-hearted enough to derive joy from seeing others joyful. I could not therefore resist the temptation of writing to you; I argued with myself it is very pleasant to me to write and it will not be exactly painful, though it may be tiresome to Monsieur to read. Do not be too angry with my circumlocution and inelegancies of expression, and believe me

Your attached pupil—F.E.Henri."

Having read this letter, I mused on its contents for a few moments, whether with sentiments pleasurable or otherwise I will hereafter note, and then took up the other. It was directed in a hand to me unknown, small and rather neat; neither masculine nor exactly feminine; the seal bore a coat of arms, concerning which I could only decipher that it was not that of the Seacombe family, consequently the epistle could be from none of my almost forgotten, and certainly quite forgetting patrician relations. From whom then was it? I removed the envelope; the note folded within ran as follows:

"I have no doubt in the world that you are doing well in that greasy Flanders; living probably on the fat of the unctuous land; sitting like a black-haired, tawny-skinned, long-nosed Israelite by the flesh-pots of Egypt; or like a rascally son of Levi near the brass cauldrons of the sanctuary, and every now and then plunging in a consecrated hook and drawing out of the sea of broth the fattest of heave-shoulders and the fleshiest of wave-breasts; I know this because you never write to any one in England. Thankless dog that you are! I by the sovereign efficacy of my recommendation, got you the place where you are now living in clover and yet not a word of gratitude, or even acknowledgement have you ever offered in return; but I am coming to see you, and small conception can you, with your addled aristocratic brains, form of the sort of moral kicking I have, ready packed in my carpet-bag, destined to be presented to you immediately on my arrival.

Meantime I know all about your affairs, and have just got information, by Brown's last letter, that you are said to be on the point of forming an advantageous match with a pursy, little Belgian schoolmistress, a Mdlle. Zénobie or some such name. Won't I have a look at her when I come over? And this you may rely on, if she pleases my taste, or if I think it worth while in a pecuniary point of view, I'll pounce on your prize and bear her away triumphant in spite of your teeth. Yet I don't like dumpies either, and Brown says she is little and stout; the better fitted for a wiry, starved-looking chap like you.

Be on the look-out for you know neither the day nor hour when your —— (I don't wish to blaspheme, so I'll leave a blank) cometh.

Yours truly, Hunsden Yorke Hunsden."

"Humph!" said I, and ere I laid the letter down, I again glanced at the small, neat handwriting, not a bit like that of a mercantile man, nor indeed of any man except Hunsden, himself. They talk of affinities between the autograph and the character; what affinity was there here? I recalled the writer's peculiar face and certain traits I suspected, rather than knew, to appertain to his nature, and I answered "A great deal."

Hunsden then was coming to Brussels, and coming I knew not when; coming charged with the expectation of finding me on the summit of prosperity, about to be married, to step into a warm nest, to lie comfortably down by the side of a snug, well-fed little mate: "I wish him joy of the fidelity of the picture he has painted," thought I. "What will he say when, instead of a pair of plump turtle-doves, billing and cooing in a bower of roses, he finds a single lean cormorant, standing mateless and shelterless on poverty's bleak cliff? Oh confound him! Let him come, and let him laugh at the contrast between rumour and fact: were he the Devil himself, instead of being merely very like him, I'd not condescend to get out of his way, or to forge a smile or a cheerful word wherewith to avert his sarcasm." Then I recurred to the other letter; that struck a chord whose sound I could not deaden by thrusting my fingers into my ears, for it vibrated within; and though its swell might be exquisite music, its cadence was a groan.

That Frances was relieved from the pressure of want, that the curse of excessive labour was taken off her, filled me with happiness; that her first thought in prosperity should be to augment her joy by sharing it with me, met and satisfied the wish of my heart. Two results of her letter were then pleasant; sweet as two draughts of nectar; but applying my lips for the third time to the cup and they were excoriated as with vinegar and gall.

Two persons whose desires are moderate may live well enough in Brussels on an income which would scarcely afford a respectable maintenance for one, in London; and that—not because the necessaries of life are so much dearer in the latter capital, or taxes so much higher than in the former, but because the English surpass in folly all the nations on God's earth, and are more abject slaves to Custom, to Opinion, to the desire to keep up a certain appearance, than the Italians are to Priestcraft, the French to vain-glory, the Russians to their Czar, or the Germans to black beer. I have seen a degree of sense in the modest arrangement of one homely Belgian household that might put to shame the elegance, the superfluities, the luxuries, the strained refinements of a hundred genteel English mansions. In Belgium, provided you can make money—you may save it; this is scarcely possible in England; Ostentation there lavishes in a month what Industry has earned in a year. More shame to all classes in that most bountiful and beggarly country for their servile following of Fashion! I could write a chapter or two on this subject, but must forbear, at least for the present. Had I retained my £60 per annum I could, now that Frances was in possession of £50, have gone straight to her this very evening and spoken out the words which, repressed, kept fretting my heart with fever; our united income would, as we should have managed it, have sufficed well for our mutual support; since we lived in a country where economy was not confounded with meanness, where frugality in dress, food and furniture was not synonymous with vulgarity in these various points. But the placeless usher, bare of resource, and unsupported by connections must not think of this; such a sentiment as love, such a word as marriage were misplaced in his heart and on his lips. Now for the first time did I truly feel what it was to be poor; now did the sacrifice I had made in casting from me the means of living put on a new aspect; instead of a correct, just, honourable act, it seemed a deed at once light and fanatical: I took several turns in my room under the goading influence of most poignant remorse; I walked a quarter of an hour from the wall to the window; and at the window, Self-reproach seemed to face me; at the wall, Self-disdain: all at once out-spoke Conscience:

"Down stupid tormentors!" cried she. "The man has done his duty; you shall not bait him thus by thoughts of what might have been; he relinquished a temporary and contingent good to avoid a permanent and certain evil; he did well. Let him reflect now, and when your blinding dust and deafening hum subside, he will discover a path."

I sat down; I propped my forehead on both my hands; I thought and thought an hour—two hours; vainly; I seemed like one sealed in a subterranean vault, who gazes at utter blackness; at blackness ensured by yard-thick stone walls around and by piles of building above, expecting light to penetrate through granite and through cement firm as granite. But there are chinks, or there may be chinks in the best adjusted masonry; there was a chink in my cavernous cell; for eventually I saw, or seemed to see a ray; pallid indeed, and cold, and doubtful, but still a ray, for it shewed that narrow path which Conscience had promised. After two, three hours' torturing research in brain and memory, I disinterred certain remains of circumstances, and conceived a hope that by putting them together an expedient might be framed and a resource discovered. The circumstances were briefly these.

Some three months ago, M. Pelet had, on the occasion of his fête, given the boys a treat, which treat consisted in a party of pleasure to a certain place of public resort in the outskirts of Brussels, of which I do not at this moment remember the name, but near it were several of those lakelets called étangs; and there was one étang, larger than the rest, where on holidays people were accustomed to amuse themselves by rowing round it in little boats. The boys having eaten an unlimited quantity of "gaufres", and drank several bottles of Louvain beer, amid the shades of a garden made and provided for such crams, petitioned the Director for leave to take a row on the étang. Half a dozen of the eldest succeeded in obtaining leave, and I was commissioned to accompany them as Surveillant. Among the half dozen happened to be a certain Jean

Baptiste Vandenhuten; a most ponderous young Flamand, not tall, but even now, at the early age of sixteen, possessing a breadth and depth of personal development, truly national. It chanced that Jean was the first lad to step into the boat; he stumbled, rolled to one side, the boat revolted at his weight and capsized. Vandenhuten sank like lead, rose, sank again; my coat and waistcoat were off in an instant; I had not been brought up at Eton and boated and bathed and swam there ten long years for nothing; it was a natural and easy act for me to leap to the rescue. The lads and the boatmen yelled; they thought there would be two deaths by drowning instead of one; but as Jean rose the third time, I clutched him by one leg and the collar and in three minutes more, both he and I were safe landed. To speak heaven's truth, my merit in the action was small indeed, for I had run no risk and subsequently did not even catch cold from the wetting; but when M. and Mde. Vandenhuten, of whom Jean Baptiste was the sole hope, came to hear of the exploit, they seemed to think I had evinced a bravery and devotion which no thanks could sufficiently repay: Madame, in particular, was "certain I must have dearly loved their sweet son, or I would not thus have hazarded my own life to save his." Monsieur, an honest-looking though phlegmatic man, said very little, but he would not suffer me to leave the room, till I had promised that in case I ever stood in need of help, I would, by applying to him, give him a chance of discharging the obligation under which he affirmed I had laid him. These words then were my glimmer of light; it was here I found my sole outlet; and in truth though the cold light roused, it did not cheer me; nor did the outlet seem such as I should like to pass through. Right, I had none to M. Vandenhuten's good offices; it was not on the ground of merit I could apply to him; no, I must stand on that of necessity: I had no work; I wanted work; my best chance of obtaining it lay in securing his recommendation: this I knew could be had by asking for it; not to ask, because the request revolted my pride and contradicted my habits, would, I felt, be an indulgence of false and indolent fastidiousness: I might repent the omission all my life; I would not then be guilty of it.

That evening, I went to M. Vandenhuten's; but I had bent the bow and adjusted the shaft in vain; the string broke. I rang the bell at the great door (it was a large, handsome house in an expensive part of the town); a man-servant opened; I asked for M. Vandenhuten; M. Vandenhuten and family were all out of town, gone to Ostend, did not know when they would be back. I left my card and retraced my steps.

CHAPTER XXII

A WEEK is soon gone; le jour des noces arrived; the marriage was solemnized at St. Jacques; Mdlle. Zoraïde became Mde. Pelet née Reuter, and in about an hour after this transformation, "the happy pair", as newspapers phrase it, were on their way to Paris, where, according to previous arrangement, the honeymoon was to be spent. The next day I quitted the Pensionnat; myself and my chattels (some books and clothes) were soon transferred to a modest lodging I had hired in a street not far off; in half an hour my clothes were arranged in a commode, my books on a shelf, and the "flitting" was effected. I should not have been unhappy that day had not one pang tortured me; a longing to go to the Rue Notre Dame aux Neiges, resisted, yet irritated by an inward resolve to avoid that street till such time as the mist of doubt should clear from my prospects.

It was a sweet September evening; very mild, very still; I had nothing to do; at that hour, I knew Frances would be equally released from occupation; I thought she might possibly be wishing for her master, I knew I wished for my pupil: Imagination began with her low whispers infusing into my soul the soft tale of pleasures that might be:

"You will find her reading or writing," said she. "You can take your seat at her side; you need not startle her peace by undue excitement; you need not embarrass her manner by unusual action or language. Be as you always are; look over what she has written; listen while she reads; chide her, or quietly approve; you know the effect of either system; you know her smile when pleased; you know the play of her looks when roused; you have the secret of awakening what expression you will, and you can choose amongst that pleasant variety. With you she will sit silent as long as it suits you to talk alone; you can hold her under a potent spell; intelligent as she is, eloquent as she can be, you can seal her lips and veil her bright countenance with diffidence; yet you know she is not all monotonous mildness; you have seen, with a sort of strange pleasure, revolt, scorn, austerity, bitterness lay energetic claim to a place in her feelings and physiognomy; you know that few could rule her as you do; you know she might break but never bend under the hand of Tyranny and Injustice but Reason and Affection can guide her by a sign. Try their influence now. Go—they are not passions; you may handle them safely."

"I will *not* go," was my answer to the sweet temptress. "A man is master of himself to a certain point but not beyond it. Could I seek Frances to-night, could I sit with her alone in a quiet room and address her only in the language of Reason and Affection?"

"No," was the brief, fervent reply of that Love which had conquered and now controlled me.

Time seemed to stagnate; the sun would not go down; my watch ticked, but I thought the hands were paralyzed:

"What a hot evening!" I cried, throwing open the lattice, for indeed I had seldom felt so feverish. Hearing a step ascending the common stair, I wondered whether the "locataire" now mounting to his apartments were as unsettled in mind and condition as I was or whether he lived in the calm of certain resources, and in the freedom of unfettered feelings. What! was he coming in person to solve the problem hardly proposed in inaudible thought? He had actually knocked at the door—at *my* door; a smart, prompt rap; and almost before I could invite him in, he was over the threshold, and had closed the door behind him.

"And how are you?" asked an indifferent, quiet voice in the English language; while my visitor, without any sort of bustle or introduction, put his hat on the table, and his gloves into his hat, and drawing the only arm-chair the room afforded, a little forward, seated himself tranquilly therein.

"Can't you speak?" he inquired in a few moments, in a tone whose nonchalance seemed to intimate that it was much the same thing whether I answered or not. The fact is, I found it desirable to have recourse to my good friends "les besicles"; not exactly to ascertain the identity of my visitor, for I already knew him, confound his impudence! but to see how he looked—to get a clear notion of his mien and countenance. I wiped the glasses very deliberately, and put them on quite as deliberately; adjusting them so as not to hurt the bridge of my nose, or get entangled in my short tufts of dun hair. I was sitting in the window-seat, with my back to the light, and I had *him* vis-à-vis; a position he would much rather have had reversed, for at any time he preferred scrutinizing, to being scrutinized. Yes it was *He* and no mistake; with his six feet of length arranged in a sitting attitude; with his dark travelling surtout with its velvet collar; his gray pantaloons, his black stock, and *his* face, the most original one Nature ever modelled, yet the least obtrusively so; not one feature that could be termed marked, or odd, yet the effect of the whole unique. There is no use in attempting to describe what is indescribable. Being in no hurry to address him, I sat and stared at my ease.

"Oh that's your game—is it?" said he at last. "Well—we'll see which is soonest tired." And he slowly drew out a fine cigar-case, picked one to his taste, lit it, took a book from the shelf convenient to his hand, then leaning back, proceeded to smoke and read as tranquilly as if he had been in his own room in Grove-Street X——
——shire England. I knew he was capable of continuing in that attitude till midnight, if he conceived the whim, so I rose, and taking the book from his hand, I said:

"You did not ask for it, and you shall not have it."

"It is silly and dull," he observed— "so I have not lost much." Then, the spell being broken, he went on "I thought you lived at Pelet's; I went there this afternoon, expecting to be starved to death by sitting in a boarding-school drawing-room, and they told me you were gone, had departed this morning; you had left your address behind you though, which I wondered at; it was a more practical and sensible precaution than I should have imagined you capable of—Why did you leave?"

"Because M. Pelet has just married the lady whom you and Mr. Brown assigned to me as my wife."

"Oh indeed!" replied Hunsden with a short laugh; "so you've lost both your wife and your place?"

"Precisely so."

I saw him give a quick, covert glance all round my room; he marked its narrow limits, its scanty furniture; in an instant he had comprehended the state of matters, had absolved me from the crime of prosperity. A curious effect this discovery wrought in his strange mind; I am morally certain that if he had found me installed in a handsome parlour, lounging on a soft couch, with a pretty, wealthy wife at my side, he would have hated me; a brief, cold, haughty visit would in such a case have been the extreme limit of his civilities, and never would he have come near me more so long as the tide of fortune bore me smoothly on its surface; but the painted furniture, the bare walls, the cheerless solitude of my room relaxed his rigid pride, and I know not what softening change had taken place both in his voice and look ere he spoke again.

"You have got another place?"

"No."

"You are in the way of getting one?"

"No."

"That is bad—have you applied to Brown?"

"No indeed."

"You had better—he often has it in his power to give useful information in such matters."

"He served me once very well—I have no claim on him, and am not in the humour to bother him again."

"Oh if you're bashful and dread being intrusive—you need only commission me. I shall see him to-night; I can put in a word."

"I beg you will not, Mr. Hunsden; I am in your debt already; you did me an important service when I was at X—— —got me out of a den where I was dying—that service I have never repaid and at present I decline positively adding another item to the account."

"If the wind sits that way—I'm satisfied. I thought my unexampled generosity in turning you out of that accursed counting-house would be duly appreciated some day; 'Cast your bread on the waters and it shall be found after many days,' say the Scriptures. Yes, that's right, lad—make much of me—I'm a nonpareil—there's nothing like me in the common herd. In the meantime, to put all humbug aside and talk sense for a few moments, you would be greatly the better of a situation, and what is more, you are a fool if you refuse to take one from any hand that offers it."

"Very well, Mr. Hunsden; now you have settled that point, talk of something else. What news from X——?"

"I have not settled that point, or at least there is another to settle before we get to X——: is this Miss Zénobie" ("Zoraïde," interposed I) "—well Zoraïde—is she really married to Pelet?"

"I tell you yes—and if you don't believe me—go and ask the curé of St. Jacques."

"And your heart is broken?"

"I am not aware that it is—it feels all right—beats as usual."

"Then your feelings are less superfine than I took them to be, you must be a coarse, callous character, to bear such a thwack without staggering under it."

"Staggering under it? What the deuce is there to stagger under in the circumstances of a Belgian schoolmistress marrying a French schoolmaster—? The progeny will doubtless be a strange hybrid race—but that's their look out—not mine."

"He indulges in scurrilous jests, and the bride was his affianced one!"

"Who said so?"

"Brown."

"I'll tell you what, Hunsden—Brown is an old gossip."

"He is—but in the meantime—if his gossip be founded on less than fact—if you took no particular interest in Miss Zoraïde—why, O youthful pedagogue! did you leave your place in consequence of her becoming Madame Pelet?"

"Because—" I felt my face grow a little hot; "because—in short, Mr. Hunsden, I decline answering any more questions." And I plunged my hands deep in my breeches pocket.

Hunsden triumphed—his eyes—his laugh—announced victory.

"What the deuce are you laughing at, Mr. Hunsden?"

"At your exemplary composure—well lad, I'll not bore you; I see how it is—Zoraïde has jilted you—married some one richer, as any sensible woman would have done if she had had the chance."

I made no reply—I let him think so, not feeling inclined to enter into an explanation of the real state of things and as little to forge a false account; but it was not easy to blind Hunsden; my very silence instead of convincing him that he had hit the truth, seemed to render him doubtful about it—he went on:

"I suppose the affair has been conducted as such affairs always are amongst rational people: you offered her your youth and your talents—such as they are—in exchange for her position and money—I don't suppose you took appearance, or what is called *love* into the account—for I understand she is older than you, and Brown says—rather sensible-looking than beautiful. She—having then no chance of making a better bargain, was at first inclined to come to terms with you—but Pelet—the Head of a flourishing School, stepped in with a higher bid—she accepted—and he has got her—a correct transaction—perfectly so—business-like and legitimate. And now we'll talk of something else."

"Do," said I, very glad to dismiss the topic, and especially glad to have baffled the sagacity of my cross-questioner—if indeed I had baffled it—for though his words now led away from the dangerous point—his eyes, keen and watchful, seemed still preoccupied with the former idea.

"You want to hear news from X——? And what interest can you have in X——? You left no friends there—for you made none. Nobody ever asks after you—neither man nor woman—and if I mention your name in company, the men look as if I had spoken of Prester John—and the women sneer covertly. Our X—— belles must have disliked you—how did you excite their displeasure?"

"I don't know—I seldom spoke to them—they were nothing to me—I considered them only as something to be glanced at from a distance—their dresses and faces were often pleasing enough to the eye—but I could not understand their conversation, nor even read their countenances. When I caught snatches of what they said I could never make much of it—and the play of their lips and eyes did not help me at all."

"That was your fault, not theirs. There are sensible, as well as handsome women in X——, women it is worth any man's while to talk to, and with whom I can talk with pleasure; but you had and have no pleasant address; there is nothing in you to induce a woman to be affable: I have remarked you sitting near the door in a room full of company, bent on hearing not on speaking; on observing not on entertaining; looking frigidly shy at the commencement of a party; confusingly vigilant about the middle and insultingly weary towards the end. Is that the way, do you think, ever to communicate pleasure or excite interest? No—and if you are generally unpopular —it is because you deserve to be so."

"Content!" I ejaculated.

"No—you are not content—you see Beauty always turning its back on you—you are mortified and then you sneer—I verily believe all that is desirable on earth, Wealth, Reputation, Love—will for-ever to you be the ripe grapes on the high trellis: you'll look up at them—they will tantalize in you the lust of the eye—but they are out of reach—you have not the address to fetch a ladder, and you'll go away calling them sour."

Cutting as these words might have been under some circumstances—they drew no blood now. My life was changed; my experience had been varied since I left X——, but Hunsden could not know this; he had seen me only in the character of Mr. Crimsworth's clerk; a dependant amongst wealthy strangers, meeting disdain with a hard front, conscious of an unsocial and unattractive exterior, refusing to sue for notice which I was sure would be withheld, declining to evince an admiration which I knew would be scorned as worthless. He could not be aware that since then youth and loveliness had been to me every-day objects; that I had studied them at leisure and closely, and had seen the plain texture of truth under the embroidery of appearance; nor could he, keen-sighted as he was, penetrate into my heart, search my brain, and read my peculiar sympathies and antipathies; he had not known me long enough, or well enough to perceive how low my feelings would ebb under some influences, powerful over most minds; how high, how fast they would flow under other influences, that perhaps acted with the more intense force on me, because they acted on me alone. Neither could he suspect for an instant the history of my communications with Mdlle. Reuter; secret to him and to all others was the tale of her strange infatuation: her blandishments, her wiles had been seen but by me, and to me only were they known; but they had changed me, for they had proved that I *could* impress. A sweeter secret nestled deeper in my heart; one full of tenderness and as full of strength; it took the sting out of Hunsden's sarcasm; it kept me unbent by shame, and unstirred by wrath:—but of all this I could say nothing—nothing decisive at least. Uncertainty sealed my lips, and during the interval of silence by which alone I replied to Mr. Hunsden, I made up my mind to be for the present wholly misjudged by him, and misjudged I was; he thought he had been rather too hard upon me, and that I was crushed by the weight of his upbraidings; so to reassure me he said, doubtless I should mend some day; I was only at the beginning of life yet; and since happily I was not quite without sense, every false step I made would be a good lesson.

Just then I turned my face a little to the light; the approach of twilight and my position in the window-seat, had for the last ten minutes, prevented him from studying my countenance, as I moved however, he caught an expression which he thus interpreted:

"Confound it! How doggedly self-approving the lad looks! I thought he was fit to die with shame and there he sits grinning smiles, as good as to say: 'Let the world wag as it will—I've the philosopher's stone in my waistcoat-pocket, and the elixir of life in my cupboard; I'm independent of both Fate and Fortune!' "

"Hunsden—you spoke of grapes; I was thinking of a fruit I like better than your X—— hot-house grapes—an unique fruit, growing wild, which I have marked as my own, and hope one day to gather and taste: it is of no use your offering me the draught of bitterness, or threatening me with death by thirst; I have the anticipation of sweetness on my palate; the hope of freshness on my lips; I can reject the unsavoury, and endure the exhausting."

"For how long?"

"Till the next opportunity for effort, and as the prize of success will be a treasure after my own heart—I'll bring a bull's strength to the struggle."

"Bad-luck crushes bulls as easily as bullaces, and I believe the fury dogs you: you were born with a wooden spoon in your mouth, depend on it."

"I believe you; and I mean to make my wooden spoon do the work of some people's silver ladles—grasped firmly and handled nimbly even a wooden spoon will shovel up broth."

Hunsden rose: "I see," said he. "I suppose you're one of those who develop best unwatched, and act best unaided—work your own way. Now I'll go." And without another word he was going; at the door he turned:

"Crimsworth-Hall is sold," said he.

"Sold!" was my echo.

"Yes—you know of course that your brother failed three months ago?"

"What! Edward Crimsworth?"

"Precisely—and his wife went home to her father's; when affairs went awry his temper sympathized with them; he used her ill; I told you he would be a tyrant to her some day; as to him—"

"Aye as to him—what is become of him?"

"Nothing extraordinary—don't be alarmed; he put himself under the protection of the court, compounded with his creditors—10d. in the pound; in six weeks set up again, coaxed back his wife and is flourishing like a green bay-tree."

"And Crimsworth-Hall—was the furniture sold too?"

"Everything—from the grand piano down to the rolling-pin."

"And the contents of the oak dining-room—were they sold?"

"Of course—why should the sofas and chairs of that room be held more sacred than those of any other?"

"And the pictures?"

"What pictures? Crimsworth had no special collection that I know of—he did not profess to be an amateur."

"There were two portraits, one on each side the mantelpiece; you cannot have forgotten them, Mr. Hunsden; you once noticed that of the lady."

"Oh I know! the thin-faced gentlewoman with a shawl put on like drapery. Why as a matter of course it would be sold among the other things. If you had been rich—you might have bought it—for I remember you said it represented your Mother: you see what it is to be without a sou."

I did; "But surely," I thought to myself, "I shall not always be so poverty-stricken; I may one day buy it back yet. Who purchased it? Do you know?" I asked.

"How is it likely? I never inquired who purchased anything; there spoke the unpractical man—to imagine all the world is interested in what interests himself! Now good-night—I'm off for Germany to-morrow morning; I shall be back here in six weeks and possibly I may call and see you again; I wonder whether you'll be still out of place!" He laughed—as mockingly, as heartlessly as Mephistopheles, and so laughing, vanished.

Some people, however indifferent they may become after a considerable space of absence, always contrive to leave a pleasant impression just at parting; not so Hunsden; a conference with him affected one like a draught of Peruvian bark; it seemed a concentration of the specially harsh, stringent, bitter; whether, like bark, it invigorated, I scarcely knew.

A ruffled mind makes a restless pillow; I slept little on the night after this interview; towards morning I began to doze, but hardly had my slumber become sleep, when I was roused from it by hearing a noise in my sitting-room, to which my bed-room adjoined, a step and a shoving of furniture; the movement lasted barely two minutes; with the closing of the door it ceased. I listened; not a mouse stirred; perhaps I had dreamt it; perhaps a locataire had made a mistake, and entered my apartment instead of his own. It was yet but five o'clock; neither I nor the day were wide awake, I turned and was soon unconscious. When I did rise, about two hours later, I had forgotten the circumstance; the first thing I saw however on quitting my chamber, recalled it; just pushed in at the door of my sitting room, and still standing on end was a wooden packing-case, a rough deal affair, wide but shallow; a porter had doubtless shoved it forward but seeing no occupant of the room, had left it at the entrance.

"That is none of mine," thought I approaching, "it must be

meant for somebody else." I stooped to examine the address: "Wm. Crimsworth Esq. No. —— —— St. Brussels." I was puzzled, but concluding that the best way to obtain information was to ask within, I cut the cords and opened the case. Green baize enveloped its contents, sewn carefully at the sides; I ripped the pack-thread with my pen-knife, and still, as the seam gave way, glimpses of gilding appeared through the widening interstices. Boards and baize being at length removed, I lifted from the case, a large picture, in a magnificent frame; leaning it against a chair, in a position where the light from the window fell favourably upon it, I stepped back—already I had mounted my spectacles. A portrait-painter's sky (the most sombre and threatening of welkins), and distant trees of a conventional depth of hue, raised in full relief a pale, pensive looking female face, shadowed with soft dark hair, almost blending with the equally dark clouds; large, solemn eyes looked reflectively into mine; a thin cheek rested on a delicate little hand; a shawl, artistically draped, half hid, half shewed a slight figure. A listener (had there been one) might have heard me after ten minutes' silent gazing, utter the word "Mother!" I might have said more—but with me, the first word uttered aloud in soliloquy, rouses consciousness; it reminds me that only crazy people talk to themselves, and then I think out my monologue, instead of speaking it. I had thought a long while, and a long while had contemplated the intelligence, the sweetness and—alas! the sadness also of those fine, grey eyes; the mental power of that forehead; and the rare sensibility of that serious mouth, when my glance, travelling downwards, fell on a narrow billet, stuck in the corner of the picture, between the frame and the canvass. Then I first asked "Who sent this picture? Who thought of me, saved it out of the wreck of Crimsworth-Hall and now commits it to the care of its natural keeper?" I took the note from its niche; thus it spoke:

"There is a sort of stupid pleasure in giving a child sweets, a fool his bells, a dog a bone. You are repaid by seeing the child besmear his face with sugar; by witnessing how the fool's ecstasy makes a greater fool of him than ever; by watching the dog's nature come out over his bone. In giving William Crimsworth his Mother's picture, I give him sweets, bells and bone, all in one; what grieves me is, that I cannot behold the result; I would have added five shillings more to my bid if the auctioneer could only have promised me that pleasure. H.Y.H.

P.S. You said last night you positively declined adding another item to your account with me; don't you think I've saved you that trouble?"

I muffled the picture in its green baize covering, restored it to the case and having transported the whole concern to my bedroom, put it out of sight under my bed. My pleasure was now poisoned by pungent pain; I determined to look no more till I could look at my ease. If Hunsden had come in at that moment I should have said to him "I owe you nothing, Hunsden—not a fraction of a farthing—you have paid yourself in taunts."

Too anxious to remain any longer quiescent, I had no sooner breakfasted, than I repaired once more to M. Vandenhuten's, scarcely hoping to find him at home, for a week had barely elapsed since my first call, but fancying I might be able to glean information as to the time when his return was expected. A better result awaited me than I had anticipated, for though the family were yet at Ostend, M. Vandenhuten had come over to Brussels on business for the day. He received me with the quiet kindness of a sincere though not excitable man; I had not sat five minutes alone with him in his bureau, before I became aware of a sense of ease in his presence, such as I rarely experienced with strangers: I was surprised at my own composure for after all I had come on business to me exceedingly painful, that of soliciting a favour; I asked on what basis the calm rested—I feared it might be deceptive; erelong I caught a glimpse of the ground, and at once I felt assured of its solidity; I knew where I was. M. Vandenhuten was rich, respected and influential; I—poor, despised and powerless; so we stood to the world at large, as members of the world's society; but to each other, as a pair of human beings, our positions were reversed. The Dutchman (he was not Flamand but pure Hollandais) was slow, cool, of rather dense intelligence, though sound and accurate judgment; the Englishman far more nervous, active, quicker both to plan and to practise, to conceive and to realize: the Dutchman was benevolent; the Englishman susceptible; in short our characters dovetailed—but my mind having more fire and action than his, instinctively assumed and kept the predominance. This point settled, and my position well ascertained, I addressed him on the subject of my affairs with that genuine frankness which full confidence can alone inspire; it was a pleasure to him to be so appealed to; he thanked me for giving him this opportunity of using a little exertion in my behalf: I went on to explain to him that my wish was not so much to be helped, as to be put into the way of helping myself—of him I did not want exertion—that was to be my part—but only information and recommendation; soon after I rose to go; he held out his hand at parting—an action of greater significance with foreigners than with Englishmen; as I exchanged a smile with him, I thought the benevolence of his truthful face was better than the intelligence of my own: characters of my order experience a balm-like solace in the contact of such souls as animated the honest breast of Victor Vandenhuten.

The next fortnight was a period of many alternations; my existence during its lapse resembled a sky of one of those autumnal nights which are specially haunted by meteors and falling stars. Hopes and fears, expectations and disappointments descended in glancing showers from zenith to horizon; but all were transient, and darkness followed swift each vanishing apparition. M. Vandenhuten aided me faithfully; he set me on the track of several places, and himself made efforts to secure them for me; but for a long time solicitation and recommendation were vain; the door either shut in my face when I was about to walk in, or another candidate, entering before me, rendered my further advance useless. Feverish and roused, no disappointment arrested me; defeat following fast on defeat served as stimulants to will; I forgot fastidiousness, conquered reserve, thrust pride from me: I asked, I persevered, I remonstrated, I dunned. It is so that openings are forced into the guarded circle where Fortune sits dealing favours round. My perseverance made me known; my importunity made me remarked; I was inquired about; my former pupils' parents, gathering the reports of their children, heard me spoken of as talented, and they echoed the word; the sound, bandied about at random, came at last to ears which but for its universality it might never have reached, and at the very crisis when I had tried my last effort and knew not what more to do, Fortune looked in at me one morning, as I sat in drear and almost desperate deliberation on my bedstead, nodded with the familiarity of an old acquaintance, though God knows I had never met her before, and threw a prize into my lap.

In the second week of October 18— I got the appointment of English professor to all the classes of —— College, Brussels, with a salary of 3000 francs per annum and the certainty of being able, by dint of the reputation and publicity accompanying the position, to make as much more by private lessons. The official notice, which communicated this information, mentioned also that it was the strong recommendation of M. Vandenhuten, négociant, which had turned the scale of choice in my favour. No sooner had I read the announcement than I hurried to M. Vandenhuten's bureau, pushed the document under his nose, and when he had perused it, took both his hands, and thanked him with unrestrained vivacity. My vivid words and emphatic gesture moved his Dutch calm to unwonted sensation; he said he was happy, glad to have served me, but he had done nothing meriting such thanks; he had not laid out a centime; only scratched a few words on a sheet of paper. Again I repeated to him: "You have made me quite happy and in a way that suits me; I do not feel an obligation irksome, conferred by your kind hand; I do not feel disposed to shun you because you have done me a favour; from this day you must consent to admit me to your intimate acquaintance, for I shall hereafter recur again and again to the pleasure of your society."

"Ainsi soit-il," was the reply, accompanied by a smile of benignant content; I went away with its sunshine in my heart.

CHAPTER XXIII

IT WAS two o'clock when I returned to my lodgings; my dinner, just brought in from a neighbouring hotel, smoked on the table; I sat down, thinking to eat; had the plate been heaped with potsherds and broken glass instead of boiled beef and haricots, I could not have made a more signal failure: appetite had forsaken me. Impatient of seeing food which I could not taste, I put it all aside into a cupboard, and then demanded: "What shall I do till evening?" for before six p.m. it would be vain to seek the Rue Notre-Dame-aux-Neiges—its inhabitant (for me it had but one) was detained by her vocation elsewhere. I walked in the streets of Brussels and I walked in my own room from two o'clock till six; never once in that space of time did I sit down. I was in my chamber when the last named hour struck; I had just bathed my face and feverish hands, and was standing near the glass; my cheek was crimson, my eye was flame; still all my features looked quite settled and calm. Descending swiftly the stair and stepping out, I was glad to see Twilight drawing on in clouds; such shade was to me like a grateful screen, and the chill of latter Autumn, breathing in a fitful wind from the north-west, met me as a refreshing coolness. Still I saw it was cold to others, for the women I passed were wrapped in shawls, and the men had their coats buttoned close.

When are we quite happy? Was I so then? No; an urgent and growing dread worried my nerves and had worried them since the first moment good-tidings had reached me. How was Frances? It was ten weeks since I had seen her, six since I had heard from her, or of her. I had answered her letter by a brief note, friendly but calm, in which no mention of continued correspondence or further visits was made. At that hour my bark hung on the topmost curl of a wave of fate, and I knew not on what shoal the onward rush of the billow might hurl it; I would not then attach her destiny to mine by the slightest thread; if doomed to split on the rock, or run aground on the sand-bank, I was resolved no other vessel should share my disaster: but six weeks was a long time—and could it be that she was still well and doing well? Were not all sages agreed in declaring that happiness finds no climax on earth? Dared I think that but half a street now divided me from the full cup of Contentment—the draught drawn from waters, said to flow only in heaven?

I was at the door; I entered the quiet house; I mounted the stairs; the lobby was void and still, all the doors closed; I looked for the neat green mat; it lay duly in its place:

"Signal of hope!" I said and advanced. "But I will be a little calmer; I am not going to rush in and get up a scene directly." Forcibly staying my eager step, I paused on the mat:—

"What an absolute hush! Is she in? Is anybody in?" I demanded to myself. A little tinkle as of cinders falling from a grate replied; a movement—a fire was gently stirred, and the slight rustle of life continuing, a step paced equably backwards and forwards, backwards and forwards in the apartment. Fascinated, I stood, more fixedly fascinated when a voice rewarded the attention of my strained ear—so low, so self-addressed, I never fancied the speaker otherwise than alone; Solitude might speak thus in a desert, or in the hall of a forsaken house.

"'And ne'er but once, my son,' he said,
    Was yon dark cavern trod;
In persecution's iron days,
    When the land was left by God.
From Bewley's bog, with slaughter red,
    A wanderer hither drew;
And oft he stopped and turned his head,
    As by fits the night-winds blew.
For trampling round by Cheviot-edge,
    Were heard the troopers keen;
And frequent from the Whitelaw ridge
    The death-shot flashed between'." &c. &c.

The old Scotch ballad was partly recited, then dropt; a pause ensued; then another strain followed, in French, of which the purport, translated ran as follows:

I gave, at first, Attention close;
    Then interest warm ensued;
From interest as improvement rose,
    Succeeded gratitude.

Obedience was no effort soon,
    And labour was no pain;
If tired, a word, a glance alone
    Would give me strength again.

From others of the studious band,
    Erelong he singled me;
But only by more close demand,
    And sterner urgency.

The task he from another took,
    From me, he did reject;
He would no slight omission brook,
    And suffer no defect.

If my companions went astray,
    He scarce their wanderings blamed;
If I but faltered in the way,
    His anger fiercely flamed.

Something stirred in an adjoining chamber; it would not do to be surprised eaves-dropping; I tapped hastily, and as hastily entered. Frances was just before me; she had been walking slowly in her room and her step was checked by my advent: Twilight only was with her, and tranquil, ruddy Firelight; to these Sisters, the Bright and the Dark, she had been speaking, ere I entered, in poetry. Sir Walter Scott's voice, to her a foreign far-off sound, a mountain-echo, had uttered itself in the first stanzas—the second, I thought from the style and the substance, was the language of her own heart. Her face was grave; its expression concentrated; she bent on me an unsmiling eye, an eye just returning from abstraction, just awaking from dreams: well-arranged was her simple attire, smooth her dark hair, orderly her tranquil room; but what—with her thoughtful look, her serious self-reliance, her bent to meditation and haply inspiration, what had she to do with love? "Nothing," was the answer of her own sad though gentle countenance; it seemed to say "I must cultivate fortitude and cling to poetry; one is to be my support and the other my solace through life; human affections do not bloom, nor do human passions glow for me." Other women have such thoughts; Frances, had she been as desolate as she deemed, would not have been worse off than thousands of her sex. Look at the rigid and formal race of old maids—the race whom all despise—they have fed themselves, from youth upwards, on maxims of resignation and endurance; many of them get ossified with the dry diet; Self-Control is so continually their thought, so perpetually their object that at last it absorbs the softer and more agreeable qualities of their nature, and they die mere models of austerity, fashioned out of a little parchment and much bone. Anatomists will tell you that there is a heart in the withered old maid's carcase—the same as in that of any cherished wife or proud mother in the land—can this be so? I really don't know—but feel inclined to doubt it.

I came forward; bade Frances good-evening and took my seat. The chair I had chosen, was one she had probably just left; it stood by a little table where were her open desk and papers. I know not whether she had fully recognized me at first, but she did so now, and in a voice, soft but quiet, she returned my greeting; I had shewn no eagerness, she took her cue from me and evinced no surprise; we met as we had always met, as Master and pupil, nothing more. I proceeded to handle the papers, Frances, observant and serviceable, stept into an inner room, brought a candle, lit it, placed it by me; then drew the curtain over the lattice, and having added a little fresh fuel to the already bright fire, she drew a second chair to the table and sat down at my right hand, a little removed. The paper on the top was a translation of some grave French author into English, but underneath lay a sheet with stanzas; on this I laid hands. Frances half rose, made a movement to recover the captured spoil, saying that was nothing; a mere copy of verses. I put by resistance with the decision I knew she never long opposed, but on this occasion her fingers had fastened on the paper; I had quietly to unloose them; their hold dissolved to my touch; her hand shrunk away; my own would fain have followed it, but for the present I forbade such impulse. The first page of the sheet was occupied with the lines I had overheard; the sequel was not exactly the writer's own experience—but a composition by portions of that experience suggested; thus while egotism was avoided, the fancy was exercised, and the heart satisfied. I translate as before, and my translation is nearly literal: it continued thus:

When sickness stayed awhile my course,
He seemed impatient still,
Because his pupil's flagging force
Could not obey his will.

One day when summoned to the bed
Where Pain and I did strive,
I heard him, as he bent his head,
Say "God—she *must* revive!"

I felt his hand with gentle stress
A moment laid on mine,
And wished to mark my consciousness
By some responsive sign.

But powerless then to speak or move,
I only felt within,
The sense of Hope, the strength of Love
Their healing work begin.

And as he from the room withdrew
My heart his steps pursued,
I longed to prove by efforts new
My speechless gratitude.

When once again I took my place,
Long vacant, in the class,
Th'unfrequent smile across his face
Did for one moment pass.

The lessons done; the signal made
Of glad release and play,
He, as he passed, an instant stayed
One kindly word to say.

"Jane, till to-morrow you are free
From tedious task and rule;

This afternoon I must not see
  That yet pale face in school.

Seek in the garden-shades a seat
  Far from the play-ground din;
The sun is warm, the air is sweet;
  Stay till I call you in."

A long and pleasant afternoon
  I passed in those green bowers;
All silent, tranquil and alone
  With birds and bees and flowers.

Yet when my Master's voice I heard
  Call from the window "Jane!"
I entered, joyful, at the word,
The busy house again.

He, in the hall, paced up and down;
  He paused as I passed by;
His forehead stern relaxed its frown;
  He raised his deep-set eye.

"Not quite so pale," he murmured low:
  "Now, Jane, go rest awhile."
And as I smiled, his smoothened brow
  Returned as glad a smile.

My perfect health restored, he took
  His mien austere again,
And as before, he would not brook
  The slightest fault from Jane.

The longest task, the hardest theme
  Fell to my share as erst,
And still I toiled to place my name
  In every study first.

He yet begrudged and stinted praise,
  But I had learnt to read
The secret meaning of his face,
  And that was my best meed.

Even when his hasty temper spoke
  In tones that sorrow stirred,
My grief was lulled as soon as woke
  By some relenting word.

And when he lent some precious book,
Or gave some fragrant flower,
I did not quail to Envy's look,
Upheld by Pleasure's power.

At last our school ranks took their ground;
The hard-fought field, I won;
The prize, a laurel-wreath, was bound
My throbbing forehead on.

Low at my master's knee I bent,
The offered crown to meet;
Its green leaves through my temples sent
A thrill as wild as sweet.

The strong pulse of Ambition struck
In every vein I owned;
At the same instant, bleeding broke
A secret, inward wound.

The hour of triumph was to me
The hour of sorrow sore;
A day hence I must cross the sea,
Ne'er to re-cross it more.

An hour hence, in my Master's room,
I, with him sat alone,
And told him what a dreary gloom
O'er joy, had parting thrown.

He little said; the time was brief,
The ship was soon to sail,
And while I sobbed in bitter grief,
My master but looked pale.

They called in haste; he bade me go,
Then snatched me back again;
He held me fast and murmured low
"Why will they part us, Jane?"

"Were you not happy in my care?
Did I not faithful prove?
Will others to my darling bear
As true, as deep a love?

"O God watch o'er my foster child!
O guard her gentle head!

When winds are high and tempests wild
Protection round her spread!

"They call again; leave then my breast;
Quit thy true shelter, Jane,
But when deceived, repulsed, oppress,
Come home to me again!"

I read—then dreamily made marks on the margin with my pencil, thinking all the while, of other things; thinking that "Jane" was now at my side; no child but a girl of nineteen, and she might be mine, so my heart affirmed; Poverty's curse was taken off me; Envy and Jealousy were far away and unapprised of this our quiet meeting; the frost of the Master's manner might melt, I felt the thaw coming fast, whether I would or not, no further need for the eye to practise a hard look, for the brow to compress its expanse into a stern fold. It was now permitted to suffer the outward revelation of the inward glow, to seek, demand, elicit an answering ardour. While musing thus, I thought that the grass on Hermon never drank the fresh dews of Sunset more gratefully than my feelings drank the bliss of this hour.

Frances rose, as if restless; she passed before me to stir the fire which did not want stirring; she lifted and put down the little ornaments on the mantelpiece; her dress waved within a yard of me; slight, straight and elegant, she stood erect on the hearth.

There are impulses we can control, but there are others which control us, because they attain us with a tiger-leap and are our masters ere we have seen them. Perhaps though, such impulses are seldom altogether bad; perhaps Reason, by a process as brief as quiet, a process that is finished ere felt, has ascertained the sanity of the deed Instinct meditates, and feels justified in remaining passive while it is performed. I know I did not reason, I did not plan or intend, yet whereas, one moment I was sitting solus on the chair near the table, the next, I held Frances on my knee, placed there with sharpness and decision, and retained with exceeding tenacity.

"Monsieur!" cried Frances, and was still, not another word escaped her lips; sorely confounded she seemed during the lapse of the first few moments; but the Amazement soon subsided; Terror did not succeed, nor Fury; after all she was only a little nearer than she had ever been before, to one she habitually respected and trusted; embarrassment might have impelled her to contend, but Self-respect checked resistance where resistance was useless.

"Frances, how much regard have you for me?" was my demand. No answer; the situation was yet too new and surprising to permit speech. On this consideration I compelled myself for some seconds to tolerate her silence, though impatient of it: presently I repeated the same question, probably not in the calmest of tones; she looked at me; my face doubtless was no model of composure, my eyes no still wells of tranquillity.

"Do speak," I urged; and a very low, hurried yet still arch voice said:

"Monsieur, vous me faites mal; de grâce lâchez un peu ma main droite."

In truth I became aware that I was holding the said "main droite" in a somewhat ruthless grasp: I did as desired and for the third time asked more gently:

"Frances, how much regard have you for me?"

"Mon maître, j'en ai beaucoup," was the truthful rejoinder.

"Frances, have you enough to give yourself to me as my wife? To accept me as your husband?"

I felt the agitation of the heart, I saw "the purple light of love" cast its glowing reflection on cheek, temples, neck; I desired to consult the eye, but sheltering lash and lid forbade.

"Monsieur," said the soft voice at last, "Monsieur désire savoir si je consens—si—enfin, si je veux me marier avec lui?"

"Justement."

"Monsieur sera-t-il aussi bon mari qu'il a été bon maître?"

"I will try, Frances."

A pause—then with a new, yet still subdued inflexion of the voice; an inflexion which provoked while it pleased me; accompanied too by a "sourire à la fois fin et timide" in perfect harmony with the tone:

"C'est à dire, Monsieur sera toujours un peu entêté, exigeant, volontaire—?"

"Have I been so, Frances?"

"Mais oui; vous le savez bien."

"Have I been nothing else?"

"Mais oui; vous avez été mon meilleur ami."

"And what, Frances, are you to me?"

"Votre dévouée élève, qui vous aime de tout son cœur."

"Will my pupil consent to pass her life with me? Speak English now, Frances."

Some moments were taken for reflection; the answer pronounced slowly, ran thus:

"You have always made me happy; I like to hear you speak; I like to see you; I like to be near you; I believe you are very good, and very superior; I know you are stern to those who are careless and idle, but you are kind, very kind to the attentive and industrious, even if they are not clever. Master, I should be *glad* to live with you always;" (and she made a sort of movement, as if she would have clung to me, but restraining herself she only added with earnest emphasis) "Master, I consent to pass my life with you."

"Very well, Frances." I drew her a little nearer to my heart; I took a first kiss from her lips, thereby sealing the compact, now framed between us; afterwards she and I were silent, nor was our silence brief. Frances' thoughts during this interval, I know not, nor did I attempt to guess them; I was not occupied in searching her countenance, nor in otherwise troubling her composure; the peace I felt, I wished her to feel; my arm, it is true, still detained her, but with a restraint that was gentle enough, so long as no opposition tightened it; my gaze was on the red fire; my heart was measuring its own content; it sounded and sounded, and found the depth fathomless.

"Monsieur," at last said my quiet companion; as stirless in her happiness, as a mouse in its terror; even now in speaking she scarcely lifted her head.

"Well, Frances?" I like unexaggerated intercourse; it is not my way to overpower with amorous epithets, any more than to worry with selfishly importunate caresses.

"Monsieur est raisonnable, n'est-ce pas?"

"Yes—especially when I am requested to be so in English; but why do you ask me? You see nothing vehement or obtrusive in my manner—am I not tranquil enough?"

"Ce n'est pas cela—" began Frances—"English!" I reminded her. "Well—monsieur, I wished merely to say that I should like of course to retain my employment of teaching. You will teach still I suppose, Monsieur?"

"Oh yes! it is all I have to depend on."

"Bon! I mean Good. Thus we shall have both the same profession—I like that—and my efforts to get on will be as unrestrained as yours—will they not, Monsieur?"

"You are laying plans to be independent of me," said I.

"Yes, Monsieur, I must be no incumbrance to you—no burden in any way."

"But, Frances—I have not yet told you what my prospects are—I have left M. Pelet's—and after nearly a month's seeking, I have got another place, with a salary of three thousand francs a year, which I can easily double by a little additional exertion; thus you see it would be useless for you to fag yourself by going out to give lessons; on six thousand francs you and I can live and live well."

Frances seemed to consider: there is something flattering to man's strength, something consonant to his honourable pride in the idea of becoming the Providence of what he loves—feeding and clothing it, as God does the lilies of the field; so to decide her resolution, I went on:

"Life has been painful and laborious enough to you so far, Frances; you require complete rest; your twelve hundred francs would not form a very important addition to our income, and what sacrifice of comfort to earn it! Relinquish your labours; you must be weary, and let me have the happiness of giving you rest."

I am not sure whether Frances had accorded due attention to my harangue; instead of answering me with her usual respectful promptitude, she only sighed and said:

"How rich you are, Monsieur!" and then she stirred uneasily in my arms. "Three thousand francs!" she murmured, "while I get only twelve hundred!" She went on faster, "However it must be so for the present; and, Monsieur, were you not saying something about my giving up my place? Oh no! I shall hold it fast!" and her little fingers emphatically tightened on mine. "Think of my marrying you to be kept by you, Monsieur! I could not do it—and how dull my days would be! You would be away teaching in close, noisy school-rooms from morning till evening, and I should be lingering at home unemployed and solitary; I should get depressed and sullen and you would soon tire of me."

"Frances, you could read and study; two things you like so well."

"Monsieur, I could not; I like a contemplative life, but I like an active life better; I must act in some way and act with you. I have taken notice, Monsieur, that people who are only in each other's company for amusement, never really like each other so well, or esteem each other so highly, as those who work together, and perhaps suffer together."

"You speak God's truth," said I, at last; "and you shall have your own way, for it is the best way. Now, as a reward for such ready consent, give me a voluntary kiss."

After some hesitation, natural to a novice in the art of kissing, she brought her lips into very shy and gentle contact with my forehead; I took the small gift as a loan, and repaid it promptly and with generous interest.

I know not whether Frances was really much altered since the time I first saw her, but as I looked at her now, I felt that she was singularly changed for me; the sad eye, the pale cheek, the dejected and joyless countenance I remembered as her early attributes were quite gone and now I saw a face dressed in graces; smile, dimple and rosy tint rounded its contours and brightened its hues. I had been accustomed to nurse a flattering idea that my strong attachment to her proved some particular perspicacity in my nature; she was not handsome, she was not rich, she was not even accomplished, yet was she my life's treasure; I must then be a man of peculiar discernment. To-night my eyes opened on the mistake I had made; I began to suspect that it was only my tastes which were unique not my power of discovering and appreciating the superiority of moral worth over physical charms; for me, Frances had physical charms; in her there was no deformity to get over; none of those prominent defects of eyes, teeth, complexion, shape which hold at bay the admiration of the boldest male champions of intellect (for women can love a downright ugly man—if he be but talented); had she been either "édentée, myope, rugueuse ou bossue" my feelings towards her might still have been kindly but they could never have been impassioned; I had affection for the poor little misshapen Sylvie—but for her I could never have had love. It is true Frances' mental points had been the first to interest me and they still retained the strongest hold on my preference, but I liked the graces of her person too: I derived a pleasure purely material from contemplating the clearness of her brown eyes, the fairness of her fine skin, the purity of her well-set teeth, the proportion of her delicate form; and that pleasure I could ill have dispensed with. It appeared then, that I too was a sensualist, in my temperate and fastidious way.

Now, reader, during the last two pages I have been giving you honey fresh from flowers, but you must not live entirely on food so luscious; taste then a little gall—just a drop, by way of change.

At a somewhat late hour, I returned to my lodgings; having temporarily forgotten that man had any such coarse cares as those of eating and drinking, I went to bed fasting. I had been excited and in action all day, and had tasted no food since eight that morning; besides for a fortnight past, I had known no rest either of body or mind; the last few hours had been a sweet delirium, it would not subside now and, till long after midnight, broke with troubled ecstacy the rest I so much needed. At last I dozed, but not for long; it was yet quite dark when I awoke and my waking was like that of Job when a spirit passed before his face, and like him, "The hair of my flesh stood up." I might continue the parallel, for in truth, though I saw nothing yet "A thing was secretly brought unto me, and mine ear received a little thereof; there was silence and I heard a voice," saying:

"In the midst of Life, we are in Death."

That sound and the sensation of chill anguish accompanying it, many would have regarded as supernatural, but I recognized it at once as the effect of reaction. Man is ever clogged with his Mortality and it was my mortal nature which now faltered and plained; my nerves which jarred and gave a false sound, because the soul, of late rushing headlong to an aim, had overstrained the body's comparative weakness. A horror of great darkness fell upon me; I felt my chamber invaded by one I had known formerly, but had thought for ever departed: I was temporarily a prey to Hypochondria. She had been my acquaintance, nay my guest, once before in boyhood; I had entertained her at bed and board for a year; for that space of time I had her to myself in secret; she lay with me, she eat with me, she walked out with me, shewing me nooks in woods, hollows in hills, where we could sit together, and where she could drop her drear veil over me, and so hide sky and sun, grass and green tree; taking me entirely to her death-cold bosom, and holding me with arms of bone. What tales she would tell me, at such hours! What songs she would recite in my ears! How she would discourse to me of her own Country—The Grave—and again and again promise to conduct me there ere long; and drawing me to the very brink of a black, sullen river, shew me on the other side, shores unequal with mound, monument and tablet, standing up in a glimmer more hoary than moonlight. "Necropolis!" she would whisper, pointing to the pale piles, and add "It contains a mansion, prepared for you."

But my boyhood was lonely, parentless; uncheered by brother or sister, and there was no marvel that just as I rose to youth, a sorceress, finding me lost in vague mental wanderings, with many affections and few objects, glowing aspirations and gloomy prospects, strong desires and slender hopes, should lift up her illusive lamp to me in the distance and lure me to her vaulted home of horrors. No wonder her spells *then* had power, but *now* when my course was widening, my prospect brightening; when my affections had found a rest; when my desires, folding wings, weary with long flight, had just alighted on the very lap of Fruition, and nestled there warm, content, under the caress of a soft hand—why did Hypochondria accost me now?

I repulsed her, as one would a dreaded and ghastly concubine coming to embitter a husband's heart towards his young bride; in vain; she kept her sway over me for that night and the next day, and eight succeeding days. Afterwards my spirits began slowly to recover their tone; my appetite returned, and in a fortnight I was well. I had gone about as usual all the time and had said nothing to anybody of what I felt, but I was glad when the evil spirit departed from me, and I could again seek Frances and sit at her side freed from the dreadful tyranny of my demon.

CHAPTER XXIV

ONE FINE, frosty Sunday in November, Frances and I took a long walk; we made the tour of the city by the Boulevards, and afterwards, Frances being a little tired, we sat down on one of those wayside seats placed under the trees, at intervals, for the accommodation of the weary. Frances was telling me about Switzerland, the subject animated her, and I was just thinking that her eyes spoke full as eloquently as her tongue, when she stopped and remarked:

"Monsieur, there is a gentleman who knows you."

I looked up; three fashionably dressed men were just then passing; Englishmen, I knew by their air and gait as well as by their features; in the tallest of the trio I at once recognized Mr. Hunsden; he was in the act of lifting his hat to Frances; afterwards he made a grimace at me and passed on.

"Who is he?"

"A person I knew in England."

"Why did he bow to me? He does not know me."

"Yes he does know you, in his way."

"How, Monsieur?" (she still called me Monsieur; I could not persuade her to adopt any more familiar term.)

"Did you not read the expression of his eyes?"

"Of his eyes? No. What did they say?"

"To you they said 'How do you do Wilhelmina Crimsworth?' To me 'So you have found your counterpart at last; there she sits, the female of your kind!'"

"Monsieur, you could not read all that in his eyes; he was so soon gone."

"I read that and more, Frances; I read that he will probably call on me this evening, or on some future occasion shortly; and I have no doubt he will insist on being introduced to you; shall I bring him to your rooms?"

"If you please, Monsieur—I have no objection; I think indeed I should rather like to see him nearer; he looks so original."

As I had anticipated, Mr. Hunsden came that evening. The first thing he said was:

"You need not begin boasting, Monsieur le Professeur; I know about your appointment to —— College and all that; Brown has told me." Then he intimated that he had returned from Germany but a day or two since; afterwards he abruptly demanded whether that was Mde. Pelet-Reuter with whom he had seen me on the Boulevards. I was going to utter a rather emphatic negative, but on second thoughts I checked myself, and seeming to assent, asked what he thought of her?

"As to her, I'll come to that directly; but first I've a word for you; I see you are a scoundrel; you've no business to be promenading about with another man's wife; I thought you had sounder sense than to get mixed up in foreign hodge-podge of this sort—"

"But the lady—?"

"She's too good for you evidently; she is like you, but something better than you; no beauty though—yet when she rose (for I looked back to see you both walk away) I thought her figure and carriage good—these foreigners understand grace. What the devil has she done with Pelet? She has not been married to him three months—he must be a spoon!"

I would not let the mistake go too far; I did not like it much. "Pelet? How your head runs on M. and Mde. Pelet! You are always talking about them: I wish to the gods you had wed Mdlle. Zoraïde yourself!"

"Was that young gentlewoman not Mdlle. Zoraïde?"

"No—nor Mde. Zoraïde either."

"Why did you tell a lie then?"

"I told no lie, but you are in such a hurry; she is a pupil of mine, a Swiss girl."

"And of course you are going to be married to her? Don't deny that—."

"Married! I think I shall—if Fate spares us both ten weeks longer. That is my little wild strawberry, Hunsden, whose sweetness made me careless of your hot-house grapes."

"Stop! no boasting—no heroics—I won't bear them. What is she? To what *caste* does she belong?"

I smiled; Hunsden unconsciously laid stress on the word *caste* and in fact, republican, lord-hater as he was, Hunsden was as proud of his old ——shire blood, of his descent and family standing, respectable and respected through long generations back; as any peer in the realm of his Norman race and Conquest-dated title. Hunsden would as little have thought of taking a wife from a *caste* inferior to his own, as a Stanley would think of mating with a Cobden. I enjoyed the surprise I should give; I enjoyed the triumph of my Practice over his Theory, and leaning over the table, and uttering the words slowly but with repressed glee, I said concisely:

"She is a lace-mender."

Hunsden examined me; he did not *say* he was surprised, but surprised he was; he had his own notions of good-breeding; I saw he suspected I was going to take some very rash step, but repressing declamation or remonstrance, he only answered:

"Well—you are the best judge of your own affairs; a lace-mender may make a good wife as well as a lady, but of course you have taken care to ascertain thoroughly that since she has not education, fortune or station, she is well furnished with such natural qualities as you think most likely to conduce to your happiness. Has she many relations?"

"None in Brussels."

"That is better; relations are often the real evil in such cases; I cannot but think that a train of inferior connections would have been a bore to you to your life's end."

After sitting in silence a little while longer, Hunsden rose, and was quietly bidding me good evening, the polite, considerate manner in which he offered me his hand (a thing he had never done before) convinced me that he thought I had made a terrible fool of myself, and that, ruined and thrown away as I was, it was no time for sarcasm or cynism, or indeed for anything but indulgence and forbearance.

"Good-night, William," he said in a really soft voice, while his face looked benevolently compassionate. "Good night, lad; I wish you and your future wife much prosperity, and I hope she will satisfy your fastidious soul."

I had much ado to refrain from laughing as I beheld the magnanimous pity of his mien; maintaining however a grave air, I said,

"I thought you would have liked to have seen Mdlle. Henri?"

"Oh that is the name! Yes—if it would be convenient, I should like to see her—but—" he hesitated—

"Well—?"

"I should on no account wish to intrude."

"Come then," said I; we set out; Hunsden no doubt regarded me as a rash, imprudent man, thus to shew my poor little grisette sweetheart, in her poor little unfurnished grenier; but he prepared to act the real gentleman, having, in fact the kernel of that character under the harsh husk it pleased him to wear by way of mental mackintosh. He talked affably and even gently as we went along the street; he had never been so civil to me in his life. We reached the house, entered, ascended the stair; on gaining the lobby, Hunsden turned to mount a narrower stair which led to a higher story; I saw his mind was bent on the attics.

"Here, Mr. Hunsden," said I quietly, tapping at Frances' door. He turned; in his genuine politeness he was a little disconcerted at having made the mistake; his eye reverted to the green mat, but he said nothing.

We walked in, and Frances rose from her seat near the table to receive us; her mourning attire gave her a recluse, rather conventual, but withal very distinguished look; its grave simplicity added nothing to beauty but much to dignity; the finish of the white collar and manchettes sufficed for a relief to the merino gown of solemn black; ornament was forsworn. Frances curtsied with sedate grace, looking, as she always did look when one first accosted her, more a woman to respect than to love; I introduced Mr. Hunsden and she expressed her happiness at making his acquaintance in French. The pure and polished accent; the low yet sweet and rather full voice produced their effect immediately; Hunsden spoke

French in reply; I had not heard him speak that language before; he managed it very well. I retired to the window-seat; Mr. Hunsden, at his hostess's invitation, occupied a chair near the hearth; from my position I could see them both, and the room too, at a glance. The room was so clean and bright, it looked like a little polished cabinet; a glass filled with flowers in the centre of the table, a fresh rose in each china cup on the mantel-piece gave it an air of fête. Frances was serious, and Mr. Hunsden subdued, but both mutually polite; they got on at the French swimmingly: ordinary topics were discussed with great state and decorum; I thought I had never seen two such models of propriety, for Hunsden (thanks to the constraint of the foreign tongue), was obliged to shape his phrases and measure his sentences with a care that forbade any eccentricity. At last England was mentioned and Frances proceeded to ask questions. Animated by degrees, she began to change, just as a grave night-sky changes at the approach of sunrise: first it seemed as if her forehead cleared, then her eyes glittered, her features relaxed and became quite mobile, her subdued complexion grew warm and transparent; to me, she now looked pretty; before, she had only looked ladylike.

She had many things to say to the Englishman, just fresh from his island-country, and she urged him with an enthusiasm of curiosity, which erelong thawed Hunsden's reserve, as fire thaws a congealed viper. I use this not very flattering comparison because he vividly reminded me of a snake waking from torpor, as he erected his tall form, reared his head, before a little declined, and putting back his hair from his broad Saxon forehead, shewed unshaded the gleam of almost savage satire which his interlocutor's tone of eagerness and look of ardour had sufficed at once to kindle in his soul and elicit from his eyes. he was himself, as Frances was herself, and in none but his own language would he now address her:

"You understand English?" was the prefatory question.

"A little."

"Well then you shall have plenty of it; and first, I see you've not much more sense than some others of my acquaintance," (indicating me with his thumb) "or else you'd never turn rabid about that dirty little country called England; for rabid, I see you are; I read Anglophobia in your looks and hear it in your words. Why, Mademoiselle, is it possible that anybody with a grain of rationality should feel enthusiasm about a mere name, and that name England? I thought you were a lady-abbess five minutes ago, and respected you accordingly, and now I see you are a sort of Swiss Sybil, with high tory and high church principles!"

"England is your country?" asked Frances.

"Yes."

"And you don't like it?"

"I'd be sorry to like it! A little corrupt, venal, lord-and-king-cursed nation, full of mucky pride (as they say in ——shire) and helpless pauperism; rotten with abuses, worm-eaten with prejudices!"

"You might say so of almost every state; there are abuses and prejudices everywhere, and I thought fewer in England than in other countries."

"Come to England and see. Come to Birmingham and Manchester; come to St. Giles in London and get a practical notion of how our system works. Examine the foot-prints of our august aristocracy—see how they walk in blood, crushing hearts as they go. Just put your head in at English cottage doors, get a glimpse of Famine crouched torpid on black hearth-stones; of Disease lying bare on beds without coverlets; of Infamy wantoning viciously with Ignorance, though indeed Luxury is her favourite paramour and princely halls are dearer to her than thatched hovels—"

"I was not thinking of the wretchedness and vice in England, I was thinking of the good side—of what is elevated in your character as a nation."

"There is no good side; none at least of which you can have any knowledge—for you cannot appreciate the efforts of Industry, the achievements of Enterprise or the discoveries of Science; narrowness of education and obscurity of position quite incapacitate you from understanding those points, and as to historical and poetical associations, I will not insult you, Mademoiselle, by supposing that you alluded to such humbug."

"But I did—partly."

Hunsden laughed his laugh of unmitigated scorn.

"I did, Mr. Hunsden. Are you of the number of those to whom such associations give no pleasure?"

"Mademoiselle, what is an association? I never saw one; what is its length, breadth, weight, value—aye *value*—What price will it bring in the market?"

"Your portrait, to any one who loved you, would for the sake of association be without price."

That inscrutable Hunsden heard this remark and felt it rather acutely too somewhere, for he coloured, a thing not unusual with him, when hit unawares on a tender point; a sort of trouble momentarily darkened his eye, and I believe he filled up the transient pause succeeding his antagonist's home thrust, by a wish that some one did love him as he would like to be loved; some one whose love he could unreservedly return.

The lady pursued her temporary advantage.

"If your world is a world without associations, Mr. Hunsden, I no longer wonder that you hate England so: I don't clearly know what Paradise is, and what Angels are; yet taking it to be the most glorious region I can conceive, and Angels the most elevated existences—if one of them—if Abdiel the Faithful himself" (she was thinking of Milton) "were suddenly stripped of the faculty of association, I think he would soon rush forth from 'the ever-during gates,' leave Heaven and seek what he had lost in Hell—yes—in the very Hell from which he turned 'with retorted scorn'."

Frances' tone in saying this was as marked as her language and it was when the word "hell" twanged off from her lips, with a somewhat startling emphasis, that Hunsden deigned to bestow one slight glance of admiration: he liked something strong, whether in man or woman; he liked whatever dared to clear conventional limits; he had never before heard a lady say "hell" with that uncompromising sort of accent and the sound pleased him from a lady's lips; he would fain have had Frances to strike the string again, but it was not in her way; the display of eccentric vigour never gave her pleasure, and it only sounded in her voice or flashed in her countenance when extraordinary circumstances, and those generally painful, forced it out of the depths where it burned latent. To me, once or twice, she had in intimate conversation, uttered venturous thoughts in nervous language, but when the hour of such manifestation was past, I could not recall it; it came of itself and of itself departed. Hunsden's excitations she put by soon with a smile, and recurring to the theme of disputation said:

"Since England is nothing—why do the continental nations respect her so?"

"I should have thought no child would have asked that question," replied Hunsden, who never at any time gave information without reproving for stupidity those who asked it of him; "if you had been my pupil, as I suppose you once had the misfortune to be that of a deplorable character not a hundred miles off, I would have put you in the corner for such a confession of ignorance. Why, Mademoiselle, can't you see that it is our *gold* which buys us French politeness, German good-will and Swiss servility?" And he sneered diabolically.

"Swiss!" said Frances, catching the word. "Servility! Do you call my countrymen servile?" And she started up; I could not suppress a low laugh; there was ire in her glance and defiance in her attitude. "Do you abuse Switzerland to me, Mr. Hunsden? Do you think I have no associations? Do you calculate that I am prepared to dwell only on what vice and degradation may be found in Alpine villages, and to leave quite out of my heart the social greatness of my countrymen, and our blood-earned freedom and the natural glories of our Mountains? You're mistaken—you're mistaken—"

"Social greatness? call it what you will; your countrymen are sensible fellows; they make a marketable article of what to you is an abstract idea; they have, ere this, sold their social greatness and also their blood-earned freedom to be the servants of foreign kings."

"You never were in Switzerland—?"

"Yes—I have been there twice."

"You know nothing of it—"

"I do."

"And you say the Swiss are mercenary, as a parrot says 'Poor

Poll,' or as the Belgians here say the English are not brave, or as the French accuse them of being perfidious: there is no justice in your dictums."

"There is truth."

"I tell you, Mr. Hunsden, you are a more unpractical man than I am an unpractical woman, for you don't acknowledge what really exists; you want to annihilate individual patriotism and national greatness as an Atheist would annihilate God and his own soul, by denying their existence."

"Where are you flying to? You are off at a tangent—I thought we were talking about the mercenary nature of the Swiss."

"We were—and if you proved to me that the Swiss are mercenary to-morrow (which you cannot do) I should love Switzerland still."

"You would be mad then, mad as a March hare to indulge in a passion for millions of ship-loads of soil, timber, snow and ice."

"Not so mad as you who love nothing."

"There's a method in my madness; there's none in yours."

"Your method is to squeeze the sap out of Creation and make manure of the refuse, by way of turning it to what you call use."

"You cannot reason at all," said Hunsden; "there is no logic in you."

"Better to be without logic than without feeling," retorted Frances who was now passing backwards and forwards from her cupboard to the table, intent, if not on hospitable thoughts at least on hospitable deeds, for she was laying the cloth and putting plates, knives and forks thereon.

"Is that a hit at me, Mademoiselle? Do you suppose I am without feeling?"

"I suppose you are always interfering with your own feelings and those of other people, and dogmatizing about the irrationality of this, that, and the other sentiment, and then ordering it to be suppressed because you imagine it to be inconsistent with logic."

"I do right."

Frances had stept out of sight into a sort of little pantry; she soon reappeared.

"You do right? Indeed—no! You are much mistaken if you think so. Just be so good as to let me get to the fire, Mr. Hunsden; I have something to cook." (An interval occupied in settling a casserole on the fire—then, while she stirred its contents:) "Right! as if it were right to crush any pleasurable sentiment that God has given to man—especially any sentiment that, like Patriotism, spreads man's selfishness in wider circles." (Fire stirred, dish put down before it.)

"Were you born in Switzerland?"

"I should think so, or else why should I call it my country?"

"And where did you get your English features and figure?"

"I am English too—half the blood in my veins is English; thus I have a right to a double power of patriotism, possessing an interest in two noble, free and fortunate countries."

"You had an English Mother?"

"Yes, yes; and you, I suppose, had a mother from the Moon or from Utopia, since not a nation in Europe has a claim on your interest."

"On the contrary, I'm a universal patriot; if you could understand me rightly; my country is the world."

"Sympathies so widely diffused must be very shallow: will you have the goodness to come to table? Monsieur," (to me who appeared to be now absorbed in reading by moonlight) "Monsieur, supper is served."

This was said in quite a different voice to that in which she had been bandying phrases with Mr. Hunsden—not so short, graver and softer.

"Frances—what do you mean by preparing supper; we had no intention of staying."

"Ah Monsieur, but you have stayed and supper is prepared; you have only the alternative of eating it."

The meal was a foreign one of course; it consisted in two small but tasty dishes of meat, prepared with skill and served with nicety, a salad and "fromage françois" completed it. The business of eating interposed a brief truce between the belligerents, but no sooner was supper disposed of, than they were at it again. The fresh subject of dispute ran on the spirit of religious intolerance which Mr. Hunsden affirmed to exist strongly in Switzerland, notwithstanding the professed attachment of the Swiss to freedom: here Frances had greatly the worst of it—not only because she was unskilled to argue, but because her own real opinions on the point in question happened to coincide pretty nearly with Mr. Hunsden's and she only contradicted him out of opposition. At last she gave in, confessing that she thought as he thought; but bidding him take notice that she did not consider herself beaten.

"No more did the French at Waterloo," said Hunsden.

"There is no comparison between the cases," rejoined Frances. "Mine was a sham fight."

"Sham or real, it's up with you."

"No, though I have neither logic nor wealth of words, yet in a case where my opinion really differed from yours, I would adhere to it when I had not another word to say in its defence; you should be baffled by dumb determination. You speak of Waterloo; your Wellington ought to have been conquered there according to Napoleon; but he persevered in spite of the laws of war and was victorious in defiance of military tactics—I would do as he did."

"I'll be bound for it you would—probably you have some of the same sort of stubborn stuff in you."

"I should be sorry if I had not; he and Tell were brothers, and I'd scorn the Swiss, man or woman, who had none of the much-enduring nature of our heroic William in his soul."

"If Tell was like Wellington, he was an ass."

"Does not *ass* mean *baudet*?" asked Frances turning to me.

"No, no," replied I, "it means an *esprit-fort* and now," I continued, as I saw that fresh occasion of strife was brewing between these two, "it is high time to go."

Hunsden rose; "Good bye," said he to Frances, "I shall be off for this glorious England to-morrow, and it may be twelve months or more before I come to Brussels again; whenever I do come I'll seek you out, and you shall see if I don't find means to make you fiercer than a dragon—you've done pretty well this evening but next interview you shall challenge me outright. Meantime you're doomed to become Mrs. William Crimsworth, I suppose; poor young lady! but you have a spark of spirit; cherish it and give the Professor the full benefit thereof."

"Are you married, Mr. Hunsden?" asked Frances suddenly.

"No—I should have thought you might have guessed I was a Benedick by my look."

"Well—whenever you marry don't take a wife out of Switzerland; for if you begin blaspheming Helvetia and cursing the Cantons—above all if you mention the word *ass* in the same breath with the name Tell (for ass *is* baudet I know—though Monsieur is pleased to translate it, esprit-fort) your Mountain Maid will some night smother her Breton-bretonnant, even as your own Shakspeare's Othello smothered Desdemona."

"I am warned," said Hunsden; "and so are you, lad," (nodding to me); "I hope yet to hear of a travesty of the Moor and his gentle lady in which the parts shall be reversed according to the plan just sketched—you, however, being in my night-cap. Farewell, Mademoiselle!" He bowed on her hand, absolutely like Sir Charles Grandison on that of Harriet Byron, adding: "Death from such fingers would not be without charms."

"Mon Dieu!" murmured Frances, opening her large eyes and lifting her distinctly arched brows, "c'est qu'il fait des compliments! Je ne m'y suis pas attendu." She smiled half in ire, half in mirth, curtsied with foreign grace, and so they parted.

No sooner had we got into the street than Hunsden collared me: "And that is your lace-mender?" said he. "And you reckon you have done a fine, magnanimous thing in offering to marry her? You—a scion of Seacombe have proved your disdain of social distinctions by taking up with an ouvrière! And I pitied the fellow—thinking his feelings had misled him and that he had hurt himself by contracting a low match!"

"Just let go my collar, Hunsden."

On the contrary he swayed me to and fro; so I grappled him round the waist; it was dark; the street lonely and lampless; we had then a tug for it, and after we had both rolled on the pavement and with difficulty picked ourselves up, we agreed to walk on more soberly.

"Yes—that's my lace-mender," said I; "and she is to be mine for life—God willing."

"God is not willing—you can't suppose it; what business have you to be suited so well with a partner? And she treats you with a sort of respect too, and says 'Monsieur,' and modulates her tone in addressing you, actually as if you were something superior! She could not evince more deference to such a one as me; were she favoured by Fortune to the supreme extent of being my choice instead of yours."

"Hunsden, you're a puppy. But you've only seen the title-page of my happiness; you don't know the tale that follows; you cannot conceive the interest and sweet variety and thrilling excitement of the narrative."

Hunsden—speaking low and deep, for we had now entered a busier street—desired me to hold my peace, threatening to do something dreadful if I stimulated his wrath further by boasting. I laughed till my sides ached. We soon reached his hotel; before he entered it, he said:

"Don't be vain-glorious. Your lace-mender is too good for you but not good enough for me: neither physically nor morally does she come up to my ideal of a woman. No; I dream of something far beyond that pale-faced, excitable little Helvetian (by the by she has infinitely more of the nervous, mobile Parisienne in her than of the robust 'jungfrau'). Your Mdlle. Henri is in person *chétive*—in mind *sans caractère* compared with the queen of my visions. You indeed may put up with that minois chiffonné, but when I marry I must have straighter and more harmonious features, to say nothing of a nobler and better developed shape than that perverse, ill-thriven child can boast."

"Bribe a seraph to fetch you a coal of fire from heaven if you will," said I, "and with it kindle life in the tallest, fattest, most boneless, fullest-blooded of Rubens' painted women—leave me only my Alpine peri, and I'll not envy you."

With a simultaneous movement, each turned his back on the other; neither said "God bless you;" yet on the morrow the sea was to roll between us.

CHAPTER XXV

In two months more Frances had fulfilled the time of mourning for her Aunt. One January Morning—the first of the New Year holiday—I went in a fiacre, accompanied only by M. Vandenhuten, to the Rue Notre Dame aux Neiges, and having alighted alone and walked up-stairs, I found Frances apparently waiting for me, dressed in a style scarcely appropriate to that cold, bright, frosty day. Never till now had I seen her attired in any other than black or sad-coloured stuff—and there she stood by the window, clad all in white—and white of a most diaphanous texture; her array was very simple to be sure, but it looked imposing and festal because it was so clear, full and floating: a veil shadowed her head and hung below her knee; a little wreath of pink flowers fastened it to her thickly tressed Grecian plat and thence it fell softly on each side of her face. Singular to state, she was or had been crying—when I asked her if she were ready she said "Yes, Monsieur," with something very like a checked sob; and when I took a shawl, which lay on the table, and folded it round her, not only did tear after tear course unbidden down her cheek, but she shook to my ministration like a reed. I said I was sorry to see her in such low spirits and requested to be allowed an insight into the origin thereof. She only said "It was impossible to help it," and then voluntarily though hurriedly putting her hand into mine, accompanied me out of the room, and ran down stairs with a quick, uncertain step, like one who was eager to get some formidable piece of business over. I put her into the fiacre—M. Vandenhuten received her and seated her beside himself; we drove all together to the protestant chapel, went through a certain service in the Common prayer book and she and I came out married: M. Vandenhuten had given the bride away.

We took no bridal trip; our modesty, screened by the peaceful obscurity of our station, and the pleasant isolation of our circumstances, did not exact that additional precaution. We repaired at once to a small house I had taken in the faubourg nearest to that part of the city where the scene of our avocations lay.

Three or four hours after the wedding ceremony, Frances, divested of her bridal snow, and attired in a pretty lilac gown of warmer materials—a piquant black silk apron, and a lace collar with some finishing decoration of lilac ribbon, was kneeling on the carpet of a neatly-furnished, though not spacious parlour, arranging, on the shelves of a chiffonnière, some books, which I handed to her from the table. It was snowing fast out-of-doors; the afternoon had turned out wild and cold—the leaden sky seemed full of drifts and the street was already ankle-deep in the white down-fall. Our fire burned bright, our new habitation looked brilliantly clean and fresh—the furniture was all arranged and there were but some articles of glass, china—books &c. to put in order—Frances found in this business, occupation till tea-time and then after I had distinctly instructed her how to make a cup of tea in rational English style and after she had got over the dismay occasioned by seeing such an extravagant amount of material put into the pot—she administered to me a proper British repast, at which there wanted neither candles nor urn, firelight nor comfort.

Our week's holiday glided by and we re-addressed ourselves to labour. Both my wife and I began in good earnest with the notion that we were working-people, destined to earn our bread by exertion and that of the most assiduous kind. Our days were thoroughly occupied; we used to part every morning at eight o'clock and not meet again till five p.m.: but into what sweet rest did the turmoil of each busy day decline! Looking down the vista of Memory, I see the evenings passed in that little parlour, like a long string of rubies circling the dusk brow of the Past. Unvaried were they as each cut gem—and like each gem, brilliant and burning.

A year and a half passed. One Morning (it was a fête and we had the day to ourselves), Frances said to me, with a suddenness peculiar to her when she had been thinking long on a subject and at last, having come to a conclusion, wished to test its soundness by the touchstone of my judgment:

"I don't work enough."

"What now?" demanded I, looking up from my coffee which I

had been deliberately stirring while enjoying in anticipation a walk I purposed to take with Frances, that fine summer day (it was June), to a certain farm house in the country, where we were to dine. "What now?" and I saw at once in the serious ardour of her face, a project of vital importance.

"I am not satisfied," returned she. "You are now earning eight thousand francs a year," (it was true; my efforts, punctuality, the fame of my pupils' progress, the publicity of my station had so far helped me on) "while I am still at my miserable twelve hundred francs—I *can* do better, and I *will*."

"You work as long and as diligently as I do, Frances."

"Yes, Monsieur, but I am not working in the right way, and I am convinced of it."

"You wish to change—you have a plan for progress in your mind; go and put on your bonnet, and while we take our walk, you shall tell me of it."

"Yes, Monsieur."

She went—as docile as a well-trained child; she was a curious mixture of tractability and firmness: I sat thinking about her, and wondering what her plan could be, when she re-entered.

"Monsieur, I have given Mimie" (our bonne) "leave to go out too, as it is so very fine; so will you be kind enough to lock the door and take the key with you?"

"Kiss me, Mrs. Crimsworth," was my not very apposite reply—but she looked so engaging in her light summer dress and little cottage bonnet, and her manner in speaking to me was then, as always, so unaffectedly and suavely respectful, that my heart expanded at the sight of her, and a kiss seemed necessary to content its importunity.

"There, Monsieur."

"Why do you always call me, Monsieur? Say, William."

"I cannot pronounce your W.; besides Monsieur belongs to you; I like it best."

Mimie having departed in clean cap and smart shawl, we too set out, leaving the house solitary and silent, silent, at least, but for the ticking of the clock. We were soon clear of Brussels; the fields received us, and then the lanes, remote from carriage-resounding chaussées. Erelong we came upon a nook, so rural, green and secluded, it might have been a spot in some pastoral English province; a bank of short and mossy grass, under a hawthorn, offered a seat too tempting to be declined; we took it, and when we had admired and examined some English-looking wild-flowers growing at our feet, I recalled Frances' attention and my own to the topic touched on at breakfast.

"What was her plan?" A natural one—the next step to be mounted by us, or at least by her, if she wanted to rise in her profession. She proposed to begin a school. We already had the means for commencing on a careful scale, having lived greatly within our income. We possessed too, by this time, an extensive and eligible connection, in the sense advantageous to our business, for though our circle of visiting acquaintance continued as limited as ever, we were now widely known in schools and families, as teachers. When Frances had developed her plan she intimated in some closing sentences her hopes for the future. If we only had good health and tolerable success we might, she was sure, in time realize an independency, and that, perhaps, before we were too old to enjoy it; then both she and I would rest, and what was to hinder us from going to live in England? England was still her Promised Land.

I put no obstacle in her way; raised no objection; I knew she was not one who could live quiescent and inactive or even comparatively inactive. Duties she must have to fulfil, and important duties; work to do, and exciting, absorbing, profitable work; strong faculties stirred in her frame and they demanded full nourishment, free exercise: mine was not the hand ever to starve or cramp them; no, I delighted in offering them sustenance and in clearing them wider space for action.

"You have conceived a plan, Frances," said I, "and a good plan; execute it; you have my free consent, and wherever and whenever my assistance is wanted, ask and you shall have."

Frances' eyes thanked me almost with tears; just a sparkle or two, soon brushed away; she possessed herself of my hand too, and held it for some time very close clasped in both her own, but she said no more than, "Thank you, Monsieur."

We passed a divine day, and came home late, lighted by a full summer moon.

Ten years rush now upon me with dusty, vibrating, unresting wings; years of bustle, action, unslacked endeavour; years in which I and my wife, having launched ourselves in the full career of Progress, as Progress whirls on in European Capitals, scarcely knew repose, were strangers to amusement, never thought of indulgence, and yet, as our course ran side by side, as we marched hand in hand, we neither murmured, repented, nor faltered. Hope indeed cheered us; health kept us up; harmony of thought and deed smoothed many difficulties, and finally, success bestowed every now and then encouraging reward on diligence. Our school became one of the most popular in Brussels, and as by degrees we raised our terms and elevated our system of education, our choice of pupils grew more select, and at length included the children of the best families in Belgium. We had too an excellent connection in England, first opened by the unsolicited recommendation of Mr. Hunsden, who having been over, and having abused me for my prosperity in set terms, went back, and soon after sent a leash of young ——shire heiresses—his cousins;—as he said, "to be polished off by Mrs. Crimsworth."

As to this same Mrs. Crimsworth—in one sense she was become another woman, though in another she remained unchanged. So different was she under different circumstances I seemed to possess two wives. The faculties of her nature, already disclosed when I married her, remained fresh and fair; but other faculties shot up strong, branched out broad, and quite altered the external character of the plant. Firmness, activity and enterprise covered with grave foliage poetic feeling and fervour; but these flowers were still there, preserved pure and dewy under the umbrage of later growth and hardier nature: perhaps I only in the world knew the secret of their existence, but to me they were ever ready to yield an exquisite fragrance and present a beauty, as chaste as radiant.

In the day-time my house and establishment were conducted by

Madame the Directress, a stately and elegant woman, bearing much anxious thought on her large brow; much calculated dignity in her serious mien: immediately after breakfast I used to part with this lady; I went to my college, she to her school-room; returning for an hour in the course of the day, I found her always in class, intently occupied; silence, industry, observance attending on her presence. When not actually teaching, she was overlooking and guiding by eye and gesture; she then appeared vigilant and solicitous. When communicating instruction her aspect was more animated; she seemed to feel a certain enjoyment in the occupation. The language in which she addressed her pupils—though simple and unpretending, was never trite or dry; she did not speak from routine-formulas—she made her own phrases as she went on, and very nervous and impressive phrases they frequently were; often, when elucidating favourite points of history, or geography she would wax genuinely eloquent in her earnestness. Her pupils—or at least the elder and more intelligent amongst them, recognised well the language of a superior mind, they felt too, and some of them received the impression of elevated sentiments—there was little fondling between Mistress and girls, but some of Frances' pupils in time learnt to love her sincerely, all of them beheld her with respect: her general demeanour towards them was serious; sometimes benignant when they pleased her with their progress and attention, always scrupulously refined and considerate—in cases where reproof or punishment was called for she was usually forbearing enough—but if any took advantage of that forbearance —which sometimes happened—a sharp, sudden and lightning-like severity taught the culprit the extent of the mistake committed. Sometimes a gleam of tenderness softened her eyes and manner, but this was rare, only when a pupil was sick, or when it pined after home, or in the case of some little motherless child, or of one much poorer than its companions whose scanty wardrobe and mean appointments brought on it the contempt of the jewelled young countesses and silk-clad Misses. Over such feeble fledglings the Directress spread a wing of kindliest protection—it was to their bedsides she came at night to tuck them warmly in—it was after them she looked in winter to see that they always had a comfortable seat by the stove—it was they who by turns were summoned to the salon to receive some little dole of cake or fruit, to sit on a foot-stool at the fire-side—to enjoy home-comforts and almost home-liberty for an evening together, to be spoken to gently and softly, comforted, encouraged, cherished—and when bed-time came, dismissed with a kiss of true tenderness. As to Julia and Georgiana G—— —daughters of an English baronet—as to Mdle. Mathilde de —— heiress of a Belgian Count, and sundry other children of patrician race, the Directress was careful of them as of the others, anxious for their progress, as for that of the rest—but it never seemed to enter her head to distinguish them by a mark of preference—one girl of noble blood she loved dearly, a young Irish baroness, Lady Catherine ——, but it was for her enthusiastic heart and clever head—for her generosity and her genius—the title and rank went for nothing.

My afternoons were spent also in college with the exception of an hour that my wife daily exacted of me for her establishment and with which she would not dispense—she said that I must spend that time amongst her pupils to learn their characters, to be "au courant" with every thing that was passing in the house, to become interested in what interested her, to be able to give her my opinion on knotty points when she required it, and this she did constantly, never allowing my interest in the pupils to fall asleep, and never making any change of importance without my cognizance and consent. She delighted to sit by me when I gave my lessons (lessons in literature), her hands folded on her knee, the most fixedly attentive of any present. She rarely addressed me in class, when she did—it was with an air of marked deference—it was her pleasure, her joy to make me still the Master in all things.

At six o'clock p.m. my daily labours ceased—I then came home, for my home was my heaven—ever at that hour, as I entered our private-sitting-room—the lady-directress vanished from before my eyes, and Frances Henri, my own little lace-mender, was magically restored to my arms; much disappointed she would have been if her master had not been as constant to the tryste as herself, and if his truthful kiss had not been prompt to answer her soft "Bon soir, Monsieur."

Talk French to me she would, and many a punishment she has had for her wilfulness—I fear the choice of chastisement must have been injudicious, for instead of correcting the fault, it seemed to encourage its renewal. Our evenings were our own; that recreation was necessary to refresh our strength for the due discharge of our duties; sometimes we spent them all in conversation, and my young Genevese, now that she was thoroughly accustomed to her English professor, now that she loved him too absolutely to fear him much, reposed in him a confidence so unlimited, that topics of conversation could no more be wanting with him, than subjects for communion with her own heart. In those moments, happy as a bird with its mate, she would shew me what she had of vivacity, of mirth, of originality in her well-dowered nature. She would shew too some stores of raillery, of "malice", and would vex, tease, pique me sometimes about what she called my "bizarreries anglaises", my "caprices insulaires", with a wild and witty wickedness that made a perfect white demon of her while it lasted. This was rare, however, and the elfish freak was always short: sometimes when driven a little hard in the war of words, for her tongue did ample justice to the pith, the point, the delicacy of her native French, in which language she always attacked me—I used to turn upon her with my old decision, and arrest bodily the sprite that teased me. Vain idea! no sooner had I grasped hand or arm, than the elf was gone; the provocative smile quenched in the expressive brown eyes, and a ray of gentle homage shone under the lids in its place: I had seized a mere vexing fairy and found a submissive and supplicating little mortal woman in my arms. Then I made her get a book, and read English to me for an hour by way of penance. I frequently dosed her with Wordsworth in this way and Wordsworth steadied her soon; she had a difficulty in comprehending his deep, serene and sober mind; his language too was not facile to her; she had to ask questions; to sue for explanations; to be like a child and a novice and to acknowledge me as her senior and director. Her instinct instantly penetrated and possessed the meaning of more ardent and imaginative writers; Byron excited her; Scott, she loved; Wordsworth, only, she puzzled at, wondered over, and hesitated to pronounce an opinion upon.

But whether she read to me, or talked with me; whether she teased me in French or entreated me in English; whether she jested with wit, or inquired with deference, narrated with interest, or listened with attention; whether she smiled *at* me or *on* me—always at nine o'clock I was left—abandoned. She would extricate herself from my arms, quit my side, take her lamp and be gone. Her mission was up-stairs; I have followed her some times and watched her. First she opened the door of the Dortoir (the pupils' chamber)—noiselessly she glided up the long room between the two rows of white beds—surveyed all the sleepers; if any were wakeful—especially if any were sad—spoke to them and soothed them—stood some minutes to ascertain that all was safe and tranquil; trimmed the watch-light which burned in the apartment all night, then withdrew, closing the door behind her without sound. Thence she glided to our own chamber; it had a little cabinet within; this she sought, there too appeared a bed, but one, and that a very small one—her face (the night I followed and observed her) changed as she approached this tiny couch—from grave it warmed to earnest; she shaded with one hand the lamp she held in the other; she bent above the pillow and hung over a child asleep—its slumber (that evening at least, and usually, I believe) was sound and calm; no tear wet its dark eye-lashes, no fever heated its round cheek, no ill dream discomposed its budding features. Frances gazed, she did not smile, and yet the deepest delight filled, flushed her face; feeling, pleasurable, powerful worked in her whole frame which still was motionless—I saw indeed her heart heave, her lips were a little apart, her breathing grew somewhat hurried; the child smiled—then at last the Mother smiled too and said in low soliloquy "God bless my little son!" She stooped closer over him, breathed the softest of kisses on his brow, covered his minute hand with hers—and at last started up and came away—I regained the parlour before her. Entering it two minutes later she said quietly as she put down her extinguished lamp:

"Victor rests well: he smiled in his sleep; he has your smile Monsieur." The said Victor was of course her own boy, born in the third year of our marriage: his christian name had been given him in honour of M. Vandenhuten who continued always our trusty and well-beloved friend.

Frances was then a good and dear wife to me, because I was to her a good, just and faithful husband: what she would have been had she married a harsh, envious, careless man; a profligate, a prodigal, a drunkard or a tyrant is another question and one which I once propounded to her; her answer, given after some reflection, was:

"I should have tried to endure the evil or cure it for a while; and when I found it intolerable and incurable, I should have left my torturer suddenly and silently."

"And if law or might had forced you back again?"

"What to a Drunkard—a profligate—a selfish spendthrift—an unjust fool?"

"Yes."

"I would have gone back; again assured myself whether or not his vice and my misery were capable of remedy—and if not, have left him again."

"And if again forced to return and compelled to abide?"

"I don't know," she said hastily. "Why do you ask me, Monsieur?"

I would have an answer, because I saw a strange kind of spirit in her eye, whose voice I determined to waken.

"Monsieur, if a wife's nature loathes that of the man she is wedded to, marriage must be slavery. Against slavery all right thinkers revolt—and though torture be the price of resistance, torture must be dared; though the only road to freedom lie through the gates of Death—those gates must be passed, for freedom is indispensable. Then, Monsieur, I would resist as far as my strength permitted; when that strength failed I should be sure of a refuge;

Death would certainly screen me both from bad laws and their consequences."

"Voluntary death, Frances?"

"No, Monsieur—I'd have courage to live out every throe of anguish Fate assigned me and principle to contend for Justice and Liberty to the last."

"I see you would have made no patient Grizzle—and now supposing Fate had merely assigned you the lot of an old maid; what then? How would you have liked celibacy?"

"Not much certainly—an old maid's life must doubtless be void and vapid, her heart strained and empty; had I been an old maid I should have spent existence in efforts to fill the void and ease the aching—I should have probably failed. and died weary and disappointed, despised and of no account, like other single women. But I'm not an old maid—" she added quickly, "I should have been though but for my master—I should never have suited any man but Professor Crimsworth—no other gentleman French English or Belgian, would have thought me amiable or handsome, and I doubt whether I should have cared for the approbation of many others, if I could have obtained it. Now I have been Professor Crimsworth's wife eight years and what is he in my eyes? is he honourable, beloved—?" She stopped, her voice was cut off—her eyes suddenly suffused. She and I were standing side by side; she threw her arms round me and strained me to her heart with passionate earnestness: the energy of her whole being glowed in her dark and then dilated eye, and crimsoned her animated cheek; her look and movement were like inspiration; in one there was such a flash, in the other such a power.

Half an hour afterwards, when she had become calm, I asked where all that wild vigour was gone which had transformed her erewhile and made her glance so thrilling and ardent; her action so rapid and strong. She looked down, smiling softly and passively:

"I cannot tell where it is gone, Monsieur," said she; "but I know that whenever it is wanted it will come back again."

Behold us now at the close of the ten years and we have realized an independency. The rapidity with which we attained this end had its origin in three reasons. Firstly; we worked so hard for it. Secondly; we had no incumbrances to delay success. Thirdly; as soon as we had capital to invest, two well-skilled counsellors, one in Belgium, one in England, viz. Vandenhuten and Hunsden, gave us each a word of advice as to the sort of investment to be chosen. The suggestion made was judicious, and being promptly acted on, the result proved gainful; I need not say how gainful; I communicated details to Messrs. Vandenhuten and Hunsden; nobody else can be interested in hearing them. Accounts being wound up and our professional connection disposed of, we both agreed that as Mammon was not our Master, nor his service that in which we desired to spend our lives; as our desires were temperate and our habits unostentatious, we had now abundance to live on, abundance to leave our boy, and should besides always have a balance on hand which properly managed by right sympathy and unselfish activity might help Philanthropy in her enterprises and put solace into the hand of Charity.

To England we now resolved to take wing; we arrived there safely; Frances realized the dream of her life-time. We spent a whole summer and autumn in travelling from end to end of the British islands and afterwards passed a winter in London. Then we thought it high time to fix our residence; my heart yearned towards my native county of ——shire; and it is in ——shire I now live; it is in the library of my own home I am now writing. That home lies amid a sequestered and rather hilly region, thirty miles removed from X——, a region whose verdure the smoke of mills has not yet sullied, whose waters still run pure, whose swells of moorland preserve in some ferny glens, that lie between them, the very primal wildness of nature, her moss, her bracken, her blue-bells; her scents of reed and heather; her free and fresh breezes. My house is a picturesque and not too spacious dwelling, with low and long windows, a trellised and leaf-veiled porch over the front-door; just now, on this summer-evening, looking like an arch of roses and ivy. The garden is chiefly laid out in lawn, formed of the sod of the hills, with herbage short and soft as moss, full of its own peculiar flowers, tiny and starlike embedded in the minute embroidery of their fine foliage. At the bottom of the sloping garden there is a wicket which opens upon a lane as green as the lawn, very long, shady and little frequented; on the turf of this lane generally appear the first daisies of spring—whence its name, Daisy-lane, serving also as a distinction to the house. It terminates (the lane I mean) in a valley full of wood; which wood—chiefly oak and beech—spreads shadowy about the vicinage of a very old mansion, one of the Elizabethan structures, much larger as well as more antique than Daisy-lane, the property and residence of an individual familiar both to me and to the reader. Yes—in Hunsden-wood—for so are those glades and that grey building, with many gables and more chimnies, named—abides Yorke Hunsden—still unmarried—never, I suppose, having yet found his ideal, though I know at least a score of young ladies within a circuit of forty miles, who would be willing to assist him in the search.

The estate fell to him by the death of his father five years since; he has given up trade after having made by it sufficient to pay off some incumbrances by which the family heritage was burdened. I say he abides here, but I do not think he is resident above five months out of the twelve; he wanders from land to land and spends some part of each winter in Town: he frequently brings visitors with him when he comes to ——shire and these visitors are often foreigners; sometimes he has a German Metaphysician, sometimes a French Savant; he had once a dissatisfied and savage-looking Italian who neither sang nor played and of whom Frances affirmed that he had "tout l'air d'un conspirateur." What English guests Hunsden invites, are all either men of Birmingham or Manchester, hard men, seemingly knit up in one thought—whose talk is of free-trade. The foreign visitors too are politicians, they take a wider theme—European progress—the spread of liberal sentiments over the continent; on their mental tablets, the names of Russia, Austria and the Pope are inscribed in red ink. I have heard some of them talk vigorous sense—yea I have been present at polyglott discussions in the old, oak-lined dining-room at Hunsden-wood, where a singular insight was given of the sentiments entertained by resolute minds respecting old Northern despotisms and older Southern

Superstitions—also I have heard much twaddle, enounced chiefly in French and Deutsch, but let that pass—Hunsden himself tolerated the drivelling theorists; with the practical men he seemed leagued, hand and heart.

When Hunsden is staying alone at the Wood, (which seldom happens) he generally finds his way two or three times a week to Daisy Lane. He has a philanthropic motive for coming to smoke his cigar in our Porch on summer evenings; he says he does it to kill the earwigs amongst the roses, with which insects but for his benevolent fumigations, he intimates, we should certainly be over-run. On wet days too, we are almost sure to see him; according to him, it gets on time to work me into lunacy by treading on my mental corns, or to force from Mrs. Crimsworth, revelations of the dragon within her, by insulting the memory of Hofer and Tell.

We also go frequently to Hunsden-Wood and both I and Frances relish a visit there highly. If there are other guests, their characters are an interesting study; their conversation is exciting and strange; the absence of all local narrowness both in the host and his chosen society—gives a metropolitan, almost a cosmopolitan freedom and largeness to the Talk; Hunsden himself is a polite man in his own house; he has, when he chooses to employ it, an inexhaustible power of entertaining guests—his very mansion too is interesting, the rooms look storied, the passages legendary, the low-ceiled chambers, with their long rows of diamond-paned lattices, have an old-world, haunted air: in his travels he has collected store of articles of vertu, which are well and tastefully disposed in his panelled or tapestried rooms: I have seen there one or two pictures and one or two pieces of statuary which many an aristocratic connoisseur might have envied.

When I and Frances have dined and spent an evening with Hunsden, he often walks home with us. His wood is large and some of the timber is old and of huge growth; there are winding ways in it which, pursued through glade and brake, make the walk back to Daisy-Lane, a somewhat long one: many a time, when we have had the benefit of a full moon, and when the night has been mild and balmy, when moreover a certain nightingale has been singing, and a certain stream, hid in alders, has lent the song a soft accompaniment, the remote church-bell of the one hamlet in a district of ten miles, has tolled midnight ere the lord of the wood left us at our porch. Free-flowing was his talk at such hours, and far more quiet and gentle than in the day-time and before numbers: he would then forget politics and discussion and would dwell on the Past-times of his house, on his family history, on himself and his own feelings—subjects each and all invested with a peculiar zest, for they were each and all unique. One glorious night in June, after I had been taunting him about his ideal bride and asking him when she would come and graft her foreign beauty on the old Hunsden-oak—he answered suddenly—"You call her ideal—but see—here is her shadow—and there cannot be a shadow without a substance."

He had led us from the depth of the "winding way" into a glade from whence the beeches withdrew, leaving it open to the sky—an unclouded moon poured her light into this glade and Hunsden held out under her beam an ivory miniature.

Frances with eagerness examined it first—then she gave it to me—still however pushing her little face close to mine and seeking in my eyes what I thought of the portrait. I thought it represented a very handsome and very individual-looking female face with, as he had once said, "straight and harmonious features"—it was dark; the hair, raven-black, swept not only from the brow, but from the temples—seemed thrust away carelessly as if such beauty dispensed with, nay, despised arrangement: the Italian eye looked straight into you, and an independent, determined eye it was—the mouth was as firm as fine; the chin ditto. On the back of the miniature was gilded "Lucia".

"That is a real head," was my conclusion. Hunsden smiled.

"I think so," he replied. "All was real in Lucia."

"And she was somebody you would have liked to marry but could not?"

"I should certainly have liked to marry her and that I *have* not done so is a proof that I *could* not."

He re-possessed himself of the miniature, now again in Frances' hand, and put it away.

"What do *you* think of it?" he asked of my wife as he buttoned his coat over it.

"I am sure Lucia once wore chains and broke them," was the strange answer. "I do not mean matrimonial chains," she added correcting herself, as if she feared misinterpretation, "but social chains of some sort—the face is that of one who has made an effort, and a successful and triumphant effort, to wrest some vigorous and valued faculty from insupportable constraint—and when Lucia's faculty got free, I am certain it spread wide pinions and carried her higher than—" She hesitated—

"Than what?" demanded Hunsden.

"Than 'les convenances' permitted you to follow."

"I think you grow spiteful—impertinent."

"Lucia has trodden the stage," continued Frances. "You never seriously thought of marrying her—you admired her originality, her fearlessness—her energy of body and mind, you delighted in her talent whatever that was, whether song, dance or dramatic representation—you worshipped her beauty—which was of the sort after your own heart—but I am sure she filled a sphere from whence you would never have thought of taking a wife."

"Ingenious—" remarked Hunsden. "Whether true or not is another question—meantime don't you feel your little lamp of a spirit wax very pale beside such a girandole as Lucia's?"

"Yes."

"Candid at least—and the professor will soon be dissatisfied with the dim light you give—?"

"Will you, Monsieur?"

"My sight was always too weak to endure a blaze, Frances," and we had now reached the wicket.

I said a few pages back that this is a sweet summer evening—it is—there has been a series of lovely days, and this is the loveliest; the hay is just carried from my fields, its perfume still lingers in the air: Frances proposed to me an hour or two since to take tea out on the lawn; I see the round table, loaded with china, placed under a certain beech; Hunsden is expected—nay I hear he is come—there is his voice—laying down the law on some point with authority; that of Frances replies—she opposes him of course. They are disputing about Victor, of whom Hunsden affirms that his mother is making a milk-sop. Mrs. Crimsworth retaliates:

"Better a thousand times he should be a milk-sop than what he—Hunsden, calls 'a fine lad'," and moreover she says that "if Hunsden were to become a fixture in the neighbourhood, and were not a mere comet, coming and going, no one knows how, when, where, or why, she should be quite uneasy till she had got Victor away to a school at least a hundred miles off; for that with his mutinous maxims and unpractical dogmas, he would ruin a score of children." I have a word to say of Victor ere I shut this manuscript in my desk—but it must be a brief one, for I hear the tinkle of silver on porcelain.

Victor is as little of a pretty child as I am of a handsome man, or his mother of a fine woman; he is pale and spare, with large eyes, as dark as those of Frances, and as deeply set as mine. His shape is symmetrical enough, but slight; his health is good. I never saw a child smile less than he does, nor one who knits such a formidable brow when sitting over a book that interests him, or while listening to tales of adventure, peril or wonder narrated by his Mother, Hunsden or myself. But though still, he is not unhappy—though serious, not morose; he has a susceptibility to pleasurable sensations almost too keen, for it amounts to enthusiasm. He learned to read in the old-fashioned way out of a spelling-book at his Mother's knee, and as he got on without driving by that method, she thought it unnecessary to buy him ivory letters, or to try any of the other inducements to learning now deemed indispensable. When he could read he became a glutton of books, and is so still. His toys have been few, and he has never wanted more—for those he possesses he seems to have contracted a partiality amounting to affection; this feeling directed towards one or two living animals of the house strengthens almost to a passion.

Mr. Hunsden gave him a mastiff-cub which he called Yorke

after the donor; it grew to a superb dog whose fierceness, however, was much modified by the companionship and caresses of its young master. He would go nowhere, do nothing without Yorke; Yorke lay at his feet while he learned his lessons, played with him in the garden, walked with him in the lane, and wood, sat near his chair at meals, was fed always by his own hand, was the first thing he sought in the morning, the last he left at night. Yorke accompanied Mr. Hunsden one day to X—— and was bitten in the street by a dog in a rabid state. As soon as Hunsden had brought him home and had informed me of the circumstance, I went into the yard and shot him where he lay, licking his wound: he was dead in an instant; he had not seen me level the gun; I stood behind him. I had scarcely been ten minutes in the house when my ear was struck with sounds of anguish: I repaired to the yard once more, for they proceeded thence. Victor was kneeling beside his dead mastiff, bent over it, embracing its bull-like neck, and lost in a passion of the wildest woe: he saw me:

"Oh papa! I'll never forgive you! I'll never forgive you!" was his exclamation. "You shot Yorke—I saw it from the window—I never believed you could be so cruel—I can love you no more!"

I had much ado to explain to him, with a steady voice, the stern necessity of the deed; he still with that inconsolable and bitter accent which I cannot render, but which pierced my heart, repeated:

"He might have been cured—you should have tried—you should have burnt the wound with hot iron, or covered it with caustic. You gave no time; and now it is too late—he is dead!"

He sank fairly down on the senseless carcase; I waited patiently a long while, till his grief had somewhat exhausted him; and then I lifted him in my arms and carried him to his Mother—sure that she would comfort him best. She had witnessed the whole scene from a window; she would not come out for fear of increasing my difficulties by her emotion, but she was ready now to receive him. She took him to her kind heart, and on to her gentle lap; consoled him but with her lips, her eyes, her soft embrace—for some time; and then when his sobs diminished—told him that Yorke had felt no pain in dying; and that if he had been left to expire naturally, his end would have been most horrible; above all, she told him that I was not cruel (for that idea seemed to give exquisite pain to poor Victor), that it was my affection for Yorke and him which had made me act so, and that I was now almost heart-broken to see him weep thus bitterly.

Victor would have been no true son of his father, had these considerations—these reasons, breathed in so low, so sweet a tone, married to caresses so benign, so tender, to looks so inspired with pitying sympathy—produced no effect on him. They did produce an effect—he grew calmer, rested his face on her shoulder, and lay still in her arms. Looking up, shortly, he asked his Mother to tell him over again what she had said about Yorke having suffered no pain, and my not being cruel; the balmy words being repeated, he again pillowed his cheek on her breast, and was again tranquil.

Some hours after, he came to me in my library, asked if I forgave him and desired to be reconciled. I drew the lad to my side and there I kept him a good while, and had much talk with him—in the course of which he disclosed many points of feeling and thought I approved of in my son—I found, it is true, few elements of the "good fellow" or the "fine fellow" in him; scant sparkles of the spirit which loves to flash over the wine-cup, or which kindles the passions to a destroying fire—but I saw in the soil of his heart healthy and swelling germs of compassion, affection, fidelity—I discovered in the garden of his intellect a rich growth of wholesome principles—reason, justice, moral courage promised—if not blighted, a fertile bearing. So I bestowed on his large forehead and on his cheek—still pale with tears—a proud, and contented kiss, and sent him away comforted. Yet I saw him the next day, laid on the mound under which Yorke had been buried, his face covered with his hands; he was melancholy for some weeks—and more than a year elapsed before he would listen to any proposal of having another dog.

Victor learns fast. He must soon go to Eton, where, I suspect, his first year or two will be utter wretchedness: to leave Me, his Mother and his home will give his heart an agonized wrench—then the fagging will not suit him—but emulation, thirst after knowledge—the glory of success will stir and reward him in time. Meantime I feel in myself a strong repugnance to fix the hour which will uproot my sole olive-branch and transplant it far from me—and when I speak to Frances on the subject I am heard with a kind of patient pain, as though I alluded to some fearful operation, at which her nature shudders, but from which her fortitude will not permit her to recoil. The step must, however, be taken, and it *shall* be, for, though Frances will not make a milksop of her son, she will accustom him to a style of treatment, a forbearance, a congenial tenderness, he will meet with from none else. She sees, as I also see—a something in Victor's temper, a kind of electrical ardour and power, which emits, now and then, ominous sparks—Hunsden calls it his spirit and says it should not be curbed—I call it the leaven of the offending Adam and consider that it should be if not *whipped* out of him, at least soundly disciplined, and that he will be cheap of any amount of either bodily of mental suffering which will ground him radically in the art of self-control: Frances gives this *something* in her son's marked character no name, but when it appears in the grinding of his teeth; in the glittering of his eye—in the fierce revolt of feeling against disappointment, mischance, sudden sorrow or supposed injustice—she folds him to her breast, or takes him to walk with her alone in the wood, then she reasons with him like any philosopher, and to reason Victor is ever accessible; then she looks at him with eyes of love—and by love Victor can be infallibly subjugated—but will reason or love be the weapons with which in future the world will meet his violence? Oh no! for that flash in his black eye—for that cloud on his bony brow—for that compressure of his statuesque lips, the lad will some day get blows instead of blandishments—kicks instead of kisses—then for the fit of mute fury which will sicken his body and madden his soul—then for the ordeal of merited and salutary suffering—out of which he will come (I trust) a wiser and a better man.

I see him now—he stands by Hunsden—who is seated on the lawn under the beech—Hunsden's hand rests on the boy's collar and he is instilling God knows what principles into his ear. Victor looks well just now—for he listens with a sort of smiling interest, he never looks so like his mother as when he smiles—pity the sunshine breaks out so rarely! Victor has a preference for Hunsden—full as strong as I deem desirable—being considerably more potent, decided and indiscriminating than any I ever entertained for that personage myself. Frances too regards it with a sort of unexpressed anxiety—while her son leans on Hunsden's knee or rests against his shoulder—she roves with restless movement round like a dove guarding its young from a hovering hawk. She says, she wishes Hunsden had children of his own—for then he would better know the danger of inciting their pride and indulging their foibles.

Frances approaches my library window—puts aside the honeysuckle which half covers it, and tells me tea is ready—seeing that I continue busy, she enters the room, comes near me quietly and puts her hand on my shoulder.

"Monsieur est trop appliqué."

"I shall soon have done."

She draws a chair near, and sits down to wait till I have finished—her presence is as pleasant to my mind as the perfume of the fresh hay and spicy flowers, as the glow of the westering sun, as the repose of the Midsummer eve are to my senses.

But Hunsden comes—I hear his step and there he is, bending through the lattice, from which he has thrust away the woodbine with unsparing hand—disturbing two bees and a butterfly—

"Crimsworth! I say, Crimsworth! Take that pen out of his hand, Mistress—and make him lift up his head—"

"Well, Hunsden? I hear you—"

"I was at X—— yesterday—your brother Ned is getting richer than Croesus by railway speculations—they call him in the Piece-Hall a Stag of ten: and I've heard from Brown—M. and Mde. Vandenhuten and Jean Baptiste talk of coming to see you next month. He mentions the Pelets too—he says their domestic harmony is not the finest in the world—but in business they are doing 'on ne peut mieux' which circumstance he concludes will be a sufficient consolation to both for any little crosses in the affections.

Why don't you invite the Pelets to ——shire, Crimsworth? I should so like to see your first flame, Zoraïde—Mistress—don't be jealous—but he loved that lady to distraction. I know it for a fact. Brown says she weighs twelve stones now—you see what you've lost, Mr. Professor. Now Monsieur and Madame—if you don't come to tea—Victor and I will begin without you."

"Papa—come!"

APPENDIX

'EMMA'

INTRODUCTION

THIS manuscript, a rough pencil draft of about 7,000 words, was Charlotte Brontë's last attempt to begin a new work of fiction after *Villette*. In that novel she had used the major theme of the still unpublished *The Professor*—the master–pupil relationship; and in May and June of 1853, a few months after the publication of *Villette*, she tried to rework its secondary theme, that of the two brothers, in the three fragments known as *Willie Ellin.*[1] Abandoning this attempt, she turned in November 1853 to another *Professor* motif—the treatment of a motherless, isolated pupil in a girls' school. As early as 1839 she had written of 'Miss Percy', a pupil at 'M[rs] Turner's Seminary at Kensington', whose 'Father . . . seldom came to see her . . . but when he did come, his carriage, his fine horses, and his own very distinguished appearance, never failed to make a deep impression on M[rs] Turner's organ of Veneration'.[2] A version of this story had been sent to Hartley Coleridge in 1840, and it was rewritten as a part of the second chapter of 'Ashworth', possibly in the same year or early in 1841. The heroine's father, Alexander Percy, or Ashworth, was a direct descendant of the rogue and adventurer Northangerland in Charlotte's Angrian tales, and the precursor of Mr Fitzgibbon in 'Emma'.

This 'last sketch', as Thackeray called it, was written at a very unsettled period in Charlotte Brontë's life, when she was secretly corresponding with Mr Nicholls; and she wrote only twenty much revised pages, leaving the second chapter unfinished. Some time after her marriage she showed the story to her husband, who described the occasion in a letter to George

[1] Printed in *BST* (1936), 3–22.

[2] Pierpont Morgan Library manuscript MA 2696; printed in *Ashworth*, edited by Melodie Monahan (*Studies in Philology* lxxx, no. 4, 1983), 97.

Smith of 11 October 1859 as follows: 'One Evening at the close of 1854 as we sat by the fire listening to the howling of the wind around the house my poor wife suddenly said, "If you had not been with me I must have been writing now"—She then ran upstairs, brought down & read aloud the beginning of her New Tale—When she had finished I remarked, "The Critics will accuse you of repetition, as you have again introduced a school." She replied, "O I shall alter that—I always begin two or three times before I can please myself"—But it was not to be—'[3] 'I shall alter' sounds like a firm intention to go on writing; but, 'very fully occupied' in helping in her husband's practical pursuits and with little time for thinking,[4] it seems that she achieved no more. Mrs Gaskell wrote, in a letter of 17 March 1858, that Mr Nicholls 'always *groaned literally*—when she talked of continuing' 'Emma';[5] but he always denied that he had discouraged his wife's writing. Certainly his letters after her death show an affectionate pride in her work: on 11 November 1859 he thanked George Smith for returning the manuscript of 'Emma'—'I prize it much as being the last thing of the kind written by the Author.'[6]

In 1856, after Charlotte's death, Nicholls had allowed Mrs Gaskell to see 'Emma' as well as *The Professor*. She found it 'excessively interesting',[7] and recalled it two years later when she wished to add something to a proposed new edition of the *Life* 'to make the book more attractive, & likely to sell'.[8] 'I don't know how far it would answer your purpose,' she wrote to George Smith, '—or how far you could obtain Mr Nicholls

[3] Letter from Nicholls to George Smith, 11 Oct. 1859. We gratefully acknowledge our indebtedness to John Murray for access to these and other unpublished letters in the archives of the firm.

[4] C. Brontë to E. Nussey, 7 Sept. 1854, and to Margaret Wooler, 19 Sept. 1854: *LL*, iv. 150, 152–3.

[5] E. C. Gaskell to G. Smith, 17 Mar. 1858: CP 496.

[6] Letter in Murray Archives; later quotations from Nicholls's letters are from the same source.

[7] E. C. Gaskell to E. Shaen, 7 and 8 Sept. 1856: CP 409.

[8] E. C. Gaskell to G. Smith, 17 Mar. 1858: ibid., pp. 495, 496.

consent,—to add as an *appendix*—(that's where I fear he would not give his consent,) *to the life*\whh he does not like/, the fragment of a tale she left.'

In the event, 'Emma' was not published until April 1860, when it was printed with a preliminary essay by Thackeray in *The Cornhill Magazine*, George Smith's comparatively new venture into journalism, launched in January of that year. To this form of publication, at any rate, Mr Nicholls had given a cordial and courteous assent: 'I willingly comply with your request to be allowed to print the fragment referred to in your letter,' he wrote to Smith on 11 October 1859, adding that the manuscript was 'in so small a hand as only to be deciphered by one well acquainted with the style of writing—I shall therefore transcribe it; & hope to be able to send you both the copy & the original in a few days— . . . I shall indeed be glad if Mr Thackeray will write an introduction, as I feel sure that he both can & will do justice to the character & genius of the writer—'

Nicholls had transcribed the manuscript by 14th October, when he sent off the copy he had made to George Smith, promising to forward the original subsequently: 'The transcribing has been rather difficult, but I have done it faithfully.' Three days later he sent the original, and commented, 'You will perceive that the last page has been crossed out, I thought it better to retain it, as the fragment would be less complete without it—' His suggestion was accepted, for the *Cornhill* text concludes with this deleted matter, describing Mr Ellin's protection of the distressed child. Mr Nicholls was a conscientious but not an expert reader of his wife's 'small hand'; several minor misreadings in the *Cornhill* text, such as 'proposed' for 'professed', 'anywhere' for 'everywhere', presumably derive from his transcript. It is not clear whether he was also responsible for regularizing the inconsistent proper names of the draft, and (less justifiably) polishing away stylistic roughness by omitting phrases, changing a 'caller' into a 'visitor', 'offered connections' into 'proffered connection', and so on. Possibly Thackeray or Smith had a hand in such revisions: if they did, Nicholls would be unlikely to object: he approved of later 'improvements' in poems by Charlotte and Emily that he sent to the *Cornhill*, and had a great admiration for Thackeray.

Both Mr Nicholls and Mr Brontë appreciated Thackeray's preliminary essay, 'The Last Sketch', in which Charlotte's 'noble English, burning love of truth' and 'passionate honour' were warmly praised. Thackeray used Mr Nicholls's account of the reading of the manuscript almost word for word, and completed his essay by recalling the fascination of *Jane Eyre*: 'Hundreds of those who, like myself, recognized and admired that masterwork of a great genius, will look with a mournful interest and regard and curiosity upon this, the last fragmentary sketch from the noble hand which wrote *Jane Eyre*.'

'Emma' has usually been reprinted from the *Cornhill*. We have based our transcription on the original manuscript, now in the Taylor Collection at Princeton University, and our notes indicate some of the many revisions. These reveal, for example, that Charlotte at first intended her heroine to be an orphan, introduced by 'Captain Selby' as the daughter of a 'deceased friend', and that the girl was to be 'exquisitely' graceful—a suitable 'decoy-bird' to attract other pupils to the school. We retain the inconsistent proper names of the draft along with its peculiarities of grammar and spelling, but we have indented paragraphs where necessary.[9]

Nov$^{\underline{br}}$ 27 1853

Emma

We all seek an ideal in life: a pleasant fancy began to visit me in a certain year that perhaps the number of human beings is few who do not find their quest at some era of life for some space more or less brief. I had certainly not found mine in youth though the strong belief I held of its existence sufficed through all my brightest and freshest time to keep me hopeful. I had not found it in maturity. I was become resigned never to find it. I

[9] We thank Princeton University Libraries for allowing us to transcribe the manuscript of 'Emma' in the Robert H. Taylor Collection.

had lived certain dim years entirely tranquil and inexpectant—and now—I was not sure—but something was hovering round my hearth which pleased me wonderfully

Look at it reader. Come into my parlour and judge for yourself whether I do right to care for this thing. First you may scan me if you please. We shall go on better together after a satisfactory introduction and due apprehension of identity

My name is Mrs Chalfont. I am a widow. My house is good and my income such as need not check the impulse either of Charity or a moderate hospitality—I am not young, nor yet old There is no silver yet in my hair, but its yellow lustre is gone. In my face wrinkles are yet to come but I have almost forgotten the days when it wore any bloom. I married when I was very young. I lived for fifteen years a life which—whatever its trials—could not be called stagnant Then for five years I was alone—and having no children—desolate. Lately Fortune placed in my way an interest and a companion by a somewhat curious turn of her wheel.

The neighbourhood where I live is pleasant enough—its scenery agreeable—and its society civilized though not numerous. About a mile from my house there is a lady's school established but lately—not more than three years since—The conductress of this school was of my acquaintance—and though I cannot say that they occupied the very highest place in my opinion for they had brought back from some months residence abroad for finishing purposes a good deal that was fantastic affected and pretentious yet I awarded to them some portion of that respect which seems the fair due of all women who face Life bravely and try to make their own way by their own efforts

About a year after the Misses Featherheds opened their school when the number of their pupils was yet exceedingly limited and when no doubt they were looking out anxiously enough for augmentation—the entrance-gate to their little drive was one day thrown back to admit a carriage "a very handsome fashionable carriage" Miss Mabel Featherstone said in narrating the circumstance afterwards—and drawn by a pair of really splendid horses The sweep up the drive—The loud ring at the doorbell—the bustling entrance into house—the ceremonious admission to the drawing-room roused excitement enough in Fuchsia Lodge—Miss Featherhed repaired to the reception room in a pair of new gloves—carrying in her hand* a handkerchief of French cambric

She found a gentleman seated on her sofa—who as he rose up—appeared a tall fine-looking personage—at least she thought him so as he stood with his back to the light. He introduced himself as Mr Ormond—inquired if Miss Fetherhed had a vacancy and intimated that he brought her a pupil wished to intrust to her care a new pupil in the shape of his daughter. This was welcome news—for there was many a vacancy in Miss Fetherhed's school-room—indeed her establishment was as yet limited to three to the very select number of 3—and she and her sisters were looking forward with anything but confidence to the balancing of accounts at the close of their first half-year—Few objects could have been more agreeable to her then than that to which by a wave of the hand Mr Fitzgibbon now directed her attention—the figure of a child standing near the drawing-room window†

* pair of new gloves—carrying in her hand] pair of new gloves—<and curtsied deeply to a person whom in the first glow of the incident she used to describe as "most aristocratic looking"—but whom subsequently when events had taken an unexpected turn—she acknowledged to be pursy, to breathe hard and asthmatically and to have red watery eyes. This personage announced himself as Captain Selby and proceeded to introduce a pale scared looking but elegant little girl whom he held by the hand. Miss Richmond" he said daughter of a friend of his deceased and who had left him guardian of his orphan> carrying in her hand

† the drawing-room window] the drawing-room window<—resting her elbow on its sill—Indeed the child had attractions for the principal of a more flourishing establishment than Fuchsia Lodge—though very young—she promised to possess all the points of a shew-pupil—a decoy-bird—As she stood her face and eyes looked very serious—but in her air—her dress—her very attitude there was a curious impress of the stylish little lady. None could appreciate appearances more fully than the Misses Featherhed—in fact they cared for very little else—and it was their consistent unremitting unflagging attention to outside varnish which afterwards brought them into such vogue and from obscure beginnings made theirs in due time the most fashionable and flourishing school for twenty miles round. It was that which enabled them afterwards quite to throw into the shade the Misses Sterling's school where the girls were

Had Miss Fetherhed's establishment boasted fuller ranks—had she indeed entered well on that course of prosperity—which in after years an undeviating attention to externals enabled her so triumphantly to realize—an early thought with her would have been to judge whether the acquisition now offered was likely to answer well as a shew-pupil—she would have instantly marked her look, dress &c. and inferred her value from these indicia. In these anxious commencing times however Miss Fetherhed could scarcely afford herself the luxury of such appreciation. A new pupil represented 40£ a year independently of masters' terms—and £40 a year was a sum Miss F—— needed and was glad to secure—besides the fine carriage, the fine gentleman and the fine name—gave gratifying assurance enough and to spare of eligibility in the offered connections.

It was admitted then that there were vacancies in Chalfont Grove—that Miss Fitzgibbon could be received at once that she was to learn all that the school-prospectus professed to teach—to be liable to every extra—in short to be as expensive and consequently as profitable a pupil as any Directresse's heart could wish. All this was arranged as upon velvet—smoothly and liberally—Mr Fitzgibbon shewed in the transaction none of the hardness of the bargain-making man of business—and as little of the penurious anxiety of the straitened professional man Miss Fetherhed felt him to be "quite the gentleman", everything disposed her to {be} partially inclined towards the little girl—whom he on taking leave formally committed to her guardianship—and as if no circumstance should be wanting to complete

---

compelled to learn grammar and to study history to mend or make garments—and where besides there existed a general impolitic system of treating pupils according to their intrinsic merits without the slightest reference to the wealth and status of their connections—the credit to be obtained by their own appearance—or the profit accruing from the terms on which they were recieved. Miss Fetherhed then looked with inexpressible complacency towards little Miss Fitzgibbon. The child had a graceful and flexible figure her short skirts shewed limbs exquisitely turned—never owned sylph or fairy finer ankles and feet. From under her large hat fell the most luxuriant hair richly {?} waved either by nature or art—her little face was fair and delicate and her eyes were very soft—well-cut {?} and dark.⟩

the happy impression the address left written on a card served to fill up the measure of Miss Fetherhed's satisfaction

Conway Fitzgibbon Esqr. The Park. Midland County. That very day 3 decrees were passed in the new-comer's favour.

1$^{\underline{st}}$ That she was to be Miss Fetherhed's bedfellow
2$^{\underline{nd}}$ to sit next her at table.
3$^{\underline{rd}}$ To walk out with her

In a very few days it became evident that A fourth secret clause had been added to these {?} viz. that Miss Fitzgibbon was to be favoured, petted and screened on all feasible occasions.

An ill-conditioned pupil who before coming to Chalfont had passed a year under the care of certain old-fashioned Misses Sterling of Hartwood and from them had picked up unpractical notions of justice—took it upon her to utter an opinion on this system of favouritism

"The Misses Sterling" she injudiciously said "never distinguished any girl because she was richer or better dressed than the rest—they would have scorned to do so. *They* always rewarded girls according as they behaved well to their schoolfellows and minded their lessons—not according to the number of their silk dresses and fine laces and feathers."

For it must not be forgotten that Miss Fitzgibbon's trunks when opened disclosed a splendid wardrobe—so fine were the various articles of apparel indeed that instead of assigning for their accommodation the painted deal drawers of the school bedroom—Miss Fetherhed had them arranged in a mahogany bureau in her own room. With her own hands too she would on Sundays array the little favourite in her quilted silk pelisse—her hat and feathers her ermine boa and little French boots and gloves. And very self-complacent she was when she led the young heiress (a letter from M^{r} F—— received since his first visit had communicated the additional particulars that this daughter was his only child and would be the inheritrix of his estates including The Park—Midland County) when she led her—I say into the church and seated her stately by her side at the top of the gallery-pew—Unbiassed observers might indeed have wondered what there was to be proud of and puzzled their wits to detect the special merits of this little woman in her silk coat—for to speak truth Miss F was far from being the beauty of the school—there were two or three blooming little faces amongst her companions much lovelier than hers. Had she been a poor child—Miss Fetherhed herself would not have liked her physiognomy at all—rather indeed would it have repelled than attracted her and though Miss F—— hardly confessed the circumstance to herself—but on the contrary strove hard not to be conscious of it—there were moments when she became sensible of a certain strange weariness in continuing her system of partiality. It hardly came natural to her to shew this special distinction in this particular instance. An undefined wonder would smite her sometimes that she did not take more real satisfaction in flattering & caressing this embryo heiress—that she did not like better to have her always at her side, under her special charge On principle—Miss F—— continued the plan she had begun—on *principle* for she argued with herself—this is the most aristocratic and richest of my pupils—She brings me the most credit and the most profit—therefore I aught in justice to shew her a special indulgence—which she did—but with a gradually increasing peculiarity of feeling.

Certainly the undue favours showered on little Miss Fitzgibbon brought their object no real benefit—Unfitted for the character of playfellow by her position of favourite—her fellow-pupils rejected her company as decidedly as they dared—active rejection was not long necessary—it was soon seen that passive avoidance would suffice—the pet was not social. No—even Miss Fetherhed never thought her social. When she sent for her to shew her fine clothes in the drawing-room when there was company—and especially when she had her in to her parlour of an evening—to be her own companion—Miss Fetherhed used to feel curiously perplexed. She would try to talk affably to the young heiress to draw her out—to put her in spirits—to amuse her To herself the governess could render no reason why her efforts soon flagged—but this was invariably the case. However Miss F.—— was a woman of courage and be the protègé what she might intrinsically—she was at least extrinsically rich and the patroness did not fail to continue *on principle* her system of preference.

A favourite has no friends—and the observation of a gentleman who about this time called at the Lodge and chanced to see Miss Fitzgibbon was "That child looks consummately unhappy" He was watching Miss Fitz—— as she walked by herself fine and solitary—while her schoolfellows were merrily playing—

"Who is the miserable little wight?" he asked

He was told her name and dignity

"Wretched little soul!" he repeated—and he watched her pace down the walk and back again—marching upright—her hands in her ermine muff—her fine pelisse shewing a gay sheen to the winter-sun—her large Leghorn hat shading such a face as fortunately had not its parallel on the premises

"Wretched little soul!" reiterated this gentleman—He opened the drawing-room window watched the bearer of the muff, till he caught her eye then summoned with his finger She came He stooped his head down to her—she lifted her face up to him

"Don't you play little girl?" "No Sir."

"No! why not—do you think yourself better than other children

No answer

"Is it because people tell you you are rich you won't play?

The young lady was gone—he stretched his hand to arrest her but she wheeled beyond his reach—and ran quickly out of sight—.

"An only child" pleaded Miss Fetherhed—"possibly rather spoilt by papa you know—one must excuse a little pettishness.

"Hump! I am afraid there is not a little to excuse

CHAP. 2ND

Mr- Ellin—the gentleman mentioned in the last chapter—was a man who went where he liked, and being a gossiping leisurely person—he liked to go almost everywhere—He could not be rich—he lived so quietly—and yet he must have had some money—for without apparent profession he contrived to keep a house and a servant—He always spoke of himself as having once been a worker—but if so—that could not have been very long since—for he still looked far from old—Sometimes of an evening—under a little social conversational excitement he would look quite young—but he was changeable in mood and complexion and expression—and had chameleon eyes sometimes blue and merry—sometimes grey & dark—& anon green and gleaming On the whole—he might be called a fair man—of average height rather thin and rather wiry. He had not resided more than two years in the present neighbourhood; his antecedents were unknown then—but as the Rector a man of good family and standing and of undoubted scrupulousness in the choice of acquaintance had introduced him he found everywhere a prompt reception of which nothing in his conduct had yet seemed to prove him unworthy. Some people indeed dubbed him "a character" and fancied him "eccentric" but others could not see the appropriateness of the epithets—he always seemed to them very harmless and quiet not always perhaps so perfectly unreserved and comprehensible as might be wished—he had a discomposing expression in his eye—and sometimes—in conversation—an ambiguous diction—but still, they believed, he meant no harm.

Mr Ellin often called on the Misses Fetherhed; he sometimes took tea with them—he appeared to like tea and muffins—and not to dislike the kind of conversation which usually accompanies that refreshment—he was said to be a good shot—a good angler—he proved himself an excellent gossip—he liked gossip well. On the whole he liked women's society and did not seem to be particular in requiring difficult accomplishments or rare endowments in his female acquaintance. the Misses Fetherhed for instance were not much less shallow than the china saucer which held their tea-cups—yet Mr Ellin got on perfectly well with them and had apparently great pleasure in hearing them discuss all the details of their school.

He knew the names of all their young ladies too—and would

shake hands with them if he met them walking out—he knew their examination days and gala days—and more than once accompanied Mr Cecil the curate—when he went to examine in ecclesiastical history.

This ceremony took place weekly on Wednesday afternoons—after which Mr Cecil sometimes stayed to tea—and usually found two or three lady-parishioners invited to meet him—Mr Ellin was also pretty sure to be there. Rumour gave one of the Misses Fetherhed to the curate in anticipated wedlock and furnished his friend with a second in the same tender relation—so that {it} is to be conjectured they made a social pleasant party under such interesting circumstances. These evenings rarely passed without Miss Fitzgibbon being introduced—all worked muslin, and streaming sash and elaborated ringlets—others of the pupils would also be called in perhaps to sing to shew off a little at the piano—or sometimes to repeat poetry—Miss Fetherhead conscientiously cultivated display in her young ladies—thinking she thus fulfilled a duty to herself and them—at once spreading her own fame and giving the children self-possessed manners. It was curious to note how on these occasions good genuine natural qualities still vindicated their superiority to counterfeit artificial advantages—while "dear Miss Fitzgibbon" dressed up and flattered as she was could only sidle round the circle with the crest-fallen air which seemed natural to {her}—just giving her hand to the guests—then almost snatching it away—and sneaking in unmannerly haste to the place allotted to her at Miss Fetherhed's side—which place she filled like a piece of furniture—neither smiling nor speaking the evening through—while such was *her* deportment—certain of her companions—as May Franks—Jessy Newton &c. handsome open-countenanced little damsels—fearless because harmless—would enter with a smile of salutation and a blush of pleasure make their pretty reverence at the drawing-room door stretch a friendly little hand to such visitors as they knew—and sit down to the piano to play their well-practised duet with an innocent obliging readiness which won them all hearts

There was a girl called Diana—the girl alluded to before as having once been Miss Sterling's pupil—a dashing, brave girl—much-loved and a little feared by her comrades—she had good faculties both physical and mental—was clever—honest and dauntless. In the school-room she set her young brow like a rock against Miss Fitzgibbon's pretensions—she found also heart and spirit to withstand them in the drawing-room. One evening when the curate had been summoned away by some piece of duty directly after tea—and there was no stranger present but Mr Ellin—Diana had been called in to play a long difficult piece of music which she could execute like a master. She was still in the midst of her performance—when Mr Ellin having for the first time perhaps recognized the existence of the heiress by asking if she was cold—Miss Fetherhed took the opportunity of launching into a strain of commendation on Miss Fitzgibbon's inanimate behaviour—terming it ladylike modest, & exemplary—whether Miss Fetherhed's constrained tone betrayed how far she was from really feeling the approbation she expressed—how entirely she spoke from a sense of duty—and not because she felt it possible to be in any degree really charmed by the personage she praised—or whether Diana who was by nature hasty had a sudden fit of irritability is not quite certain—but she turned on her music-stool.

"Ma'am" said she to Miss Fetherhed, "that girl does not deserve so much praise. Her behaviour is not at all exemplary. In the school-room she is insolently distant. For my part—I denounce her airs—there is not one of us but is as good or better than she—though we may not be as rich."

And Diana shut up the piano—took her music-book under her arm—curtsied and vanished.

Strange to relate—Miss Fetherhed said not a word at the time—nor was Diana subsequently reprimanded for this outbreak. Miss Fitzgibbon had now been 3 months in the school—and probably the governess had had leisure to wear out her early raptures of partiality

Indeed As time advanced this evil often seemed likely to right itself—again and again it seemed that Miss Fitzgibbon was about to fall to her proper level—but then somewhat provokingly to the lovers of reason and justice—some little incident would occur to invest her insignificance with artificial interest—Once it was the arrival of a great basket of hothouse fruit—melons—grapes and pines—as a present to Miss Fetherhed in Miss Fitzgibbon's name—whether it was that a share of these luscious productions was imparted too freely to the nominal donor—or whether she had had a surfeit of cake on the occasion of Miss Mabel Fetherhed's birth-day—It so befel that in some disturbed state of the digestive organs—Miss Fitzgibbon took to sleep-walking—She one night terrified the school into a panic—by passing through the bedrooms—all white in her night-dress—moaning and holding out her hands as she went.

Dr Cecil was then sent for—his medicine probably did not suit the case—for within a fortnight after the somnambulistic feat—Miss Fetherhed—going up stairs in the dark—trode on something which she thought was the cat—and on calling for a light—found her darling Matilda Fitzgibbon curled round on the landing—blue, cold and stiff—without any light in her half-open eyes—or any colour on her lips, or any movement in her limbs. She was not soon roused from this fit—her senses seemed half-scattered—and Miss Fetherhed had now an undeniable excuse for keeping her all day on the drawing-room sofa—and making more of her than ever.

There comes a day of reckoning both for petted heiresses and partial governesses.

One clear winter morning as Mr Ellin was seated at breakfast enjoying his bachelor's easy chair and damp fresh London newspaper—a note was brought to him marked "private" and "in haste" The last injunction was vain—for William Ellin did nothing in haste—he had no haste in him—he wondered anybody should be so foolish as to hurry—life was short enough without it—he looked at the little note—three-cornered, scented and feminine—he knew the handwriting; it came from the very lady Rumour had so often assigned him as his own. The bachelor took out a morocco case—selected from a variety of little instruments a pair of tiny scissors, cut round the seal—

and read "Miss Fetherhed's comp^{ts}– to Mr Ellin and she should be truly glad to see him for a few minutes if at leisure. Miss F requires a little advice she will reserve explanations till she sees Mr E."

Mr E. very quietly finished his breakfast—then as it was a very fine December day—hoar and crisp but serene and not bitter—he carefully prepared himself for the cold—took his cane and set out—He liked the walk—the air was still—the sun not wholly ineffectual, the path firm and but lightly powdered with snow He made his journey as long as he could by going round through many fields—and through winding unfrequented lanes When there was a tree in the way conveniently placed for support—he would sometimes stop—lean his back against the trunk—fold his arms and muse. If Rumour could have seen him—she would have affirmed that he was thinking about Miss F——; perhaps when he arrives at the Lodge his demeanour will inform us whether such an idea be warranted

At last he stands at the door and rings the bell—he is admitted and shewn into the parlour—a smaller and more private room than the drawing-room—Miss Wilcox occupies it—she is seated at her writing-table—she rises not without an air and a grace—to receive her caller—This air and grace she learnt in France—for she was in a Parisian school for six months—and learnt there a little French and a stock of gestures and courtesies. No—it is certainly not impossible that Mr Ellin may admire Miss Wilcox—she is not without prettiness—any more than are her sisters—and she and they are one and all smart and shewy—Bright stone-blue is a colour they like in dress—a crimson bow rarely fails to be pinned on somewhere to give contrast—positive colours generally grass-greens—red violets—deep yellows are in favour with them greys and fawns—all harmonies are at a discount. Many people would think Miss Wilcox—standing there in her blue merino dress and pomegranate ribbon a very agreeable woman. She has regular features—the nose a little sharp—the lips a little thin good complexion, light red hair. She is very business-like, very practical; she never in her life knew a refinement of feeling or of thought—she is entirely limited respectable &—self-satisfied—She has a cool eye prominent—sharp and shallow pupil unshrinking and inexpansive pale irid—light eyelashes, light brow. Miss Wilcox is a very proper and decorous person—but she could not be delicate or modest because she is naturally destitute of sensitiveness. Her voice when she speaks—has no vibration—her face has no expression, her manner no emotion. Blush or tremor—she never knew.

"What can I do for you Miss Wilcox?" says Mr Ellin—approaching the writing-table and taking a chair beside it

"Perhaps you can advise me" was the answer—"or perhaps you can give me some information. I feel so thoroughly puzzled—and really fear all is not right."

"Where and how."

"I will have redress if it be possible" pursued the lady "but how to set about obtaining it—? draw to the fire—Mr Ellin—it is a cold day"

They both drew to the fire. She continued:

"You know the Christmas holidays are near?"

He nodded

"Well about a fortnight since—I wrote—as is customary to the friends of my pupils—notifying the day when we break up and requesting that if it was desired any girl should stay the vacation—intimation should be sent accordingly. Satisfactory and prompt answers came to all the notes except one—that addressed to Conway Fitzgibbon Esqr May Park, Midland County—Matilda Fitzgibbon's father you know."

"What—won't he let her go home?"

"Let her go home—my dear Sir! You shall hear. Two weeks elapsed during which I daily expected an answer. none came—I felt annoyed at the delay as I had particularly requested a speedy reply. This very morning I had made up my mind to write again—when—what do you think the post brought me?"

"I should like to know."

"My own letter—actually my own—returned from the Post-Office—with an intimation—such an intimation—but read for yourself—"

She handed to Mr Ellin an envelope—he took from it the returned note and a paper—the paper bore a hastily scrawled line or two; it said in brief terms—that there was no such place in Midland County as May Park—and that no such person had ever been heard of there as Conway Fitzgibbon Esqr

On reading this Mr Ellin slightly opened his eyes—

"I hardly thought it was so bad as that—" said he

"What—you did think it was bad then? You suspected something was wrong?"

"Really I scarcely know what I thought or suspected. How very odd—no such place as May Park! The grand mansion the grounds—the oaks—the deer vanished clean away and then Fitzgibbon himself!—but you saw Fitzgibbon—he came in his carriage—?"

"In his carriage—" echoed Miss Wilcox "a most stylish equipage—and himself a most distinguished person—do you think after all there is some mistake.

"Certainly a mistake—but when it is rectified—I don't think Fitzgibbon or May Park will be forthcoming—Shall I run down to Midland County and look after these two precious objects.?

"Oh would you be so good Mr Ellin? I knew you would be so kind—personal inquiry—you know—there's nothing like it."

"Nothing at all. Meantime what shall you do with the child—the pseudo-heiress—if pseudo she be—shall you correct her—let her know her place?"

"I think—" responded Miss Wilcox reflectively—"I think not exactly as yet—my plan is to do nothing in a hurry we will inquire first—if after all—she should turn out to be connected as was at first supposed—one had better not do anything which one might afterwards regret—no—I shall make no difference with her till I hear from you again

"Very good. As you please" said Mr Ellin with that coolness which made him so convenient a counsellor in Miss Wilcox' opinion. In his dry laconism she found the response suited to her outer worldliness. She thought he said enough if he did not oppose her. The comment he stinted so avariciously—she did not want

Mr Ellin "ran down" as he said to Midland County—It was an errand that seemed to suit him—for he had curious predilections as well as peculiar methods of his own. Any secret quest was to his taste; perhaps there was something of the amateur detective in him. He could conduct an inquiry and draw no attention His quiet face never looked inquisitive nor did his sleepless eye betray vigilance.

He was absent about a week. The day after his return he appeared in Miss Wilcox presence as cool as if he had seen her but yesterday—Confronting her with that fathomless face he liked to shew her—he first told her {he} had done nothing.

Let Mr Ellin be as enigmatical as he would—he never puzzled Miss Wilcox. She never saw enigma in the man. Some people feared because they did not understand him—to her it had not yet occurred to begin to spell his nature or analyze his character. If she had an impression about him—it was that he was an idle but obliging man—not aggressive—of few words—but often convenient. Whether he were clever & deep or deficient and shall{ow}—close or open—odd or ordinary—she saw no practical end to be answered by inquiring and therefore did not inquire

"Why had he done nothing?" she now asked.

"Chiefly because there was nothing to do."

"Then he could give her no information?"

"Not much—only this indeed, Conway Fitzgibbon was a man of straw, May Park a house of cards—There was no vestige—of such man or mansion in Midland-County or in any other shire in England. Tradition herself had nothing to say about either the name or the place. The oracle of old deeds and registers when consulted had not responded

"Who can he be then that came here and who is this child?

"That's just what I can't tell you. An incapacity which makes me say I have done nothing."

"And how am I to get paid.?"

"—can't tell you that either

"A quarter's board & education owing and masters terms besides pursued Miss Wilcox "How infamous! I can't afford the loss."

"And if we were only in the good old times" said Mr Ellin "where we ought to be—you might just send Miss Matilda out to the Plantations in Virginia—sell her for what she's worth and pay yourself—

"Matilda indeed and Fitzgibbon! a little impostor! I wonder what her real name is—?

"Betty Hodge? Poll Smith? Hannah Jones?" suggested Mr Ellin

"Now" cried Miss Wilcox "give me credit for sagacity! It's very odd—but try as I would—and I made every effort—I never could really like that child. She has had every indulgence in this house—and I am sure I made the greatest sacrifice of feeling to principle in shewing her such attention—for I could not make anyone believe the degree of antipathy I have all along felt towards her."

"Yes—I can believe it—I saw it."

"Did you? Well—It proves that my discernment is rarely at fault. Her game is up now however—and time it was I have said nothing to her yet—but now—"

"Have her in whilst I am here—" said Mr Ellin "Has she known of this business? Is she in the secret? Is she herself an accomplice or a mere tool? Have her in."

Miss Wilcox rung the bell, demanded Matilda Fitzgibbon and the false heiress soon appeared. She came in her ringlets—her sash, her furbelowed dress—adornments alas! no longer acceptable

"Stand there!" said Miss Wilcox sternly, checking her as she approached the hearth. "Stand there on the further side of the table. I have a few questions to put to *you*—and your business will be to answer them. And mind—let us have nothing but the truth. *We will not endure lies.*

Ever since Miss Fitzgibbon had been found in the fit—her face had retained a peculiar paleness—and her eyes a dark orbit. When thus addressed she began to shake and blanch like conscious guilt personified

"Who are you?" demanded Miss Wilcox "What do you know about yourself?"

A sort of half interjection escaped the girl's lips—it was a sound expressing partly fear—and partly the shock the nerves feel when an evil very long expected—at last and suddenly arrives.

"Keep yourself still and reply if you please" said Miss Wilcox—whom nobody should blame for lacking pity—because Nature had not made her compassionate. "What is your name—we know you have no right to that of Matilda Fitzgibbon

She gave no answer.

"I do insist upon a reply. Speak you shall—sooner or later So you had better do it at once."

This inquisition had evidently a very strong effect upon the subject of it—she stood as if palsied—trying to speak—but apparently not competent to articulate.

Miss Wilcox did not fly into a passion—but she grew very stern and urgent spoke a little loud—and there was a dry clamour in her raised voice which seemed to beat upon the ear and bewilder the brain. Her interest had been injured—her pocket wounded—she was vindicating her rights—and she had no eye to see and no nerve to feel but for the point in hand Mr Ellin appeared to consider himself strictly a looker-on—he stood on the hearth very quiet. As to the soi-disant Matilda Fitzgibbon—speech still seemed for her out of the question. never such a pale face was seen at a legal bar*—never such a quivering frame stood in a dock.

* very quiet. As to the soi-disant . . . never such a pale face was seen at a legal bar—]very quiet. As to the soi-disant Matilda Fitzgibbon—speech still seemed for her out of the question. ⟨At last the culprit spoke—a low voice escaped her lips

"Oh my head!" she cried lifting her hand to her forehead—She staggered but caught the door and did not fall.

Some accusers might have been startled by such a cry—even silenced—no{t} so Miss Wilcox. she was neither cruel nor violent—but she was coarse because insensible—having just drawn breath she went on, harsh as ever.

Mr Ellin leaving the hearth—deliberately paced up the room as if he were tired of standing still and would walk a little for a change—In returning & passing near the door and the criminal—a faint breath seemed to seek his ear whispering his name

"Oh Mr Ellin!"

The child dropped as she spoke. A curious voice—not like Mr Ellin's—

though it came from his lips—asked Miss Wilcox to cease speaking and say no more. He gathered from the floor what had fallen on it. She seemed overcome but not unconscious. Resting beside Mr. Ellin in a few minutes she again drew breath. She raised her eyes to him.

"Come my little one—have no fear" said he Reposing her head against him—she gradually became reassured—it did not cost him another word to bring her round—even that strong trembling was calmed by the mere effect of his protection. He told Miss Wilcox with remarkable tranquillity but still with a certain decision that the little girl must be put to bed—He carried her up-stairs—and saw her laid there himself. Returning to Miss Wilcox, he said

"Say no more to her—Beware or you will do more mischief than you think or wish. That kind of nature is very different from yours—It is not possible that you should like it—but let it alone—We will talk more on the subject to-morrow Let me question her—>

never such a pale face was seen at a legal bar—

EXPLANATORY NOTES

Page 1: *Preface*: the text of the Preface given here is from an undated pencil draft composed by Charlotte Brontë shortly after the publication in October 1849 of *Shirley*. See the introduction to the Clarendon edition of *The Professor*, pp. xxiii, xxxv–vi.

Page 1, l. 17: *by the sweat of his brow*: Genesis 3: 19: 'In the sweat of thy face shalt thou eat bread, till thou return unto the ground.'

Page 1, l. 19: *the hill of Difficulty*: one of the obstacles faced by Christian in Bunyan's *The Pilgrim's Progress* (1678). Halfway up the hill is 'a pleasant *Arbour*, made by the Lord of the Hill, for the refreshment of weary Travailers' (*The Pilgrim's Progress*, ed. J. B. Wharey, 2nd edn., rev. R. Sharrock (Oxford, 1960), 42). Echoes of this passage also occur on pp. 50 and 175. For a discussion of the parallels between *The Professor* and *The Pilgrim's Progress*, see Michael D. Wheeler, 'Literary and Biblical Allusion in "The Professor,"' *BST*, 86 (1976), 46–57.

Page 2, l. 12: "*He that is low need fear no fall*": 'He that is down, needs fear no fall' (*The Pilgrim's Progress*, pt. ii, 238).

Page 3, l. 2: *the following copy of a letter*": Charlotte Brontë's unfinished story 'John Henry' includes a letter by the narrator, William Calvert Moore, to his half-brother John, a companion of Eton days, in which he describes his wish to escape the patronage of the Seacombe family and the proposal by their friends Greatorix and Calvert that he enter the Church. See the Introduction, p. xvi above, and *Shirley*, App. D, 814–20.

Page 3, l. 9: *animal magnetism*: a phrase given currency in the late eighteenth century by the theories of the Austrian physician Friedrich Anton Mesmer (1734–1815), who maintained that the universe was permeated by magnetic forces which affected the human nervous system, and which could be channelled to cure diseases. *Blackwood's Magazine* for September 1817 opens with a long letter on the subject.

Page 3, l. 11: *Pylades and Orestes*: in Greek mythology, Pylades was Orestes' loyal and constant friend, and accompanied him on his mission of vengeance to slay Clytemnestra. See Aeschylus' play *The Choephori*.

Page 4, l. 5: *how the world has wagged with me*: cf. *As You Like It*, II. vii. 23; also *ODEP*, 919.

Page 5, l. 11: *Crœsus*: the last King of Lydia (6th century BC), proverbial for his wealth.

Page 6, l. 24: *(railroads were not then in existence)*: this places the beginning of the novel's action at some time before 1830, when the opening of the Manchester–Liverpool line marked the beginning of passenger traffic on the railways.

Page 8, l. 33: *'no man can serve two masters'*: Matthew 6: 24, Luke 16: 13. Other references to this verse occur on pp. 18 and 237.

Page 10, l. 14: *irid*: iris of the eye; a rare word, but used elsewhere by Charlotte Brontë, e.g. in *The Professor*, 136, 155, and *Villette*, 16. Jane Stedman suggests that Charlotte may have 'assimilated' the technical term *irides* from Bewick's *British Birds* ('Charlotte Brontë and Bewick's "British Birds" ', *BST* 76 (1966), 39).

Page 10, l. 17: *after the roses and lilies are faded*: cf. Campion's lyric, 'There is a garden in her face, | Where roses and white lilies grow.'

Page 13, l. 16: *lion-like generosity*: perhaps an allusion to Aesop's fable of the lion and the mouse, in which the lion shows mercy to the tiny creature. See also *ODEP*, 467.

Page 14, l. 12: *laden with pieces*: laden with cloth, which was sold by the 'piece', the length in which the cloth was woven. Cf. 'the Piece-Hall,' p. 246 and note.

Page 14, l. 23: *having removed his mackintosh*: if the novel's opening is set in the period before 1830 (see note to p. 6), this is a minor anachronism; although Charles Macintosh patented his new waterproof material in 1823, the coat bearing his name was not in general use until after 1830.

Page 17, l. 2: *a strait gate enough*: cf. Matthew 7: 13–14, Luke 13: 24.

Page 18, l. 30: *posed*: puzzled.

Page 18, l. 32: *owned no God but Mammon*: see note to p. 8 above.

Page 19, l. 17: *a distant move*: an aloof bow.

Page 20, l. 23: *retroussé*: snub, turned-up.

Page 20, l. 28: *a manufacturer and a millowner*: Hunsden's occupation, his first name (Yorke), and his mixture of roughness and refinement suggest that he was an early version of Hiram Yorke, the testy mill-owner in *Shirley*. Charlotte Brontë's model for both characters was Joshua Taylor of Gomersal, owner of a cloth mill at Hunsworth, and father of Charlotte's close friend Mary Taylor. See the *Life*, i. 176, and *Shirley*, 50–60.

Page 22, l. 1: *odalisques*: concubines, female slaves. Cf. the description of Paulina in *Villette*, 'seated, like a little Odalisque, on a couch' (38).

Page 23, l. 5: *bumps of ideality . . . conscientiousness*: terms drawn from the pseudo-science of phrenology, whose practitioners claimed to be able to read character by examining the conformation of the skull. According to the theories of Gall and Spurzheim, founders of phrenology at the beginning of the nineteenth century, a person's mental qualities and capacities reside in different parts of the brain, and exist in proportion to the size of each part. For Charlotte's account of her own visit to a phrenologist in 1851, see *LL*, iii. 256–9.

Page 23, l. 22: (*a stout person in a turban*: head-dresses modelled on the oriental turban were popular in the early nineteenth century. In *Villette*, Dr Bretton's lottery prize is 'a lady's head-dress—a most airy sort of blue and silver turban, with a streamer of plumage on one side, like a light snowy cloud' (317). Cf. also Lady Ingram's 'shawl turban of some gold-wrought Indian fabric' (*Jane Eyre*, 215).

Page 23, l. 33: *the partially decayed fortunes of his house*: Joshua Taylor (see note to p. 20, l. 28 above) owned a bank which failed in 1825, and 'set his mind on paying all creditors, and effected this during his lifetime as far as possible' (Ellen Nussey, cited in *LL*, ii. 232). On p. 238 Hunsden is said to have earned enough by trade 'to pay off some incumbrances by which the family heritage was burdened'.

Page 24, l. 15: *quiz*: one who is odd or eccentric in character or appearance.

Page 27, l. 5: *must Lot have left Sodom*: see Genesis 19.

Page 27, l. 12: *Rebecca on a camel's hump*: see Genesis 24: 61–4.

Page 27, l. 27: *Alack and well-a-day!*: cf. Herrick's 'Mad Maid's Song', *Hesperides*: 'Ah woe is me, woe, woe is me, | Alack and welladay!'

Page 28, l. 16: *happed*: stacked or heaped up so as to keep the fire in (Scots and northern dialect). Cf. Scott, *The Monastery* (1820), iv: 'now it's time I should hap up the wee bit gathering turf, as the fire is ower low'.

Page 28, l. 28: *sundry modern authors*: The breadth of Hunsden's reading is evidently intended to suggest the free-thinking qualities of intellect he shared with Joshua Taylor (see note to p. 20, l. 28 above). The authors listed reflect liberal and progressive tendencies: Adolphe Thiers (1797–1877), radical statesman and historian, author of *L'Histoire de la Révolution française* (1823–7); Abel-François Villemain (1790–1870), liberal politician and literary historian; Paul de Kock (1794–1871), prolific author of popular novels portraying low and middle-class life in Paris; George Sand, pseudonym of Armandine-Lucile-Aurore Dupin (1804–76), the most widely admired French authoress of the nineteenth century; Eugène Sue (1804–57), socialist and writer of much melodramatic fiction; Johann Wolfgang von Goethe (1749–1832), poet, dramatist, and novelist, the leading figure of the Romantic movement in Europe; Friedrich von Schiller (1759–1805), dramatist, poet, and philosopher; Johann Heinrich Daniel Zschokke (1771–1848), social and political reformer, and a writer best known for his tales; Johann Paul Friedrich (Jean Paul) Richter (1763–1825), novelist and noted humorist.

Page 28, l. 30: *works on Political Economy*: although Charlotte Brontë may have had in mind such standard works as Adam Smith's *Wealth of Nations* (1776) or Malthus's *Principles of Political Economy* (1820), she would probably have been more familiar with the *Illustrations of Political Economy* (1832–4) by Harriet Martineau, whom she greatly admired and who would become a friend of hers in 1850.

Page 29, l. 34: "*morale*": one's mental, moral, or spiritual powers.

Page 31, l. 23: *Juggernaut*: an avatar of Vishnu, whose idol is annually pulled through the streets of Puri in India on a great car, under the wheels of which fanatical worshippers were said to throw themselves.

Page 34, l. 25: *Brown's nor Smith's nor Nicholl's nor Eccles'*: names with strong Haworth associations: John Brown was Mr Brontë's sexton; James William Smith was curate to Mr Brontë from 1842 to 1844; Arthur Bell Nicholls (Charlotte Brontë's future husband) succeeded Smith in 1845.

Page 35, l. 9: *the souls of just men made perfect*: cf. Hebrews 12: 22–3.

Page 35, l. 19: *his tale of bricks*: see Exodus 5: 8. 'Tale' means total number.

Page 36, l. 19: *Greasehorn!*: flatterer (Yorkshire dialect).

Page 37, l. 32: *fugleman*: leader, spokesman; from the military term for a soldier placed before others to lead them in drill.

Page 38, l. 19: *get away to your parish, you pauper*: to be eligible for relief under the poor laws of the nineteenth century, paupers had to be resident in a parish for at least a year, or acquire a 'settlement' within the parish by means of birth, marriage, or inheritance.

Page 41, l. 6: *sparkless cinders*: cf. Shelley, *Adonais* (1821), l. 360: 'With sparkless ashes load an unlamented urn'.

Page 46, l. 9: "*A singular regeneration . . . inner and outer man*: see Ephesians 3, especially v. 16.

Page 47, l. 1: *the organ of Caution*: another phrenological reference; see note to p. 23, l. 5 above.

Page 50, l. 5: *I felt like a morning traveller* etc.: an echo of the earlier allusion to *The Pilgrim's Progress*; see note to Preface, p. 1.

Page 50, l. 22: *diligence*: a public stage-coach; *fiacre*: a cab.

Page 51, l. 16: *the great bell of St. Paul's*: a similar description appears in *Villette*, 63; in both cases, Charlotte Brontë was drawing on memories of her first visit to London in February 1842 en route to the Pensionnat Heger in Brussels.

Page 51, l. 32: *bed-gown*: a short, loose-fitting jacket worn over the petticoat while working; see also the note for 'cotton camisole', p. 63, l. 19.

Page 54, l. 5: *Pelet*: possibly suggested by the adjective 'pelé', bald or hairless. Charlotte Brontë's model for this character may have been Joachim-Joseph Lebel, the French-born director of the boardinghouse of the Athénée Royal, overlooking the garden of the Pensionnat Heger (see note to p. 58, l. 27 below). One of Lebel's colleagues at the Athénée Royal was Constantin Heger, who taught literature there as well as at his wife's school.

Page 54, l. 22: *General Belliard*: Augustin-Daniel Belliard (1769–1832) was a distinguished soldier in the service of Napoleon; subsequently, under Louis-Philippe, he became French ambassador in Brussels, and was instrumental in guiding Belgium towards independence and keeping it free from Dutch invasion. For a contemporary lithograph of the Parc and the statue of General Belliard, see Gérin, 188.

Page 54, l. 24: *Rue d'Isabelle*: this was the real name of the street on which the Pensionnat Heger was situated. See the *Life*, i. 256, and Gérin, 187–9.

Page 54, l. 29: *externats*: day-girls, non-resident pupils.

Page 55, l. 17: *1000 francs per annum*: the equivalent of about £40 at the contemporary rate of exchange. On 24 July 1844 Charlotte Brontë wrote to Constantin Heger: 'On vient de m'offrir une place comme première maitresse dans un grand pensionnat à Manchester, avec un traitement de £100 ie. 2,500 frs. par an—' (*LL*, ii. 10). Gérin (193) reports that Constantin Heger's initial salary at the Athénée Royal in 1829 was 500 francs per annum, increased to 800 francs the following year.

Page 56, l. 1: "*fine et spirituelle*": delicate and lively. Cf. *Shirley*: 'Her features ... were, to use a few French words, "fins, gracieux, spirituels" ' (222).

Page 57, l. 28: "*voix de poitrine*": chest voice.

Page 57, l. 29: *affreux!*": frightful, hideous.

Page 58, l. 13: *l'adresse*: skill, shrewdness.

Page 58, l. 20: *light not being taxed in Belgium*: window taxes, first levied in England in 1697, were not repealed until 1851.

Page 58, l. 27: "*La fenêtre fermée ... demoiselles*": cf. *Villette*, 149, which describes the rear of the boarding-houses of the neighbouring boys' college as seen from the garden of Madame Beck's pensionnat: '... all blank stone, with the exception of certain attic loop-holes high up, opening from the sleeping-rooms of the women servants, and also one casement in a lower story said to mark the chamber or study of a master'. This is the room from which M. Paul Emanuel watches the girls and their teachers in the garden below, studying 'human nature—female human nature' (*Villette*, 526).

Page 58, l. 28: *les convenances exigent*: propriety demands.

Page 59, l. 7: "*pas de géant*": giant's stride: a pole with ropes attached to a revolving head.

Page 59, l. 30: *it was Zoraïde*: Charlotte Brontë had already used the name 'Zorayda' in her Angrian tales 'The Foundling' (1833) and 'A Leaf from an Unopened Volume' (1834); see Christine Alexander, *The Early Writings of Charlotte Brontë* (Oxford, 1983), 93, 121. It may have been suggested by the story of Zoraida, an Algerian maid who becomes a Christian and elopes with her lover, in *Don Quixote*, pt. I, bk. iv, chs. 13 and 14. There may also be an intentional echo of 'Zoë', Mme Heger's middle name.

Page 60, l. 13: *Their intellectual faculties were generally weak*: for similar strictures on Belgian pupils, see pp. 62, 92 above, and *Villette*, 109–16. Charlotte Brontë's contempt for the Belgians grew in part out of her patriotism, but was also influenced by her experience at the Pensionnat Heger, where she felt a sense of isolation and alienation in a Catholic environment. In 1842 she wrote to Ellen Nussey from Brussels: 'If the national character of the Belgians is to be measured by the character of most of the girls in the school, it is a character singularly cold, selfish, animal and inferior—They are besides very mutinous and difficult for the teachers to manage—and their principles are rotten to the core—we avoid them—which is not difficult to do—as we have the brand of Protestantism and Anglicism upon us' (*LL*, i. 267).

Page 60, l. 14: *animal propensities*: in the jargon of phrenology, 'propensities' meant 'impulses leading to actions', and included such qualities as Destructiveness and Secretiveness; see George Combe, *Elements of Phrenology*, 3rd edn. (Edinburgh, 1828). For other instances, see pp. 81 and 91 above; and cf. *Jane Eyre*, 391, 455.

Page 60, l. 34: *Ste. Gudule*: the church of St Michael and Ste Gudule, built in the thirteenth century, stood to the north of the Pensionnat Heger. For a photograph of the Pensionnat Heger and Ste Gudule, see *Villette*, 87.

Page 61, l. 13: "*The boy is father to the Man*": cf. 'The Child is father of the Man', in Wordsworth's poem, 'My Heart Leaps Up' (1807).

Page 61, l. 15: *the political history of their ancestors*: Crimsworth is alluding to the long history of Belgium's servitude to foreign rulers until its achievement of independence in 1830–1.

Page 62, l. 6: *ushers*: under-masters.

Page 63, l. 19: *cotton camisole*: a woman's loose jacket or morning-gown, not the sleeveless underbodice of more recent usage. Cf. the 'striped cotton camisole' worn by Hortense Moore in *Shirley*, 73.

Page 64, l. 6: *its ways are not our ways*: cf. Isaiah 55: 8: 'For my thoughts are not your thoughts, neither are your ways my ways, saith the Lord.'

Page 64, l. 15: "*Plaît-il?*": I beg your pardon?

Page 64, l. 19: *salle of the Grande Harmonie*: a minor anachronism; the Société de la Grande Harmonie of Brussels gave concerts in a hall which was opened in March 1842. Charlotte Brontë attended a concert there in December 1843.

Page 65, l. 8: *fauteuil*: armchair.

Page 65, l. 32: *maîtresse d'auberge*: hostess of an inn.

Page 67, l. 15: *maîtresse-femme*: capable, managing woman.

Page 68, l. 5: *pomme cuite*: baked apple.

Page 70, l. 5: *pendule*: an ornamental clock. Cf. Lucy Snowe's first impressions of Madame Beck's salon: 'The next moment I sat in a cold, glittering salon, with porcelain stove unlit, and gilded ornaments, and polished floor. A pendule on the mantel-piece struck nine o'clock' (*Villette*, 88).

Page 70, l. 13: *chiffonnière*: an ornamental cupboard with a sideboard top.

Page 70, l. 20: *It was however Mademoiselle Reuter*: Zoraïde Reuter, like her successor Modeste Maria Beck in *Villette*, was modelled in part on Claire Zoë Heger, née Parent (1804–90), the directress of the Pensionnat Heger in Brussels, who was rather cool and reserved in manner: see the *Life*, i. 311. Though she was friendly enough towards Charlotte and Emily Brontë during their stay at the pensionnat in 1842, her mood changed the following year when Charlotte, now without her sister, began to show signs of an infatuation with her husband. For an account of the Hegers and their school, see Gérin, 189–94.

Page 71, l. 32: *Ledru*: perhaps a play on 'dru', meaning lively or lusty.

Page 73, l. 10: "*Comme vous avez l'air rayonnant!*": How radiant you look!

Page 73, l. 17: *ne vous laissez . . . impressions*: don't give way to vivid impressions.

Page 74, l. 1: *mousseline-laine*: woollen fabric of light texture.

Page 74, l. 2: *manchettes*: cuffs.

Page 74, l. 3: *brodequins*: laced boots.

Page 74, l. 20: *armoire*: cupboard.

Page 74, l. 32: *estrade*: dais, platform.

Page 75, l. 33: *prête à pâmer de rire*: ready to die with laughter.

Page 75, l. 35: *blanc-bec*": greenhorn, beginner.

Page 76, l. 13: *Eulalie, Hortense, Caroline*: cf. 'Mesdemoiselles Blanche, Virginie, and Angélique', the 'three titled belles' who try to disrupt Lucy Snowe's first class (*Villette*, 109–11).

Page 77, l. 13: *a smile "de sa façon"*: a characteristic smile.

Page 77, l. 14: *Pauline Borghese ... Lucrèce de Borgia*: Pauline Borghese (1780–1825), sister of Napoleon Bonaparte, was a renowned beauty; Charlotte Brontë had probably seen reproductions of Canova's famous statue of her as 'Venus Triumphant'. Lucrezia Borgia (1480–1519), daughter of Pope Alexander VI and sister of Cesare Borgia, was reputed to have led a violent and wanton youth, though in later life she became an important patron of the arts and learning.

Page 79, l. 9: *beaufet ... armoire vitrée*: sideboard and glazed cupboard.

Page 79, l. 13: *cabas*: small bags or baskets.

Page 81, l. 13: *Talleyrand*: Charles Maurice Talleyrand de Périgord (1754–1838) was a consummate politician renowned for his guile and resourcefulness, who held high office both under Napoleon and in the ministries of the restored Bourbon monarchs.

Page 82, l. 1: *crafty little politician*: this aspect of Mlle Reuter's character is given fuller development in the depiction of Madame Beck in *Villette*: see 99–102.

Page 82, l. 11: *maigre-day*: in the Roman Catholic Church, a day on which flesh may not be eaten.

Page 82, l. 13: *stock-fish*: cod or similar fish cured by splitting and drying in the open air, without salt.

Page 82, l. 16: *in heaven above or in the earth beneath*: Exodus 20: 4 (BCP, Holy Communion).

Page 82, l. 23: *mauvais sujet!*": bad lot, ne'er-do-well.

Page 82, l. 25: *que je vous gronde un peu*": so that I may scold you a little.

Page 83, l. 10: *bêtes de somme*: beasts of burden.

Page 83, l. 30: "*Honi soit qui mal y pense*": shame to him who thinks evil of this; the motto of the Order of the Garter.

Page 84, l. 12: *n'est-ce pas . . . supérieurement?*": wouldn't that suit you extremely well?

Page 85, l. 6: *bonnet grec*: a rimless smoking-cap or fez, normally worn indoors; M. Paul's usual headgear in *Villette*.

Page 86, l. 14: *une jolie espiègle*: a pretty rogue.

Page 86, l. 24: *houri!*: a nymph in the Mohammedan Paradise; a voluptuously beautiful woman. Cf. 'the dark heaven of Houris' eyes', in Byron's *The Giaour* (1813).

Page 87, l. 16: *gay strain of Béranger's*: Pierre-Jean Béranger (1780–1857) wrote many light, popular *chansons*, witty or satiric verses which were set to music.

Page 88, l. 13: *the genus "jeune fille"*: cf. Lucy Snowe's distinction 'between the novelist's and poet's ideal "jeune fille," and the said "jeune fille" as she really is' (*Villette*, 109).

Page 89, l. 2: *Very little open quarrelling*: cf. Charlotte Brontë's letter to Branwell, dated 1 May 1843: 'Nobody ever gets into a passion here. Such a thing is not known. The phlegm that thickens their blood is too gluey to boil. They are very false in their relations with each other, but they rarely quarrel, and friendship is a folly they are unacquainted with' (*LL*, i. 297).

Page 89, l. 28: *bottines*: ankle-boots.

Page 91, l. 23: *Pope Alexander the sixth*: the infamous Rodrigo Borgia (1431–1503), pope from 1492–1503, and the father of Cesare and Lucrezia Borgia (see note to p. 77, l. 14 above). Charlotte Brontë may have been familiar with Spurzheim's analysis of the conformation of his skull: 'This cerebral organization is despicable in the eyes of a phrenologist. The animal organs compose by far its greatest portion. . . . The cervical and whole basilar region of the head are particularly developed, the organs of the perceptive faculties are pretty large, but the sincipital region is exceedingly low, particularly at the organs of benevolence, veneration and conscientiousness. Such a head is unfit for any employment of a superior kind, and never gives birth to sentiments of humanity. The sphere of its activity does not extend beyond those enjoyments which minister to the animal portion of human nature' (*Phrenology, In Connexion With The Study Of Physiognomy* (Boston, 1833), 71).

Page 91, l. 28: *fibrous and bilious*: according to Spurzheim, the bilious temperament 'is characterized by black hair, a dark, yellowish, or brown skin, black eyes, moderately full, but firm muscles, and harshly-expressed forms. Those endowed with this constitution have a strongly marked and decided expression of countenance' (*Phrenology, In Connexion with the Study of Physiognomy*, 16–17).

Page 91, l. 31: "*regard*": look, aspect.

Page 91, l. 36: *worky-day*: a dialectal form of 'workaday', formed by analogy with 'holiday'. Cf. *Antony and Cleopatra*, I. ii. 55: 'Prythee tell her but a worky day Fortune.'

Page 94, l. 14: *Mesdemoiselles Zéphyrine, Pélagie and Suzette*: these correspond to the three teachers described more fully in *Villette* (175–6), one of whom, like Zéphyrine, is a 'prodigal and profligate' Parisienne. For descriptions of the originals on whom the teachers were modelled, see *LL*, i. 260, 298–9.

Page 95, l. 1: *Jack o'lanthorns*: will-o'-the-wisps.

Page 96, l. 1: *the casket ... jewel within*: cf. *All's Well That Ends Well*, II. v. 26.

Page 98, l. 1: '*inconvenant*': unseemly or improper.

Page 98, l. 4: *clear-obscure*: chiaroscuro, gradations or contrasts of light and shade.

Page 98, l. 20: *the persiennes of one croisée*: the slatted shutters of one casement-window.

Page 102, l. 6: *gambadoes*: sudden or fantastic actions; from French 'gambader', to leap or caper.

Page 102, l. 28: *half-pistolet*: in Belgian usage, a 'pistolet' is a small bread roll.

Page 103, l. 10: *Consolations of Philosophy*: the capitals suggest an allusion to the *De Consolatione Philosophiae* of Boethius.

Page 103, l. 12: *balm ... at Gilead*: Jeremiah 8: 22, 46: 11.

Page 108, l. 10: *Marie, "vierge céleste*: Charlotte Brontë had scant respect for Catholic ritual; in July 1842, during her stay at the Pensionnat Heger, she wrote to Ellen Nussey of the 'mummeries' of Catholicism, and condemned the 'idiotic, mercenary, aspect of *all* the priests' (*LL*, i. 267).

Page 109, l. 3: *Scipio-like self-control*: it was said of Scipio Africanus the elder (235–183 BC) that when a fair princess fell into his hands after the capture of New Carthage, he avoided temptation by refusing to see her, and restored her to her parents. Cf. *Paradise Regained*, ii. 199–200.

Page 110, l. 21: *his only ewe-lamb*: see 2 Samuel 12: 1–7.

Page 114, l. 4: *carré*: the 'hall, large, lofty, and square' described on p. 74 above. In *Villette*, the carré is defined as 'a large square hall between the dwelling-house and the pensionnat' (106).

Page 115, l. 29: *(Vide, the history of Scotland.)*: the passage cited is taken, with some minor changes, from Sir Walter Scott's *Tales of a Grandfather*, 1st ser. (Edinburgh, 1828), II. vii. 105. It is part of Scott's account of the assassination of James I of Scotland at Perth in 1436.

Page 121, l. 19: *Alfred tending cakes*: the pencil draft of a poem by Charlotte Brontë based on the same apocryphal story, and with many similarities of idea and expression, is at BPM (Bonnell 106). See *The Poems of Charlotte Brontë*, ed. V. A. Neufeldt (New York and London, 1985), 230–1.

Page 122, l. 26: *a great, black bull or a shadowy goblin dog*: In a fragment in BPM (Bonnell 104) that may be a part of her poem on Alfred (see previous note), Charlotte writes of ill omens 'Like wolf—black bull or goblin hound', and of an apparition with wings that betokens an impending death. Cf. Jane Eyre's description of her encounter with 'a great dog . . . exactly one mask of Bessie's Gytrash' (*Jane Eyre*, 136). In 'Percy' (a fragment dated 30 Dec. 1837) Branwell Brontë had described the Gytrash as a creature appearing variously as 'a black dog dragging a chain, a dusky calf, nay, even a rolling stone' (cited by Gérin, *Branwell Brontë* (1961), 136). *Blackwood's Magazine* for November 1830 includes an article on 'The Spectral Dog—An Illusion'. For other accounts of spectral dogs as omens of death, see K. M. Briggs, *A Dictionary of British Folk Tales*, pt. B (1971), i. 3–19.

Page 123, l. 10: *took on him the form of man*: cf. Philippians 2: 6–7.

Page 124, l. 14: *cahier*: exercise book.

Page 125, l. 7: *tabouret*: stool.

Page 130, l. 29: *Berlin wools*: Berlin wool is a soft woollen yarn used for knitting or embroidery.

Page 131, l. 33: *moved to me*: bowed in salutation.

Page 133, l. 10: *the bourgeois*: citizens, inhabitants.

Page 133, l. 22: *I am isolated; I am too a heretic*: in April 1843 Charlotte Brontë, writing to Ellen Nussey, described her situation at the Hegers in similar terms: '. . . there are privations and humiliations to submit to—there is monotony and uniformity of life—and above all there is a constant sense of solitude in the midst of numbers—the Protestant the Foreigner is a solitary being whether as teacher or pupil' (*LL*, i. 295).

Page 135, l. 7: *penny-fee*: money, wages (Scots dialect).

Page 135, l. 10: *the very breath of her nostrils*: cf. Isaiah 2: 22.

Page 137, l. 32: *virgin forest and great, new-world river*: the subject and treatment of Frances's devoir may have been suggested by the writings of Chateaubriand, in such works as *Atala* (1801) and *Le Génie du Christianisme* (1802). As a pupil at the Hegers' school, Charlotte Brontë had copied out selections from both these works: from *Atala* she transcribed a passage headed 'La Cataracte de Niagara', and from *Le Génie* an excerpt with the heading 'Prière du Soir à bord d'un Vaisseau' (exercise book at BPM, Bonnell 115).

Page 138, l. 32: *castor*: a fur hat.

Page 139, l. 1: *a concurrent*: the noun is used here in its French sense of competitor or rival.

Page 139, l. 15: *ambition . . . mind of a woman*: in December 1836 Charlotte Brontë had written to the Poet Laureate, Robert Southey, asking his opinion of her poems; in his reply, Southey warned her against seeking literary fame: 'Literature cannot be the business of a woman's life, and it ought not to be. The more she is engaged in her proper duties, the less leisure will she have for it, even as an accomplishment and a recreation' (*Life*, i. 178).

Page 140, l. 4: *coûte que coûte*: at all costs.

Page 140, l. 32: *grisette*: working girl; cf. Madame Beck's portresse Rosine Matou, 'an unprincipled though pretty little French grisette' (*Villette*, 143).

Page 142, l. 10: *la vie champêtre*: country life.

Page 143, l. 12: *état d'instituteur*: profession of schoolteacher.

Page 144, l. 24: *the great Mogul*: the title bestowed by Europeans on the Mohammedan-Tartar emperors of India.

Page 145, l. 30: *the 'basse ville'*: the 'lower town' was the older part of Brussels, a largely working-class district with narrow winding streets and picturesque houses dating back to the sixteenth century. Lucy Snowe visits the Basse-Ville, which she calls 'old and grim': see *Villette*, 559–60. Mlle Reuter's suggestion about Frances's address is meant to mislead, for the street on which Frances lives (see note to p. 158, l. 28) is in the upper town, not the 'basse ville'.

Page 148, l. 6: *perfected by love purified from fear*: see 1 John 4: 18.

Page 148, l. 19: *the silent system*: the rule of silence, introduced into English prisons early in the nineteenth century.

Page 149, l. 36: *never see you more*: the phrasing and sentiments of Frances's letter are strongly reminiscent of Charlotte Brontë's letters to Constantin Heger in 1844–5: on 18 Nov. 1845, for example, she wrote 'truly I find it difficult to be cheerful so long as I think I shall never see you more' (*LL*, ii. 69).

Page 151, l. 10: *petit commissionaire*: errand-boy, messenger.

Page 151, l. 19: *Allée verte*: a promenade in the northern part of Brussels, near the Porte d'Anvers.

Page 151, l. 20: *St. Jacques*: the church of St Jacques-sur-Caudenberg, to the south of the Rue d'Isabelle and the Pensionnat Heger. For Ste Gudule, see note to p. 60 above.

Page 151, l. 20: *the two protestant chapels*: Anglicans in Brussels might worship at the Chapel Royal, which Charlotte and Emily attended, or at St George's Chapel, the church preferred by Charlotte's friends the Wheelwrights. See Gérin, 199–200, and *LL*, i. 302.

Page 151, l. 31: "*encadrées*": bordered, framed.

Page 152, l. 14: *salut at the church of Coburg)*: 'salut' is the evening service. 'Coburg' is probably a slip for 'Caudenberg'; the church of St Jacques-sur-Caudenberg in the Place Royale is a short walk from the Chapel Royal in the Place du Musée.

Page 152, l. 22: *couc?*: Flemish 'koek', meaning cake.

Page 152, l. 23: *anglice*: in English.

Page 152, l. 24: *porte de Louvain*: one of the seven gates originally giving access to the once fortified city of Brussels.

Page 152, l. 33: *campaign*: tract of open country (archaic).

Page 153, l. 22: "*The protestant Cemetery*: this was situated outside Brussels on the Chaussée de Louvain. It was here that Martha Taylor, younger sister of Charlotte's friend Mary Taylor, was buried in October 1842. Charlotte, Emily, and Mary visited the grave together on 30 October 1842: see *Mary Taylor, Friend of Charlotte*

Brontë: Letters from New Zealand and Elsewhere, ed. Joan Stevens (Auckland, 1972), 39–41; and *LL*, i. 274–5, 282. Martha Taylor appears as 'Jessie Yorke' in *Shirley*, where allusion is made to her 'grave new-made in a heretic cemetery' (460).

Page 154, l. 4: *fitful, wandering airs*: cf. 'He comes with western winds, with evening's wandering airs', from Emily Brontë's poem 'Julian M. and A. G. Rochelle' (*The Complete Poems of Emily Jane Brontë*, ed. C. W. Hatfield (New York, 1941), 238). A shorter version of the poem appears in *Poems by Currer, Ellis, and Acton Bell* (1846) under the title 'The Prisoner. A fragment'.

Page 156, l. 34: *my lost sheep*: cf. Matthew 18: 11–12.

Page 158, l. 28: "*Rue Notre Dame aux Neiges*": Charlotte Brontë places Frances's lodging in a dingy street of small working-class houses not far from the Rue d'Isabelle and the Pensionnat Heger.

Page 158, l. 32: *heavy, prone and broad*: 'prone' carries the sense of steeply descending, headlong; cf. *Villette*, 564: 'this storm . . . rushed down prone'.

Page 161, l. 24: *sweet . . . as manna*: see Exodus 16: 31.

Page 162, l. 21: "*secret top of Oreb or Sinai*": *Paradise Lost*, i. 6–7.

Page 163, l. 23: *look to England as my Canaan*: Frances's words are an ironic echo of Charlotte Brontë's comment to Ellen Nussey on her desire to attend school in Belgium: 'Brussels is still my promised land' (10 Dec. 1841, *LL*, i. 247).

Page 169, l. 7: *in a fine frenzy . . . fool and the lunatic*: see *A Midsummer Night's Dream*, v. i. 7 ff.

Page 169, l. 17: *comminations*: threats of divine punishment or vengeance.

Page 169, l. 35: *his ladye-love*: for a similarly ironic allusion to the language of love ballads, see Byron, *The Giaour*: 'I cannot prate in puling strain | Of ladye-love and beauty's chain.'

Page 170, l. 14: *mœurs de Caton*: the morals of Cato (the Roman censor who, in the first century BC, sought to reform the lax morality of the Roman nobility).

Page 170, l. 24: *Helot humility*: the Helots were serfs in ancient Sparta.

Page 171, l. 6: "*Que le dédain lui sied bien!*": how well disdain becomes him!

Page 171, l. 12: *"Il me fait ... ses besicles"*: with his spectacles, he quite puts me in mind of a brown owl.

Page 171, l. 23: *the iron of jealousy ... his soul*: cf. Psalm 105: 18 (BCP).

Page 173, l. 23: *porte de Flandre*: the gate on the north-west side of Brussels, about a mile from the Rue d'Isabelle. Charlotte Brontë would have passed through this gate on her arrival in Brussels, and on her visits to Koekelberg where the Taylor sisters were at school. See Gérin, 202–3.

Page 174, l. 8: *a mind degraded*: there is little doubt that in this account of the 'results produced by a course of interesting and romantic domestic treachery', Charlotte Brontë is alluding to the experience of her brother Branwell, who had been dismissed from his post as tutor in the Robinson family in July 1845, allegedly on the discovery of his affair with Lydia Robinson, his employer's wife. After his return to Haworth, Branwell had entered on the course of drugs and alcohol that would lead him to his death on 24 September 1848 at the age of 30. Many of Charlotte's letters at this time refer to his dissipation and lack of self-government: see, e.g., *LL*, ii. 43, 57–8, 65–6, 74, 76–7. For accounts of Branwell's relations with Mrs. Robinson, see the *Life*, I. xiii; Francis A. Leyland, *The Brontë Family, With Special Reference to Patrick Branwell Brontë* (London, 1886), ii. 33–93; and Gérin, *Branwell Brontë*, 216–43.

Page 175, l. 5: *Rough and steep was the path* etc.: another allusion to *The Pilgrim's Progress*; see note to p. 1, l. 19 above.

Page 176, l. 25: *owe no man anything*: cf. Romans 13: 8.

Page 178, l. 23: *heave-shoulders ... wave-breasts*: see Leviticus 10: 14–15.

Page 178, l. 35: *Zénobie*: like 'Zoraïde' (see note to p. 59, l. 30 above), this is a name with strong Angrian associations: Lady Zenobia Ellrington figures prominently in Charlotte Brontë's juvenilia as a renowned bluestocking passionately enamoured of the Duke of Zamorna, and in several stories attempts to separate him from his beloved Marian Hume. See Alexander, *Early Writings* (1983) 61, 71, 81. The historical Zenobia was queen of Palmyra, made captive by Aurelian in AD 272.

Page 179, l. 2: *in spite of your teeth*: a proverbial expression: see *ODEP*, 766.

Page 179, l. 6: *you know neither the day nor hour*: see Matthew 24: 36, 25: 13; Luke 12: 46.

Page 181, l. 31: "*gaufres*": waffles.

Page 184, l. 9: *commode*: chest of drawers.

Page 184, l. 10: "*flitting*": removal (Scots and northern dialect).

Page 185, l. 18: "*locataire*": lodger, tenant.

Page 186, l. 8: *surtout*: overcoat.

Page 186, l. 13: *indescribable*: for a conjectural reading of a heavily deleted passage in the manuscript at this point, see the Note on the Text, on p. xxviii above.

Page 187, l. 32: '*Cast your bread . . . after many days*': Ecclesiastes 11: 1.

Page 189, l. 26: *Prester John*: a legendary Christian priest and king, reported in medieval legend to have reigned in Asia, and later identified with the King of Abyssinia.

Page 190, l. 14: *the ripe grapes*: from Aesop's fable of the fox and the grapes.

Page 191, l. 23: *the philosopher's stone*: the substance thought by medieval alchemists to be the agent that would turn base metals into gold.

Page 192, l. 1: *bullaces*: wild plums.

Page 192, l. 23: *flourishing like a green bay-tree*": Psalm 37: 36 (BCP).

Page 192, l. 31: *amateur*: as in 'amateur des beaux-arts', lover or patron of art.

Page 193, l. 11: *out of place!*": unemployed.

Page 193, l. 17: *Peruvian bark*: the bark of the cinchona tree, from which quinine is procured.

Page 197, l. 15: *négociant*: merchant.

Page 199, l. 3: *happiness finds no climax on earth?*: cf. Spenser: 'here on earth is no sure happinesse,' *Faerie Queene*, VI. xi. 1.

Page 199, l. 21: '*And ne'er but once, my son*': the opening lines of Scott's 'The Covenanter's Fate'.

Page 200, l. 1: *I gave, at first, Attention close*: an earlier version of these stanzas, together with the rest of the poem on pp. 202–5, appears in an exercise book used by Charlotte Brontë in Brussels in

1843. The substantive variants in this draft (Bonnell-BPM 118), including two stanzas omitted from the version printed in *The Professor*, are given in the textual notes to the Clarendon edition. Appendix IV of the Clarendon edition also gives the text of the related poem 'At first I did attention give', a modified form of which became Rochester's song in *Jane Eyre*. For discussion of these poems, see the Appendix to the Oxford English Novels edition of *Jane Eyre*, ed. Margaret Smith (Oxford, 1973), 461–4; E. Chitham and T. Winnifrith, *Brontë Facts and Brontë Problems* (London, 1983), 1–13; and T. Winnifrith (ed.), *The Poems of Charlotte Brontë* (Oxford, 1984).

Page 200, l. 27: *a mountain-echo*: cf. Wordsworth, 'Yes, it was the mountain Echo' (1807).

Page 201, l. 5: *the rigid and formal race of old maids*: this subject is treated more fully (and more sympathetically) in *Shirley*, 194–205, 440–4. See also Frances's comments on p. 236.

Page 203, l. 8: *green bowers . . . bees and flowers*: cf. Wordsworth, 'The Green Linnet' (1807).

Page 205, l. 17: *the grass on Hermon . . . dews of Sunset*: see Psalm 133. Mount Hermon is in southern Syria, close to the border of Lebanon.

Page 206, l. 14: *de grâce*: for pity's sake.

Page 206, l. 23: "*the purple light of love*": 'O'er her warm cheek and rising bosom move | The bloom of young desire and purple light of love' (Gray, 'The Progress of Poesy', ll. 40–1).

Page 206, l. 33: "*sourire à la fois fin et timide*": a smile at once shrewd and bashful.

Page 206, l. 35: *entêté, exigeant, volontaire*: obstinate, hard to please, self-willed.

Page 208, l. 24: *the lilies of the field*: see Matthew 6: 28.

Page 210, l. 5: "*édentée, myope, rugueuse ou bossue*": toothless, short-sighted, wrinkled, or hunch-backed.

Page 210, l. 29: "*The hair of my flesh stood up*": Job 4: 15.

Page 210, l. 31: "*A thing was secretly brought . . . a voice*": a conflation of Job 4: 12 and 16.

Page 210, l. 34: "*In the midst of Life*: from the service for the Burial of the Dead, BCP.

Page 211, l. 5: *A horror of great darkness fell upon me*: see Genesis 15: 12.

Page 211, l. 8: *Hypochondria*: nervous depression. Charlotte Brontë described her own subjection to 'the tyranny of Hypochondria' in a letter to her former teacher Margaret Wooler in 1846 (*LL*, ii. 116–17). See also *Villette*, 303–5, where Lucy Snowe describes Leopold I, king of the Belgians, as 'a silent sufferer—a nervous melancholy man. Those eyes had looked on the visits of a certain ghost—had long waited the comings and goings of that strangest spectre, Hypochondria.'

Page 212, l. 6: *when the evil spirit departed from me*: an allusion to the story of David and Saul, in 1 Samuel 16: 23.

Page 214, l. 21: *a spoon!"*: one who is simple or foolish, especially in amorous matters. Cf. 'spoonie' in *Jane Eyre*, 173.

Page 215, l. 9: *Stanley . . . Cobden*: Lord Stanley, 14th Earl of Derby (1799–1869) and Richard Cobden (1804–65) were Parliamentary opponents in the controversy surrounding the repeal of the Corn Laws in 1845–6. Stanley, an avowed Protectionist, resigned from the Tory cabinet in December 1845 when Peel indicated his intention of modifying the Corn Laws. Cobden, a leader of the Anti-Corn Law League and a proponent of free trade, was an outspoken critic of the English aristocracy and its stranglehold on the economy.

Page 215, l. 33: *cynism*: rare in English; Charlotte Brontë's use of it here may have been influenced by French 'cynisme'.

Page 216, l. 14: *grenier*: garret.

Page 217, l. 23: *fire thaws a congealed viper*: the common viper or adder, the only poisonous snake found in England, hibernates in the winter months.

Page 218, l. 7: *a sort of Swiss Sybil*: the references to 'a lady-abbess' and 'high tory and high church principles' suggest an anachronistic allusion to the eponymous heroine of Disraeli's novel *Sybil: or The Two Nations* (1845). A few lines below, Hunsden's invitation to Frances to visit the English poor and 'get a glimpse of Famine crouched torpid on black hearth-stones' recalls Sybil Gerard's ministering visit to the Warners' 'squalid lair' with its starving inhabitants and its fireless grate (I. xiii, xiv).

Page 218, l. 19: *St. Giles in London*: the parish of St. Giles was infamous for its slums, its poverty, and its many gin shops. Dickens describes the area in 'Seven Dials' and 'Gin Shops', in *Sketches By Boz* (1836).

Page 219, l. 22: *Abdiel the Faithful*: 'So spake the Seraph Abdiel faithful found', *Paradise Lost*, v. 896.

Page 219, l. 24: '*the ever-during gates*' ... '*with retorted scorn*'": from *Paradise Lost*, vii. 206 and v. 906.

Page 220, l. 4: *nervous language*: strong, vigorous language, as elsewhere in Charlotte Brontë; cf. p. 231 above, and *Jane Eyre*, 449.

Page 220, l. 31: *servants of foreign kings*": Swiss mercenaries served various European powers from the fifteenth century to the nineteenth, with especial distinction in France, where the royal bodyguard of Swiss Guards defended the Tuileries against a revolutionary mob in August 1792.

Page 221, l. 1: *the French accuse them of being perfidious*: a reference to the phrase 'Perfide Albion', ascribed to Napoleon, though its origin appears to be a sermon preached *c.*1655 by Bossuet, in which he exclaimed, 'L'Angleterre, ah! la perfide Angleterre!'

Page 221, l. 18: *a method in my madness*: see *Hamlet*, II. ii. 205.

Page 221, l. 25: *intent ... on hospitable thoughts*: cf. *Paradise Lost*, v. 332: 'She turns, on hospitable thoughts intent.'

Page 223, l. 16: *your Wellington*: Charlotte Brontë inherited her father's admiration of the Duke of Wellington, who figures prominently in her early juvenilia (see Alexander, *The Early Writings of Charlotte Brontë*, *passim*). Her strongest praise appears in *Shirley*, where the narrator describes the Duke as 'a demi-god' (728).

Page 223, l. 22: *Tell ... our heroic William*: the legendary hero of the struggle by Switzerland to free itself from Austrian rule in the fourteenth century.

Page 223, l. 26: *baudet?*: jackass, dolt.

Page 223, l. 27: *esprit-fort*: a strong-minded person.

Page 224, l. 4: *guessed I was a Benedick*: in *Much Ado About Nothing*, Benedick is the cynical young nobleman of Padua who has forsworn women.

Page 224, l. 11: *Breton-bretonnant*: an inhabitant of Brittany who speaks the old Breton dialect.

Page 224, l. 17: *Sir Charles Grandison ... Harriet Byron*: Sir Charles Grandison, the aristocratic hero of Samuel Richardson's novel *The History of Sir Charles Grandison* (1753–4), woos and wins Harriet Byron by his nobility of character and exemplary manners. He takes her hand on many occasions; the phrase 'He bowed upon her Hand' appears in vol. VI, letter lii (ed. Jocelyn Harris (Oxford, 1972), iii.

227). For Charlotte Brontë's interest in Richardson, see the Introduction, p. xviii above.

Page 224, l. 22: *Je ne m'y suis pas attendu*: I did not expect it.

Page 224, l. 28: *ouvrière!*: work-woman.

Page 225, l. 24: *'jungfrau'*: maiden.

Page 225, l. 24: *chétive*: puny.

Page 225, l. 26: *minois chiffonné*: pleasing but irregular features.

Page 225, l. 30: *Bribe a seraph to fetch you a coal of fire*: see Isaiah 6: 6.

Page 225, l. 31: *fattest ... of Rubens' painted women*: a similarly disparaging reference to 'the army of [Rubens'] fat women' appears in *Villette*, 371.

Page 225, l. 33: *my Alpine peri*: in Persian mythology, the Peri were a race of beautiful spirits descended from the fallen angels. Charlotte Brontë would have read of them in Thomas Moore's *Lalla Rookh, An Oriental Romance* (1817), to which she alludes in both *Jane Eyre* and *Villette*, and which includes a section on 'Paradise and the Peri'.

Page 229, l. 2: *chaussées*: roadways.

Page 229, l. 11: *She proposed to begin a school*: Charlotte Brontë and her sisters had formed a similar plan in 1841. With the financial assistance of their aunt, Elizabeth Branwell, they intended to complete their education in Brussels, then to open a school. Only the first part of their scheme was realized; after Charlotte's return to Haworth from the Pensionnat Heger in January 1844, the sisters advertised 'The Misses Brontë's Establishment for the Board and Education of a Limited Number of Young Ladies', but received no applications. See the *Life*, i. 231–50, 314–26.

Page 233, l. 16: "*malice*": used in the French sense of mischievousness, roguishness.

Page 233, l. 19: *white demon*: an innocent demon. Cf. *OED*, 'white witch'.

Page 233, l. 24: *the sprite that teased me*: this and similar phrases in the same paragraph ('the elfish freak', 'a mere vexing fairy') anticipate Rochester's view of Jane Eyre: see *Jane Eyre*, 307, 325, 328, 336–8.

Page 234, l. 11: *Dortoir*: dormitory.

Page 236, l. 7: *patient Grizzle*: Grizzle, or Griselda, is the traditional model of wifely patience and obedience. Boccaccio tells her story in the *Decameron*, as does Chaucer's Clerk in *The Canterbury Tales*. Cf. *The Taming of the Shrew*, II. i. 287: 'For patience she will prove a second Grissel.'

Page 237, l. 11: *Mammon was not our Master*: see note to p. 8 above.

Page 238, l. 7: *one of the Elizabethan structures*: Charlotte Brontë may have been thinking of Oakwell Hall, near Birstall in the West Riding of Yorkshire, which was first built in the fourteenth century and then remodelled in the sixteenth. It provided the model for 'Fieldhead' in *Shirley*.

Page 238, l. 24: *Savant*: scholar.

Page 238, l. 24: *savage-looking Italian*: English interest in the long struggle for Italian independence was especially high in 1844 when it was learned that the exiled Italian patriot Mazzini, then living in London, had been corresponding with a group of revolutionaries led by Attilio and Emilio Bandiera. The Bandieras' attempt to instigate an uprising ended in July 1844 with their capture and execution in Calabria. The British government admitted to opening Mazzini's letters and communicating their contents to the Neapolitan authorities; this led to angry debates in Parliament and a letter of denunciation in *The Times* by Thomas Carlyle. See *The Times*, 17 June 1844, 4–5; 19 June 1844, 6; 5 July 1844, 1–2.

Page 238, l. 30: *liberal sentiments ... the Pope*: the election of a seemingly reformist pope, Pius IX, in June 1846 brought much talk of Italian liberation from Austrian domination. In 1848, however, the Pope was driven from Rome by revolutionary rioting, and in 1850 returned to rule the Papal States with the help of French troops.

Page 239, l. 14: *Hofer*: Andreas Hofer (1767–1810) led the people of the Tyrol against the French and the Bavarians, but after some early successes, he was betrayed and executed.

Page 240, l. 15: *the "winding way"*: this, with the earlier references to the song of the nightingale, the 'balmy' night, and the tolling bell, suggest that Charlotte Brontë was thinking of Keats's 'Ode to a Nightingale': 'Through verdurous glooms and winding mossy ways'.

Page 240, l. 29: *"Lucia"*: Enid L. Duthie suggests that Frances's analysis of 'Lucia' points to a character 'strikingly similar to Madame de Staël's Corinne' (*The Foreign Vision of Charlotte Brontë* (1975), 128). *Corinne* was published in 1807. That Charlotte was familiar with this novel is suggested by the loose insertion of two conjugate leaves from vol. i of *Corinne* in the copy of *Russell's*

General Atlas of Modern Geography that she used in Brussels, now in the Pierpont Morgan Library. Her German Notebook of 1843 (Bonnell-BPM, 118) contains brief pencilled notes entitled 'Lucia', which include ideas later used in *The Professor* and *Shirley*.

Page 241, l. 25: *girandole*: a branched support for candles, either as a candlestick or in the form of a wall-bracket. Cf. *Jane Eyre*, 238.

Page 243, l. 26: *burnt the wound with hot iron*: in the *Life*, Mrs Gaskell records Charlotte Brontë's account of her sister Emily's being bitten by a rabid dog, and her 'taking up one of Tabby's red-hot Italian irons to sear the bitten place' (i. 318–19). The incident is incorporated into *Shirley*, 578–9.

Page 245, l. 4: *my sole olive-branch*: see Psalm 128: 4 (BCP).

Page 245, l. 15: *the offending Adam ... whipped out of him*: cf. *Henry V*: 'Consideration like an angel came, | And whipped the offending Adam out of him' (I. i. 28–9).

Page 245, l. 16: *will be cheap of*: will get off lightly with (Scots dialect).

Page 246, l. 17: *appliqué*: hardworking.

Page 246, l. 30: *railway speculations*: speculation in railway stocks was at its height in the mid-forties; Charlotte Brontë herself had invested in York–North Midland stock floated by George Hudson, the 'railway king', and lost money when Hudson's empire collapsed in 1849. See her letters to Margaret Wooler, 30 Jan. 1846 (*LL*, ii. 76); George Smith, 27 Sept. 1849 (BPM, Seton-Gordon), and 4 Oct. 1849 (*LL*, iii. 27; BPM, Seton-Gordon).

Page 246, l. 30: *the Piece-Hall*: the cloth exchange, where cloth was sold by the piece.

Page 246, l. 31: *a Stag of ten*: a stag with antlers having ten points is highly prized by huntsmen. In Stock Exchange slang, a 'stag' is an investor who speculates in new issues to make a quick profit.

THE WORLD'S CLASSICS

A Select List

SERGEI AKSAKOV: A Russian Gentleman
Translated by J. D. Duff
Edited by Edward Crankshaw

HANS ANDERSEN: Fairy Tales
Translated by L. W. Kingsland
Introduction by Naomi Lewis
Illustrated by Vilhelm Pedersen and Lorenz Frølich

ARTHUR J. ARBERRY (Transl.): The Koran

LUDOVICO ARIOSTO: Orlando Furioso
Translated by Guido Waldman

ARISTOTLE: The Nicomachean Ethics
Translated by David Ross

JANE AUSTEN: Emma
Edited by James Kinsley and David Lodge

Northanger Abbey, Lady Susan, The Watsons, *and* Sanditon
Edited by John Davie

Persuasion
Edited by John Davie

ROBERT BAGE: Hermsprong
Edited by Peter Faulkner

WILLIAM BECKFORD: Vathek
Edited by Roger Lonsdale

KEITH BOSLEY (Transl.): The Kalevala

CHARLOTTE BRONTË: Jane Eyre
Edited by Margaret Smith

JOHN BUNYAN: The Pilgrim's Progress
Edited by N. H. Keeble

FRANCES HODGSON BURNETT: The Secret Garden
Edited by Dennis Butts

FANNY BURNEY: Cecilia
or Memoirs of an Heiress
Edited by Peter Sabor and Margaret Anne Doody

THOMAS CARLYLE: The French Revolution
Edited by K. J. Fielding and David Sorensen

LEWIS CARROLL: Alice's Adventures in Wonderland
and Through the Looking Glass
Edited by Roger Lancelyn Green
Illustrated by John Tenniel

GEOFFREY CHAUCER: The Canterbury Tales
Translated by David Wright

ANTON CHEKHOV: The Russian Master and Other Stories
Translated by Ronald Hingley

JOHN CLELAND:
Memoirs of a Woman of Pleasure (Fanny Hill)
Edited by Peter Sabor

WILKIE COLLINS: Armadale
Edited by Catherine Peters

JOSEPH CONRAD: Chance
Edited by Martin Ray

Victory
Edited by John Batchelor
Introduction by Tony Tanner

NORMAN DAVIS (Ed.): The Paston Letters

DANIEL DEFOE: Colonel Jack
Edited by Samuel Holt Monk and David Roberts

CHARLES DICKENS: Christmas Books
Edited by Ruth Glancy

Sikes and Nancy and Other Public Readings
Edited by Philip Collins

FËDOR DOSTOEVSKY: Crime and Punishment
Translated by Jessie Coulson
Introduction by John Jones

ARTHUR CONAN DOYLE:
Sherlock Holmes: Selected Stories
Introduction by S. C. Roberts

ALEXANDRE DUMAS *fils*: La Dame aux Camélias
Translated by David Coward

MARIA EDGEWORTH: Castle Rackrent
Edited by George Watson

GEORGE ELIOT: Felix Holt, The Radical
Edited by Fred C. Thompson

Middlemarch
Edited by David Carroll

Scenes of Clerical Life
Edited by Thomas A. Noble

SUSAN FERRIER: Marriage
Edited by Herbert Foltinek

SARAH FIELDING: The Adventures of David Simple
Edited by Malcolm Kelsall

GUSTAVE FLAUBERT: Madame Bovary
Translated by Gerard Hopkins
Introduction by Terence Cave

ELIZABETH GASKELL: Cousin Phillis and Other Tales
Edited by Angus Easson

My Lady Ludlow and Other Stories
Edited by Edgar Wright

J. W. VON GOETHE: Faust, Part One
Translated by David Luke

OLIVER GOLDSMITH: The Vicar of Wakefield
Edited by Arthur Friedman

THOMAS HARDY: A Pair of Blue Eyes
Edited by Alan Manford

ALEXANDER HERZEN: Childhood, Youth and Exile
Introduction by Isaiah Berlin

HESIOD: Theogony *and* Works and Days
Translated by M. L. West

HOMER: The Iliad
Translated by Robert Fitzgerald
Introduction by G. S. Kirk

THOMAS HUGHES: Tom Brown's Schooldays
Edited by Andrew Sanders

HENRIK IBSEN: An Enemy of the People, The Wild Duck, Rosmersholm
Edited and Translated by James McFarlane

HENRY JAMES: The Ambassadors
Edited by Christopher Butler

M. R. JAMES: Casting the Runes and Other Ghost Stories
Edited by Michael Cox

RICHARD JEFFERIES: After London or Wild England
Introduction by John Fowles

JOCELIN OF BRAKELOND:
Chronicle of the Abbey of Bury St. Edmunds
Translated by Diana Greenway and Jane Sayers

GWYN JONES (Transl.):
Eirik the Red and Other Icelandic Sagas

BEN JONSON: Five Plays
Edited by G. A. Wilkes

RUDYARD KIPLING: The Day's Work
Edited by Thomas Pinney

CHARLES LAMB: Elia *and* The Last Essays of Elia
Edited by Jonathan Bate

J. SHERIDAN LE FANU: Uncle Silas
Edited by W. J. McCormack

MIKHAIL LERMONTOV: A Hero of our Time
Translated by Vladimar Nabokov with Dmitri Nabokov

MATTHEW LEWIS: The Monk
Edited by Howard Anderson

KATHERINE MANSFIELD: Selected Stories
Edited by D. M. Davin

CHARLES MATURIN: Melmoth the Wanderer
Edited by Douglas Grant
Introduction by Chris Baldick

HERMAN MELVILLE: The Confidence-Man
Edited by Tony Tanner

Moby Dick
Edited by Tony Tanner

PROSPER MÉRIMÉE: Carmen and Other Stories
Translated by Nicholas Jotcham

MICHELANGELO: Life, Letters, and Poetry
Translated by George Bull with Peter Porter

MOLIÈRE: Don Juan and Other Plays
Translated by George Graveley and Ian Maclean

JOHN HENRY NEWMAN: Loss and Gain
Edited by Alan G. Hill

MARGARET OLIPHANT:
A Beleaguered City and Other Stories
Edited by Merryn Williams

EDGAR ALLAN POE: Selected Tales
Edited by Julian Symons

JEAN RACINE: Britannicus, Phaedra, Athaliah
Translated by C. H. Sisson

ANN RADCLIFFE: The Italian
Edited by Frederick Garber

M. E. SALTYKOV-SHCHEDRIN: The Golovlevs
Translated by I. P. Foote

SIR WALTER SCOTT: The Heart of Midlothian
Edited by Claire Lamont

The Two Drovers and Other Stories
Edited by Graham Tulloch
Introduction by Lord David Cecil

SIR PHILIP SIDNEY:
The Countess of Pembroke's Arcadia (The Old Arcadia)
Edited by Katherine Duncan-Jones

TOBIAS SMOLLETT: The Expedition of Humphry Clinker
Edited by Lewis M. Knapp
Revised by Paul-Gabriel Boucé

ROBERT LOUIS STEVENSON: Treasure Island
Edited by Emma Letley

ANTHONY TROLLOPE: The American Senator
Edited by John Halperin